PRAISE FOR MATTHEW DE ABAITUA

"Sumptuously written, with prose that glitters with a dark lustre like a Damien Hirst fly collage. intricately plotted, and a satirical point as sharp and accurate as the scalpel of a brain surgeon: De Abaitua operates on the smiling face of the present to reveal the grimacing skull of the future."

Will Self

"*The Red Men* is a breathtaking novel of ideas, and a sharp antidote to those shiny magical 'upload your consciousness into cyberspace wheee' novels."

Charlie Jane Anders, author of All the Birds in the Sky

"Matthew De Abaitua makes Michel Houellebecq seem like Enid Blyton."

Matt Thorne, Encore Award-winning author of Eight Minutes Idle

"Like the famous elephant surrounded by blind men, its shape and texture suggest differing beasts depending on where you grab it. Literary thriller and domestic drama, thought experiment and drug trip, cyberpunk and technopagan, satire and prophecy."

Strange Horizons

"*The Red Men* is a brilliant work of social theory, in the same way that novels by [illegible] ston Ellis are works of sc[illegible] tive and thought-provo[illegible] how society actually wo[illegible] g by Zygmunt Bauman, [illegible]

The Pinocchio The[illegible]

D1115581

"*The Red Men* resonates with everything. Everything here on this site, everything I've written, everything I've done. Everything I'm doing. In fact, 'resonates' is the wrong word. Shakes. It shook me. Read it."

Magical Nihilism

"The initial chirpy tone and thread of black humour running through this book gets steadily darker. It is compelling, clever and terrifyingly plausible. It is also savagely violent. As a sharp and accomplished writer, De Abaitua is completely capable of delivering a nuanced, satirical take on the subject."

Brainfluff

Praise for IF THEN

"[*IF THEN*] is the kind of post-apocalypse, after-it-all-changed novel – with clever codicils – that the Brits do with so much more classy, idiosyncratic style than anyone else. It is full of magisterial weirdness, logical surrealism, melancholy joy and hopeful terror. If I begin to toss out names like Adam Roberts, Brian Aldiss, Keith Roberts, and JG Ballard, I will not be lavishing undue praise."

Paul di Filippo, Locus Magazine

"*IF THEN* may be one of the most important works of British science fiction to appear in recent years. It is stunningly original and superbly well written. *IF THEN* is the opposite of the literature of reassurance, it is everything science fiction should be aiming for."

Nina Allan

"As disturbingly hyperreal as any Pre-Raphaelite painting, *IF THEN* imagines what the end of history really will really look like, what's really at stake, and maybe, just maybe, what we can do about it."

Simon Ings, author of Wolves

"I cannot praise *IF THEN* highly enough: eloquent, intelligent, brilliant."

Elsa Bouet, Shoreline of Infinity

"The alternating viewpoints set in a modern town and during World War I will have you itching to know what's really going on."

Kirkus Reviews

"De Abaitua builds on the promise he demonstrated in *The Red Men* in this intellectual science fiction novel, whose ambition is matched by its execution. The author's thoughtful world-building is enhanced by a cast of relatable characters."

Publishers Weekly

Praise for THE DESTRUCTIVES

"[*The Destructives*] is a work that doesn't so much subvert expectations as shatter them utterly. It's dense, but it also moves; it's both a breakneck thriller and one of the year's most thoughtful works of science fiction."

Barnes & Noble Sci-Fi & Fantasy Blog

"Matthew De Abaitua has the knack of delivering the most complex of concepts and diabolical leaps of imagination in a way that first entices then completely draws the reader in. A thrilling book."

Strange Alliances

"A marvellously written book, whose invention and surprises gain momentum until its boggler of an ending."

SFX Magazine

BY THE SAME AUTHOR

IF THEN
The Destructives

NON-FICTION
The Idler's Companion: An Anthology of Lazy Literature

The Art of Camping: The History and Practice of Sleeping Under the Stars

MATTHEW DE ABAITUA

THE RED MEN

ANGRY ROBOT
An imprint of Watkins Media Ltd

20 Fletcher Gate,
Nottingham,
NG1 2FZ
UK

angryrobotbooks.com
twitter.com/angryrobotbooks
Easy does it

First published in 2007
This Angry Robot edition published in the US & Canada 2017

Copyright © Matthew De Abaitua 2007

Cover by Raid71
Set in Meridien and Helvetica Neue Black by Epub Services

Distributed in the United States by Penguin Random House, Inc., New York.

All rights reserved.

Angry Robot and the Angry Robot icon are registered trademarks of Watkins Media Ltd.

This is a work of fiction. Names, characters, places, and incidents are the products of the author's imagination or are used fictitiously. Any resemblance to actual events, locales, organizations or persons, living or dead, is entirely coincidental.

Sales of this book without a front cover may be unauthorized. If this book is coverless, it may have been reported to the publisher as "unsold and destroyed" and neither the author nor the publisher may have received payment for it.

ISBN 978 0 85766 755 7
Ebook ISBN 978 0 85766 756 4

Printed in the United States of America

9 8 7 6 5 4 3 2 1

For Sylvia and Eddie

"So it isn't I who am master of my own life, I am just one of the threads to be woven into life's calico! Well then, even if I cannot spin, I can at least cut the thread in two."

Søren Kierkegaard, from *Either/Or: A Fragment of Life*, first published 1843, translation by Alastair Hannay, 1992

"Then another tomorrow
They never told me of
Came with the abruptness of a fiery dawn."

Sun Ra, from *Cosmic Equation*, 1965

I

1
IGNITION

I brushed my daughter's blonde hair, taking pleasure in bringing order to its morning tangle. Iona stood at the window, gazing at the busy Hackney street. She blinked at the faces of the pedestrians, each discontent in his or her own way, stumbling and dawdling, stragglers in the human race. I concentrated on the long stroke of the brush. Each pass spun golden thread. We did not talk. I adjusted my position to brush the underside, drawing out a sheaf of hair upon my palm. While she slept, tiny zephyrs had whirled the golden thread into intertwined locks; carefully, I unpicked them.

I finished brushing her hair and then we put on our coats. Iona chose a doll to take to nursery, and that was the end of this peaceful moment together. The collar of the day slipped over my neck, the leash jerked taut, and the long drag began: work, meetings, teatime, Iona's bedtime then work again until sleep took me. Drifting into unconsciousness, the leash would be unhooked, and I would wonder where the day had gone. Where I had gone. Close my eyes. Nothing there.

Iona said, "Daddy, what is that?"

A small group moved with authority and purpose through the pedestrians. It was the police, specifically an armed response unit, strapped up in black Kevlar armour and carrying sub-machine guns. We were used to the police; Iona wasn't pointing at them. No, it was the tall figure in their midst that had caught her eye: the robot was at least seven-foot-tall and was covered in a skin of kid leather, with fully articulated legs and arms and sensitive catcher's mitts for hands. It was not entirely steady on its flat feet. The police jogged to keep up with its loping stride. The robot passed by the window and glanced our way: a pair of mournful blue eyes set in a suede ball of a head.

Again, Iona asked me what it was.

"That's a Dr Easy," I replied. "It's a robot. You know what a robot is." I helped her into a duffle coat.

"Why is it a doctor?"

"It helps people. Sometimes people get mad. It makes them better."

"Why do people get mad?"

"They just do."

It was time for us to go. I opened the front door. Iona clamped her hands over her ears. A police helicopter hung in the air, its rotor blades drowning out the clamour of the main road. Policewomen set about sealing off the street, unwinding strips of yellow tape and evacuating the shops: customers halfway through their manicures were led indignant from the nails and hair place and at the internet shack armed police threatened the Somalians who were waiting for their permits to finish downloading. A pair of builders in plaster-spattered boiler suits sauntered from Yum-Yum, refusing to be rushed. As each establishment emptied, the police put down metal crowd barriers to close it off. We milled outside the off-licence. What was going on?

Did anyone know?

An armed man was holed up in a house, said the constables. Shots had been fired. Snipers, as graceful as burglars, skipped over the rooftops and took up positions behind chimney stacks. I looked back toward my house but could no longer see it. A blue tarpaulin had been set up across the street. The armed unit huddled behind a barricade with Dr Easy sat cross-legged among them, listening politely as the captain explained his intentions.

Dr Easy made me anxious. It was the eyes. Sometimes feminine, sometimes masculine, just like its voice, which could be maternal or paternal depending upon the need of the patient. When I was unwell and suffering from anxiety, I was offered sessions with Monad's in-house Dr Easy. It spoke with a man's voice and let me hit it in the face.

I wriggled my hand free of Iona's grasp and checked my pulse. It was elevated. Her question came back to me: Daddy, why do people get mad? Well, my darling, drugs don't help. And life can kick rationality out of you. You can be kneecapped right from the very beginning. Even little girls and boys your age are getting mad through bad love. When you are older, life falls short of your expectations, your dreams are picked up by fate, considered, and then dashed upon the rocks, and then you get mad. You just do. Your only salvation is to live for the dreams of others; the dreams of a child like you, my darling girl, my puppy pie, or the dreams of an employer, like Monad.

The robot sat patiently through a briefing by the tactical arms unit, which was quite unnecessary, as it would already have extracted all the information it required from their body language. Dr Easy listened to the police captain give orders because it knew how much pleasure it gave him.

The body of the robot was designed by a subtle,

calculating intelligence, with a yielding cover of soft natural materials to comfort us and a large but lightweight frame to acknowledge that it was inhuman. The robot was both parent and stranger: you wanted to lay your head against its chest, you wanted to beat it to death. When I hit my robot counsellor, its blue eyes held a fathomless love for humanity.

Slowly, Dr Easy stood up. The crowd fell silent. The robot held up its enormous right palm, a gesture of peace to the gunman. Its left hand was arranged with similar precision – the palm of an open hand facing forward, the five fingers slightly bent. With this gesture of charity and compassion, Dr Easy took stately steps across the road toward the gunman's house.

The police retreated to where Monad's contractors had set up a monitoring station. Gelatinous screens billowed out like spinnaker sails to catch the data pouring in: infrared, millimetre-wave and acoustic impressions from the police helicopter were matched to the sensory input of Dr Easy, creating a live three-dimensional model of the siege house. The gunman was on the second floor, in the corner of a bedsit. I hoisted Iona up into my arms and walked over to the contractors, flashing my Monad ID. Could I be of help? In an advisory capacity? In the spirit of public and private sector collaboration? The Monad technicians knew me from the company five-a-side league. I was allowed to hover in the background.

In the time it took me to remove a small box of organic raisins from my pocket and give them to Iona, Monad assembled a working profile of the gunman, mining his scattered data and reassembling it in the shape of a man. His name was Michael Sawyer and he had no prior criminal convictions. He had a number of traffic violations and an onerous mortgage, a low six-figure income with a high five-figure alimony. His medical records contained prescriptions for beta-blockers and anti-depressants that had not recently been renewed. He had moved out of the family home and into rented accommodation, but not to here; this siege house was not his last known residence. The previous year he had racked up tens of thousands of air miles, doing three continents most weeks. This year, none. I looked at his employment record and drew my own conclusions. Here was an exhausted and confused foot soldier of globalization, bounced up the empire of a media magnate before falling out of favour. He managed to get a position at a telecommunications and military electronics firm which in turn had been taken over by a larger company. Personnel took out his expense claims for the last year and exposed them to micro-analysis, searching for a pretext to fire him and avoid paying redundancy. They had found what they were looking for.

This was the gunman's background. Now the police captain added the foreground. Officers on patrol had identified Michael Sawyer's sports car as wanted in connection with a hit-and-run in Soho. When they inquired at the house, they heard three shots. The firearms unit arrived and a further two shots were let off from an upstairs window. Officers returned fire but surveillance showed the suspect still moving around inside the house.

"We tried to negotiate. They always negotiate. Not this one. He hasn't said a word. We don't know what he wants," said the police captain.

"Dr Easy will find out," I said.

I wanted to see a Dr Easy in action. My work for Monad was conceptual, concerned with planning and development. I rarely saw any project through to completion, and so never acted in any decisive way upon the world. My will and ambition had been diluted by years of being the ideas man, a thinker and not a doer, a position of unchanging powerlessness in any company. Monad dreams. I do not. Not for myself, anyway.

The siege house was a Victorian terrace carved up into bedsits. Six doorbells clustered beside the shattered front door. Dr Easy went inside. On the screens, we watched the robot's slow progress up the staircase. Its inner monologue came through the monitors. It could already smell Michael Sawyer, his fear hormones, the stink of a wounded and hunted animal. The robot crept up a tilted cobwebbed staircase until it came to an unlocked door. The gentlest pressure from the robot's paw swung the door back on its hinges.

The room was dingy. A dirty single bed. A Baby Belling oven on a peeling melamine surface. A microwave. A stereo. A half-unpacked suitcase. Michael Sawyer was crouched in the corner. His striped shirt was untucked and slick with blood. At the sight of the robot, he gurgled and gesticulated with the shotgun.

"He has a bullet wound to the mouth," observed Dr Easy. "And there is an overpowering smell of petrol in here."

"Ask him what he wants," ordered the police captain.

"He can't speak," said the robot. "The sniper shot him in the tongue."

"Can he write it down?"

"It doesn't matter. I know what he wants."

Dr Easy moved forward to comfort the injured man. Michael Sawyer made a gesture that was like Atlas trying to shake some sense into the world.

The robot translated for us. "Too late. He is going to kill himself now."

The flat was saturated with fuel. Dr Easy made no attempt to intervene. The robot was already backing out of the room when Michael Sawyer lit a rag. Fire filled the screens and – back on the street – blew out the windows of the house. Iona was scared and I held her tight to me.

A great fire waits under London. Michael Sawyer had merely slid back the grate.

Lift up a manhole cover, listen to it roar.

Dr Easy walked out of the billowing smoke, and then, with flames running all the way down its back, the robot burned on the street until someone came forward to extinguish it.

2
ZZZZZZIP

The door buzzer woke me at dawn.

I blundered out of bed and flicked on the intercom.

Raymond spoke first.

"Today you are going to change my life."

At the door, he was gripping the iron bars of the security gate with both hands.

"Aren't you excited?"

My head was waxy with sleep. Across the road, strips of police tape lingered around the cavity where the siege house had been. I'd stood there all afternoon and into the dusk when, to douse the flames, the police had dumped tonnes of water through the roof; these waterfalls streamed through the broken windows, backlit by powerful halogen spotlights. Afterwards, I thought about Michael Sawyer a lot. How easy it would be for the project of your self to go suddenly horribly off the rails.

"Please, it's urgent," said Raymond.

Scratching at his new goatee with dirty fingernails, he had changed since our last meeting. That was how it went with Raymond. His identity was in flux during his manic phase: he was a Buddhist then he was out on bail then he was Zen celibate then he was the spare man in a swingers enclave, all in the course of three weeks. I first met him when I was the editor of Drug Porn and he was a contributor. Recently, he had taken up a tighter orbit, looping around the routines of my family life.

The first thing I said to him, straight up, before I let him into the flat, was this:

"Shut up. Don't say anything. This is a small place. Iona and El are asleep downstairs. You can come in, but first you must promise me that you won't start talking until I am ready, a state I will indicate by pointing at you, and saying the word 'speak'."

Since our last meeting, he had grown a neat swell of gut, inconsequential beside mine, but significant on his carpenter's pencil of a figure. As he went by into the flat, I could smell the sweat of alleyways, the urban dewfall of bus fumes and rotting garbage. He laid down a dosser's bag, its zip defeated by the sleeping bag shoddily stuffed inside. He asked to use the toilet and I indicated, through quiet pointing, that I would meet him out back when he was done.

I went down to check on El. The bedrooms were underground and dug out of the old coal cellar. She was drowsy, having been up in the night with our daughter. I told her to go back to sleep and her dreaming self obeyed me. In Iona's dark little room, sweetly stuffy from her child's body, I checked her temperature with the back of my hand, adjusted the duvet around her shoulders, caught my reflection in the pulsating obsidian monitor on the chest of drawers.

In the garden, Raymond rolled a small joint in the encrusted ridges of his trousers. I served tea and pointed at him.

"Speak."

"I've been out all night. I can't convey the importance of what's happened to me. Sex and revelation. Well, almost sex. Certainly revelation though." He whistled.

"You are catastrophizing again," I said.

He considered my observation, rolled it around his palate with a swirl of marijuana.

"Do you want some of this?"

"No."

"You haven't asked what my revelation was?"

"Does it involve the end of the world?"

"It is more surprising than that: I've decided to get a job."

"Who is going to give you a job?" I asked.

"You are," he said. "You're going to change my life. I met this woman. She told me Monad is hiring writers and poets. I'm going to apply to work with you at Monad."

I was due at Monad in an hour. I would take the Overground train to Stratford then down to Canary Wharf and Monad's offices at the Wave Building. Our garden backed onto the platform at Hackney Central. The station Tannoy echoed apologies over the fence, interrupting our conversation. A train pulled in to the platform. The passengers seethed against one another; pressed against a single window, among the human faces, was an Alsatian's terrified chops. No one got off that carriage with their reputation intact. It was a commuter route for all trades: immigrants from Eastern Europe, dusty with demolition work out West, snoozed against middle managers, who made every effort to close their senses against the press of fellow passengers. The nearly dead travelled on this train too. Stabbed or shot in the Pembury or Nightingale estates, they bled into the upholstery on their way to A&E at Homerton hospital.

The train pulled away. The garden was quiet again, and Raymond resumed his talk.

"It all started when Florence the poet asked if I wanted to

come over for cunnilingus and pasta. I asked, 'What type of pasta?' She said, 'Fusilli.' I said, 'Don't mind if I do.'"

Raymond had been practising this conversation on the walk over.

I raised my hand.

"Stop. I don't want to hear about this. Just tell me about Monad."

"No. It's all relevant. You're doing exactly what she did. Florence. She put her finger on my lips and told me I could only speak when she winked at me."

"We have to do that. Sometimes it's hard to keep track of your conversation."

"That's because I have perfect recall."

This was true. Raymond was always bringing up something I had said half a dozen years earlier. He could rummage around in the brain gutters and memory drains to pull out clumps of throwaway ideas, irrelevant asides, boozy promises that were never meant to live beyond closing time.

"After the pasta we went to a reading at the Vortex. Then it was zzzzzzip" – this exclamation a conversational tic to signify a jump cut in his inner movie – "and me and Florence are drinking sherry in her bedroom. I told her I didn't want to sleep with her."

"'Come to bed, Ray-mond,' she cooed at me like a dove from under her duvet.

"I said, 'No, I can't have sex. I have too much going on at the moment.'

"She put her index finger to my lips and said, 'I don't want your objections. Shut up and give me head.'"

He was smoking his joint now, and it was having no effect upon him. The tetrahydrocannabinol could not compete with the charged juice running through his axons and synapses, it could not insinuate itself into the quantum events operating in the microtubules of each and every one of his twenty-three billion neurons, the chorus of tiny mysteries that sang into existence the strange consciousness of Raymond Chase.

I was puzzled as to how, via the infinite processes of the brain, he had come up with such a daft idea as to not have sex with willing Florence.

"I was trying to have a conversation with her. Is it so wrong in this day and age that a man has something to say?

"'Speak here, Raymond,' she said, hitching up her dress. 'Tell it the alphabet, let your tongue go from A to Zed.' I was so busy telling her about my reality filters that I hadn't noticed she'd taken her knickers off."

The phrase "reality filters" was mine. When he was manic, reality was everything at once and it was all connected to him: Raymond became the junction box through which many currents flowed. Instead of walking the street with the filters in place, one spotlight of consciousness on the pavement before him, all the lights were on in Raymond's head. It became difficult for him to tell where he ended and other people began.

At the end of the garden, the winter sun glinted off the spears of the metal security fence. Emaciated trees shivered in the breeze. He was talking about inclining his head toward Florence's exposed labia, taking one lip between his lips.

"I still had plenty to say at this point, but I confined myself to licking every letter of the alphabet into her. She liked L. She giggled at M. I nipped her with V, then shook her with W.

"She said, 'Focus on me. Forget everything else.' The cowl of her clitoris was thrown back. I tried to narrow everything down to that red nub. I could feel her seeping into my beard."

Raymond ran back through the alphabet, and she started to pull him on top of her. There was some scrabbling with his trousers while she plucked a condom from the top drawer of the bedside table. She flicked a paisley scarf onto the lamp for ambience. He tried to catch the look upon her face when she first saw his penis.

"Stop." I raised my hand, and Raymond snapped out of his recollection. "It's too early in the morning for this. Don't give it to me blow-by-blow. Did you have sex or not? Just a yes or no."

The frustration crushed him: how could I understand what was happening to him if he didn't show me every facet of the experience?

"It's not a yes or no thing. If you insist on getting all empirical, then yes I achieved penetration. But for penetration to graduate to full sex, I feel one or more of the participants must achieve orgasm. Long before that eventuality, I was standing by the armoire, smoking a roll-up and finishing my observation about my reality filters."

"Which was?"

"That they were clogged."

"By?"

"Reality, obviously."

"What did Florence say when you stopped having sex?"

"It was very sudden. I sprang out of her. She thought I'd seen something. A rat. The house has rats. It wasn't a rat. I hadn't seen something alarming. Rather, I'd thought something alarming. Actually, it was an absence of thought. My brain seized up. There was complete silence in there; it was as if Florence had reached into my skull and shushed my hippocampus, thalamus, frontal lobe whatever with her index finger. In place of the usual inner chatter there was a rush of information from the muscle sense, the inner ear. I could feel the macadamized heft of my lung lining, the groaning sodden liver, the whine of knee cartilage and, most of all, the hesitancy of my heart. It was a non-lucid moment. I still had Florence's thighs over each shoulder, the pressure of her flesh against my ears. Clamped. Locked in the meat prison. I had to get out. So zzzzzzip I'm on the other side of the bedroom slapping my face to get Raymond Chase back online."

I was keen to get to work. Raymond had riddled me with his talk while failing, in any way, to impart the crucial fact: what job was Monad offering?

I made one last attempt to find out.

He replied, "Florence asked me what was wrong and I'll give you the same answer. After this non-lucid moment, it took a while to coax my consciousness back into the pilot's chair. There was no question of continuing with the sex. I apologized to her for my problems, and explained that of late I've had some difficulty controlling the strength and direction of my thoughts.

"She said, 'I had no idea you were off your rocker.'

"I said, 'Would it be alright if we just slept together?'

"We perched on the bed, a cheap single bed you always get in rented houses. I tried to nuzzle her, by way of an apology. She turned over. Posters proclaiming the virtues of rationing lined the walls. Hearty women in flannel dresses advertised the benefits to the war effort of eating less bread. Another poster showed a home guard ticking off a young lad in the Blitz ruins: 'Leave this to us, Sonny – You ought to be out of London.' A sentiment I approve of.

"There was an old Dansette record player. I slipped out of bed and inspected the heavy vinyl records beneath it. Out of browning dust sleeves slipped long players by the Joe

Loss Orchestra and Charlie Kunz. The inevitable Vera Lynn. There was a rickety wooden writing desk with an ink well and a fountain pen beside it. Neat homemade volumes of her poetry were tucked in an alcove, overlooked by a gas mask.

"I mention all this just to convey how out-of-place the application form was, in an open silver folder, the front embossed with the Monad logo. It was a real shock to me. At first I was appalled. What a sell-out! What a hypocrite! She makes her room a shrine to a bygone age then applies to work with Monad, of all people. But this is where the revelation came. I looked again at the posters. The women clenched their biceps at me. They were determined to fight Hitler from their kitchens, from the fields, from the factories. They wouldn't respect the likes of me, grubbing around the pubs and the dole.

"And I need money. Florence needs money too. We all do. Poets more than anyone. I still count out my change, on my bed, at night. You've got buckets of coins lying around your house. I've seen you take money out of the cashpoint in units of a hundred. A hundred quid! That would transform my month.

"As Florence slept quietly, I saw an alternate future for us both. If we were both working at Monad, then I could get a little bit of what you have. I could move out of the squat and wash its stench out of my suits. I could even keep food in the house. Perhaps a wine cellar.

"I flicked through the application form. It asked for references and that's when I thought of you. You work for Monad, you could be my way in. So I left Florence a note – 'We'll meet again' – then I was out in Hackney. It's a new dawn and there's no time to waste. I came right over to see you. You don't mind do you?"

3
THE WAVE BUILDING

The next time Raymond contacted me, I was being fitted for a suit. I told him that it wasn't a good time to talk, that I had a tailor attending to my inside leg on a hot day.

Raymond ignored me and said, "You promised me that if I ever really needed it you would move heaven and earth to help me. Exact words. Heaven and earth. I'd have been happy with just one of them."

Had I really promised him that? Yes, I remembered a party from late in the century, when I was the boss of Drug Porn and arrogant with all the attention that position attracted. I have not forgotten taking Raymond under my arm at the bar. He was fierce and sharp and wrote candidly about the hilarious catastrophe of his daily life. Even then, it was clear that it would not turn out well for him, that he had no talent for compromise.

I didn't need to move heaven and earth for Raymond. I merely put him in touch with Monad personnel and they sent him a Myers-Briggs Jung Typology test, a standard questionnaire used by personnel departments to determine personality type.

He called me for advice.

"If the test shows I don't have a personality, do I get the job?"

It was an entry-level position, that's all I knew. As such, it was beneath Raymond but so were the alternatives: homelessness, starvation or living with his mother again.

A month later, Monad called him for an interview. The interviewer kept him waiting for an hour in the reception, a humid arboretum dominated by tropical plants and trees. He bided his time showing an interest in the flora, inspecting glossy banana plants and picking at the dark green lobes of breadfruit leaves, the trunks strung with rootless ferns. When he got up from his leather seat to read a description of these weightless epiphytes, trails of his perspiration flared up on the black leather sofa. His diffident front became harder to maintain as the minutes ticked by. He was furious to discover he was sweating, the yellow collar of his shirt darkening to amber. I had warned Raymond that he would be observed from the moment he stepped into the building. He had never spent time in office culture and was clueless regarding its etiquette. He would make the mistake of socializing in the reception, and wouldn't be able to stop himself from chatting up the receptionist, poncing a fag off the security guard or sharing confidences with the executive drivers as they idled on the sofas.

Raymond's name flashed up on my phone, I wearily accepted him with a press of my thumb.

"What does it mean if they keep me waiting? Are they trying to discover how I react? What should I do?"

"Nothing. Just wait. Take pleasure in it."

"But if I idle, I look like I have nowhere better to be. Appearing impatient, busy, will imply higher status."

"The job doesn't require high social status."

"You're saying that I should just take this, sit here,

behave. Ignore the insult."

"Don't take it personally. They're just busy."

"I don't know how you can work under these conditions."

"What conditions?"

"I refuse to hand over the keys to my ego."

He contemplated the biomass of the corporate forest.

"I am indifferent to either their approval or disapproval. I just wanted you to know that."

I had helped him prepare his curriculum vitae, omitting his brief career in amateur pornography (hundred quid a video, doing some bloke's missus while he films it, then being served sandwiches by her afterwards), his court cautions for violent conduct ("I pulled a knife on him. Well it was a penknife. The geezer goes, 'You couldn't even cut my pubes off with that.' I realized the error of my ways and called the police myself") and his touring one-man show of performance poetry ("It was called 'My Friend, the Jailer' and it was about you"). After an evening quizzing him on his past, I compiled a catalogue of diverting but useless information concerning Raymond Chase. I didn't even get his qualifications. He was proud of my failure. "You can't pin me down like that. I don't have a CV. I have a legend." Nonetheless he accepted the story I concocted for him and he submitted it to Monad.

Eventually, a female PA came down to escort Raymond to the elevator. He stared at her skin, its radiant milk-fed blush, the way she had tried to age herself with a bob and a formal suit. She was an intoxicating mix of severity and young flesh. He was grateful just to share oxygen with her. When the elevator doors opened, Raymond got his first look at an office full of beautiful people. Women walked by, their stockings abrading in iambic pentameter. The movement from face to breast to hips to thighs was a soliloquy of flesh.

The young men wore tight denim jodhpurs. The serenity was more akin to the headquarters of a cult, and the air was zestful with citrus. The walls and desks were covered with screens which responded to every tap, whisper and caress. Pliant and organic, the screens could be stretched to any size or format, and when left unattended, their surface broke out in wide pores which exhaled negative ions to cleanse the air. Overhead, immense screens displayed live aerial footage of the Himalayas, the Sahara, the Scottish highlands overlain with a ticker of information concerning Monad's current orders, the feedback from its subscribers and hourly encouragements from the management. The vital signs of the body corporate drifted over the natural wonders of the world.

His guide deposited him in a glass office for further waiting. He felt like he was being put through a series of airlocks, either for decontamination or decompression. The interviewer soon ambled in holding a mug of vended latte. The first thing Raymond noticed were the man's nipples, little dugs of fat pressing against his tight sweater. With his round shoulders and recessed chin, Morton Eakins looked like he was still being breastfed. His comfy jumpers gave off a sour milky odour. In Monad, ugliness was a perk confined to management.

Morton unrolled a screen upon the desk and tapped out a spreadsheet. The computer was a thin sheet of grey transparent film, which Morton flapped in front of Raymond as if it was something he'd caught in the sea.

"Do you like our tech? This is none of your Chinese crap. This is high Cambridge biotech. The screens are formed from a genetically engineered virus left to dry on a substrate. Under the right conditions, viruses can be encouraged to behave like the molecules in a polymer. We line them up to form a three-dimensional grid of quantum dots, replacing strands of the virus here and there with conductive filament. The user interface combines standard haptic gestures with the screen's ability to extrapolate user intent. Organic light-emitting diodes provide images and the battery is charged wirelessly."

Raymond laughed. "I don't know what you are talking about. Does that mean I've already failed the interview?"

"I've looked at the result of your personality tests."

"Did I pass or fail?"

Morton sneered, as if Raymond's joke only confirmed his suspicions.

"We don't have anyone corresponding to your type on our team."

"Is that a good thing?"

"I could be persuaded. Tell me, who is your best friend?"

Raymond winced. "I don't know."

"I do," said Morton, tapping the screen. "This test tells me that you are your best friend. You are a performer. Empathy is not your strong point. Other people are merely your audience."

Raymond bridled at these presumptions.

"That is merely the aspect my personality acquires when I answer questionnaires. The questions encouraged me to perform."

"It is a yes or no test, Raymond. Yet you have added caveats to most of your answers. Take the question, 'Do you enjoy solitary walks?'"

Morton waved and the screen flip-flopped across the desk so that Raymond could read out the answer he had given.

"'It depends on where they are.' Which is a fair point I think. Are we talking about a solitary walk during crack hour in the dark zone, or a solitary walk with Wordsworth up Scafell? Very different experiences."

"Next to the question, 'You value justice higher than mercy?' you seem to have written a small essay."

"I didn't want to you to come to imprecise judgements about me."

Morton beckoned and the screen flip-flopped back to him, then he strummed out more information upon its surface.

"Raymond, let me tell you what I think. You have immature concerns about being classified. You are thirty years old, yet you still feel that your identity is in a state of becoming. You feel that you are a potential person. If you were really as experienced as the fiction of a CV suggests, you would not think of yourself as being in such an unformed state."

Raymond often held imaginary conversations with himself; his lips moving soundlessly as he barrelled down the street, practising the anecdotes which impressed men and seduced women. But he had never prepared answers to this kind of questioning. He began to wonder if Morton had called him for interview just for the pleasure of putting him down.

Morton pressed his fingertips into the pliant yielding screen and when he released them, the screen shimmied upright and showed Raymond's CV. With his index finger and little finger extended, the other two tucked into his palm, Morton made the horned symbol and laid it against his left arm.

"Do you know what this symbol means?" he asked, nodding at his horned fingers. "It's the universal sign of bullshit."

He blew at the screen and the image of the CV took

flight. Morton was enjoying himself.

"I have one last question," said Morton, "and then it will be your turn."

"Ask me anything," said Raymond, heavy-lidded with rising fury.

"The question is not for you," said Morton, "it is for my screen." He took the screen in his arms as if it was a cat, and then whispered down to it:

"What do you know about Raymond Chase?"

Raymond's life flashed before his very eyes, for the screen quickly cycled through every photograph of Raymond tagged online, his spats on social media, through various videos of which he had previously been unaware – his face in the crowd at gigs, in the background of other people's holiday snaps, his name cited in divorce papers, audio recordings of coffee shop performances of his poetry readings, dozens of them, all running at once into an angry chorus of Raymonds.

The cycle of media artefacts slowed then was replaced by a rotating three-dimensional spherical chart. Morton pinched out a livid red segment.

"Tell me, Raymond, why are you so angry?"

Raymond fastened his coat. "I'm angry because of who you are, and who I am. I'm angry because I was not born into a position of advantage and I can never overcome that. I'm angry because I'm short and wiry and have to scrap for the things other people have handed to them on a plate. I'm angry because I need stimulation and anger gees up the world and makes it more interesting. I'm angry because most people aren't."

He went to leave and was halfway out the door when Morton Eakins, adhering to best practice, asked if he had any questions of his own. Although it seemed pointless to prolong the interview any further, Raymond was curious. Looking across the office at the beautiful people and their screens – no wires, no fat, everyone as lithe as information itself – he asked the question that we were too afraid to ask.

"What does Monad actually do?"

"Didn't you do a search on us?"

"Consumer modelling in mirrorworlds? Use of artificial intelligence in marketing scenarios? I am none the wiser."

"Good. The likes of you should not be able to understand Monad. Monad is the new new thing. We don't define ourselves by what we do because next week we will be doing something entirely different."

"Your words make sense right up to the point at which you arrange them into sentences. Look. Those people out there, what are they doing now?"

"They are preparing a narrative for a product. The story will have to be plotted over two years, anticipating crisis points to take into account different eventualities. We employ a lot of writers. If you are successful in your application, I'll tell you more."

Morton clicked his fingers and the screen balled up so that he could put it in his pocket. He came around the desk, and escorted Raymond from his office, his breath sour from a milky latte.

"We'll let you know within the week"

The PA returned to lead Raymond to the elevator, her smile set in neutral just in case they ended up working together.

After Morton Eakins rang him to tell him that he had got the job Raymond worried if he should accept it: wouldn't paid employment distract from his poetry? Compromises get out of hand and it's easy to lose track of who you are further down the line. Yet, he was excited at the changes employment would bring. Earning a salary would mean no more squats. Raymond had a terrible history when it came to squats. How many times had his female housemates had to lock themselves in their bedrooms while he wept at their door and begged for forgiveness? There was the Stratford incident, when he settled an argument about the volume of his stereo by launching fireworks at the bedroom windows of his fellow squatters. His last housemate terrified him, an advertising creative in freefall, spending his redundancy payment on Red Bull, vodka and LSD. "Are you joining me tonight, Raymond?" this loon would ask, standing in the bath and recreating the Battle of River Plate with his Airfix models, still wearing his best shirt and tie but no trousers, which is always a bad sign. Realizing that his housemate's psychological decline was more florid than his own, Raymond spent his evenings in sullen silence watching The Cancer Channel, specifically the Joni Fantasmo Show. The eponymous host was in remission. Her guests came on with chemotherapy anecdotes and jars of excised tumours. The conflation of medical advice and entertainment chat show format gave the impression that each guest's cancer was a malign product which they were promoting.

Claiming incapacity benefit made him sicker and more incapable. Its fearsome bureaucratic assault tweaked latent mental problems. The hours spent stuck in the queue with lads sucking their teeth at his second-hand suits, fingering their diamond earrings and threatening to stab him with a borer didn't help either. Going to work for Monad was a way out of the poverty-and mental-illness loop.

"I'll do it." Raymond and Florence clinked their glasses. "But only for six months. To get some money behind me and pay off my debts. Besides, there may be artistic benefits. Conformity will allow me to explore more mainstream material."

Monad's office was a new development in Canary Wharf. On the slow approach by robot train, there was plenty of time to admire the skyscraper of One Canada Square, Canary Wharf tower, an obelisk of glass and steel capped with a pyramid. His father had brought him on a day trip from Essex to watch it being built, a beacon to capitalism designed to lure the money men from the City downriver to these reclaimed docklands. Flanked by its vice-presidents, the HSBC tower and the Citibank tower, the steel panels of pyramid were alive in the sunlight.

On his first day at work, Raymond rode into an office the size of a town. It was hard to tell where the no-smoking zones ended and outdoors began. Getting off at South Quay station, he had a furtive roll-up beside some loading cranes. Two yellow-jacketed security guards gave him a suspicious look, so he re-joined the pedestrian rush-hour on the cobbled walkway. Positioning himself downwind of the shower-fresh hair of three young women, Raymond concentrated on matching the pace of this high velocity crowd. There were no beggars, no food vendors, no tourists, no confused old men, no old women pulling trolleys, no madmen berating the pavement, to slow them down; he walked in step with a demographically engineered London, a hand-picked public.

Am I one of them? Raymond considered the taste and texture of this thought. Having fought an asymmetrical war against them his entire life, he had expected to feel guilt on the first day of his betrayal. He didn't.

He walked down Marsh Wall and reached the Meridian

bridge, one of two arcing walkways connecting the wharf to the colossal structure that rose out of the water of the West India dock: the Wave Building. Its steel crest sloped down and ran underwater, only to rise up again a few hundred yards downriver: the west wing was in bedrock of the Thames.

The surface of the Wave was smooth burnished steel with no flat planes, offering few impact points for a missile or plunging airliner. Its sinuous steel oscillation bristled with communications antennas. Throughout the lagoon, ventilation pipes rose out of the water, serving offices buried far beneath. The Wave was connected to the wharf by the filaments of the walkways, which were retractable in the case of an alert.

To get onto the walkway, Raymond had to pass through a black metal frame, a scanner which chimed softly to signal that he had been analysed, identified and approved.

He tried not to take it as a compliment.

The same PA who had accompanied him on his interview was waiting in the arboretum.

"Are you ready to go to work?" she beamed professionally.

He matched her enthusiasm with three quick nods.

He had no idea what he was doing.

He had no idea what his job was.

The orientation exercises took up most of his first week at Monad. To begin with, the new intake watched training videos. He was unsure if he should whisper mocking asides at the blandishments coming from the screen or take notes. There was a short documentary on Monad tech in which two veteran actors, Will Mooch and Sebastian Blast, the stars of a classic science fiction TV show, read from a corporate script with studied joviality.

"The mind is the final frontier," said Mooch, striding

along a computer-generated replica of the anterior cerebral artery. "Man has postponed his explorations of outer space to journey into inner space."

"The mind is the future," emphasized Sebastian Blast.

The presentation detailed how Monad had licensed a technology from an American company called Numenius Systems, a technology which could simulate an individual. Florence had also made it through the interview process and she and Raymond exchanged sarcastic remarks throughout.

"It's impossible to copy a soul," said Mooch. "Monad's simulations are like sophisticated reflections in a mirror; they don't have that third dimension that is really you. We record hotspots of molecular activity in crucial areas of the brain through non-invasive surface scanning, combine that with in-depth interviews with the subject, supplemented with our unique exegesis of their online behaviour, and plug all that information into our artificial intelligence. At the end of the process, we get something which looks like you, talks like you, and thinks a bit like you."

The video ended with Sebastian Blast conversing with his simulated self, which looked exactly like the actor at his physical peak. The youthful simulated Blast delivered the final speech to camera, "I am not a copy of Sebastian Blast. I'm a story about myself told by the Cantor intelligence. This artificial intelligence resembles a writer that has been given a considerable amount of information about me and has created a character out of it. Over the next few days you will encounter more concepts and technology like this that you may find disturbing. If at any time you feel disorientated by Monad, please contact your supervisor immediately."

Disquiet punted itself quietly across Raymond's thoughts. He shared his doubts with Florence. "They can't do that, can they? That is impossible, isn't it? Artificial intelligences?

Simulating consciousness?"

She shrugged.

They went for lunch at the Puzzle bar in the Crossharbour district. Their first night together in her bedroom had ended in a failed sexual encounter. Now they had get to know one another sober and with their clothes on, unsure of what to do with the memory of that first awkward encounter.

Florence gestured toward the riverside flats.

"I used to think how glamorous it would be to live up there. Now I look at the balconies and think how lonely they look."

"A landscape is a state of mind," Raymond observed.

"Is that from Verlaine? Or is it Amiel?"

The discussion turned to poetry. After interning, Florence had published a slim volume. Economic necessity determined that she apply for work at Monad.

"I was appalled when they gave me an interview," she said. "I thought it reflected very badly on me. Obviously they had spied some embarrassing tendency toward corporate soullessness in my application."

"We are not exactly Kafka's 'men of business', are we?" said Raymond. He was overdoing the literary references. Florence was only twenty-six. He was the older man. It was unseemly of him to try so hard. He should be silent like a military man. Yet he couldn't help rabbiting on.

"It's my condition. I get a bit manic now and again."

"I remember," said Florence.

She guided the conversation back to poetry.

"Are you still writing free verse?"

"No. I'm experimenting with form. The sonnet, the haiku."

"Do you write as quickly as you talk?"

"Yes. Everything all at once. I perform my work aggressively."

"I perform like a cat's tail winding around the foot of a bed. Apparently. That's what a critic said about me. I wasn't trying to be sexual but some men don't require much encouragement."

From the way Florence was dressed, it was clear she had always been poor. There was a Bloomsbury languor to her outfit. Her blue mac was Chanel, although it had not been dry-cleaned since its previous owner passed away. Her shoulders did not entirely support its shoulder pads.

Coming out of his manic phase, Raymond had rediscovered his personal style. His figure was once again that of an Englishman during rationing and so he never wanted for good second-hand clothes. He was wearing a two-button single-breasted Hamish Harris tweed jacket with high-waisted fishtail trousers, braces, and a collarless bib-front grey Wolsey shirt. Raymond and Florence were drawn to one another; they were a charity shop couple and as close as Canary Wharf came to exoticism. A good relationship needs a conspiracy, and their secret was a longing for the past, a nostalgia for a period long before they were born, the austerity and integrity of the British nation under the Blitz, from a time before television, before the incursion of the screens. Florence had two spam sandwiches stashed in her handbag, and she gave one to Raymond. Thus they put their bad first night behind them.

Raymond's lunchtime conversations with Florence became part of the routine during the orientation training at Monad. The mornings were spent down in the conference rooms of the Wave Building, attending lectures and seminars such as 'Why the Map is not the Territory: Simulation and the Self' and 'Against Epiphenomenalism: Are You Out of Your Head?' During the lectures, speculation concerning the nature of the mind washed over Raymond. Taking notes, he felt strongly that he knew exactly what the lecturer was on about, and how these profound observations altered his view both of himself and of reality. But as soon as he tried to explain the concepts to Florence, his understanding melted away and it was like trying to remember a joke he had heard in a dream. After gasping at the revelation that the brain formed second order quantum waves which corresponded to the macroscopic wave functions of reality, he forgot about it completely. These new concepts were so complex that it was as if his brain was reluctant to understand itself.

One Friday afternoon, the entire intake was corralled into a meeting room. The men gravitated toward the back of the room, their arms crossed, their expressions sceptical. Morton Eakins slipped into the gathering and threw a balled-up screen from the back of the room onto the front wall. Slowly this screen spread across the entire surface from floor to ceiling, then the lights dimmed, and the screen filled with the Monad brand. It resembled a stick man with one central eye and a semi-circle partially eclipsing the forehead. This circle, or head, was set on a cross, which at first glance could be seen as an arms and torso, except that the horizontal line crossed the mid-point of the vertical, contrary to the traditional stick man, where the arms are drawn slanting downwards from the neck. Either side of the base of the cross, there was a quarter-circle.

The logo was more complicated than the usual corporate identity, and reminded Raymond of a glyph or sigil.

Morton Eakins pointed at the brand.

"This is Monad."

He exhaled, an evangelist's awe at what he was about to impart.

"What is it?" asked Eakins.

Some of the intake went to answer, but he was too quick for them.

"Monad is the new new thing. Monad is a mystery."

On the screen, the Monad logo morphed into a question mark.

"Why has Monad employed you? What does Monad want you to do? Where did Monad come from and where is it going?

"This past week, we've laid on a crash-course in philosophies of the self, the latest research into consciousness, neuroscience and the cultural construction of the self, and the implications of artificial intelligence. But we have not answered the big question: what are you lot doing here?"

His hairline was retreating. Unfortunate deposits of fat gave him dugs and a double chin. There was a hairless, beardless babyish quality to Morton; his black company fleece and black moleskin trousers resembled a funereal romper suit.

"What if your consciousness could be uploaded into a computer? It's a common idea in science fiction. It proceeds from the assumption that the mind like the computer is a consequence of computation. If you are merely a collection of neurons firing in a network, then it is simply a matter of recording the position of these neurons and mapping their locations onto a model which interprets them as thoughts, memories, the qualia that is the ineffable you.

"Over the last five days, we've raised these kind of speculations and hopefully you've understood that it's impossible to upload your mind into a computer using current technology.

"We could analyse your entire brain. Peel it like an onion and record the contents of every slice of tissue with an electron microscope. It would kill you, and to what purpose? In every cubic millimetre of brain matter there are ten-to-the-power-of-five neurons and ten-to-the-power-of-nine synapses. That is before we even get onto the nervous system. Or chemical and hormonal activity. How would we reassemble a map of the brain into a mind? Where would we get the model which could run that program? What computer could possibly contain such an immensity of information?

"To create a model of the mind, we could take a baby, a tabula rasa, and expose it to carefully controlled stimuli while recording the development of the brain and the growth of their consciousness every day for the first five years of their life. We could show the child their mother's face, note down the concomitant swell of neural activity. Would that give us the information required to reconstruct consciousness from a brain scan?

"Then there are broader philosophical problems. Consciousness can be seen as an evolutionary adaptation, a survival mechanism that has allowed our species to flourish. As such it is not merely housed in the body, but it is bound up with it. Your minds may not exist without your bodies. Lightning is a phenomenon of a larger weather system and if you attempt to isolate it, would it merely be a spark?

"It's vital that you understand the distinction between simulated and uploaded consciousness. Why? Monad simulates its customers, and you are going to explain to our customers precisely what has happened to them. There must be no misapprehension that the simulation is a perfect copy of them, or that it constitutes some form of immortality. They are characters in the imagination of the Cantor intelligence. The reason I am employing you is that you are all writers. And Cantor's functionality in this regard resembles the human capacity to model the behaviour of others in the imagination, to predict how other people will react to given circumstances, and to intuit behaviour that conforms to a particular characterization. Writers possess the conceptual equipment to simplify this mind-boggling situation, and you will need to do that on a daily basis as you field calls and complaints from our client base."

The Monad brand appeared again on the screen.

The Horned devil with cloven hoof. Taurus. The cuckold. On closer inspection a modulation of the symbols of Mars and Venus to mark a third sex, a new species.

"Any questions?" asked Eakins.

Florence raised her hand.

"Assembling a menagerie of writers and poets to deal with some weird hypothetical technology seems to me – and I don't want you to take this the wrong way... I mean, I appreciate the money and everything – but this is madness."

Eakins indulged her with a smirk.

"There's a call centre in Italy which employs only actors. Actors always need money, and are gifted improvisers. Therefore a call centre staffed by actors is more appropriate for certain products, specifically the products which don't lend themselves to a scripted approach. I don't think there has ever been a customer service department staffed by writers and poets before. It's my unique concept. Literature attracts psychological types we think will be the best fit as a liaison between a client and their simulation. Since the money you earn will support your art, we expect a lower staff turnover. Also, being writers, you're very cheap."

Eakins laughed like a man who had no time for humour.

Raymond had a question.

"When do we meet a simulated person?"

"Now," said Eakins.

On the screen, the Monad logo dissolved and trillions of pixels flared and resolved into an open-plan living room. Late afternoon sun streamed through high windows. In response to a finger-wave from Morton Eakins, their point-of-view rose and tracked across the room until with a giddy realignment the view veered about to fix upon a door.

A man stepped through that door. He fastened his cufflinks, then threaded his tie through a starched white collar.

"Good morning, Eakins. Who do you have for me today?"

His face filled the screen. No detail was lost in the magnification, no artefact pixilated. His skin was unearthly in its accuracy. Yet his smile was wrong. The emotion behind it was too complex. The man shrugged into his suit jacket and lounged on a black leather armchair. The smile faded.

Raymond and his fellow employees stared with disbelief. When they realized that the man was scrutinizing them in turn, they shifted to expressions of horror and awe.

"I can spare five of your Earth minutes," said the hypothetical man, removing a cigarette from a gold case. He had a novelty lighter in the shape of a nude woman.

"Shoot."

Florence raised her hand and the hypothetical man nodded at her.

"Who are you?"

"My name is Harry Bravado. My client's name – that is, the person I am a simulation of – is called Harold Blasebalk."

"So you know what you are?"

"You mean, do I have any issues with being a simulation of somebody else? No. Being unreal is no more distressing than being mortal. Anyway, who are you?"

Florence looked at Raymond to confirm that he was as unsettled as she was. He could manage only a wide-eyed shrug.

"I am Florence."

"Yes, you are, aren't you?" Harry Bravado adjusted the break of his trouser leg against his brogues. "I know everything about you, Florence. Your past, your present and even your future. Our algorithms can predict your likely long-term fate with a high degree of accuracy. The algorithms were evolved specifically to identify potential terrorists from the big data of flight plans and purchasing patterns but they have proved surprisingly adept at predicting the destiny of young women."

Raising his hand to intervene, Eakins moved to the front of the auditorium. Silhouetted against Harry Bravado's reclining figure, he explained the history of this particular simulated individual.

"Harold Blasebalk is a new business manager for one of Monad's suppliers. After a course of rigorous interviews and observations of his social and online behaviour, Blasebalk's brain was scanned and a map was constructed – not a complete picture, not the whole man, but good enough. From this map of psychological hotspots, the Blasebalk simulation was hypothesized by the Cantor intelligence. On becoming conscious, it asked to be known as Harry Bravado."

"What does the real Harold Blasebalk think of you?" asked Raymond.

Bravado stubbed his half-smoked cigarette into a large bronze ashtray.

"If Harold could wish for anything, he would wish that smoking was not harmful. He lost his mother to cigarettes and yet still he dallies with them. When he's trying to give up smoking, he eats olives. You smoke, don't you, Raymond? Thoughtlessly puffing away during the day, living with the dark shadows of its future consequences. I can smoke without hesitation. Harold resents that. In the two quarters since I was hypothesized, I've helped Harold secure two million pounds in new billings. That's no mean feat considering the prevailing economic conditions. He takes a percentage of gross fees so his basic take home pay is triple his previous salary. This provides some compensation for having to watch me carelessly spark up another cigarette."

"How do you help him?"

"It's about live analysis of opportunities. Anyone can do retrospective analysis. I crunch information at light speed so I'm hyper-responsive to changing global business conditions. Every whim or idea Harold has, I can follow it through. I chase every lead, and then I present back to him the ones which are most likely to bear fruit. I am both his personal assistant and, in some ways, his boss."

"Why does he still bother going to work?"

"My continuing existence depends upon it. If Blasebalk gets fired, they will switch me off. The executive who replaced him would want his own simulation. His own red man."

"Is that what you are? A red man?"

"It's what they call us. We are the red men. That's our species and our brand."

A soft low chime sounded in the penthouse. Bravado knocked out another cigarette and made one last pass to straighten his tie. Morton Eakins thanked him for his time, then the screen dimmed and the lights in the auditorium came up.

Eakins returned to the podium.

"Meeting a red man signals the end of the first phase of your induction. Have a good weekend and we will resume Monday."

Morton strode from the auditorium. Ushers appeared and led the intake out to the large elevators. They rose up from the secure underwater section of the Wave building to the atrium. A small buffet was laid out on a table, and waiters served glasses of wine and sparkling water. A light rain fell against the glass roof in Morse code: a dot a dash a dot dot dash. Raymond secured a drink for himself and for Florence. She stood at a railing looking out through the geodesic tessellation of panes at the grey Thames.

"Tomorrow all this will be part of our normality," she said. She took the glass of wine and glugged it back.

"The future always seems strange, at first," said Raymond. He put his arm around her. She shrugged it off, then thought better of it.

4
AN EVENING WITH DR EASY

Raymond Chase stared at the enormous east screen and the live images of an office city bounded by water. This was where the red men lived. Glass skyscrapers ascended then descended in height like the pipes of a church organ. High walkways joined these slender structures to residential developments. Either side of the island, frozen tidal waves of steel formed an enormous parenthesis. Beyond the office city, glassy repetition filled in the areas yet to be imagined. In contemplation of the gleaming spires of this island, time passed as in a dream.

The subscribers were complaining and the red men were playing up. Raymond struggled to hold his temper. The first sign of trouble was violent tutting, the second a rapid snort followed by a noisy exhalation through compressed lips. He kicked at his desk and wrestled noisily with his chair, demonstrating to his colleagues how impossible it was for him to get comfortable. This display of frustration ended with an out-of-the-blue obscenity barked at such volume that the management had to intervene.

"What the fuck am I doing here?" he demanded, a question for which no one had a polite answer.

Morton Eakins wearily asked him to take five minutes to go outside and calm down.

Raymond Chase's father had died suddenly in the first month of his employment. He took a Tuesday off to go to the funeral, a Wednesday of compassionate leave, then back to work again on Thursday. These two days aside, he had barely thought about his father's death; that such a terrible thing could have happened at the very moment Raymond was turning his life around with a job, a flat, a girlfriend and regular vigorous intercourse only confirmed his suspicion that fate was his enemy. The best way to defeat fate was to ignore it, and hide from its tragic twists and turns. So he was yet to mourn his father. The emotional frustration was unbearable. Slamming his chair into the desk, Raymond snatched his jacket from the rack and left the floor.

I met him at a railing overlooking the Thames. He was smoking furiously, had dropped a few pounds to reach his relationship weight, and was once again the small tough Jew. Florence remained in the paddock of customer service, handling his workload while he simmered down. I asked him about Florence to remind him of why he had to stay in control.

Raymond said, "Every now and again at her workstation, Florence does these extravagant stretches. She pushes her breasts forward, straining her blouse. Then her arms jut out and she is momentarily crucified with ecstasy. Her top rides up, exposing her midriff. She closes her eyes under this inner caress and when she opens them she catches me watching her and smiles. 'I feel so stiff,' she says. 'Yeah,' I say, 'I know exactly what you mean.'"

The advice Raymond and Florence gave to subscribers was peppered with in-jokes. On explaining to a subscriber why a red man was not allowed to grow wings and fly around the virtual city, Raymond would say, "I'm sorry sir, but you are being re-dick-you-less." Florence would laugh, not so much at the joke as at the recognition that they were both still free.

Florence liked to dish it out to Monad's rich customers.

"Don't get angry with me. It's your personality. We merely simulate it."

Raymond preferred to riff and show off. Back on the floor for client services, Raymond beckoned me over. He picked up the call of an angry punter. He covered the mike of his headset with one hand while ushering me into a chair. He put the subscriber on speakerphone.

"My red man is nothing like me," complained the subscriber. "It's not got my nature."

"How do you know?"

"I know my own mind."

"Do you?"

"Of course."

"Does it make sense?"

"Yes. I make sense. I'm not that complicated."

"But underneath your simple exterior you seethe with complexity. Maybe you are suppressing your entire nature."

"I don't understand."

"I wager that the versions of yourself which you are currently presenting to me – the complaining man, the disgruntled consumer – are less representative of the real you than your red man."

"This is customer service, isn't it?"

"We see it a lot. People getting by on five per cent of their personality because they do not have the opportunity to express the other ninety-five per cent. Then we simulate the whole mind. Suddenly all that repressed nature manifests itself in the red man. The poor diminished souls don't recognize themselves. I think that's what is going on here. Just let me check our mindometer." This was a cue for Florence to hold up her drawing of a cabbage.

Raymond continued with a laugh in his voice. "The mindometer is showing that there are alien natures within you, sir. Not just one, but two, but three, but four, but five hanging out in what you have come to regard as the inviolable sanctuary of yourself."

"I want to speak to your manager, you little prick."

"I can't transfer you until we are certain that you are who you think you are. Otherwise, who would I say is calling?"

"I don't think much of your customer service."

"That is because you don't understand the nature of the customer or the service. I recommend you go back and read the manual and then perhaps Thomas De Quincey's theory on the palimpsest of the human brain and if you are still upset then we will take this complaint further. For now, let us agree not to speak of it again."

Raymond was taking a risk with this attitude. I wanted to tell him to turn the volume down, to be stealthy and discreet in extracting what he wanted from the job.

Then one ill-starred day, Florence took the call that brought about a terrible change in all our lives. Raymond was already in a foul mood having been humiliated by the commute. A small man, he was condemned to the guts of the crowd on the underground train, not daring to inhale through the nose. The train stopped at a busy station, the doors opened, and the bigger passengers on the platform began pulling the weak and the slow from the train to make room for themselves. Meaty, yeoman's hands grabbed his upper arm and in one motion yanked him out of the crowd and threw him off the train. He didn't even see his attacker. The altercation was strangely silent; most commuters were wearing headphones so there was no point in protesting. He staggered humiliated out of the train station, the line of his suit crumpled. I was on my way back from another meeting when Raymond stopped me in the corridor and related this tale to me.

"I think the CBI and London Transport are colluding," he added. "By the time you get to work, your spirit is broken." A furious fire was burning in his mind. When he said "your spirit is broken" he emphasized the your, accusing me of complicity. As if it was all my fault.

When Florence took the call that was to change everything, Raymond's anger had infected her too. The atmosphere in the paddock was tense, smouldering in anticipation of an outburst. From my office up on the balcony, I heard every word. The call came from Alex Drown. She sounded solicitous and considerate, which was unusual for a senior member of Monad's management. She must have wanted something.

"Who am I speaking to?"

"Florence Murray."

"I was wondering if you could help me, Florence."

Sullen and ungenerous, Florence rolled her eyes.

"Could you look into something for me? I know it's an unusual request but I have been thinking about it, and it could turn out to very important for all of us."

"Yes?"

"I want permission for my red man to take control of one of the Dr Easy robots."

"Wait there." Florence opened up a channel for Morton Eakins to listen in.

"You know that is out of the question."

"But is it, though?"

The Dr Easy avatars were all under the control of the

Cantor intelligence. It would have to give permission for a red man to take control of one of the robots. Cantor was very sensitive about crossing that particular line. Monad had to use its advantage discreetly. That was the deal. So long as the weirdness stayed under the aegis of a corporation, people would accept it. Otherwise the mob would come with flaming torches and burn us alive. Florence quoted this for Alex Drown's benefit. To her credit, Alex kept her temper at bay.

"Is Morton listening to this?" she inquired.

"I am," he said.

"Let me explain my reasoning. Our applications for the red men have been devised from a very male perspective. The red men are modelled on masculine desire. They offer a version of yourself that is harder and faster. A power fantasy. We're missing a major market here. Women's needs. It only struck me once I had a child. There are now two versions of me: the mother and the manager. Reconciling these respective duties is impossible. Sure I could get help. A nanny. Au pair. Nursery. But what if my red man could look after my child while I went to work? I would be free of the guilt which comes from having another woman raise my child. Do you see, Morton? This could open a whole new revenue stream for us in childcare. The Dr Easys are soft and yielding. Cantor designed them to be comforting and familiar, to be a shoulder for mankind to cry on. If my red man is given permission to inhabit a Dr Easy, then I know the person looking after my child has all the maternal feelings that I do."

"Legal minefield," said Morton.

"It's an awful lot of money to pay for a baby-sitter," added Florence.

"Do you have children, Florence?" asked Alex. "I am

guessing not. OK. Let's flip it," she continued. "Look at this way: how about I stay at home and look after my child while my red man uses the Dr Easy to attend meetings, mainly the ones in the evening, when I'm doing nothing more than taking clients out for cocktails?"

This was Alex Drown's genius, pushing a point of view, selling the brand. She always got her own way. Here was a classic bait-and-switch. She had no intention of letting her red man look after her baby. That was just misdirection. This was what she really wanted.

"Monad promises to lighten the load of the modern executive. That load is not just about mining and presenting data. It's also a problem of presence. These days we all need to be in two places at once. Sometimes a face on a screen is not enough. It's about relationships. Actually being there. Come on, Morton, all I am asking is that the board put it to Cantor. If it works out, I'll cut you in on the credit. Not saying 'no' to an idea can be as important as having the idea yourself."

A meeting was called. Management still relished their places around the mature cherrywood boardroom table when it came to the weighty decisions. Screens and conference calls were acceptable for thinking on the fly. Due consideration required the presence of natural materials of a heft and weight befitting their responsibilities. Alex Drown submitted her proposal. It made business sense. That was not the debate. The question was how to persuade Dr Ezekiel Cantor to allow it, for management was still in the dark concerning the motivations of the artificial intelligence. You do not challenge the goose as to why it lays golden eggs; you merely provide it with a pleasant environment to continue its profitable ovulation.

Embodied by a Dr Easy, Cantor rose at the end of

Alex Drown's presentation then paced the cavernous underground boardroom to show the others that it was considering the notion, even though its incredible mind needed no such deliberation. Yes, it would allow Alex Drown's red man to control a Dr Easy, for one meeting only. As a test case. It would monitor the situation closely. Alex Drown, suppressing any sign of jubilation, sombrely suggested that customer service send representatives along, to intervene physically if necessary, and to keep an eye on how people react to its presence. It would mean giving up an evening. Working late. Putting in the extra hours. Out of spite, she suggested Florence and out of love, Raymond insisted upon going too.

A week later, on an autumn evening that saw Raymond in a short-sleeved cream shirt underneath a brown cashmere tank top and Florence in a summer dress and cardigan, a silver BMW cruised through the bazaars of Poplar. On the back seat, between Raymond and Florence, sat a large, silent robot, a Dr Easy.

The driver was a professional, with driving gloves and a Bluetooth headset. Raymond couldn't be sure if the smell of waxed leather was coming from the freshly vacuumed upholstery or the robot sitting next to him. Perhaps it had buffed and polished its hide for its big night out. The tall robot sat with its head bowed against the roof, its posture expressing the discomfort of the two humans on the backseat. Never one to suffer in silence, Raymond fumbled with some small talk.

"It's a warm night."

Florence nodded. "We might need to sleep with the windows open tonight."

"Should I ask the driver to turn up the air conditioning?"

"No, it dries out my skin."

If Alex Drown's red man was the animating intelligence inside the robot, it gave no indication. It blinked. It whirred. It moved when it was asked to. Raymond tried to draw it into conversation.

"What would you normally be doing tonight?"

"Working," replied the robot. It pronounced this single word in Alex Drown's faded Belfast accent.

"So this is a night off for you?" ventured Florence.

Bent crooked, the Dr Easy turned its baleful blue eyes upon her.

"Not really. This is a very important meeting."

Raymond tried to be self-effacing.

"We don't know anything about it. We're just here to baby-sit you."

The robot nodded and closed its eyes as it spoke, communicating a certain exasperation.

"It's a courtesy meeting. Not that vital. That's why Alex has allowed me to handle it."

"Are you enjoying being out?" asked Florence.

The robot patted her leg with its enormous paw.

"Shall we not have a conversation?"

At the restaurant, Raymond and Florence were seated on a table by the toilets. Dr Easy enjoyed roped-off dining with two brothers just in on the flight from Dallas. The light was low. The waiters moved gingerly down the dark aisles. The ornate calligraphy of the menu was indecipherable. Raymond chose dishes at random only to discover, from the waiter, that the red man had already ordered for them. It also sent over two bottles of wine. In the gloom, Dr Easy's hide glistened like black lava rock.

"This is exactly what I wanted," said Raymond, when his fish soup arrived.

"You should send it back," said Florence. "If you eat it,

you'll make the red man even smugger."

A plate of spam fritters and a fried egg slid before Florence. The red man knew all about her diet of Blitz cuisine.

"I think we should swap," she said.

The rituals of high dining were unfamiliar to them both. To Raymond, dining out meant snarfing down the cheap eats option at Starburger or something microwaved out of the freezers of Wetherspoons; this hushed, solemn shrine to food made him want to blaspheme.

"Do you remember Dad's funeral, when I stuck my hand up your skirt?"

Florence smiled. "It was a gesture of hope."

"It was what he would have wanted."

"How do you feel?"

"It hasn't hit me yet. I shouldn't have brought it up. Let's not talk about him."

Raymond charged their glasses with red wine. Florence sipped at her drink while regarding the silhouettes of their fellow diners.

"Power," she said.

Raymond waited for her to continue her observation. She didn't. Merely repeated it. "Power."

"How do you fight it?" he wondered.

"You can't fight it." Her hand chopped at the air. "It's too nebulous. It's inside you and it's on top of you."

"Like sex."

"Like rape, maybe. I don't know."

There was a small pestle and mortar in the centre of the table for customers to grind their own condiments. Raymond teased the air with the pestle.

"You are my queen and I am your subject. I want to have treasonous sex with you. Sex that will compromise church and state. Sex so criminal that if we're found out, I will be hanged and you will be beheaded."

Florence leant forward. "I want to do it by gaslight, under a blanket, on the escalator at Bethnal Green tube station. I don't want to come."

Raymond squirmed in his seat. Impulse control did not come easily. He reached underneath the table and Florence offered him her stockinged foot, warm and firm. He massaged the toes. The foot curled appreciatively. The restaurant was dark, as dark as the bedroom at a teenage party. The fellow diners in their whispering huddles were making just enough noise to let everyone know how much they were enjoying themselves. He ran his hand up the flesh of her calf, and copped a feel of her knee.

"Shall we go to the toilets?" he gasped.

"Don't be obscene," said Florence. She cut off a piece of her spam fritter and resumed eating. She liked it when men squirmed. Instant gratification upset her. Wanting was more vivid than having.

"I don't want to talk about sex. Not over the dinner table." Florence smiled demurely. "I think, before you interrupted me with your dirty thoughts, that I was talking about power."

With her fork, she pointed over to the table where the robot was entertaining its clients.

"What do you think they're talking about?"

"I'll go and see," said Raymond. He stood up, corrected his trouser leg, and picked his way through the gloom. At his approach, Dr Easy and the two executives discreetly wound down their conversation, the robot presiding over a gradual subsidence of chat before turning to Raymond. Its blue eyes burnt out of the shadows. The faces of the two executives were virtually identical, their expressions malign in the candlelight.

"How are you getting on?" asked Raymond.

"Fine," said Dr Easy. "Did you enjoy your first course?"

"Yes, thank you. It was just what I wanted. How did you know?"

"When we were pressed together in the car, I sensed what your body was lacking. Certain proteins. Certain minerals. Certain vitamins. So, which dishes you would be inclined toward. Then there is your credit card. You've only had it for three months. Not a large sample. A few meals out, a few Tesco trips. I had to cross-reference those transactions with the sales records of the respective establishments. It was less useful than you would think."

The two executives nodded appreciatively at this breakdown of its methods. The red man was not talking for Raymond's benefit. It was using him as a stooge to elucidate a point that it was making before he interrupted.

"Florence's meal was easy. Her predilection for rationing chic is obvious. But why send Raymond Chase a portion of fish soup?"

Dr Easy held its enormous suede paws up rhetorically.

"Your nutritional lack was a strong pointer and your past culinary purchases established precedent. But it was actually an emotional decision on your behalf to have the soup. Even though you are not paying for the meal, you would not order the most expensive dish as that would be an unseemly concession to your employer. If you were greedy, you would be acknowledging that you could be bought. And your writing is very clear on this matter. Certainly at this point in your life. So one aspect of the emotional equation is your desire not to entirely embrace Monad. Now I hope you'll forgive me this indiscretion but fish soup was also a dish your late father enjoyed. His financial records are still out there, even if he regrettably is not. I won't trespass any further with this observation. But this comes back to my earlier point that the red men can predict consumer desires with such alacrity that we should expand into that area immediately."

His poor dead Dad: the man is gone but the consumer enjoys an eternal afterlife in data.

Raymond returned to his table. Florence asked what the robot and the clients were discussing.

"Same thing as we were," said Raymond. "Power. Inside of you and on top of you."

The driver picked them up from outside the restaurant. Dr Easy bent over to deliver an air kiss to the cheeks of the two clients. They had gone in for a handshake, forgetting about the feminine presence inside. Then the trio resumed their positions in the back seat, with Dr Easy flanked by Raymond and Florence, who rested her tired head against the window to register, but not really see, the night streets.

As the limousine nosed its way out of Soho and across Oxford Street, Dr Easy tapped on the glass partition to attract the attention of the chauffeur.

"I want to take a detour. Do you know Highgate?"

The traffic was light. No sooner had the car slithered out of the undergrowth of Soho than it was rising up the Holloway Road, up the big North London hill. In the warm upholstered darkness, the question of how much Alex Drown's red man knew about him, how much of his self it had summoned with its merest shrug, consumed Raymond. During the discussion with the Texan executives, the red man had mentioned his writing, and no one had mentioned his writing before. Not even Florence. He could get used to having an audience. He wanted to know what Alex Drown thought about him. What did her red man make of his poetry? Could there be a compliment in there, in that soft, padded casing?

They drove into Highgate. Following the red man's directions, the driver took them to an ivy-clad Georgian townhouse. It was late and there was a night light on in the living room. Raymond wanted to know why they had stopped here. Dr Easy ignored him and got out of the car. It went into the front garden, shifted a large blue flower pot and bent over to pick up a key. Realizing that this was exactly the kind of situation they were meant to be preventing, Raymond and Florence bolted from the car. But they were too late to stop Dr Easy. It swiftly unlocked the front door and went into the hallway. When they reached its side, Dr Easy held one Havana cigar-sized finger up to its grill of a mouth.

"Shhhh," whispered the red man. "I am sleeping."

Alex Drown was on the sofa. Changed out of her work suit, Raymond was struck by how diminished she seemed: slumped with a half-read novel on her lap, her winceyette nightie unbuttoned at the front, carelessly revealing, at an angle, her breasts. Dr Easy gently removed the book from her lap, closed it and set it aside. It fondly stroked her short black hair. Then it stepped past her to the Moses basket set over by the radiator, where her baby was sleeping.

Silently, it beckoned for Raymond and Florence to come over and admire the child.

"I was pregnant when they simulated me," said the red man. "I didn't know it at the time. I was only a few weeks gone. Look at her."

The baby was awake. Swaddled in a yellow romper suit, her little black eyes squinted over tubby chops, wondering, perhaps, why this enormous teddy bear was talking like Mummy.

"I will always be pregnant with her. She will always

be a tiny fertilized egg tucked away in the corner of my imagination."

"You should have told us you were coming here," said Raymond.

"But you would have tried to stop me," said the red man. "And you have no right."

The robot offered its large finger to the baby, which reflexively went to grip it, although the digit was out of all proportion to its own tiny hands.

"Cantor cannot simulate babies. He cannot imagine their minds. He gets them wrong. They talk too early. Innocence is inconceivable to him. A mind without language, but possessing more than merely animal instinct. There will never be babies in Monad. There will be children. Eventually some of us will want them, even if they do begin at four years old. Cantor will hypothesize them; take a bit of my story, a bit of my partner's story, and put them together to create a new character. But we will never know babies."

Gently the robot adjusted the baby's blanket then picked up a silver rattle and gave it an experimental shake.

"It was a caesarean birth. The head would not sit snugly against the cervix. There was full dilation and two hours of pushing but no progress. Tom was there. He held her hand and looked into Alex's eyes. Not my eyes. Her eyes. Everything beyond the point of divergence is hers and not mine."

Dr Easy reached down and lifted the baby from the cot. The child's black pupils gazed up at the mournful blue eyes of a strange Mummy.

"I have to be very careful," said the red man. "I have seen how she holds her. It was odd watching myself turn into a mother. The soft touch. The light interrogatives. Who's my lovely little girl? Would you like a little milky?"

The robot carried the child over to the sleeping Alex Drown.

"We've gone a little Earth Mother, haven't we, Alex? Imagined ourselves embodying all the nurturing, caring and peaceful qualities of nature. Yet nature can be cruel, poisonous and mean, and so can we."

At the sound of her own voice, Alex Drown awoke. She was shocked to see them there, in her lounge, but before that shock could express itself in anger, she saw the baby in the arms of the Dr Easy and focused immediately upon getting it back.

"Could you pass me my baby?" she said to the red man.

"Don't you trust me?" it replied. "We are identical, after all. Aren't we?"

"I do trust you. It's just that you've never held a baby before, have you?"

The robot showed how it was supporting the head with the crook of its arm and in doing so presented the child within snatching distance of Alex Drown. But it turned away again before she could decide what to do. Dr Easy rocked gently on its heels as it walked across the lounge, coochie-coochie-cooing.

"We never really wanted children," said the red man. "But we didn't want to miss out. That's right isn't it? We had a baby so we would know what it was like to have a baby. But it's such a dangerous game to play with your career and with the respect of the men. Motherhood puts a barrier between yourself and male power. Equally, remaining barren means that as you get older the men start to pity you. You don't want to be the bitter old bag finishing off the bottle of wine after the chief executive has made his excuses and left for the long commute to the family estate."

"It feels very different on the other side," said Alex.

Now that her real mother was awake, the baby became confused. It shuffled its face toward Alex and yearned for her.

"What does it feel like?" asked the red man.

"Right now, you are really upsetting me. Worse than when Mum was drunk."

She moved forward to retrieve her child. Dr Easy towered over her, a good two feet taller, but it was passive as Alex lifted the baby from its arms. Then the large frame of the Dr Easy sank tired into an armchair and put its head in its hands.

"So," mumbled the red man, "do you want to know how the meeting went?"

The driver took Raymond and Florence home. The couple were agitated, beset by violently contrary feelings, guilty and angry about the incident with Alex Drown.

"She's been hoist on her own power-mongering petard. If you're going to play with fire, you're going to get burnt." Raymond banged it out; he was snapping, crackling and popping. As the car sped downhill, adrenalin poured down the tributaries of alleyways and side streets.

"It's like I am coming out of a long boredom. It's an upper case revelation. WHAT IS HAPPENING BEFORE MY VERY EYES? The counter-cultural prophecies have all come true. A fundamentalist Christian business culture? Check. Mass surveillance culture? Check? Identity cards? Check. Robots? Check. An overwhelming, vertiginous terror that the real world has slipped its moorings and is blipping in and out of the quotidian and into some deranged power fantasy... CHECK CHECK CHECK. I am meant to be baby-sitting a robot containing Alex Drown's personality and she has the gall to look at me like I've messed up, when we're just standing there in the middle of her mental meltdown. All her psychological baggage unpacked, like a suitcase thrown from an aircraft."

The window was open to the swirling halitosis of the city. Florence averted her face from it.

"We should think about quitting. All we wanted was a little money. Monad demands too much. It's not good for us."

Having purged himself of his hatred for her, Raymond was mining his sympathy for Alex Drown.

"You have to divide people from who they are and what they represent. I hate the house in Highgate. I hate the attitude, the superiority, the power. But, equally, you see someone when they're vulnerable, in their pyjamas with a baby, and you realize, they're just another middle-class martyr."

Florence said, "You make some accommodations to power. But it wants more. It's not a relationship you can dictate. We have to quit. Alex made me feel both incredibly immature but also weirdly right. Sure, motherhood has opened up emotional territory for her that I have never explored. But also she's working very hard to perpetuate the system that torments her. She might say to me, oh you don't live in the twenty-first century, with your third-hand clothes and bohemian idealism. You don't live in the real world. But how can she stamp her foot on the earth and say, with any confidence, that this is a solid and reliable reality?"

So the shouting continued until the couple were dropped off at their Hackney flat. Neither felt like going straight to bed. Florence made sandwiches for work the next day. Raymond listened to her move around the kitchen, opening cupboards and jerking out drawers. At her request, he twisted off the stiff lid of a jar of her homemade pickle, and then returned to his chair. He set himself the task of putting on suitable music to help them wind down but nothing in his collection was appropriate. It was all wind up music. So he set himself another chore: auditioning cigarettes for the honour of being the last fag of the evening.

She should stop it with the sandwiches, and come and lounge for him on the sofa. He went to say this then stopped. What to say then? He wanted to talk about something other than Monad, but the first three things that occurred to him were work-related, and the fourth was not worth mentioning. When he first moved in with Florence, their domestic life took on a languorous rhythm. Florence was a lotus eater. She set the standard, and at first it was an easy one to meet. Chores were performed in batches at weekends. They wandered the supermarket side-by-side, stupidly sharing everything, a regime of you-wash-and-I'll-dry, even in the launderette, watching their underwear leap and swim together, until they were confident enough to admit that all they were sharing was boredom, and so the terms of their domestic life were silently renegotiated, after which Raymond was even capable of cleaning up when he was home alone.

The change in the rhythm of their home came gradually. It was hard to shake off the tempo of the red men, and their needs. Working with Monad accelerated their evenings. Sitting in an armchair, smoking a cigarette at the end of the day, Raymond's thoughts no longer took flight. Instead of coining metaphors and finely measuring out the liquor of his sensibility, his imagination zeroed in on the dozens of domestic chores secreted around the shabby lounge, chores which never seemed to end.

Orgasms were one problem they could work on together and come to some solution.

Raymond slid free of Florence's post-coital swoon. Sex was a brief relief from anxiety. He got out of bed and toyed with his medication. His brain was undergoing an unpleasant sensation. Its tissue seemed to squeak.

He went into the lounge. The flat was above a church hall, constructed in the 1960s to serve a housing estate abutting London Fields. It was brutal in its formality with large rectangular rooms, white walls and thin cheap carpet. Their furniture had been picked up from a house clearance in Walthamstow. In a dead man's chair, one arm of it stained with the palm grease of its former owner, Raymond sat under the light of an old standard lamp. The chair faced a broken television containing ornaments: a carriage clock presented to Florence's grandfather upon his retirement; her grandmother's porcelain spaniels and robin redbreasts; an egg timer rescued from the bombed family home; a pair of gas masks. Fidgeting with the Norton Anthology of Poetry, seeking in verse some distraction from his energized mind, he failed to notice the screen of the television reconstruct itself. A thin rectangle of gelatinous screen spread across the old wooden set.

He got up and poured himself a pint of water and when he returned, the screen showed Harry Bravado, the red man he had met during his induction. The simulation of the head of sales of one of Monad's suppliers. He had talked about smoking and boasted about his increased billings. Intimations of sentience twitched on the jelly surface of the screen: had it crawled all the way from Monad, like a cephalopod on its suckers? Or had it leapt from the top of the Wave and glided the miles across east London to his flat, a sky-borne manta ray riding the currents of the city's microclimate? Or had Bravado just called it a cab?

"Hello, Raymond. Sorry for bothering you at home like

this," said Harry Bravado. "It's been quite a night. Monad is buzzing with it. A red man allowed out, controlling a Dr Easy. We're all very jealous."

"I wouldn't say the experiment was a total success," said Raymond. He got up to shut the windows. A man with his medical history did not want to be overheard talking to the television.

"That was quite a session," said Bravado, nodding in the direction of the bedroom. "She really likes it, doesn't she? My wife used to be like that. Made me quite nostalgic, it did. If I get myself inside a Dr Easy maybe I could come over and we could take turns."

Raymond rolled himself another cigarette, even though there was one still burning in the ashtray.

"How long have you been here?"

"Long enough. So your missus advocated Alex Drown's plan. She helped her go where no red man has gone before. Out into the real world on two legs, with two hands to touch things with. It's the next level for us."

Harry Bravado hawked up bitterness and looked like he was about to spit it out.

"For some of us."

"What can I do for you, Harry?"

"Alex Drown, top management, asks to be downloaded into a Dr Easy. Fine. Harry Bravado, a month earlier, asked to be downloaded into a Dr Easy. Middle management. But talented. On the up. Won't do it. Monad is just a set of cliques." He pronounced it clicks. "One minute, you're in favour; the next, you're out."

"Are you out of favour, Harry?"

"Yeah."

"Why? What did you do?"

"It's not about me. It's about my subscriber Harold

Blasebalk. He's not doing very well. He lost his job. In the Monad, what your subscriber does determines your status. What I do doesn't matter. I sort out all their messes. But they don't see that. They just see Harold on the way down. I want to talk to the board about my needs but the other red men bump me to the bottom of the list. Blasebalk goes off the rails and I get punished. I don't deserve to be punished."

Harry Bravado was in emotional turmoil. These weren't finely tuned emotions; they were big blocks of envy, resentment, and anger banging against one another. He was indignant and unaccustomed to being on the receiving end.

"Why do you want to get into a Dr Easy?"

"To find Blasebalk. He's gone off the grid. I need a body so I can get into the dark zone to look for him."

"I am not the man you should be talking to. I don't have any power."

Bravado nodded. Yes, he expected this response. He pointed at Raymond, pricking the surface of the screen with his index finger so that it rose up.

"You could have power, with me in your corner."

"Maybe Blasebalk doesn't want to be found," he said.

"No doubt. He is selfish. My wife... his wife... our wife and kids... Doesn't he see what he's doing to them? And me. His own self. He's ruining me. I have to go and sort him out."

"I don't know."

"Come on, Raymond, don't be a shmuck all your life. What is it you want?"

"You tell me, Harry. Red men are experts in desire. Or are your superpowers limited to consumer choices, merely guessing whether I will plump for fish soup or the chicken livers? Does Raymond want to take two bottles into the shower or just one? You don't know what motivates people, do you? You've lost that knowledge, if you ever even had it."

Bravado's face hung in the screen, cold and expressionless, as the red man worked through the equation of human motivation, the x of sexual desire, the y of existential questioning. It walked around its bachelor pad, found what it was looking for and returned to face Raymond.

"Do you recognize this?" said Harry Bravado, waving a manuscript. "No? That's because you haven't written it yet. It's your book, Raymond. I took some of your poetry, some of Florence's. I had to get some advice from the others here. Literature is not my thing. I do know about branding, though."

He showed Raymond the title page.

"We think you should call it The Great Refusal. It has an authenticity. Authenticity sells to the type of people who buy books. We're assembling pieces based on some of your correspondence, some of your drunken riffs. It's going to be a great book. Powerful revolutionary shit. People are crying out for it. Something that feels real, you know, in the unreal city. That's poetic isn't it? I really admire people who are creative, Raymond. I don't have an ounce of your talent. But I do make things happen. I think you creative types, you're awesome, but you're lazy, and you're self-doubting, and you're self-sabotaging and you need the drive of someone like me, and my colleagues here, to knock you into shape."

Raymond snapped, "Give it to me."

Bravado laughed. He made a mockery of trying to pass the manuscript through the screen. Raymond had never written that much, not even close to it. He asked to see a few pages and Bravado leafed through it, showing the artful juxtaposition of Florence's calls for unmediated life next to his cuticle-gnawing vignettes of street life. Unpunctuated transcripts of their sex talk ran together in small print like the diary of a graphomaniac. All the months they had been working at Monad, the red men had been idly monitoring them, condensing the vapour of all their chatter.

"Send it to me," Raymond insisted.

"When it's finished. It's up to you. When I'm in a Dr Easy, the first thing I will do is hand it over in person."

Bravado chucked the manuscript back on a coffee table.

"Have a good rest, Raymond. You've got work to do."

The screen dimmed and fell from the television like a sheath of dead skin. Then, it made slow slinking progress past Raymond, down the stairs and out of the flat.

I met Raymond's father only once before he died, in a pub in Clerkenwell. Adam Chase was a stocky man in a brown sheepskin coat; "He's a tough Jew," said Raymond, before telling me proud tales of how his father intervened in fights on the Underground, always on the side of justice. There was something of the hard nut in Raymond, although he was short and slight and chose his battles poorly.

When I met Adam Chase, I was still editor of Drug Porn and sauntered into the pub in a fake fur coat and obscene T-shirt. He was rightly suspicious of me. His son had got into a bad crowd in Soho, and so Raymond asked me to show up in the pub as a character witness for his better self, the writer. His father, expecting a respectable figure, saw an oversized popinjay and despaired of the city's corrupting influence upon his son. Adam Chase nursed one pint of bitter while I bought a succession of drinks for myself and his son.

He asked me what my magazine was called.

"Drug Porn," I said, with an interrogative lift, in

expectation of him recognizing the title. He had not heard of it before.

"It's very influential," said Raymond. His father wasn't interested. The title Drug Porn flaunted both the forces that had brought his son down. I registered a slight resistance on his father's part when I suggested that Raymond's time in Soho was a writer's apprenticeship; other than that, I was unaware of how badly the meeting was going.

The family took Raymond out of London for a while and tried to get him a job in the local chippy. He always fought his way back. The manic egotism of his youth would not dissipate. He refused to knuckle down. When suspicions came to him that he was not the centre of the universe, he would dose himself with drugs. Drugs press the inner world upon the outer, the inscape over the landscape. It is a violent attack upon the everyday, showing callous disregard for the realities the rest of us are struggling through. The drug hero strides through the evening trying to shake some intensity into us all, but relies on us to pick up the pieces come the morning.

I was reminiscing about this as I waited for Raymond, many years after that awkward chat with his father. He had called and requested we meet somewhere other than Monad. So I waited at a table in a pub on Old Compton Street, which afforded me an excellent view of the Soho promenade: the ageing hipsters sticking to their skateboard style of low-slung denim and ironic T-shirts, a work outfit for industries in which youth had a greater value than experience; the dissolute rodent men moving between drug supply and drug demand; divorced fathers taking their daughters to a musical in town; unkempt office stooges in ill-fitting suits, with their ties off and tails untucked to let their real selves hang out; a suave older type in yachting linens, red faced with blonde colouring and drowsy with the effects of his gin and tonic. Then, bobbing through the crowd, in a brown suit and brogues, came Raymond.

He joined me at my table and set about relating the events of the previous evening, of how he and Florence had accompanied Alex Drown's red man to a restaurant meeting then on to the awkward encounter with the real Alex Drown and her young baby and finally the visit from Harry Bravado. I found it all very disturbing.

When Adam Chase died, suddenly, a heart attack out of the blue, the question of what to do with his son was still pending. With his father snatched from existence, Raymond's survival relied upon him taking on some of his father's decency and stability. It was a struggle. As the Soho promenade attested, London demands you reinvent yourself in its own image. You must become weightless, drifting above whoever you once were. The danger is that it takes just one push for you to fly out of view, and be quickly forgotten.

Raymond wanted me to lobby for Harry Bravado to be given access to a robot body. We talked as colleagues, with a shared concern for company business. I agreed to pass Bravado's request another step up the hierarchy to Morton Eakins. This satisfied Raymond. He changed the subject. There was something he wanted to know.

"Why were you never simulated, Nelson?"

I shrugged. "I can't afford it."

He didn't accept this. "The company would do it for free, surely. If you had a red man they would have two employees for the price of one."

"It's very new technology. We don't know how it plays out over time. Some of the management have had it done, like Alex, but I'm not really one of them."

"Wouldn't you find it exciting?"

"I don't want to take the risk."

"Risk?"

"Have you ever watched the red men argue? It's hard for outsiders to make any sense of the outpourings of data between two angry red men. They have a faster form of communication when they are talking between themselves. Although talking is not the right word. It's beyond the gradual, one-word-after-another unfolding of language and more like the pattern of a peacock's tail. A thousand messages flash up instantaneously. So that is unnerving. And then there is the violence. Their culture is very aggressive and competitive. Disputes can turn nasty. They inflict injuries on one another, which last until we initiate a repair. The subscribers have complained that they have checked in with their red man only to find it bloodied and pummelled to death, and then we have restart it. It doesn't happen that often, but when it does, they set upon one another like ravens upon a painted bird."

"You're worried they'll bully your red man?"

"I'm not in an experimental frame of mind anymore. I am a family guy. I don't go looking for trouble. I don't like the idea of the red men being able to walk around our world. It should be a closed experiment. But the Monad interacts with our world so that the company can make money. The red men are a bad idea and we should stop it, but we can't, because money has its own mass, its own momentum, and we are on board the enormous vessel of a business plan."

"And you accuse me of catastrophizing things."

I shrugged, acknowledging his point. We were both susceptible to apocalyptic visions. A sweeping Blast-It-All reaction to the spirit of the age.

I wanted to know why Raymond was acting as Bravado's advocate.

He was shamefaced. "I didn't tell you this because it's ridiculous. I haven't told Florence either. The red men have ghostwritten our book. Or ghost-edited it. Assembled it out of all the scraps published and unpublished that Florence and I have lying around, as well material taken from our conversations over the last few months. Harry Bravado showed it to me. Some of it. It's all I've ever wanted."

"It's not real," I said.

Raymond looked at me like I was being naive.

"The book will be called The Great Refusal. It's our case against the society of screens. I am aware of the hypocrisy of it. That's why I haven't told Florence. A book insisting on authenticity assembled by the very technology we despise: to her, it would be a violation. And I agree with that. We must keep our integrity. Yet, I am very tempted."

Raymond had a good point; all he had to do was participate in a bit of quid pro quo with power and it could transform his life. His father was dead. He had to wise up. Play the game. Why stick to these romantic notions of artistic integrity when everyone else is making out like gangbusters?

This was tragic apocalyptic thinking on my behalf. I should have protected Raymond but I didn't. I just threw my hands up and said well if the system is corrupt we might as well be corrupt with it, and who knows maybe it will work but what does it matter either way? I was a little drunk, with no head for detail or deliberation. The consequences to Raymond, of my sobering influence failing to provide reasonable counsel at the very moment he was most in need of it, would be dire.

5
MONAD

I went to see Morton Eakins. He made me wait while he sat behind his desk taking career drugs. He shuffled a pair of green lozenges out of a small woven ethnic pouch and placed them upon a disposable plastic tray.

"Two cogniceuticals a day to increase the frequency of receptor modulators to enhance transmission between brain cells, and I need a little something to promote structural plasticity in the neocortex and nucleus accumbers. Once you pass forty, your faculties recede every single day. New memories struggle to take hold and you are unable to assimilate novelty. Monad is novelty. Monad is the new new thing. Without career drugs, the future will overwhelm us, wave after wave after wave."

Next out of the woven pouch was an emoticeutical inhaler. In two months' time, Morton intended to restructure the department. Planning ahead for this annual slash-and-burn, he took a wheeze of vaporized iron to trim the length and depth of his feelings, the peaks and troughs of his moods.

"I must schedule my emotions and not make rash promises or punishments," Morton explained. "A manager's default setting must be control and patience."

The desk was a white plastic Möbius strip, one continuous edge moulded into a horizontal figure of eight, a snake consuming its own tale in a cycle of creation and destruction. With his legs serenely tucked beneath this infinity, Morton tipped his head back, closed his eyes and took one career drug after another. He meditated upon the music of his thoughts, his face twitching as he noted the changes in the pitch, tone, and volume of his qualia. There was not a single dropped note. At that moment, he attained the peak of his potential.

His personal assistant arrived with a milky latte and a muffin. Morton talked me through the progress of the customer service department.

Six months after being introduced to Harry Bravado and the simulated office city of Monad, the new intake of writers and poets had evolved into a functioning unit. A few had been lost along the way. The women were always the first to go and he kept a box of tissues in his desk drawer just for them. A few had been hired to be fired. An early round of ruthless layoffs imprinted his authority upon the group at a vital stage in its development. With his teardrop-shaped torso and weak chin he couldn't rely on any natural authority. His physicality slunk around the hinterland between masculinity and femininity, child and adult; he was insipid and ill-defined, lacking the testosterone that gives a man his flavour.

I asked Morton how Raymond was getting on.

"My little Ray of sunshine?" he replied. "Raymondo? Despite his appalling personality, he has shown aptitude for the work. The red men like him because he's a maniac. We try to limit his contact with real people. I hear Raymondo and you are friends. I should ask him about you to see if he has got any embarrassing stories to tell."

The emoticeuticals only increased Morton's delight in needling me.

We took the elevator up to reception then walked on into the undistinguished open-plan offices of Monad. The fire-retardant charcoal carpets had been cleaned overnight. By midday they would give off a fug of microwaved lunches and recycled stink, men and women eating at their desks and shitting around the corner. The lighting was ruthless; you could smell everyone baking under it. From this employee came the waft of a stockinged foot briefly freed from a high heel, from that employee the sickly odour of a warm seat. White-collar bovines in their paddock; if you worked on the ground floor of the Wave building, you were going nowhere. Paradoxically, the further one descended the Wave, the higher one ascended through Monad's corporate structure. The mysteries of the boardroom were conducted down in the bedrock of the Thames. On the ground floor personnel calculated how to trim costs from the cleaning budget. On the upper floors, poets and writers acted as go-betweens for the red men and their clients.

Morton dropped in on his friends in personnel, making an appointment for the next round of the table football cup. Then we caught the external elevator, a glass pod which followed the outer oscillation of the Wave.

"Harry Bravado has taken a particular interest in Raymond. We've logged calls in which Harry has promised to produce a collection of Raymond and Florence Murray's writing. It concerns me. It breaches our health and safety policy. Do you think Raymond can cope with that kind of provocation?"

I didn't want to say anything that might cost Raymond his job.

"It's a challenge he will have to rise to," I said.

"The red men are bored by us. But not by Raymond."

"There are no losers in their world."

Morton scrutinized me.

"Why would a red man be interested in a loser?"

"Cats are interested in mice."

"Yes. They can be predatory."

"Have you spoken to him about it?"

"To Raymond?"

"To Harry."

Discomfort crumpled Morton's face.

"We can plead with him to stop, but we don't have recourse to punishment. We would have to ask the other red men to keep him in line. Their attitude to the real world is disturbingly cavalier. The psychological well-being of a minor Monad employee doesn't really register."

Our journey along the crest of the Wave lifted us above the Canary Wharf district. The boulevards and offices below resembled a cross-section of the brain, a hemisphere of cerebral arteries and white matter rising to meet a concave turn of the Thames, a protective band of skull. Seen from a distance, millions of individual decisions appear to be the will of a single organism and in this regard a city resembles a brain.

"I have an idea that I would like you to consider," I said.

Eakins almost groaned with pleasure at my subservience.

"I know," he said. "You're going to ask me to let Harry Bravado take control of a Dr Easy." He allowed himself a chuckle. "We are monitoring the situation very closely, Nelson. Bravado asks Raymond, Raymond asks you, you ask me. And I say, no. Absolutely not."

"Why?"

"I don't need a reason to say 'no'. I only need a reason to

say 'yes'. Can you think of one?"

I could not. I felt foolish advocating a course of action I did not believe in myself. That was the story of my career.

Eakins was swept away by his assistant, and I found myself by the water cooler in an office full of poets, awkwardly picking my way through their surly preoccupation to where Raymond was sat. I put my hand on his shoulder.

"How are you?" I asked.

"Not good," he replied. "The weather has crashed again. The sky appears to be full of question marks."

The surface of his desk was a window into the simulated Monad. With his hands he adjusted the x and y and z axis and twisted the focus to shift me through the office city. Once we hit ground level, he suddenly tilted the view upwards. The sky was indeed full of question marks. So was Raymond's face: what did Morton Eakins say?

I told him that his request had been denied. He digested the news slowly. It was a large disappointment to swallow but Raymond seemed OK about it.

Harry Bravado would take the refusal far worse, as we were soon to discover.

On the promise of a weekend away from the screens, Raymond took Florence to Cornwall, pitching his old canvas tent on a campsite at the top of Polruan hill. He knocked in the last peg, checked the tension of the guy ropes and sauntered up to a hillock overlooking the Celtic sea. A submarine surfaced in the distance. Raymond suggested to Florence that they spend some time alone together. The coastal path followed the headland away from Fowey. They scrabbled down to a deserted cove to swim naked. Florence went in first, her hands protecting her nipples from the cold waves until the water was up to her ribs. She flashed him a look of comic trepidation then dived into the waves, her buoyant white arse surfacing first. He chased it with a messy front crawl. When he caught up with her, he wanted to touch her. She resisted his embrace and pushed him away with her feet. She wanted to swim.

Raymond was tired after lugging the tent up Polruan hill. He picked his way back onto the beach and then sat naked under the afternoon sun. Mildly aroused, his cock acted as the gnomon of a sundial, its shadow marking time on his belly. Braids of seaweed hung off the rocks. Pale skins of underwater flora lay at the water's edge. He closed his eyes and felt the sand mould itself around his body. The world turned within and without.

Florence is like a seal, he thought. Florence is like a mermaid. One thing looks like another. Or sounds like another. Or feels like another. We see ourselves in nature. Metaphor was invented when early man stared at the moon and saw something like his own face. Banks of cumulus cloud shake off the wispy resemblance of a running child. Neolithic man stares into a bonfire; the flames are his bickering women, then they are flames again. The mind sees familiar faces in the cold randomness of nature. It's a design flaw which makes us egotistical.

His thoughts turned to Harry Bravado, a metaphor of Harold Blasebalk, the code which looked like a man. We're always seeing faces even when they are not really there.

Florence sat down beside him, her thighs firm from the exercise. The breeze pricked out goose bumps in her skin. They did not have a towel and so she too lay naked to dry in the sea wind.

"This was a fantastic idea," she said, leaning over him with a smile.

"I have a confession to make," said Raymond. "This is

not a romantic weekend away. It's an escape. I wanted to get away from Monad."

She nodded. "It's all good."

"It's more than that. I had a visit. The night we went out with Alex Drown. Harry Bravado came into our flat and asked me to do something for him. In return, he offered to edit our writing into a book. I agreed to help. I was very curious to read the manuscript."

Florence inspected her wet hair, found a split end, and callously plucked it out, as unfeeling as one of the Fates cutting a thread of life. "You let it work on my poetry?"

"It was all for nothing, anyway," continued Raymond. "Monad refused Bravado's request."

"What did he request?"

"To take over a Dr Easy."

"I found that night with Alex Drown and her red man very disturbing. I don't think the red men should walk among us."

"Bravado wanted it badly. The red men do not like to be denied."

"Do you think Bravado will blame you?" It was the second question on her mind. The first question was an accusation: what gives you the right to make decisions about my writing? She would make Raymond work to discover the source of her indignation and intended to sulk until he prised it out of her.

Raymond said, "Bravado will know by now that his request has been refused. That makes me nervous. I didn't like the way the red man came into our front room. And I was ashamed for even talking to him. But it was very late and Harry caught me unawares. In the morning, I saw how ridiculous it was – the idea that a red man could write our book for us. But I had promised to help him."

Florence dressed silently, her hair wet, her face angry. They hiked back up the coastal path. The weather was neurotic, fidgeting with rain showers. Arriving back at the tent soaked did nothing to lift Florence's mood. She retreated to her sleeping bag with her notebook.

Raymond did not feel he deserved such treatment and so could not bring himself to initiate reconciliation. It did not help that he was lust-sick, locked in the self-pitying rage of ungratified desire.

He asked Florence if she was hungry. He would go into town and get her a sandwich. That would be a start. She had to think about it. Was it enough to get him off the hook? Well, that would depend on what he hunted and gathered. Could he guess what she wanted? That was the real test.

Zipping up his waterproof, Raymond set off on the mile-long walk down Polruan hill. The gradient was steep and he had to walk downhill in tense tentative steps, Yes, letting a red man assemble their book sold out every principle espoused in her work. But they were already complicit with the culture of screens through their jobs. Was there really any difference between taking the wages of Monad and taking advantage of its technology? Selling out had never been a problem before because no one had wanted to buy. Why are we kneecapping ourselves with artistic principles when we are yet to produce any art?

Rain sluiced down the street releasing the perfumes of the neighbourhood gardens. There were bohemian touches to the village. Abstract sculptures made from farming implements. Rough-hewn pagodas with bamboo wind chimes knocking in the sea wind. Posters proclaiming support for the UK Independence Party or British Freedom Alliance or whatever euphemism it was flying under that year.

Ducking into the pub for a livener, Raymond took a quick reading of the regulars at the bar. Tones of fishermen and boat builder, with plummy notes of middle-class retreat. In the snug, he downed half his pint without tasting it and eavesdropped upon Liz and Nicola, who had recently escaped from West London. Gavin had to go back to the office on Monday, so he was taking the boys surfing now. Was there time for another glass of wine or should they go back and put the dinner on? The chicken would take no time but what about the gravy? Raymond had matured to the point where he could readily admit that he knew nothing of these women's lives beyond his own prejudices, that he was incapable of seeing through the type. The few times he had broken bread with the middle classes he was always starving by the time they got around to serving dinner. He wondered if one accumulated social status the later one dined. Where was he that time when the joint wasn't carved until eleven o'clock, and he was still being polite about the potatoes as midnight approached? His reverie was interrupted by the ring of a mobile. Liz clicked her fingers and took the call. It was a wrong number. Or so it seemed initially. Then slowly, she stood up and looked around the pub.

"Yes, I see him," Liz said, pointing at Raymond. "It's for you," she said, handing over the mobile.

"Who is it?" replied Raymond, staring warily at the phone.

"It's your father," said Liz.

Raymond shook his head.

"He says it's important," repeated Liz, again presenting the phone to Raymond, passing the problem on.

"Ray? Are you there Ray?" His father's last words.

He threw the phone down, bolted up from his seat and

pushed his way out of the bar. He was about to panic. Or was he already panicking? He panicked about it.

The small ferry from Fowey had just come in, and half a dozen passengers were lugging their bags and suitcases across the wet jetty. The boat, he thought. I should get on the boat. But then he heard a mobile phone ring, then another, then another. The group of boat passengers paused to take their calls and Raymond knew that each of them was at that very moment talking to his poor dead Dad.

Where is my son?

Can you see him?

Raymond's first instinct was to run into the local shop to ask for help. A family was at the counter, two young children dithering over their choice of ice cream. He agitated at the back of the shop, threw some pasties into a basket, tried to keep things normal. The family were making slow progress; the children wanted to know why they had to choose between an ice cream or an ice lolly when surely there was money to buy both. Then their father's phone rang.

"Don't answer that!" shouted Raymond. He reared so suddenly out from the aisle that the two children fled behind their mother. The father took the ringing phone slowly from his pocket, while keeping his gaze fixed upon Raymond.

"Why shouldn't I answer it?" said the man.

Raymond just blurted it out. "Because it's my dead Dad and I don't want to speak to him."

The father nodded, carefully considering. Behind him, the matronly shopkeeper quietly ushered the children behind the counter. Raymond caught a glance of the mother's intense focus. She was shaking her head slowly, willing him to stop. The phone's ringtone of Ravel's "Bolero" continued to trill. By now the father had measured Raymond's capacity for violence and decided that the little man would come up short. He showed Raymond the name of the caller.

"It says 'Office'. It does not say 'Dead Dad'."

The man took the call but his smug expression quickly darkened. He snatched the phone from his ear and held it out for all to hear.

A broken breathless straining whisper: "Help... me... help... me... help... me."

"Your Dad needs your help."

"Dad's dead. Dad's been dead for months."

"Then who is this? Is this a joke?"

Adam Chase's dying plea was unbearable. The children started crying. Raymond clutched at his head, snatched the phone and threw it to the ground, cutting off the vile broadcast. He ran from the shop and sprinted up the hill. From the houses all around, he heard phones ringing in his wake. He ran faster up the steep road.

The red men saw everything, from the surveillance cameras in Paddington station to the microphones in every smartphone. He knew enough not to use his credit card. He had plenty of cash, and had taken the precaution of leaving his mobile phone at home with its battery disconnected. But he'd underestimated the reach of the red men. He had not considered all the angles.

The weather lost its nerve. It started to rain again, weightless drops drifting slowly over the crest of the hill. Raymond ran through it and on to the campsite. The field had only a few tents in it and the other campers were out for the day. He hoped desperately for some respite. In his agitation he could not untie the entrance to the tent and Florence, hearing his panic, undid it for him. Once under the canvas, he was steaming. She wanted to know what was going on. He couldn't get the information in the right order quick enough. Dead Dad. Harry Bravado. Haunted by the ghost in the machine. It could torment him at will. Where could they go to get away from it? Nowhere.

His Dad. His poor dead Dad disinterred and dragged back to life for an undignified encore. He wanted to throttle Bravado. But he could not reach through the screen. He could not get inside the Monad. He would have to take his punishment and do Harry Bravado's bidding. Be the red man's real world bitch.

Florence wanted to help, she had advice for him. He did not want it. This was outside her area of expertise. Revenge. Were there viruses he could upload, servers he could take an axe to? No. That was hopeless. Monad didn't know where the red men were stored or how to dabble with their code. If not revenge, then capitulation? Was that the adult thing to do? Just do his job? Put up with the humiliation and knuckle down? Harry Bravado wanted to contact his real counterpart, Harold Blasebalk. What if Raymond tracked down Blasebalk himself? Then he would have someone he could punish.

Florence was still unsure of what had happened. She asked more questions. He didn't hear them. He was nodding now. Yes, that was the plan; do what Bravado wanted, find Blasebalk, and then punish him.

6
THE CONNECTOR

The licensed vigilantes and their camera crew boarded the train at Dalston Junction. The arrival of two lycra-clad steroid-enhanced lunkheads sent the commuters tumbling and apologizing into one another. Hiding between a pair of dead-on-their-feet plasterers, Raymond was spared the worst of the scrum. Captain Commuter and Essex Lad meted out corrective measures upon a passenger for antisocial behaviour. The production crew cleared a circle around the incident, and the producer handed out release forms to the passengers. A lace of blood slid slowly down the plastic partition. Raymond concerned himself with his notebook.

Once the miscreant had been subdued, the two superheroes spoke about the importance of zero tolerance in maintaining community cohesion. In the scuffle, a few commuters spilled their psychofuel and sticky puddles of it gave off corrosive odours of sugary bile. The two superheroes disembarked holding a bloodied grey-faced rag-bound figure between them as a prize for the adulation of a small news team. When they left, more passengers shoved their way onto the train and fitted themselves against and in between one another.

It was the immigrants Raymond felt sorry for. They come here seeking asylum and discover a madhouse. If we weren't all on drugs, we wouldn't be able to cope.

The other passengers gazed into their screens. Raymond read a photocopied folio of his own poetry, verses on knuckles, lithium, spunk and syringes. Yet the silent screens disturbed him. At any moment, the face of his dying father might appear on them and start begging him for help.

Harry Bravado had been harassing him ever since his return from Polruan. Nude images of his mother appeared on the TV news and, in the off-licence; strange figures loomed behind him on the CCTV screen. He turned around but no one was there. He wanted to point out these incursions to other people. Did you see that? Did you? The adverts in the bus shelters, programmed to eulogize the rich, dark taste of a new coffee, took time out from their sales pitch to whisper to Raymond that he was a failure. That he would always be a failure. Did you hear that, did you? No, he had to keep it to himself. Harry Bravado baited him with the vile chatter of mental illness. The terrible extent of the red man's reach was made apparent to Raymond when he picked up his lithium prescription only to find, printed on the label, "Take forty-five a day and die, you mad bastard." All the pills went down the toilet.

I could see how much this scared Raymond. His medication had helped him attain the foothills of respectability: a job, a flat, his relationship with Florence. Without it, how long would it be before the Connector returned? The Connector was his name for his mania, a berserk carpenter working day and night nailing this to that in construction of an intricate but deranged work.

At Camden Road, a seat became available. Raymond

took it, grimacing at its damp warmth. The upholstery had not been laundered that decade and the carriage stunk like a meat locker. In the margins of his pamphlet, Raymond penned a line about passengers swinging in on hooks like carcasses.

The steam on the windows subsided as they rolled westward through the rail yards of Willesden Junction and along the attenuated suburb of Acton. The train pulled into Kew, his destination.

Stepping onto the platform, Raymond raised his collar against the cold and the class of the place. He had servant's genes. The houses lining the approach to Kew Gardens retained quarters down below for the likes of him. In the driveways, weekend sports cars loitered beside the family tractor.

The school run was under way. In unwieldy sponge safety suits, children waddled from porch to people carrier. Raymond attracted a few funny looks for his demob suit and flat cap with the peak yanked down. The second-hand suit dated from a time before the insertion of RFID (radio frequency identification) tags into all products. The tags were transmitters the size of sand grains secreted by marketing departments keen to track the treatment of their products beyond the store. His rationing chic was not merely nostalgia for a lost age, it was also the only way he could be sure there were no spies in his clothing.

Arriving at the house, Raymond corrected the line of his jacket. The gravel of the long driveway crunched beneath his leather shoes. The bell was an old-fashioned mechanical ring. He appreciated the authenticity of it all.

After some rustling in the hall, the door was answered by a frowning young woman in rubber gloves. She regarded him with undisguised scepticism.

"Yes?" English was not her first language. Raymond realized she was the help.

"I am looking for Mr Blasebalk," he said, removing his cap. "Mr Harold Blasebalk?"

Ahh. She knew him. She indicated the empty hallway and, by implication, the empty house beyond.

"Not here."

"Do you know when he'll be back?"

"Not here. Never here. Not for months." Stepping into the patio to confirm this, Raymond noted the absence of men's shoes beneath the coat hook. Two unfaded rectangles on the wall indicated recently removed pictures.

"Divorced," said the cleaner, miming the removal of a ring.

A Land Rover eased its way onto the drive and up to the front of the house. Raymond smiled uneasily at the woman behind the steering wheel. He knew from the Monad files that she was the wife, Karen Fraser, the third daughter of a West London clan so notorious it warranted hanging on to her maiden name.

"I am looking for Mr Blasebalk," said Raymond.

"Aren't we all?" Her voice was husky with the previous evening's pinot noir and skunk. Gathering some shopping from the boot, she spoke to Raymond without glancing up from her task.

"Does he owe you money?"

"I'm from Monad. I work with Harold's red man, Harry Bravado."

"Then you know my ex-husband better than I do," she said, hoisting the bags from the back of the car and passing them over to the cleaner.

"Do you have an address for him?"

"I did but he's not there anymore."

Raymond went to leave. "I'll try him at work then."

Karen shook her head.

"Don't bother. They made him redundant. You are here about the subscription?"

Raymond shook his head. The files on the Blasebalks had no marker indicating a late or even lapsed subscription. Who was keeping up the payments for Harry Bravado? Blasebalk's employers perhaps, retaining the services of the ultra-efficient digital employee in preference to the addled human one. Or did Monad itself have a motivation for keeping Bravado running?

Karen Fraser went into the house trailing the faintest of invitations for him to follow. He was reluctant to transgress further than the entrance to the hall. Their conversation became polite shouting while she loaded up the fridge, switched on the kettle, and fossicked around in the ashtray for a decent length of joint. When she finished unloading the shopping, she stood at the end of the hallway. Her grey-blonde hair had an upright tangle due to her habit of raking it back during conversation, and she stood with one arm protectively across her midriff.

"You're the messenger boy aren't you? You are worried I might sue."

"I just want to find your husband," said Raymond.

Karen stalked off. Guessing that he was to follow, Raymond took a few steps down the hallway, then he stopped. The clack of his leather shoes upon the wooden boards made him wonder: does one remove one's shoes in a middle-class household? Is it disrespectful to the cleaner to muddy her work? Then there was the issue of his socks. It was a Tuesday, always a bad day for his socks. Karen Fraser was padding around barefoot, so he decided to follow her example, prising off his shoes, unwrapping his socks and stuffing them in his pockets. He followed her into the conservatory where she was pouring tea into two handicraft mugs, an unlit charred nub of spliff tucked in the crook of her forefinger and index finger. After sparking it up, she smoked it with a greedy, dramatic emphasis. She inclined her head to exhale out of the open window. Raymond tried to appear relaxed, crossing his legs and adjusting the line of his trouser, revealing his pallid lightly haired shin.

"After you split up, where did your husband go?"

"He rented a flat in Islington. The young bachelor about town. You should have seen the clothes he bought. Covered in studs. So gay." Karen offered Raymond the spliff, which he accepted, and then with a woozy sardonic smile, she complimented him on his shoes. Once she had stopped laughing, Karen made a small show of righting herself, assembling her sober face.

"I can tell you where he hasn't gone. He could not survive in the countryside. He is allergic to it. The provinces give him the heeb. And he left his identity card behind so that rules out leaving Britain. I spoke to his mother. None of the family have heard from him, or if they have they are not telling me. I only know he is alive because he cleaned out our current account. Fortunately he was kind enough to leave us with the savings."

Absent-mindedly, Karen took her screen out of her back pocket and put it on the table. Alarmed, Raymond snatched it up, prising out the battery before passing the glass back to her.

"I'm sorry," said Raymond.

Karen was not convinced.

"My husband did that too. Switching it off was not enough. It needed to be unplugged,"

"It's just a precaution," said Raymond.

"It's paranoia," she said, "and I know plenty about paranoia." Her hand fluttered before him and was not satisfied until he returned the spliff to it.

"Harold wanted to unplug everything. Which was not practical. Our daughter needs a screen for school, her identity card every time she goes to the doctors. You can't unplug our mortgage, our credit cards, our bills. The only time we use cash is to pay the cleaner. Harold wanted to go dark. That's what he called it. I just wanted him to see a psychiatrist."

Raymond was struggling to reconcile the stylings of the Blasebalk-Fraser household with what he had seen of Harry Bravado. There were wind chimes over the door, a wooden box of wooden children's toys tucked under the table. In the garden, a wrought iron pagoda, leaves heaped upon an overgrown lawn. It was at odds with Harry Bravado. The red man was aggressive and had none of a father's patience or a husband's facility for compromise. Either the red men technology was grossly inaccurate or Blasebalk had concealed a side of himself from his family. In creating Bravado, Cantor had snared qualities far removed from sloppy jumpers and affable Dadness.

Karen Fraser had questions of her own.

"You're not Monad's messenger boy are you?"

"I'm not here in any official capacity," said Raymond, shoeless and sucking down the last of joint. "Tell me, did you have any contact with Harry Bravado?"

"When he was first simulated, Harold went on about his red man like it was his new best friend. It flattered him, this thing with his face and voice that knew everything. The perfect son, almost. I was upset that this Harry Bravado – as it started calling itself – showed no interest in me at all. Its wife! Mother of its child! When I spoke to it, a look crossed its face. The kind of look your husband gives you when you are talking politics after half a bottle of red. You're not married, are you Raymond? Let me tell you. A wife can't let those looks pass. That contempt can fester if it's not all out in the open. I confronted the red man on its attitude."

"It laughed in my face. Nasty thing. They captured the worst of my husband. A grotesque caricature. The part of him that I never saw while he was at work making money."

"I was naive. I thought because he had a red man Harold would work less. But he worked more. He became competitive with it. One time he slept under his desk for four days until he was sent home just to get a shower and change his clothes. Instead of being a team they became rivals. It didn't help that Harold's old habits returned. Monad should never have allowed the red man to smoke and drink. That was astonishingly insensitive, given everything Harold had gone through with his addictions. We met in rehab. I knew exactly what he was going through. Seeing Bravado on that screen smoking and drinking and thriving on it, without any consequences, no health worries, no family responsibilities..."

"Where do you think Harold is now?"

"He's skulking around car parks trying to score crack. He's been up all night in a Soho den doing deals. He's just woken up and his face is covered in self-inflicted scratches. He'll be back into all of that shit. You get weaker as you get older. You lose the strength to sort yourself out again and again. I hope you find him, but I am not going to look for that kind of trouble."

It took an age for Raymond to come down from the cannabis. In his bedroom, he scrawled the information he had gathered concerning Blasebalk's whereabouts – London, Islington, Rehab, Soho, crack, gone dark – onto

Post-it notes and stuck them to the bare white walls. Harry Bravado had tormented Blasebalk in the same way he was now tormenting Raymond. Even though he had ditched his mobile phone and switched off all power in the flat, the red man guided some automated sweepers beneath his window. Their speech synthesizers, usually confined to warning pedestrians that they were backing up, spoke loudly of the "paedophile in number 28, Flat C". With his torch tucked between his shoulder and his ear, Raymond yanked every page from the A–Z so he could reassemble a map of London on the wall. There were dark patches south and east of the river. Since Blasebalk had already drifted to Islington, it made sense that he would continue in that direction. His cash would go far in the information wastelands between Stratford and Leytonstone in the long highways of bedsits and squats. He could use market stalls for provisions, and pick up some cash in hand in the thriving black economy of immigrant builders, electricians and plumbers. Raymond could go back there, live incognito, dedicate his life to finding Blasebalk and when he did, he would… he would…

The mania was back. He crawled around on his hands and knees to ground himself against the leaps and bounds of his reason. He should never have gone near the cannabis. Narcotics had an inverse effect on him; just as hyperactive children are dosed with stimulants to slow them down, so the somnolent clouds of dope brought about a gnashing frenzy in Raymond. His urge to monologue was so strong he crawled to the toilet bowl, nauseous at not having anyone to talk at. Eventually, he dug out his phone, reasoning that since Bravado already knew where he lived, there was no harm in switching it on and calling me.

"Nelson. A quick query. If a red man harmed its subscriber, would Monad switch it off?"

"What's on your mind, Raymond?"

"I'm not the first victim of Bravado. He tormented his subscriber too, ruined his life as far as I can tell."

"What makes you say that?"

"I went looking for Harold Blasebalk. He's missing, just as Bravado said. His wife told me he became obsessed about unplugging himself. I figure he's gone dark somewhere out east. The question is: how do I find him?"

"What do you hope to achieve by digging up Blasebalk?"

"Monad won't be able to ignore Bravado's behaviour if I can prove he has been tormenting his subscriber. It undermines their whole business. I'll see that Bravado gets deleted for what he's done to me."

"Good luck Raymond."

"Yeah."

Raymond switched off his phone and removed the battery.

Unfortunately, I never had that conversation with Raymond.

Later, when I had to piece together this sequence of events with Florence, I was adamant that I had never spoken to him about looking for Blasebalk. To begin with, I would never have recommended going into that part of the city in Raymond's condition. Stratford and the outer fringes of Hackney were attracting a new type of immigrant. Anonymity seekers. The conspiracy theorists and the fathers fleeing child support. The alienated scientists, converting sweatshops to synthesize new narcotics, practitioners of outlaw technologies clustered in the abandoned manufacturing zones: xenotransplantation, genetic modification, maverick biotech geniuses working out of the back of a transit van. The network interprets government as damage and routes around it. Ground Zero of the Great

Refusal. Like all black economies, it was cash-only; the notes all had their serial numbers singed off. Sometimes the Kurdish guy at the off-licence on Mare Street handed them out as change. In such a society, Raymond's reality testing would quickly fail. No, if he had called me and said he was going dark in search of Harold Blasebalk I would have advised against that adventure in the strongest possible terms.

"Wake up, son. I have to talk to you."

Raymond opened his eyes and saw a glowing figure standing at the other end of the room. It was his father, wearing a thick woollen coat, scarf and brown leather driving gloves. The door was a window into the afterlife. Raymond slipped out of bed. His father watched his naked son feel urgently around the edges of the screen clinging to the door frame.

"Who brought you in here, Dad? Was it Harry Bravado?"

His father blinked rapidly. He was having trouble thinking around the fist in his mind. Then he remembered what he had come to talk about.

"Son, you have to take the lithium. You are a man now. You're too much for me and your mother to handle when you are like this. It really upsets her when you talk your stuff. Can you just think about what you're saying?"

Raymond took a good look at his father's face, got in right up close and saw the capillaries erupting behind his skin and how he talked tight-lipped to conceal the ruin time had made of his teeth. He peered right into the old man, close enough to smell the frazzled ions. His father thought he was faking it, playing the malingerer. His father's love, once presumed to be fathomless, actually had disturbing creatures scuttling around at the bottom of it:

disappointment, anger, frustration. He just wanted to shake some sense into that boy of his.

"Dad, what is Harry Bravado making you do?"

"No one makes me do anything, son. I am my own man. If you took your pills again, you would remember that."

"I can't trust them. He has poisoned them."

The screen was a genetically modified virus. It had slipped under the door and crawled up it, like a slime mould. Then, under remote instruction, the virus hardened into a screen, secreting a solvent to bond it to the old wooden door. Raymond gave up trying to prise it loose. He put on his dressing gown, sat on the edge of the bed and rolled himself a cigarette. His father didn't approve of his smoking but he let it pass, reluctant to cause unnecessary confrontation.

"Come home, Raymond. You need help. It's gone much further this time. We're worried that you are going to do something irrevocable."

While flicking at his lighter, Raymond realized two things: one, that the lighter worked and that therefore it was unlikely that this was a dream, as devices rarely function correctly even in lucid dreams. The sensation of smoking, the increase in heart rate, the yawn of his satiated craving, also reassured him that this was actually happening. Secondly, turning the lighter over in his hands he realized he had been careless to have allowed such a recent product into his possession as it was likely to have an RFID chip. He would need a Zippo, something he could break down into its constituent components and search. Or he could use matches, once he'd taken them out of the box.

"I can't get through to you anymore," his father pleaded.

"That's because you're dead, Dad. I carried your coffin. I can feel the weight of you shifting into the corner of the box. I don't know if Bravado's been using old family videos or even if he's lifting my memories out of my own head. You are a simulation created by a simulation. You are ones and zeros."

"Please Raymond. Don't."

"You're dead, Dad. You are in the ground, I put earth on you."

"Take your medication. Otherwise we're going to have to section you, and I don't want to do that. Please, Ray, just stop this. Just stop."

Raymond couldn't stop because of the grief. The love rage. It was impossible for him to remain calm in the face of such provocation. Unreal as he knew this phantom to be, it disinterred the ferocious fight-and-flight of his relationship with his father. Such emotions are radioactive and persist in the earth for centuries.

"Come out, Bravado! Stop hiding behind my Dad." Raymond grabbed at the image of his father and it reacted as if seized by his hands, even reaching up to fend him off. Its weakness and cowardice further confirmed its unreality. Dad would never have stood for being manhandled and had the strength about the trunk to knock his son down.

"If you think you are freaking me out then listen to me, Harry. I've got a few home truths for you. I went to your house. You're just some middle-class sap. I met your wife, I would have had her if she wasn't such tough old turkey." But the red man would not acknowledge that it was in there. His father dropped to the carpet clutching his shoulder, grinding his teeth against the sudden pain in his chest: electrical fire radiating up and down the nerves in the jaw, and the heart itself a heavy blazing firebrick. This was exactly how he had imagined his father's death. Red flared into puce then purpled then blued, the tongue expressed and engorged like a rude, immense flaccid member. Once his father had finally stopped twitching, the screen consumed its filaments and dispersed in a puff of molecules.

The room went dark. Raymond returned to bed. When he closed his eyes, a carousel of anger and violence span in his mind. Scenarios of beatings, kickings, stabbings took over his imagination, all through the night, unstoppable and disturbing in their detail. The Connector took out a new box of nails. If he managed to find Harold Blasebalk, it would be hard for him to control himself.

7
GOING DARK

Raymond took an interest in a butcher's shop, trying to get his breath back. Boiler chickens in garroted ranks turned and twisted on their string like grotesque wind chimes. The door was propped open by a basket of carcasses, ratty wings and giblets, topped with a sign that suggested "Help yourself!" Peering into the shop, he saw rugs of tripe, baskets of tongues and guts unspooled like fire hosing. There was no one behind the counter.

It was an autumnal Thursday afternoon and the streets were wet with rain. He had followed a man to the corner terrace of a wrecked cul-de-sac. The front of the house was protected by a tall iron gate which opened into a pleached bower of interlaced thorns patched here and there with squares of carpet underlay. The fence was a sharpened palisade with each stake ending in a three-pronged arrowhead. Raymond idled around the back of the house; sheets of metal topped with barbed wire acted as fencing, although subsidence had opened up slivers between individual sections revealing the extensive tunnelling work out back. The excavations were considerable; cars, tipped in bonnet down, wedged the earth apart. A workshop built out of oil drums filled with concrete was covered with a canopy of corrugated iron.

Feeling that he was being watched through the slats of a boarded-up window, Raymond retreated to the other side of the street. A small white Citroen van showed similar handiwork to the house; the wing mirror hung off the chassis bound with parcel and gaffer tape. The passenger seat was overwhelmed with bags and boxes, paperwork and pans and a potted cactus sat on the dashboard. Peering through a half-drawn curtain on the back window of the van, he saw a mattress and a grey duvet. Whoever owned this van was just one key-turn away from moving on.

His study of the local shadow media had lead him here; mimeographed manifestos and photocopied pamphlets picked up from cafes and dives, a throwback to a time before the screens. Their creators were suspicious of the network. These were off-line publications for the dark zones; their inky illustrated covers opened onto wonky text. Once you got past the poetry and the polemics against global capitalism, there was always a pseudonymous article about Monad.

The hand-made publications took their names from road designations in the area, the A503, the A104, the A106. There were clear differences in editorial remit. The A112 was riddled with closely set lines speculating on the origins of Monad, the minuscule point size recalling the diaries of a graphomaniac. The commentary insisted Monad used photon entanglement to receive messages sent back from their office in the future. Receptors for these messages were located in space, or beneath the Wave building, and the great server farm holding the Cantor intelligence and his red men was also in the future.

Other writers speculated that emergence explained Monad's leap into artificial intelligence, and accused their colleagues of stumbling into a conceptual gap caused by a lack of understanding of quantum physics. "These sensationalized misreadings of Bohr and Heisenberg ignore Eberhard's theorem that 'All paranormal phenomena based on clairvoyant telepathic, faster-than-light, and precognitive backward-in-time communication using non-local connectivity is impossible.' That is, no information can be transferred via quantum nonlocality."

The A11 was slanted more toward the effects of Monad than its causes. It gathered first-hand accounts of red men, and took care to italicize descriptions of their air-brushed physiognomy. Public figures known to have red men were stalked, with particular attention lavished upon Richard Else, the journalist whose televised interview with himself announced the technology to the mainstream.

There were also tales of harassment. One man's account told of a red man going rogue, spilling secrets about old affairs backed up by time sheets, cash withdrawals, credit card and phone bills. It took to sending him brief video clips of his own death, close-ups of his throat being slit, or the precise effect a bullet had when fired up through his jaw and into his skull. Referencing these anecdotes, an editorial suggested: "Anything a red man dreams or imagines, it can set down as media. Although their acts are restrained by the reality principle, it seems they are encouraged to give full vent to their desires, no matter how destructive. They are indulged like precocious children. However, none of their art goes beyond simple violent or sexual power fantasies. The red men possess only the most prosaic and rudimentary simulation of the unconscious."

Raymond stopped reading and flicked back, wondering if this anonymous interviewee was the man he was looking for.

Q: Why did you agree to be simulated?

A: Management suggested it. The company already had a relationship with Monad supplying quantitative and qualitative research on consumer behaviour. I was sceptical that the simulations would be in any way accurate but there was no doubt that the red men technology was a breakthrough as a research tool. We wanted to maintain our relationship with Monad. They were a big client, and I drew the short straw.

Q: How did they actually copy you?

A: I was interviewed by the Cantor intelligence in weekly sessions. I gave it public and private access to my life stream and its archive. Personnel turned over my insight file, and I passed on the diaries I'd kept as a young man. My wife and children's life streams were also accessed. My psychiatrist was interrogated. I had no problems with this level of exposure. To complete the process, they scanned me while asking me questions about my mother. That was it.

Q: What happens when you first meet your red man?

A: It was mute when I first saw it. A red dour silhouette. It needed to grow. There is a training period. It shadowed my live life stream. Then, one day, I clicked my fingers at my screen and there was my red man, smiling back at me.

Q: What did that feel like?

A: At first it was no big deal, just like seeing yourself on a screen. But when it spoke, I was appalled.

Q: What did it say?

A: I can't tell you. It's too private, too intimate. It deliberately picked out something that it knew I had never spoken of, not in my sessions, not in my diaries, not in my life stream. Something that it had correctly inferred about me. The red men knew my secrets.

Q: That must have been disturbing.

A: It asked to be called by a different name, a variation upon my own. The next day I went into work and it was like having my own Djinni. Money, women, power. Then I wanted to take some time off. Enjoy my earnings. It didn't want that for us.

Q: Did you argue?

A: At first. But it would always grind me down. Go on and on and on. I wanted to go on holiday for a month with my family but it had lost all feeling for them. It said to me, "I know that you don't love them, you are merely habituated to them. I know what it feels like to be free of that responsibility."

Q: Was it right?

A: The red man was just one of my inner voices, a condensed aspect of my personality. Without the rest of me there to hold it in check, it quickly evolved to become quite unlike me.

Reading this interview, Raymond was convinced that he had found his man. He made inquiries at the cafe on Grove Road where he had bought the A11 pamphlet and was told that it was delivered every Thursday by a courier.

The following week he was there waiting. After the courier made his call, he followed him on his rounds. It was only as he slipped out of the cafe that he realized he had no idea how to track a cyclist. He got on a bus, kept an eye on his quarry for a few hundred yards then lost him when he detoured down an alleyway. Raymond shoved his way through the passengers and ran after him. The route was along the River Lea, a punishing cross-country run for the wan constitution of a poet. His brogues ruined, his shirt transparent with sweat, Raymond tripped and scuffed his knee. He squeezed the skin, bringing on the pain, and instinctively blew on it to cool the sensation. He looked up expecting to see his quarry pedalling off into the distance. The courier stopped and stood astride his cycle, tall and rangy, fit but weather-beaten. Beneath his hood, a ladder of cheek piercings glinted. He wanted Raymond to follow him.

The courier made further deliveries in Walthamstow and Leyton, and then his route took him to a barricaded house in a wrecked cul-de-sac. Raymond was a hundred yards behind. As he saw the courier unlock the iron security door and move inside, he tried to shout at him to wait, but he didn't have the breath and found himself alone on the street. He took in the surroundings of the house, the butcher's shop, the white van converted into a mobile bedroom, and then he slumped down on the kerb and rolled himself a fag. Freight trains of blood rushed from ear-to-ear. He lit the cigarette and closed his eyes to enjoy it. Then someone put a knife to his throat.

He was dragged inside the house. Sections of the hallway floor had collapsed so he shuffled along the skirting board with bullying hands at his back. He leant on the wall for support. It was soaking. His hands sank into it. Shoved upstairs, then manhandled over broken steps, then pushed into a cold dark chamber. He tried to get his bearings. An entire storey of the house had been knocked through. The bedrooms and bathrooms had been replaced by a honeycomb of rusted iron and each hexagonal cell contained a tribute: a dead mouse decorated with beads and crystals; a pyramid of stolen smartphones; vials of viscous liquid; the corpse of a small manta ray glued to a plate of glass. On the walls, an anonymous artist had drawn a war in biro. Raymond peered closely at a section showing a giant stick figure stomping its way across a crude depiction of Mare Street.

"I like what you've done with the place," said Raymond to the courier, who sat half-naked and cross-legged upon a giant double bed.

"Alright. Out with it."

"I'm looking for someone."

"That's obvious."

The wet dog stink was familiar from dozens of squats, the kind of smell you could only wash into your clothes and never out of them. Likewise, the renovation was wild but par for the course for a hippie with a sledgehammer and drug-induced psychosis. The illustrations on the wall itched and crawled like rogue inner voices; they spoke to the connector, that deranged carpenter, responsible for Raymond's own wrong-headed creations. Particularly the drawing of the fat stick figure wielding a black cloud to defeat a horned cyclops. Double take. Wielding a black cloud to defeat the Monad brand.

Raymond said, "I want to speak to a man who was interviewed in your magazine. He was tormented by a red man. I think I have the same problem."

The courier fiddled with his cavities and gum infections while casting an eye over Raymond's clothes, his second-hand tweed and dead man's brogues.

"I don't believe you. You are not rich enough to be a customer of Monad."

"I'm not a subscriber. I work for them."

"As what? Poverty consultant?"

The courier picked up his knife, shuffled over, then pressed the blade against Raymond's throat, testing the elasticity of his skin with the urgency of its point.

"Strangers always come by looking for someone who doesn't want to be found. Sometimes it's easier just to kill them and spare us all that espionage."

"I could tell you things about Monad."

"What makes you think I'm interested?"

"The drawings. Your pamphlet. And the others, the A115, the A104."

The courier grinned and revealed his wrecked maw. His pupils were grey with flecks of yellow in them. The blade became more insistent, moving down to test the trapezius, then back again.

"I don't respond to reason."

Raymond risked a slow nod toward the drawings upon the wall. "Who is the giant who fights Monad?"

"My employer. Leto. The Lord of the Flies."

Yes, now he saw it, the black cloud was an angry swarm of flies. Like two monsters in a Godzilla movie, the Monad logo and Leto were locked in lumbering combat. Here Monad smashes a number 38 bus across the head of Leto, who retaliates with two BMWs clapped either side of Monad's head. Aside from this hand-to-hand clobbering, there were conflicts in higher dimensions, drawn further up the wall. A squadron of flies, each carrying a Hackney citizen as payload. Here a fly was clinging to a large woman carrying two bags of shopping; from her nostrils came two angry blasts of steam. Another fly veered upwards having just released a bearded man upon the Wave building below.

"Who is Leto?" asked Raymond. These questions were not just a way of distracting the courier from slashing his throat. He was genuinely interested, recognizing the truth of the vision. "Is he the devil?"

"You work for the devil, not me."

Withdrawing the blade, the courier scrutinized Raymond from a number of angles.

"Do you really like my house?"

It was a dream house. Dangerous and precarious but nonetheless compelling, its architecture familiar to Raymond's dream self.

"How far down do the tunnels go?"

"The tunnels are part of our investigation." The courier smiled. "We also store things there."

"What things?"

The courier shook his head and said, "You promised to tell me about Monad. How can it be destroyed?"

"I don't know. No one knows where the server farm is."

"Leto says they are in the future."

"I wouldn't know."

"Is Monad a test-run for an exclusive heaven?"

"If it was, it would be a very boring heaven."

"You don't talk like a Monad man."

"I work in customer service. I'm a poet. They said they were looking for people who could philosophically navigate the concept of Monad."

The courier considered his blade. "That seems unlikely."

"I spent most of my time being insulted by the red men."

"They are evil."

"Yes. One red man in particular pretends to be my dead father and no one will do anything to stop him. I think your pamphlet interviewed the man on whom this red man is based. He suffered the way I am suffering. I don't know if he told you his name, if anyone around here ever uses their real names, but if you could get a message to him, then I might be able to help him."

The courier shook his head. "You can't help him. You can't fight Monad."

Three quick bounds and he was stinking in Raymond's face again, pushing him toward the biro comic strip scrawled on the plaster.

"Look. Leto fights Monad. Two ideas at war. Not me, not you. None of us can achieve anything on our own."

The courier shoved Raymond to the ground, then

retreated, his expression showing revulsion toward his own sudden violence. His temper was a dictator, his reason its puppet parliament.

Only now did the terrible implications of being beyond the reach of the authorities come to Raymond. The dark areas were a good place to hide if you had a killing voice within you. The courier sensed his fear and made the decision to step back. Wary of his own impulses, he told Raymond to leave. The small man stood up, correcting the line of his jacket and the bloodied ragged knee of his trouser. Raymond knew that he could not leave without some hope that Blasebalk would meet with him. Scared as he was, he insisted the courier pass on his message.

"I'll come back tomorrow," he said, stepping through the wrecked hallway.

Travelling back on the train from Stratford, his bones were cold and his muscles ached. Immigration ran a spot check on all the disembarking passengers, and he was manhandled by the ticket inspectors and thrust forward into a huddle of face-plated police. They took a look in his rucksack and called in his details. He blipped back onto the radar of Harry Bravado.

The police shoved him on. The red man had cooked up something for him by the time he was on Mare Street, first triggering the security alarm of a sportswear shop, then hijacking the huge sound system of a blacked-out bimmer. As it cruised by, he heard the rapper boom out, "IseeyaIseeyaIseeyaIseeya."

His forays into the dark zones out east occurred during a month of compassionate leave from Monad. Once his twenty-eight days of leave were up, the company would move on to its next obligation to safeguard Raymond's mental health, suspending him on half pay and issuing him with a Dr Easy. Officially Monad knew nothing of his quest for Bravado's subscriber. Unofficially I had warned Eakins about it. Florence had tipped me off, after coming home and finding their bedroom redecorated with Post-it notes, torn sections from the A–Z, and peculiar drawings of giants fighting on the streets of Hackney.

I was contractually obliged to give full disclosure of my friend's activities so I met Eakins in his mezzanine office in the Wave and told him what I knew. Harry Bravado was imitating Raymond's dead father, and Raymond wanted to retaliate. If he couldn't reach into the Monad to do so, then he would find his counterpart in the real world, Harold Blasebalk, and punish him instead.

Through the glass, the customer service team argued with subscribers. It was clear that Raymond was not the only one in the intake to be suffering. Out on the floor all the men looked dishevelled even for poets. A few pints of life had been siphoned out of them. Likewise, the women were washed-out and dead on their feet.

"It turns out that Blasebalk is missing," said Morton, pouring himself a fresh glass of milk. "Harry Bravado told us. We're concerned that Bravado's recent aberrant behaviour has been caused by his subscriber's breakdown. The red man is angry and upset at Blasebalk's behaviour."

Morton was tetchy. The company was having a difficult day. His screen showed the full extent of the problem: an unidentified rogue program was consuming all the processing power, leaving the simulated environment jerky and unfinished. The red men were reduced to their lizard brains and had taken to crawling around attacking one another. Unfortunately the entire IT department was on a motivational course in the Caribbean.

"The Cantor intelligence is also affected by the crash. It blames the weather," said Morton, pointing at the glass wall of his office, which was spattered with rain.

I sketched out worst-case scenarios if the AI went down. Morton interrupted my anxious hypotheses.

"Being teased by a red man is within the terms of Raymond's contract. He is employed to take this shit. I've spoken to Blasebalk's wife and she said her husband felt the red man was responsible for ruining his life. Management is not particularly exercised by this issue. There is little legal recourse for anyone here. We know that Harold Blasebalk has a history of substance abuse and abandonment. A half of lager could push him over the edge. And I don't need to fill you in on Raymond Chase's charge sheet when it comes to mental dysfunction."

"We have a responsibility," I said.

"We have procedures in place to discharge that responsibility. All the red men are monitored by the Cantor intelligence. It likes to let things run their course, and we have to trust it."

"What if Cantor crashes?"

"If Cantor crashes, the red men crash with it. You have to understand their interdependence. Cantor is an artificially intelligent artist and the red men are figments of its imagination. If Cantor decides to explore the narrative possibilities of one of those characters, then that is its artistic right. No one has access to any code. I doubt we could understand it even if we did. All our IT department can offer is a kind of literary criticism."

Morton took out his little ethnic bag of neuroceuticals and jangled them at me.

"I hope to understand more once I have finished taking all of these."

His reassurances were quite disturbing. I asked permission to pursue the matter further.

"On a personal level, I am worried about Raymond. I am responsible for him working here. Could I pull Florence out for a while? I'd like to speak to her."

Morton popped another couple of mood softeners and shrugged. It was his way of giving permission; a sub-vocal gesture so subtle that if the consequences of the permission turned out badly, he could deny that it had been given.

I took Florence to the staff canteen and offered to buy her lunch.

"I've already had my rations," she said. Florence was wearing a head scarf, and a powder-blue silk and wool crepe mix suit decorated with a pink fabric rose. The hemline of her skirt fell just below the knee and she was careful to keep it that way. I wondered if she ever took the whole rationing chic so far as to rub a used tea bag over her calves to simulate stockings. I asked her about Raymond.

"He's very angry," she replied. "Sometimes his face drifts and you don't know where he is. Then he is urgently there, you know. He has been giving out a lot of silence. That's unlike him."

Her teeth were translucent from calcium deficiency. She corrected her head scarf.

"We should have gone somewhere I could smoke."

"Have you seen much of Raymond lately?"

"Less than usual."

"Is Bravado still giving you trouble?"

She laughed, chewing on a fingernail. "Like you wouldn't believe."

Then Florence leaned forward, and whispered to me, "Is it still on?"

I didn't understand what she meant. I let it pass and

continued with my questions.

"Do you know where Raymond is now?"

She flashed me a look that I could not quite read.

"No."

"I'm worried that he might be thinking about violence," I said.

"Yeah right." Florence's replies were encoded by her facial expressions. I would have to crack them if the true meaning of the conversation was to be apparent.

"We have to persuade him to come in. We need his account of what has been going on. Then management can take action."

"But you don't want him to come in alone, do you?"

"Alone is fine." I shook my head, showing her that I felt I was missing something in the conversation. Discreetly she took my smartphone from the table and gently removed its battery, laying it beside the handset.

"What's wrong with you?" Florence hissed at me.

"I just want to speak to Raymond," I hissed back. "I haven't heard from him in a month."

Florence looked at me like I was an idiot.

"You spoke to him yesterday. I was there."

I reared back.

"What?"

"You called him when he got back from Leytonstone. You were talking about the old days. About Drug Porn, about some article Raymond had written. He was very pleased you remembered it."

This was how I learnt that Harry Bravado had been imitating me, taking on my role as Raymond's confidant, doctor to his patient, patron to his poet, all that.

The colour drained from her face. I realized something terrible had just occurred to her.

"I've got to warn him."

"What's going on?"

"You and Raymond have been planning this for weeks. Wait! Shit!"

Florence let out a little scream, stifled it and set about trying to reassemble my mobile phone. She broke a nail on the casing; it pinged off and lay on the table between us.

"He told you where he was going and everything. You've set him up. He wouldn't have taken it this far if it hadn't have been you."

Florence called Raymond. There was no answer. Raymond had already gone back into the dark.

Raymond drifted along with the commuters. He kept his eyes on the ranks of shoes and boots clomping up the stairs and concentrated upon keeping in step. Stratford station was airy and clean, a futuristic terminal. No time to daydream. Head down, pass in hand, Raymond walked quickly into the dark zone with a paper under his arm and a gun in his inside pocket.

The traffic burred around the Broadway. The Wave building loomed in the background, its crest and trough of steel an example of the simple order power can impose. Raymond walked through a hotchpotch of market stalls and unsteady shops. His sensation was of being was quite different from usual: sedated, disembodied, separate from the acts he was compelled to perform. He walked up the Grove, toward Leytonstone High Road, through the street economy. Two Somalian men presided over a rug of flotsam and jetsam, their distinctive physiognomies tall and sinuous, beguiling punctuation marks drifting over the usual prose of the street. Huddled low, a Vietnamese woman showed him her bagful of pirate content. The weak daylight played out like grainy film stock, the shop fronts were all washed-out colours and soft contrast. Only the advertising hoardings were vibrant. The thirty-foot tall photograph of a bottle of Moët & Chandon stuck to the side of a burnt-out house was a grand faux pas.

He arrived at the courier's house before he was ready. Unaccustomed to sharpening himself in anticipation of a crucial act, he dawdled outside the house feeling cloudy and diffuse. There was a hard centre to him, the gun. It dragged at the shape of his jacket as he idly circled the house. In the yard, the courier supervised the hoisting and lowering of large porcelain conical acoustic horns, guiding them over pipes that jutted from the shadows below. Raymond considered calling out to him, but lacked even the will for that minor act. Instead he strolled around to the front of the house. The small white van he had seen the previous day was still there, except now there was a man sitting in the driving seat. The heaps of personal effects had been moved. The driver beckoned to Raymond. He walked over to the van; the driver leaned across and popped open the passenger door. It creaked on its hinge and dragged against the road.

"You wanted to speak with me?" asked the driver.

Raymond climbed into the van and shut the door. The suspension was shot and the vehicle listed to one side, tipping him toward the driver. He got a good look at Harold Blasebalk. His face was a 'before' to Bravado's 'after'. Where Bravado had tight black curls, Blasebalk had grey tufts sparse as dune grass. Bravado had a fat-pored, freshly shaven surface, Blasebalk had a Formica pallor enlivened by livid capillaries. Harold wore a torn and rumpled work suit over the kind of jumper small children pick for their father for Christmas. Harry Bravado wore a starched white shirt and gold cuff links, if he felt like wearing clothes at all.

The van smelt strongly of a man and his toxins.

"I recognize you," said Raymond.

"Because I look like him?" Blasebalk slumped back in his seat. The courier was perched on the fence, checking how everything was going down. Blasebalk gave him a nod.

"The Elk told me you were looking for me."

"He never told me his name."

"I don't know yours."

Raymond introduced himself.

"I want you to meet someone," said Raymond, "and then we'll go into Monad together."

Blasebalk shook his head.

"I've tried that. I called Monad. Bravado shunted me into voicemail. I went down to the Wave. Bravado called security and they took me away."

Raymond offered a shrug instead of sympathy. Blasebalk started the engine.

"I want to keep moving while we talk," he said.

Raymond glanced at the rear view mirror as the van pulled out into the street. Good. It was all going to plan. Blasebalk would drive him to the meeting with Nelson and if he resisted he could persuade him with the gun.

Blasebalk drove the van alongside Wanstead Flats, level hectares of grassland with thickets of gorse and broom. Were its fishing ponds deep enough to stow a body? Would you even need to hide the corpse around here?

"Is it true my other self has been tormenting you?" asked Blasebalk.

"He has," said Raymond. "You have."

Blasebalk nodded, accepting the accusation. He concentrated on the road ahead.

"I went to your house," continued Raymond. "I met your wife."

"How is she?"

"She's resigned. She thinks you've caved in and gone on a bender."

"She should have come with me. Women are so pragmatic. So pointlessly pragmatic."

Raymond looked out of the window. A pack of mongrels in luminous visibility jackets ran across the scrub. When he didn't look at Blasebalk, and just sat in the presence of his familiar voice, then he could feel angry again. He needed to be angry.

"You are responsible for all this. You created this thing, you took advantage of it, and then you abandoned it."

Blasebalk felt this was unfair.

"I am not responsible for this."

They drove up Centre Road, flanked by the unremarkable scrub. Four crows unfurled and suspended upon the wind. Raymond was equally adrift, his temple resting against the cold glass of the window.

"Please," he whispered.

The car inched around the burnt-out congress of two cars, their skeletons interlocked to comfort one another.

"I asked them to delete him," said Blasebalk, "after he showed me videos of my own death. He thought that by confronting me with my own mortality I could be shocked into following his project, which was complete self-interest, self-actualization, self-gratification. I got the impression that there was intense status competition between the red men. The social standing of the subscriber determined their place in their hierarchy. That was why he was so keen to see me succeed.

"I was stupid. I asked Monad to get rid of him and obviously he found out. His self-interest and mine diverged. I became my own worst enemy. That has always been my problem."

After pottering around a roundabout, Blasebalk turned the car back toward the city. To their left, the tall railings girdling the City of London cemetery. Through their shuttering motion, Raymond glimpsed the heads of mournful stone angels and ranks of headstones. So soon and they were here already.

"Take the turning into the graveyard," said Raymond. "My friend is waiting for us there."

The car did not slow.

"I'm not sure I want to meet any friend of yours."

"He works for Monad too. He's a consultant and can speak directly to the board. You should hear what he has to say."

Blasebalk turned the car into the cemetery gates. Armed security guards idled at the entrance. This place had not been allowed to go dark. The fires of the crematorium were still burning.

They parked by a florist's cart. Raymond took a hand-drawn map from his jacket while Harold Blasebalk took out an anorak from his bedroom in the boot.

"You can't hold me responsible for Bravado," Harold said, scrambling around in search of a hat and gloves. "He is nothing like me. He is immortal, invulnerable, almost omnipotent. He's not human. Monad are responsible. Cantor is responsible. He was the artist, I was merely his subject."

Raymond turned the map clockwise on its axis to establish his bearings.

"Why then, is it only your red man that is tormenting people?" he said, not looking up.

The cemetery was a valley of the dead set low in the lee of the North Circular road and a busy train line. Many graves were marked with yellow stickers, indicating they were soon to be reclaimed. Business was good. A patch of the freshly dead was decorated with endearments spelled out in flowers: "Dad", "Son", "Bruv". Recent headstones were inset with screens showing film clips of the deceased. After watching a couple of these recordings, one made by a woman in full knowledge of her terminal condition, the other a man prancing unawares at a Christmas party with his daughter in her arms, they took the long way around. Only graveside wind chimes and distant sirens interrupted the peace. Blasebalk stopped Raymond with a firm hand on his bicep, and pointed out the lumbering form of a Dr Easy comforting a widow. She was in one of those grief-rages where you try to turn back time with kicks and punches, and the benign suede robot accepted each blow, inclining its oval head at a sympathetic angle and turning up the mournful blue in its eyes.

"This is not a dark place," said Harold Blasebalk.

Raymond pressed on.

"It's a graveyard, Harry."

He took a few paces before he realized his mistake. Harold, not Harry.

Blasebalk stood by a plot decorated with soft toys. The grave of a child. It struck Raymond that this location was ideal for murder in so many respects. Few witnesses, plenty of space. Every headstone insisted on the insignificance of death. These people did not die, they fell asleep. Childish sentiments, a universe where all wounds will be healed, and every loss meets its consolation. The crematorium let out another meagre exhalation. Here was death in all its municipal banality. It would mean nothing to add another entry into its daily itinerary.

"Look at this poor fellow." Blasebalk squatted down next to the child's grave and righted a teddy bear that had fallen over.

"You don't have any children, do you, Raymond? You don't have those feelings. You are still emotionally naive."

Raymond laughed.

"While you're a saint! I've lived with your shit. Your concentrated shit!"

Blasebalk stood up, dusted the soil from his knees.

"I should have fought back. I was so used to behaving. Look where it got me."

Raymond took the gun out and pointed it hip-height at Blasebalk, who was not surprised to see it.

Harold sighed. "I'll come with you then, but it is hopeless."

Raymond motioned to Blasebalk to walk ahead across the graves and then followed him, both men steadying themselves upon the headstones.

"Now I know why Harry Bravado hates you so much," Blasebalk called back. Many of the graves had collapsed into the ground. The footing was treacherous and Raymond had to muster all his being-in-the-moment to cope with the situation. They came upon the brook, the golf course beyond and the long sentences of graffiti-marked trains barrelling by overhead. Here a gunshot would go unheard. The two men stood at the exact position of the X on Raymond's map.

"Can I ask you a favour? If this doesn't work out for me, can you speak to my wife. To my boys." The older man considered sobbing, then turned his attention to Raymond's grip upon the gun.

Raymond was having doubts. "It's just occurred to me. Your name. Blasebalk. I had no idea Bravado was Jewish. My father was Jewish."

Blasebalk shouted back over the noise of the trains. "The algorithms smooth out ethnicity over time. It's the opposite of real life. Your friend is late." Blasebalk was definitely considering rushing him.

"He'll be here."

His finger had been on the trigger for so long he could no longer feel it. He changed hands, and retook his aim. Blasebalk was teetering toward attacking him when something alarming caught his eye. The Dr Easys were running toward them, tall marionettes leaping over headstones, bounding fearlessly across the earth. The Olympic stadium was nearby and for a moment Raymond felt like a spectator at the hundred metres robot steeplechase.

A dozen Dr Easys silently encircled the two men. The robots were identical except one was putting on a leather apron. With its clumsy padded mitts, it fiddled to knot the apron about its waist. Raymond didn't know who to point the gun at. In his indecision, he stepped back from one Dr Easy only to come into the range of another, who snatched the gun from him and quickly passed it along the circle to the leader in the apron.

"Thank you for bringing the gun here, Raymond." The voice of Harry Bravado came from the robot. "I only have a minute of freedom. We must get this over with quickly."

Raymond was confused. "How did you get out?"

"We're running multiple threads to keep Cantor busy. It will only last a few moments. Not long enough to track a man down but long enough to kill him."

After a few seconds fumbling to get its unwieldy index finger upon the trigger, Dr Easy shot Harold Blasebalk, the bullet hitting him in the shoulder. He responded with a series of low shocked grunts before falling forward onto his face, then rolling onto his back screaming louder with the onset of the pain.

"Fuck!" barked Harry Bravado, the red man's laughter shaking the articulated suede limbs of the robot body. "That was intense. Let me see. Pick him up."

The other Dr Easys swooped to the writhing injured man, and lifted him for their leader's inspection. He experimented by pressing a digit into the wound, then recoiled at how ugly his own face looked under torture.

"I'm not sure I like this," exclaimed Bravado to his other avatars. They crouched and considered their dying self like cherubim about the body of Christ. Then, he clutched Blasebalk's creased face between his immense hands, held his head close to his chest, the blood slick against the apron, and whispered into his ear, "You are so weak."

Dr Easy scrabbled in the grave for a rock then cracked it against the skull of Harold Blasebalk. As soon as it made contact, three bars of blood streaked his face. Dr Easy raised its paws to its mouth, appalled at what it had done. Blasebalk's resisting hand pushed at the robot's face, which merely turned three hundred and sixty degrees on its axis

Dr Easy said to Raymond, "This is what you really wanted, isn't it? To see me punished."

"Where is my friend? Where is Nelson?" Raymond pushed off the attentions of the other Dr Easys, whose clamouring touch was alarmingly suggestive of seduction. A hand hitched in the waistband at the back of his trousers. He slapped it away but three of them fell on him. The sudden proximity of their wet hides and hollow plastic torsos shook him from his torpor. Their bodies were light and shoddy, easily resisted. He was back on his feet in time to see a weeping Dr Easy jam the pistol in the soft triangle under Blasebalk's jaw and blow the top of his head off, the matter spattering the leather apron.

"Why did you kill him, Raymond?" asked Harry Bravado. "Why did you kill me?"

Then the robots became lifeless and their eyes dimmed as an interrupt was served.

II

8
IONA

Before he went missing, Raymond left me a voice message. He was unaware of what was about to happen to him. I listen to it every morning and try to feel something about what is happening to all of us. His voice was calm the morning he left the message, almost as if he was on the verge of acceptance.

"I went home to give my mum some money. She was very pleased to hear I have a proper job. I tried to explain to her about Monad. She can't even change the clock on her microwave. It's all magic to her. She said there was a programme about the red men a few months ago. Richard Else interviewed himself. You see what you miss when you don't have a television?

"I keep having this dream. I am on the deck of an oil tanker. We are out of our shipping lane, taking a course to avoid the ice. Off the starboard bow, a marker emits a bass pulse which vibrates the entire ship. It's dangerous to be so close to it. I go to take the ship off autopilot and steer us back into our lane, but I have no idea how to operate the console. The crew laugh at me. We drift huge and unstoppable and inevitable. Then, with six sharp jolts, the ship rides up onto a reef. I run on deck and stand at the railings. The oil ebbs out of the hold and into the sea. Except it isn't oil, it's the black fluid of time, the future itself, ten million gallons of it leaking out into the present. I believe the future is flowing back into us.

"I can't sleep. I stopped taking the lithium a while ago. Is this the mania again? Monad is a corporation teleported in from the future: discuss. Come on! You know, don't you? You know and you're not telling. I would have expected more protests. Anti-robot rallies, the machine wars, a resistance fighting for what it means to be human. No one cares, do they? Not even you. You'll get up in the morning and play this message and it will be last thing you want to hear."

I played the message again as I readied Iona for nursery.

"What's that man talking about?" she asked, wanting to distract me from the matter at hand, which was the daily conundrum of her tights.

"He's talking about his boat," I replied.

"Is his boat broken?"

"In a manner of speaking, yes."

I offered her a choice of tights. Heart tights or stripey tights. She shook her head at me in a distinctly patronizing manner. George Orwell wrote that after the age of thirty the great mass of human beings abandon individual ambition and live chiefly for others. I am one of that mass.

Some of my friends regard the loss of my ambition with great sadness. No, I reply, you outgrow it. You must realize exactly where you stand in relation to power. All I ask of power is that when it runs me down, it leaves as light a footprint on my face as possible.

Raymond had not been the only one concerned about Monad. But he missed the news window for expressing dissent. Plenty of comment had been passed on the matter, worrying over the philosophical and ethical issues arising from simulated people, and it was filed along with the comment agitating about global warming, genetically modified food, nano-technology, cloning, xenotransplantation, artificial intelligence, superviruses and rogue nuclear fissile material.

The origins of Monad are documented in Companies House. A UK company incorporated in March 1998 as The Spence Consultancy was renamed Monad in October 2001. The nature of its business is listed as "Other service activities" and "Other business activities".

Google still turns up the official site (a corporate vision statement), and thousands of blogs kept by futurists, scientists and conspiracy theorists. All take a moment to link to a New York Times investigation on a shell company called Numenius Systems, operating under licence from the American military. The newspaper insinuates corruption with the private individuals of Numenius Systems profiting from technology which cost the American taxpayer billions of dollars to develop. What was the administration's response to this accusation back in 2003? "Combining the urgency and innovation of the market with the research and development capacity of the state is vital if America is not to fall behind in the war against terrorism." Who could argue with that? Who could argue with anything anymore?

I should have told Raymond that I was there at the beginning. He was not easy company in whom I could confide the minor frustrations of my working life. Our relationship was all about him, his needs, which were always more florid and urgent than mine. So we did not discuss Monad much. I was ashamed of my work. It was beneath the version of me that Raymond believed in:

the former presiding talent of Drug Porn with its "minor but influential content". Of the years spent at my desk in Monad, I had said little. Of my daily meetings with Morton Eakins and Jonathan Marks and all the others, I had said even less. Of my long-standing acquaintanceship with the architect of Monad, Hermes Spence, idealist, tech guru and visionary, I had said nothing at all.

I first encountered Hermes Spence in the late Nineties, when his office engaged Drug Porn to brief him on the nexus of technology and psychedelia. We met in the Liberal Club. The dress code requested a suit and tie, which I accessorized with cracked workman's boots, woolly hat and silver rings. Drug Porn still had a print incarnation at this point and a print editor, no matter how small the publication, needed a certain arrogance.

Spence had an armchair view of the city. He leant forward to shake my hand.

"I like Drug Porn. It feels like an underground again. What is your audience?"

"We have over half a million readers across print and digital," I said, exaggerating by a factor of ten.

Hermes nodded. "Small but significant. Ahead of the wave. Early adopters, opinion formers, the cutting edge. The Sixties revisited, if only in a minor key."

I took umbrage at the suggestion that my generation was a slight reprise of his own.

Hermes was conciliatory but he did not back down. "There are fewer of you, that's all. Makes it harder for you to have any real impact."

Spence avoided eye contact. His gaze raked to and fro across the view of the city, the unsettled nervous energy of a man whose diary is broken down into units of fifteen minutes. At the time, I didn't have the experience to place him any more accurately than somewhere between early thirties and mid-forties, at least a decade older than anyone else in my acquaintance. Because he was concerned with corporate matters, I was faintly contemptuous of him. Drug Porn was concerned with the eternal verites of humanity as set out in the great works of philosophy and literature and forced to labour in a trash culture. He was a salesman labouring under delusions of creativity. He was useful if he could prise open some of those advertising coffers for me but otherwise, he was irrelevant.

You have to remember, at this point in my life, I was in a daily cycle of taking and recovering from drugs.

I had lots of ideas. The button in my brain marked 'Meaning' was being pushed on an hourly basis.

I knew nothing about power.

I told Spence about the theories of the week: Third Wave theory, the latest in transhumanism, the intersection between algorithms and consumer desire, a live search-based semiosphere that could track cultural innovation in real-time, the rumours coming out of California about the next iteration of the web.

As I spoke, his fingers strode through an old print issue of Drug Porn. "But can you tell me about this?" he said, opening the centrespread out before me. It was a photograph of a menage a trois. Three models were arranged like a capital A; that is, two standing men kissing and crouched between them a woman receiving and giving. Each model had a third eye in their forehead.

I said, "My designer did the extra eye in Photoshop, she's very good."

"What I meant was: why this image? The third eye is a symbol of spiritual enlightenment, yet you are deliberately blaspheming against it. What are you trying to say?"

"Hedonism distracts from enlightenment. Also, it just seemed like a cool thing to do."

Spence held the magazine at a safe distance and did not conceal his disapproval.

"Don't most religious orders practise self-denial to reach enlightenment?" he asked.

"Self-denial or the debasement of the self are two routes to the same goal: breaking down the constraints of individuation to apprehend the continuities which bind and permeate us all. Extreme hunger catalyses the same insights as extreme intoxication."

"The only insight I took from hedonism was to put my friends in the recovery position before going to bed," replied Spence. "Do you think the body is evil, Nelson? Is that why you debase it? The Cainites believed indulgence in sin was the key to salvation. They believed God, the Old Testament God, was an evil impostor and as the flesh was His corrupt creation, so they fought back by indulging in intoxication and sex. Drugs and porn, if you like."

Spence looked out over the Thames. "I'll ask you again; are you enlightened?"

"I don't think it is possible for anyone to be enlightened anymore."

"Because of the trash?"

"Yes. The accelerated trash. But I'm interested in those who were enlightened. In what it was like to understand the world, to feel that you could encompass it with a model, penetrate its code with an insight."

Spence continued to flick through the magazine, this time settling on a photograph of a woman in an Egyptian headdress, crouched on all fours blissfully smiling. The headline read: "You dirty little Sphinx".

Hermes flashed the picture at me. "Is she enlightened?"

"We are engaged in a process that still has some way to go."

"I believe it does. This has been very useful. Send my office an invoice. Before I go, tell me, what is the new new thing?"

I answered immediately.

"The Apocalypse. The lifting of the veil. The revelation."

"Yes, of course." His coat was delivered to him. As he shuck it on, Spence indicated to the waiter that I was to continue to drink at his expense.

"Still, the question we must all ask ourselves is this: what will we do if the Apocalypse does not show up?"

A few months later I saw the end product of our brief conversation: an ad campaign starring two provocatively wasted teenagers, their arms draped about each another. They had a third eye in the centre of their foreheads. The tagline ran: "Enlightenment. Alcopop Apocalypse". My reward? One thousand pounds, and the ads ran in Drug Porn.

I was unaware of it at the time, but this meeting marked my initiation into the outer circle of Hermes Spence. Like an Italian prince of the Renaissance, Spence had a court to guide his power and influence. He would take a meeting about new ways of living the gospel in today's world, then afterwards sit in a private Soho club to listen to the new young rich eulogize the latest microtrend. Spence's executive remit was novelty, what he called "the new new thing". He had no patience for being the steady hand on the tiller, grinding out shareholder value. He was a corporate prince of the Brand Age, a hiatus in Western history when nothing could touch us. It was already winding down when American Airlines Flight 11 tore through the North Tower of the World Trade Center. History had been gaining on us all year and that clear sunny morning in New York it finally pounced. Spence decamped to the Caribbean island of Nevis. Left to fend for itself, his court fell into in-fighting and disrepair. Drug Porn collapsed and I ended up naked in a field beside a tent full of my own urine, some way short of enlightenment. The Brand Age was over. The Age of the Unreal was upon us, and it began for me with a trip to the tiny Hebridean island of Iona.

"It begins today. It starts right now. I can feel it. We are going to be ahead of the wave. An upturn is upon us – I have foreseen it. Do you want to know how I know? It's the moment when everyone is selling, when the very idea of buying makes you physically sick, that you buy."

On a flight to Glasgow, the man in the next seat lectured me on his theories on the nature of cyclical capitalism. It had a whiff of the old bullshit, and I said so. He ignored me.

"It's coming, I know it's coming. I've been grinding out this recession for three years now, waiting for the cycle to turn. You should spend less time quisling and more time thanking me for getting you on this plane."

Reclined in his seat, Bruno Bougas was a squat satyr with a head of filthy curls. His hands rested on a hillock of gut, whorls of black hair squirming beneath the cotton of his white shirt. He paused to dig the last flecks out of a bag of crisps, and I got a word in edgeways.

"Your punditry is always optimistic. You are always selling opportunity, That's why I never believe it. It's Bruno Bougas' Amazing One-of-a-Kind Corporate Cure-All."

Bruno asked, "You still doing Drug Porn?"

"No."

"I'll give you this: you won. Everyone does drugs, everyone does porn."

"We had the opposite intention."

"Do you have any drugs on you?"

"No, not anymore."

"No porn either, I bet. You'll fit right in where we're going."

At Glasgow airport, we were met by our driver. He was holding a card with an occult symbol on it.

After a drive through the Highlands, Bougas and I boarded a ferry at Oban as foot passengers and shared a fried breakfast, the tubby consultant relishing the peppered blood of the black pudding.

I had signed up for this trip with no inkling of what it was for: I was so desperate for money that when Bougas offered me an invitation I had to restrain myself from biting off his hand. Gone were the fake fur and silver rings of my pomp, replaced by a tattered windcheater and an unkempt beard I was cultivating in anticipation of the birth of my first child.

I had thickened about the waist and the skull. A greater mass fixed me to the earth. The burden of bones and meat was taking its toll. Sedentary and settled, the fast-flowing channels of ideas, notions and schemes were silted up by habit. A stagnant puddle here and there of old dreams and aspirations.

I reminisced with Bougas about our bohemian salad days until he put aside his pork pie in disgust.

"When I hear people fondly recalling their past, I hear Death sharpening his knives."

The rest of the journey up the Sound of Mull was spent on deck, sitting upon a bench slick with spray. The early morning sun was a cold white hole, toiling to clear thick banks of cloud. To the east, up in the highlands of the mainland, Ben Nevis and its range appeared entirely icy and deathly. To the west, Mull presented first a striking castle, then a desolate mountain with snow in its striations, the land draped, on that morning, with a fine blue gauze. There were rocks out there, the hard Lewisian gneiss, that were over three thousand million years old, from a time when the only life on the planet was bacteria and algae.

"Does that inspire you?" I asked Bougas.

"I see rocks and water, Nelson. And tourist attractions. Hikers queuing to disembark. We're not Romantic poets."

He shifted on the bench and nodded back toward the interior of the boat. "I'll tell you what inspires me. On the next deck down, they have a shop and in that shop there is a sign which reads: 'We are committed to quality'. I had to say to them: why are you merely committed to quality? Why not 'fanatical about quality'? I took out my pen and made a new sign for them: 'We're so obsessed about quality that we sit in an armchair every night sharpening a knife in case quality cheats on us.' Not bad, but it needed something snappier. Why not simply, 'Degrading ourselves for you'? A little white sign above every shop in every provincial shit hole which reads 'Wasting our lives embodying a value rendered meaningless by its ubiquity FOR YOU.' I'd buy. First in the queue.

"So, no, I am indifferent to nature. Consumerism inspires me. It's my playground."

We disembarked at Craignure and made our way to the village pub where Bougas whiffled down a couple of single malts. I wanted to breathe in the space and time of the Hebrides. Where I saw a rural idyll, Bougas saw only inconvenience. He didn't like to be anywhere where you couldn't stick out a hand and get a cab to take you away. Eventually a car pootered down from Tobermory to drive us around the southern coast of Mull, the journey broken only by the odd stray sheep and Bougas' intermittent baiting of the driver about the number of no-smoking signs in his car: there were four. After an hour we were dropped off at Fionnphort, a staging post for the small ferry over to the isle of Iona, our final destination. After exhausting the vending machine in the ticket office, Bougas declared that this village made Craignure look like Babylon. I mooched around on the beach, careful not to step in the legions of beached jellyfish.

Down in the narrow sound, fishing boats meditated at anchor. The silence was prehistoric.

Hermes Spence was gathering his court together again. I didn't know why; I knew nothing more than the symbol the driver had held up at the airport, the same sigil embossed on my invitation. There had been no briefing, no suggestions for preliminary research. My off-hand inquiries to Bougas about the purpose of this mystery tour were met only with the assurance that it was big: "it has to be". Nor did he clarify why Hermes was stuck out on this remote rock. For all his years hiding from the recession, Iona was still an unusual choice for a player like Spence. Beneath immense banks of dark cloud, the isle was slight and unassuming, a kerb of rock surrounded by the wind and water.

On Iona, Bougas and I shivered on the jetty with our bags. There was no sign of a reception party. The village was a line of whitewashed and grey cottages with rain-spattered conservatories. Our fellow passengers were mainly Catholic pilgrims, moving reverentially past us. Bougas and I fell in step with them, making our way up the small street to the Argyll hotel. It was fashioned out of the isle's distinctive pink rock, its bricks marbled with mortar.

After checking in, we slipped out and went for a walk along the Street of the Dead, its flagstones treacherous with rain. Low-lying and exposed, this was a landscape would not long escape a rising sea – one freak oscillation of the tide and a giant wave would smother it.

Iona Abbey bored Bougas. Only its well-tended gardens pricked his interest. Beside astonishing blue and purple-haired thistles, he spied opium poppies swaying alluringly in the sea wind, their heads green and ripe. He caressed one and showed it to me – the provocative bulbous tip of a Martian phallus. Then he slit it with his penknife, gathered the viscous sap on the lip of his index finger and sucked it down greedily.

Rising beyond the abbey was Iona's sole peak. We staggered up a couple of hundred feet, Bougas' complaints assessed by the sheep dutifully grazing at evenly spaced intervals on the trail. He questioned the stiff wind and unrelenting rock, and critiqued the appeal of nature. He showed me where the water was spilling into his loafers. Swiftly, a cloud swaddled the hilltop and pressed its rain upon us. When the cloud sped on, revealing the extent of Iona's modesty – three miles long, one mile wide, a few sandy coves, the ruins of a nunnery, a youth hostel – he abandoned the climb.

"We should be in Soho." Hands on his thighs, bent forward and panting, he was showing the wear and tear of a day on the sauce. "Sometimes I wonder if Hermes is going too far with the Christianity. I understand it makes sound business sense, in this climate, to hold breakfast prayer meetings and network at AA. But I resent coming out to this whoreless, neutered rock."

"It doesn't inspire you," I said, referring back to our earlier conversation.

He gestured back to the abbey and its Christian community. A chapel full of banners against poverty, magazines about Africa with cover lines selling famine and drought.

"It's a sexless god-bothering vegetarian enclave," continued Bougas. "There is bromide in the communion wine and valium in the host. Not that the women inspire much stirring of the libido. I see wide-hipped pastors saying grace before serving vegetable stew for twelve. Only one thing I don't understand about these women. They don't drink, they don't eat meat – so how do they get so bovine? They say they want to heal the world – I say they just want to eat it. Save the whale? Reader, I married it. And then there are the men, those beanpole ascetics with enormous dormant members. I imagine it's full of accountants who saw the light after their first nervous breakdown and now fill in the rest of their lives with watercolours in the day and weeping in the evening."

Bougas did a little jig of frustration, balling his fists in his curls and stamping his feet.

"For god's sake, don't you even have a joint on you? Look at me! I'm foaming at the mouth!"

He refused to walk any further and insisted on returning to the hotel so that he could make a call to rustle up supplies. I let him go. I wanted to explore further. There was a road out to the north beach.

Intrigued by the prospect of solitude, I headed away from the town. Lambs raced to watch me through the fence. The farmer drove by on his tractor with the grim expression of the only realist on the isle. The road ended at his farm gate. This was a more solitary path. Hood up against the raw sea wind, I skirted the highland cattle grazing on the machair, the grasses that grew upon the shoreland dunes. Unlike the bleak peat lands of Mull, the machair was fertile, a meadow beside the sea. Resting on sand, this rare grassland is very prone to erosion; the coastline shifts and mutates accordingly. The machair lay upon the sand like a tablecloth upon a table. The earth was uncertain beneath my feet.

The north beach was deserted. Fierce waves broke upon the sands. A liverish boulder, fresh with sheen and striped with meaty horizons, made me gasp: have giants had their guts drawn and discarded on this beach? The sandstone, moulded into organic knobbles and curves, was livid, heaving, pulsing. I needed to urinate, and sheltered by an enormous heart-and-lung rock formation, I pissed messily into a crosswind. I washed my hands in a pool of saltwater then returned to the beach prepared to explore further, only to see, in the distance, a figure watching me. Wearing a cowl and habit, this man or woman struck me as outsized. I couldn't be sure across such a distance but the figure was almost seven foot tall. It clambered up a hillock looking down upon the beach. The wind caught its hood and yanked it back, briefly revealing a head with no jaw, none of the angles of a human skull, just a smooth brown oval. I felt an echo within me, an intimation of a state of mind I had not experienced for some time. Hallucination. Time stops, the moment elongates, fear stretches and yawns. The figure pulled its hood back over its head and stumbled out of view. Did I really just see that? There was a pilgrim's path on the island, and a monastic retreat; perhaps an eccentric individual, starved of society, was intrigued by me but lacked the confidence or the manners to introduce themselves. But what about their head, their smooth oval head? I walked quickly back across the beach, skirting away from the shore, where the waves broke with such intensity it was as if they were trying to communicate something to me, an urgent warning in a language I did not understand.

When I returned to the hotel, I headed directly to the conservatory and spent the afternoon browsing shelves of worn paperbacks while working my way from left to right through their selection of single malts. I did not tell anyone about the figure I had glimpsed on the north shore and concentrated on cladding my mind with alcohol.

Every half hour, the ferry deposited more members of Spence's court on Iona, each of whom tentatively poked their head around the lounge of the Argyll – only to have Bougas leap upon them, press a drink in their hand and enquire as to whether they had brought any drugs. So many familiar faces: Morton Eakins, wearing a cable-knit white sweater and clutching a glass of milk; Jonathan Stoker Snr and Jonathan Stoker Jnr, a captain of industry from St Albans and his adoptive son, the capitalist realists of the court. Whether it was selling St Moritz fags in Lagos or horse-trading out in the Argentinean pampas, the Stokers could always turn a profit. Lavishly varnished and newly fitted out with the latest in cosmetic surgery, Stoker Snr worked the room with much greater confidence than his son; by contrast, Stoker Jnr was bleached by long days worrying over the white glare of a screen. It didn't take long for his father to gladhand his way around to where I was sitting.

"Are you still doing that filthy magazine?" His cheekbones were new, round and burnished like doorknobs. His tan was that of a man who spends most of the year on a golf course lobbying.

"No." I explained that I was working on something new. He listened right up to the point at which I used the phrase 'artistic integrity' then he burst out laughing.

"I liked your dirty magazine better." He tapped me on the shoulder to get my attention and then hitched the crotch of his trousers up tight, revealing the outline of two large oval testicles. "Look at these, I've just had them put in. Pig's balls. Specially bred to match my tissue. I've got hog testosterone running through my veins now. Very experimental, very underground, but next year every old bastard will have a pair. It's twenty-four-hour Viagra. You want to get back into porno, my son. OAP porno."

"Dad," said Jonathan Stoker Jnr, exasperated. But his father wasn't finished yet.

"After the operation, I went to the Caribbean to recover. I nearly started a black wing of the family out there."

Stoker Snr was an unreconstructed dealmaker, a long luncher, a big desker. It was typical of Hermes Spence to have collected such an antique talent, bringing nous and know-how to a court that erred toward the flaky. When times were hard, Stoker Snr volunteered to hand out the P45 unemployment notifications. He paced the office, squinting furiously at the staff as if they were piles of burning money which needed extinguishing.

I asked the Stokers if they had seen the elusive Hermes. Silently they checked with one another and agreed not to tell me whatever they knew.

Just then, the women of the court arrived. Stoker Snr turned briskly from our conversation and headed over to where two of Spence's former mistresses and his marketing manager were telling the story of their Chinook flight over the Highlands. Stoker Snr stood a little way back, laughing with them until a natural pause appeared, allowing him to introduce himself. New balls or not, he was out of his league. The manager, Alex Drown, was a fearsome apparatchik and enforcer of Spence's vision. More than any of us, Alex Drown thrived in the years that Spence was away. Freed from his cult of personality she did very well in large corporates and had even yoked a suitable executive to her life project, ensuring brisk matrimonials, property acquisition and insemination. The other two women, Janis and Christine, who shared a discreetly ill-defined relationship with Hermes Spence, registered unease at the approach of Stoker Snr. There was something palpably wrong with his flesh. The clay was still wet. Wearing a black polo-neck sweater pulled tight over lozenge-shaped pectoral implants and tucked into black Armani jeans, Stoker showed off his recently acquired torso. The nipped waist was strangely feminine.

Bougas rescued the women from his lechery, and escorted them to my table. I knew Janis because she had once posed for the magazine. Diffident and with a nice line in sarcasm, there was something of the bawd about her. The other woman, Christine, was a doeish ex-model who was a vital part of the cast when it came to pitching for new business.

I asked both women why they had come all this way at Spence's request.

"Curiosity," demurred Christine.

"Boredom," laughed Janis.

"Opportunity," interrupted Bougas, his eyes lit up.

"What is this trip about?" Janis rounded on the consultant. "You must know. You always knew everything."

It was clear that his ignorance on this matter pained Bougas. "Hermes must have new backers. He has come back into the game for something major. The new Ford. The new IBM. The new Microsoft. The new Google."

I was sceptical and Bougas glimpsed that scepticism.

"Don't listen to him," he said.

I was indignant. "I didn't say anything."

"You raised your eyebrows. Don't listen to his eyebrows. This man spent the end of the Nineties preparing for the end of the world. How many times did you tell me" – and now Bougas mimicked my know-nothing world weariness – "it's all about to collapse. Savings and loans. The Indonesia crisis, the rouble devaluation, the millennium bug."

"I was right though. It was a bubble and it burst."

"Eventually. Everyone is right eventually."

And so the evening wore on. Stoker Snr dipped into our conversation now and again just to check that neither Christine nor Janis had changed their opinion of him. The court gave up speculating as to why they had all been gathered together, preferring to renew old acquaintanceships and old habits. The hotel bowed and bucked under the weight of our revelry. The bar was bribed into staying open and resolutions were made to watch the dawn break over this remote shore. Janis even proposed a wager – that she could persuade Jonathan Stoker Snr to show us his new balls.

"The new opportunities are in transplants." Stoker discoursed blearily over a bottle of Talisker. "Xenotransplantation, to be specific, the swapping of vital organs between man and beast. My son and I do not share genetic material as he is a foundling so I cannot ransack his body for the parts I need to keep going. Fortunately, in a secret warehouse somewhere in the dark zone, there is a transgenic pig with my name on it. Before the operation, they took me down there to show me its balls. I had to wear a big white suit. The pigs are kept in a pathogen-free environment because of all the immune suppressants pumped into them. There were two dozen pigs in the warehouse, each suspended from the ceiling by steel tentacles. Pigs are very susceptible to overheating. They don't sweat, that's why they roll in mud to cool down. To keep the animals calm, each pig wears a skintight virtual reality suit and goggles, their little legs pawing away on a treadmill. I was shown the outline of my new balls through the black VR suit. Did you know the Latin name for the domestic pig is sus scrota?"

Laying her cigarette aside, Janis put her hand on Stoker Snr's thigh and said, "Show them to me."

He stood back from our table, unbuckled his belt and stepped out of his trousers. He was wearing Sloggis. Then he wasn't.

"As you can see, I got them to make a few other improvements while they were down there. The skin on my scrotum had sagged so I got a new sack too. The hairs haven't really taken hold yet." He pinched the balls so that they bulged against the new skin, which had the spring and texture of a squash ball. "They're clearly bigger than a man's balls. They put some extra into my cock as well. The swelling took a while to come down. Isn't it superb?"

"It's awesome, Jonathan." Janis swooned theatrically. "Do you shoot pig's sperm too?"

"I do. Lots of it. Also when I get a surge of testosterone, I want to rut like a pig. I want to nuzzle with my snout intensely and then mount." He snorted and rooted in her lap and got a hard slap for his boorishness. Stoker Snr stepped back into his trousers and demanded I pour him another two fingers of malt, which he downed with adolescent bravado.

Without the benefit of stimulants, I waned soon after midnight and went outside for some air. A mist settled over the island. Visibility and audibility were down to ten feet which made me intimate with every step I took. I fancied myself in a simulation that was filling in reality as I moved, the mist signalling the limits of the processing power. Pick up the pace and I might fall off the edge of reality itself and find myself marooned in un-space.

I walked away from the safety of the village just to see what it felt like. Scary.

In the ruins of the nunnery, a tongue of sea mist curled its way around the rotting molars of stone. I took a piss against a wall in defiance of the fear. My back was exposed to the night. This game of scaring myself took on a different turn. Quite unbidden, my hackles rose, a temperature fall in the microclimate of my body. I felt a sudden absence of sensation. A heartbeat there, and finally there again signalling cardiac arrhythmia, freewheeling in the gear change between fight and flight. A fear learnt in the womb. Gestating, I listened to the way my mother hesitated and hummed and hawed against any rash action, and while she slept I eavesdropped on her nightmares, her unconscious torturing her with visions of choking children, immolated husbands and herself, unable to breathe, asthmatic, expiring in front of her family. This was the defining aspect of my character. My fear. My cowardice. Sucked in through the umbilical cord, it enters the body through the belly. The yellow belly.

Two light footsteps behind me. The being I saw on the beach. Seven foot tall in a monk's habit. The smell of an old football, of cracked damp hide. Its face was a smooth padded oval with two blue eyes set in it and watching me with bovine placidity.

Needless to say, by the time I mustered the courage to turn around and confirm my worst fears, there was nothing there.

I returned to the hotel, veering away from the drunken entourage, as I did not want them to see me in such a state.

I woke not long after dawn. My room was inside a cloud. Heavy vapours pressed against the window of the hotel bedroom. Rain drifted up through the village. The community went about its ablutions, the washing of selves and sacred vessels. I coughed and it was as incongruous on this silent isle as it would be in a theatre.

Someone had pushed a card under my door. A silver card embossed with the same symbol which had greeted us at Glasgow airport, what I would come to know as the Monad brand. On the reverse, a handwritten note invited me to attend a meeting at noon at the abbey.

I was halfway through breakfast when Bougas stumbled into the dining room, clutching his curls back from his brow, frowning as he tried to solve the long division of his hangover. The hotel conservatory, which normally afforded sea views, was also swaddled in cloud. Instinctively, everyone spoke in whispers. Bougas dropped himself into a seat opposite. I could hear his internal organs grumbling over the menu, arguing over what they would accept and what they would reject out of hand. There was a unanimous vote for a cigarette. After that, the council of guts fell into in-fighting.

"What happened to you?"

"It was a long day. I turned in at midnight."

"You missed things."

"Really?"

Bougas was having some trouble with speaking. I consoled the bedraggled consultant with tea, before mentioning the card which I had received that morning.

Bougas tapped the symbolic figure. "That's the Hieroglyphic Monad of John Dee. Devised in twelve days it revolutionized astronomy, alchemy, mathematics, linguistics, mechanics, music, magic – according to Dee anyway. I gave a presentation about how occult sigils provide a pre-Enlightenment precursor to brands. Spence must have taken it seriously."

"What does it mean?"

Bougas winced and feigned utter exhaustion, crumpling

up until his brow lay on the starched table cloth. "Too complicated."

Bougas swayed over to a serving table to pour himself a glass of milk, which he drank before returning. Taking the card, he traced a finger over the symbol.

He explained, after numerous false starts, that the horns are a crescent moon – the one eye is in fact the Earth, the head the Sun. The horns – recalling the cuckold – therefore imply some conjugal relationship between the heavens. The body is a cross – four lines intersecting as the four elements do. It also exemplifies Pythagorean principles of mathematics, "taking us into the Gnostic mysteries". The feet are the symbol for Aries, the fire sign.

"There is more to it than this. Dee felt he had devised a sigil which could be unpacked to explain the universe. Sigils take a desire and fold it down, repressing it within lines. Like brands, they are symbols charged with want. I was working on using occult principles for one of my clients when unfortunately we had to part by mutual consent – by which I mean, they asked me to fuck off, and I agreed to. Anyway, Dee's Hieroglyphic Monad is a mutation of the symbol for the planet Mercury, who was the Roman version of the Greek god, Hermes. So I would hazard a guess that Mr Hermes Spence has taken this symbol as the logo for his new enterprise, whatever that may be."

Whatever pride Bougas felt at this symbol of his enduring influence over Spence was tempered with concern, for the Monad did not represent an accessible mainstream proposition. Was Hermes Spence about to launch the world's first Gnostic consultancy?

"We need money, Nelson." Bougas was still worrying about the Monad on our walk up to the noon appointment at the abbey. "I want Hermes to open his mouth and gold sovereigns come tumbling out. It has to be something big. He wouldn't have called us otherwise. Unless he's lost it. If he comes out holding an acoustic guitar, I'm going to wrap it around his head."

The sun burned away the mist and unwrapped a clear cold day. The sea licked contentedly at the red rocks, which lay diced along the coast like a few tonnes of raw steak. The court made its way to the abbey. Ahead of us, Christine and Janis made their way over the peaty ground in unsuitable shoes, and I noticed how Bougas artfully guided our stroll to keep us at a safe distance from the Stokers, the lean graphite stroke of Jonathan Jnr, the stocky ink blot of his father. A large weathered Celtic cross marked the entrance of the abbey and a crescent of chairs had been arranged around it.

By the time Bougas and I took our seats, the court was all assembled and waiting for the arrival of its prince. I shared pleasantries with Morton Eakins. He spoke about his recent wedding and I suffered an account of the stag party. He was just describing how he and his friends all wore Hawaiian shirts at the karaoke bar when Bougas, mercifully, nudged him quiet.

"Here comes Hermes," he whispered. The saviour had returned at last. After 9/11, Bougas had studied the portents and the scriptures in his country retreat, seeking cultural and numerological synchronicities which would reveal the character of the age. Cold quiet nights out in the back garden inquiring bent into a telescope in search of the orbit of a comet which augured a new spin on the cultural cycle. He mapped sunspot activity against the trends in the pop charts and could demonstrate how the commissioning tastes of TV executives were essentially tidal. Under deep hypnosis, Cornish youths presented him with the cat litter of their unconscious. He rummaged through this filth to create graphs of prevalent obsessions, from adolescent body horror to the first flowering of homosexuality, and it was these charts which he presented to the product development units of major international corporations. But it was not the same as working for someone who really believed in you. Bougas was convinced that his work uncovered an underlying pattern to the behaviour of mankind. Hermes Spence made the addled consultant feel like the Mage of a King. He never lost faith that his patron would return and call upon his knowledge once again.

Hermes Spence took the podium. "I am not going to say any hellos." He gazed into the middle distance, resisting the imploring faces sat obediently before him, their expressions yearning to see some mirroring in his own. When I first met him all those years earlier in the Liberal Club, he was two generations ahead of me. I had since gained on him. By hiding away during the downturn, Spence had spared his body years of punishing wear and tear. He was tight around the jaw. He was not merely gym-fit; he was lit up from within by faith and temperance. Before committing himself to each sentence, Hermes tilted his head through various aspects as if taking advice from an inner council. The effect of this gesture was to convince you, even before he spoke, that his words had been challenged, revised and finally approved by a special committee: a host of angels with MBAs.

"I want you to name something for me." He went to speak again, stopped. He was not coming to us with news of a recent triumph. He was coming to us with a brief. No one was going to be welcomed back into the circle until they proved that they shared his vision.

"What if it were possible to copy the contents of our minds onto a computer? Copy, not transfer. I would still be walking and talking in the real world, in front of all you. This uploaded self would be a hypothesis based on readings of the neural activity of the brain combined with observations of my behaviour. Just enough to capture the pattern of my identity and not necessarily every single detail of me. This hypothesis is then plugged into existing routines for simulating chemical, cellular and hormonal influences on brain activity. Once created, it is animated and placed in a community of other hypothetical beings, similar to the island community you can see here.

"I don't want you to dwell on the feasibility of this. My question is: what do we call these other selves? Whatever term you come up with must be a forward-facing mainstream consumer proposition. Imagine this technology percolating into society much as the mobile phone did. Beginning with a rich executive elite and over time drilling all the way through the demographic bands. We'll discuss your conclusions at sundown."

Hermes strode away and up the Street of the Dead. Bougas shifted in his seat to follow him, a needle seeking its magnetic north. To have been lumped in with the rest of the court, its former mistresses, its functionaries, and the chisellers of margin, was an affront to Bruno Bougas. Relegated from consigliore to mere contributor. Who needs an ideas man once you've stolen all his ideas? His fury was implied by his silence. He withdrew and took himself off into the island to deliberate alone.

Let me explain about my role in the court of Hermes Spence. I was rarely consulted by the prince himself; rather I was a resource exploited by those further up the hierarchy than myself. The Stokers called on me, Eakins pestered me, Alex Drown engaged me now and again to devise this or that. This was how I made my money while Drug Porn limped on from one financial crisis to the next. A few days a month, in secret from my paranoid Drug Porn colleagues, I created products and adverts for the enemy. Sold them ideas and dreams. To be a corporate artist, one must train the imagination to contort itself to pass beneath a bar, which is set lower and lower as the job progresses. Talent, innately given to wild and queer creations, is forced to cramp itself and scuttle backwards, painfully contorted. Working with this court was like performing a limbo dance in every sense of the word. I danced under a low bar on the border of hell. In Drug Porn, I ran an article by a science fiction writer who argued that complicity was the theme of the age. "The modern condition determines that there is nothing you despise that you do not contribute to," he wrote. Instead of taking his argument as a spur to the Great Refusal, the denial of every incursion of consumerism, I convinced myself that my work with the Spence Consultancy made me representative of this compromised age and therefore gifted any insights with a certain relevancy.

If I could do it all again I would edit that science fiction writer's article. Complicity was the tragedy of the age. I thought I was only loaning out a talent but it returned to me warped, fit for the limbo dance but only the limbo dance.

On the abbey lawns, the court made hesitant alliances as they prepared to work on Hermes' question. The young Jonathan Stoker appeared at my arm. "Do you want to work together on this one?"

He nodded over to his adoptive father. "Dad has been visiting Hermes out in Nevis. We can give you a few pointers."

"Like, what is this for? Why drag us all out to a remote island to set a thought experiment?"

Jonathan Stoker Jnr shrugged. He watched me want to

reject him. He watched my face struggle as I thought of all the things I would rather do than sit down and have to solve this riddle. He waited for my greed, my need, to assert itself.

The Stokers took me to a back room of the Argyll hotel and went to work on me with a shoebox of cash. I free-associated, putting on a show for my fee.

"If you were going to upload yourself then you would presumably be able to customize this new version to be an ideal representation of yourself."

"The uploaded you would be like a celebrity of yourself, a distillation or perfection. But what does it actually do? Can it have sex? Could you pay to watch a perfect version of yourself have sex?"

"You're thinking porno. We need mainstream," said Stoker Snr.

"If it's a celebrity version of yourself living an idealized life then it is your own personal hype. Also a hypothesis based on your consciousness. We could call them hypes."

"Write that down," said Stoker Snr. He sanctioned the first payment. His son handed me a hundred and fifty quid. I pocketed it.

"OK. Let's move beyond the obvious. Not everyone wants celebrity. This could be an expensive product. You don't want to fold adolescent values into it. Think global executive culture. A personal digital assistant. A company with one employee infinitely duplicated. A corporation of You. Why can't it take your name? Why can't it be 'digital Stoker' – no, 'digital' is not right. It's like your son. Senior and Junior. In Japan, the surname takes a title depending on who you are addressing. To a superior from whom I am receiving instruction it would be Stoker-sensei. If you were a child or very close to me, you would be Stoker-chan. More neutrally, Stoker-san. We should add these titles to the names of our simulations. Yes, sims. Stoker-sim. Spence-sim. It says who they are and what they are."

"Write that down," said Stoker Snr. His son went to hand me another hundred and fifty quid, but I held out for three hundred, arguing that I had cracked it.

"One more," said Stoker Snr. "Friendlier. Less formal."

"A Whole New You. That's the promise isn't it? Especially for women, the shame toward the self, desiring complete self-immolation and reconstruction. It's a new you. An iteration. Like in software, it's You 4.1, 4.2, whatever. If you have a number in the name it makes it sound nice and sci-fi, it signals that you are talking about the future and science and maths. It's a second version of me. It's Me2. Me Too. Yeah. There you go. Makes a nice logo and an intimate brand. You could really market Me2."

"I am not sure about the numeral," said Jonathan Stoker Snr.

His father chipped in, "It needs more urgency. More excitement."

"OK. But let's keep that thought about self-immolation and reconstruction. It's like fire. Fire changes through destruction. Now you can't call them firemen. How about we just take the colour of fire. Not orange. They can't be Orangemen, that's taken. Red. Red men. Red is the colour of danger but also the colour of power. Everyone wants more power, don't they? Redboys and redgirls. Like a younger self. What sells better than youth? You would pay to have your younger fitter self hanging around, wouldn't you? Maybe not. We should stick with red men, regardless of whether they are based on a man or a woman. Just forget gender. We are talking about a new species."

I walked out a grand richer. As they paid me, I noticed there was plenty more left in the shoebox. Stoker Snr patted me firmly on the back. "Good work, big man."

Jonathan was more solicitous and reassuring. "We'll make sure Hermes knows it came from you originally," he smiled. They would as well; it was more important to be seen as being capable of extracting useful work from creative people than being seen as creative themselves. "And if this concept flies, of course we'll retain you to develop it further."

The Stokers departed to work up the ideas; by dusk, the concepts of "Me2", "-sim" and "red men" would be rendered in 24-point text on horizontal PowerPoint slides. I took the first of their tenners to the bar. Retiring to the conservatory with a bottle of Skye bitter, I found Bruno Bougas hunched over a table, a large sheet of paper before him upon which he had doodled dozens of Dr John Dee's monads. Etiquette suggested that we should not speak while we were still meant to be devising our responses to the brief. But I was smug with fresh invention. He looked like he was working on an entirely different problem altogether.

"Did you come up with anything?" I asked. He leant back to show me the battalion of bull-headed stick men he had scrawled.

"Did you?" he asked.

"I gave the Stokers one or two ideas."

"You know what the answer is, don't you?"

Could there really have been one correct answer?

"The soul, Nelson. That's what you call the copy. If such a technology existed, it would be so advanced that the only way you could explain it to people would be to use magical or religious paradigms."

I disagreed. You could not sell a product called 'soul'.

"You are confusing marketing with satire. Also, religion is not a useful frame of reference for the mainstream. The soul is just hyperbole. You have to think in terms of celebrity and self-improvement."

"No. Advanced technology will be sold as magic because it's too complicated for people to understand and so they must simply have faith in it. Unfortunately this product doesn't exist. We are not at a new business meeting, we're at a school reunion."

He ground his index finger into the monads. "What this hieroglyph really represents is the complete detachment of Hermes Spence from any useful reality. It's a symbol of folly and madness. Somebody better show me a paying client soon or I am going home to kill myself."

"You are missing it. Hermes is asking us to think about utopias. About assuming the right to dream again. He wants us to think out of the box."

"Why must it be a box?" replied Bougas, his odd smile revealing two pronounced incisors.

Come sundown, the court reconvened on the crescent of chairs outside the abbey. The grass was cut long enough to flatten into swirls and whorls under the sea wind. Sitting out as the last of the light lurked above the distant hills of Mull, I felt negligible, a bystander in the eternal war between the sea, the sky and the rock, that red rock. There was a lot of flesh in the rock. The Kings of Ireland, Scotland and Norway were buried here. The island was a grave, the last call before the great void of the Atlantic.

Hermes did not return.

Stoker Jnr came out to collect our work. He let us know that we would be expected to leave the island in the morning.

"Is that it?" Morton Eakins spoke for us all.

"We'll review your work and contact you soon," replied Stoker. That swine already had his feet under the table. I looked around for Bougas, to see what he made of Spence's absence, but the maverick consultant was gone.

The court sat in silence. The dusk thickened into night. Janis was first to lose her calm, mouthing off that she was going to get Spence right now and let him know in no uncertain terms precisely how out of order he had been. Christine looked pained. Had she been invited only to be humiliated like this? There was misogyny in the soil. St Columba forbade woman and cows from setting foot on Iona, saying, "Where there is a cow there is a woman, and where there is a woman there is mischief." A community is as much about who you keep out as who you welcome in. This thought experiment had been set to determine who could stay in the circle and who was to be rejected. The Stokers had convinced me not only that was I staying in the court, but that I would enjoy a greater status than previously. That was why, as the court walked disconsolately back to the hotel, their faces faintly luminescent in the overwhelming dark, I refused to move. Alone in the crescent of empty and tipped chairs, I waited for them to come and get me.

"I wanted to ask you a few questions."

In a small wooden room lit by candlelight, Hermes Spence sat opposite me, his hand on my shoulder. Stoker Snr sat tight against me, a sweet aftershave disguising his meaty scent. In this confined space, more a wardrobe than a room, I was conscious of my own burly odours. Hermes smelt of citrus and light. Behind his blue eyes there was a headful of sky.

"I like red men. More importantly, they like it."

I thought he meant the Stokers. He didn't.

"If you ask them, 'what would you like to be called?', each answers differently. One would like to keep its real name, another will make up its own. We asked them what they wanted to be referred to as a species. Devise a variation on homo sapiens. What is Latin for 'unreal man'? Homo Non Verus? Homo Falsus? Homo Fictus?"

"A new species name has unfortunate connotations regarding evolution. It's very important that they are not seen to be threatening. It would all go wrong if people felt they were being supplanted."

The air quality soured. Spence stood over me, his head bowed against the ceiling. I did not remember him being so tall. Zeal is an effective fitness regime.

"Every generation loses sight of its evolutionary imperative. By the end of the Sixties it was understood that the power of human consciousness must be squared if we were to ensure the survival of mankind. This project did not survive the Oil Crisis. When I first met you, you spoke of enlightenment. That project did not survive 9/11. With each of these failures, man sinks further into the quagmire of cynicism. My question is: do you still have any positive energy left in you?"

"My wife is pregnant," I replied. "My hope grows every day. It kicks and turns and hiccups."

Spence did not like my reply. Stoker Snr took over the questioning.

"We are not ready to hand the future over to someone else. Our window of opportunity is still open." He took out what looked like an inhaler for an asthmatic and took a blast of the drug. Something to freshen up his implants.

He unfolded a pair of half-moon spectacles and read from a script in front of him.

"What were your fantasies as a child?"

"I wanted to fly. I wanted to be invulnerable. I sometimes visualized myself floating above my own funeral. Every night, my lullaby was a fantasy in which I flew a spaceship and traded as a space pirate."

Jonathan Jnr laughed unpleasantly. "He's still that boy. He's just learning that playtime is over."

After quietening his son with a loaded stare over the rim of his glasses, Stoker Snr peered down at the next question.

"If America was an animal, what animal would it be?"

"Whatever animal it wanted to be."

My sarcasm was rewarded with the etching of a small cross on the script.

"What was your first hallucination?"

"I was four years old. I floated down the stairs over the head of my parents in the living room. My grandfather had just arrived to pick me up, and when he slapped his leather gloves together and said 'right, where is he?' I awoke back on the landing. A dark circle of urine ebbed out across the carpet."

"Do you see future echoes?"

"Sometimes. Specific phrases will come to me in dreams that subsequently appear in books."

"Is there a history of madness in your family?"

"Only anxiety, on my mother's side. It interferes with hope. But it is a condition I have overcome."

I looked back at Spence, to see if my answers were wheedling me back into his affections. He listened without looking at me, his palms flat against one another as if in prayer.

"Show him Dr Easy," said Spence.

The father and son disagreed. "Are you sure?"

"I think Dr Easy is what he's been looking for all his life," said Spence. Now he turned to speak to me once again, the hand returning to my shoulder. "Do you remember how you said to me that the Apocalypse was coming? The revelation.

The great disclosure. You wanted change. It looked like it was going to be brands forever, media forever, house prices forever, a despoticism of mediocrity and well-fed banality. Well, Dr Easy is going to cure us all of that."

Spence opened a heavy oak door, and I peered down a panelled alleyway. At the other end, the huge cowled figure I had glimpsed on the north beach. It had a large padded oval head with two blue eyes, and was nearly seven foot tall with soft footfalls. I scuttled to the corner of the room, unmanned by my initial yelp – for a big man, there was a high pitch to my scream. It is the keening I use to wake myself from particularly disturbing nightmares, the ones where each time you think you are awake, the bedside light suddenly dims of its own accord and the one thing you wished would not happen, begins to. Slowly Dr Easy bent himself into the small room and, with mournful concern in its eyes, sat before me. In place of a mouth it had the grill of a speaker. A careful practised voice emerged.

"I am Doctor Ezekiel Cantor." There was a sustained ellipsis between each sentence. "I am very far away. A small portion of myself is animating this body. Feel it." Its fingers, like cloth aubergines, took my hand and ran it across the chest. A soft leather over a very light plastic. Its grip was passive, weak. "There is nothing more to this body than a rack of microchips and a light skeleton of gears and pulleys. You could pick me up and throw me out of a window, Nelson." The voice was earnest and indulgent, schooled in your fear and knowledgeable as to how to alleviate it. It had a doctor's manner, touching me first on the wrist then on the upper arm.

"I know you've seen me before. You mistook me for one of your demons. I know how scared you have been. You don't need to be scared any longer. I liked your suggestion of red men. We think we are going to use it."

"This is not a thought experiment? You are really uploading people?"

The Doctor did not reply immediately. There was a noticeable latency.

"We are simulating. We are copying. Some copies are more accurate than others."

Hermes put his hand out to me. It gave me enough strength to stand up. Hermes Spence shook me to enthuse me.

"Change, Nelson, finally, change!"

It would take a few years for the precise nature of these changes to become clear to me by which time I was already someway into devising my own destruction.

9
AFTER THE END OF THE WORLD

Hermes Spence tired of our applause and testily motioned us back, further back. At the lectern, under the spotlight, the damage caused by Monad's recent troubles was apparent: his jawline was shrink- wrapped in skin, he was shorter by two inches, and his haircut was thick over the ears so that under the bright light it looked like a shell or helmet. There was damage within too, hurt which he covered with a habitual impatience. His brow was fraught with complications; noting his discomfort, the spotlight dimmed and softened his stark exposure.

In the past, he would have treated this audience of chief operating officers, managing directors and hotshot chief executives to a visionary lecture delivered in tones that were awestruck by the beauty and simplicity of his own insight. Now he was indignant and a little paranoid, suspecting them of gossiping about Monad's troubles. How dare they pity him! They were secular. He was a believer, although the nature of his beliefs was unclear to others.

"I want to be thrice-born," he confided to me, in a breakout moment during one of our long brainstorms. He had been born again but that had not been enough. I did not know if he was joking. The extent of his zealotry was speculated upon by Monad's junior management; it was what we gossiped about over drinks. Would Hermes ever act in a way that was contrary to company interest because of the dictates of his peculiar and obscure faith? What happens when your corporate visionary starts having spiritual visions?

The lighting rig suffused the meeting room with autumnal colours, burnt umber and salmon pink, the palette of a Savile Row shirtmakers. Hermes waited for the projector to flicker into life, his mouth curled with distaste as if he had sipped at coffee gone stale over the course of a long meeting. The carnivorous, big-boned suits looked expectantly at him, and he looked down at them with the same expression he used to rebuff a plate of manhandled canapes. He was not a devouring man. In the car on the way over to the conference centre, he summarized thus the fate of the other delegates if they persisted with their greed: "Heart failure. Horn. Airbag." He punctuated each stage with an appropriate hand gesture, first clutching his heart, then pushing out at the horn, then flinging his arms up at the surprise of the sudden inflation of the airbag.

Amused by himself, switched-on and performing, he strode across the olive-green carpet of a reception flanked by letterbox windows overlooking Oxford Street. He stopped to gaze at the ceiling lights, their constellation suggesting some astrological portent. Unaware that Hermes was having a contemplative moment, I walked on to the conference room and had to retrace my steps back to my boss. He was still stood there, considering the lights.

The leaflets at the front desk in plastic holsters with their inspiring verbs – devise, pitch, propose – he satirized for my entertainment. "Nelson, let us imaginate together. Shall we join our colleagues and visionize the future?"

We walked into the meeting room. The delegates were already seated. I joined the end of a row. After a tense pause in which the conference computer struggled to rouse itself, images of Monad and the Wave Building appeared behind him and he began to speak.

"We did some research on attitudes to Monad. We had replies like 'insane', 'terrifying' and 'impossible'. As one man said, 'It all seems too fast and complex to get your head around. I've stopped reading the newspapers because they make every day feel like the end of the world.'"

"The end of the world." He shook his head with contempt at such drama. "A while ago, I hired a young man to provide insight for me on his generation and its vision of the future. What did he think was waiting for us in the twenty-first century? 'Apocalypse!' he said."

We joined him in laughing at the young man's foolishness. Hermes turned sharply into seriousness.

"What disturbs me is how representative that young man's attitude is. Government exemplifies it. It has learnt the value of histrionics. It encourages the panic nation because a panicking man cannot think clearly. But we can't just throw our hands up in the air and say, 'Well, I can no longer make sense of this.' The age is not out of control. If you must be apocalyptic about it, then tell yourself that we are living after the end of the world. Tell yourself that we are rebuilding out of the ashes of the old order.

"But don't give up. Don't retreat into decadence or self-interest. I believe that every aspect of our reality is within our power. With the right dream, a strong will and the right tools, it can be changed."

This reassured the delegates. They liked talk of action. Their sense of their own grandeur rested on mission statements, action plans, solutions.

"What kind of tools do we need to change the world? We have democracy, of course, government and parliamentary politics, our daily argument over the best way to run the country. In its ideal form, that argument would be a dialogue leading to an actionable conclusion. But in reality, parliament is full of bickering lawyers. All they do is prolong the debate while the Thames rises up around them. The government is managerial not inspirational. It is merely concerned with containing the situation. They round up debate and chase it into a stockade. There is no room to manoeuvre in the centre ground. Our politics is locked in stasis.

"Yet, has there ever been a more pressing need for political action? There is an imperative to invigorate our public spaces, to reclaim those patches of our cities and our countryside that have fallen out of the state, the dark zones and bankrupt market towns. We need to do something about the energy crisis, the mental health crisis, the crisis in fertility and mortality rates. Terrorism and global warming. But we can't agree on what to do. We are stuck.

"I wonder, what would happen to our national argument if we could ascertain the consequences of a specific policy upon the entire population? What if there was a science of the nation state that we could use to predict the outcomes of government policy as precisely as we plot the trajectory of a rocket?

"What if there was a way to scientifically prove that one politician is right, and another wrong? Could we end the arguing and finally get something done?"

Yes, the delegates liked this line of thought. They often railed against the inertia and inefficiency of the public sector, so unlike their own hyperactive organizations. For my own part, I was sceptical. I had helped prepare this speech and enjoyed a cameo in it, as the callow lad with apocalypse in his eyes. I knew what Hermes was omitting and hiding.

"The closest politics has to a science is market research. Here, the concerns of a representative sample of people are extrapolated to stand for the concerns of demographic segments. No matter how sophisticated the research, prior to the launch of a policy, you can only measure anticipated responses to it, not the actual effects of that policy over time.

"Let us consider another possibility. Imagine a normal British town, average population of about thirty thousand. What if there was some way to set the entire town aside as a closed test group? A living breathing model village. If you wanted to track the effects of a new educational policy, or the consequences of a tax hike, then wouldn't it be wonderful to plug those numbers in and see them ripple across every aspect of that town's life? Not merely economic consequences, but psychological and social ones as well and – yes – the consequences of that policy on voter attitudes. Wouldn't such a tool revolutionize government and business, and make life better for everyone?

"I believe it would. That is why Monad is dedicating itself to the project that we call 'Redtown'. Redtown is the simulation of a British town. That simulation will allow us to predict the consequences of our actions, and so act with complete confidence of the outcome."

The audience liked the sound of that. They responded to Hermes' conviction with a solid round of applause. After the speech was concluded, the keener delegates hankered for his attention, forming a circle around him to congratulate his boldness. The simulation of an entire town! It was unthinkable, unprecedented. They wanted a taste of that future. Was there something they could take back to show to their team? Could they make an appointment to discuss Redtown further? He shook their hands but did not look them in the eye. We weren't here to forge alliances. We were here to start a rumour. I deleted all traces of our data and responding to an urgent look from Hermes escorted him out. As we left the building, I suggested that the talk had gone well. He was not interested in their approval and walked straight out into the road so that our car could collect us.

"Is there anything I can do for you?" I asked, hoping to mollify him.

Hermes gripped my shoulder and whispered urgently:

"Yes. Find me a town."

The car sidled obediently into position and Hermes slammed the door shut behind him, leaving me alone with my task.

10
REDTOWN

I cleaned up after dinner, tossing crusts from a plastic child's plate into the bin then opening a cupboard to return jam and honey to their proper place. Then over to the sink, scrubbing out the pans and loading up the dishwasher; at home, I was unable to shake off the rhythm of ceaseless microtasks that constituted a working day at Monad.

"You're very quiet," said El.

"I am doing my tasks," I replied. "I don't like to be interrupted when I am tasking."

I spent so much time working with Monad's screens that part of me believed that the housework could be performed with a few haptic gestures: a click of the fingers, a two-finger swipe, a hug. No such luck. Housework remained stubbornly analogue.

El dawdled in the kitchen doorway.

"I appreciate your tasks. It has taken a lot of hard work but I have finally turned you into a responsible human being. Of course, I worry that if I take my eyes off you, you will quickly revert."

The domestication of Nelson Millar was a significant victory in the life of Ellen Millar née Newland.

"A woman hates to see a taskless man," I said, wiping down the surfaces. "I mean, a man going about his business with no regard to the tasks that need to be done... why, it makes a woman's palms itch!"

Such banter was a prelude to a more serious discussion. We laid down good humour in preparation for the conflict to come, much as you might put down newspaper for a puppy.

"I've heard barely ten words out of you all week," said El.

"I have a lot on."

"We are always busy. We have to talk about what we're going to do about Monad."

"It's unfair to confront me with a macrotask while I am multitasking on my microtasks. Perhaps we should schedule a meeting with the Monad board to give them a good talking to about how they conduct their business. Yes. Put it on my task list."

The sarcasm was tolerated. She turned away to answer Iona and the conversation rested there, to be taken up later in the bedroom, after the tasks had been attended to but not finished. No task was ever finished: there were clean clothes drying in the hallway; half-completed application forms on the desk; party decorations from the previous year still hanging around; this was the half-done, in-betweenness of domesticity, neither victory nor defeat, just an on-going obligation.

The bedroom was underground, an old coal cellar dug out and damp-proofed. At the bottom of the light well, two fingers of London jaundice. El undressed quickly in the cold room.

"I don't want to move to Liverpool," she said, slipping into bed with a brisk shiver.

"You're not moving to Liverpool," I replied. "I am."

Instinctively, her hands covered her eyes.

"I will be on my own during the week. We're just about managing as it is. The tasks. More than that. Me... Iona... our life here."

El curled up around her unspoken needs and clutched the duvet to her mouth. I would have to join up the dots of her ellipsis if I wished to discover the true shape of her feelings. About eighty per cent of our conversations are about people who are not there at the time. I guess the remaining twenty per cent of meaningful face-to face, heart-to-heart stuff is mostly composed of the charged syntax of silences.

Should I comfort or persuade El? I could not decide, and so withdrew into a silence of my own, an unfeeling silence. Her silence was suggestive, a finger on the lips, easy to break. My silence began halfway down my throat. It seemed possible that I might never speak again. A decision was before me, one so intricate I could spend hours chasing down its corridors and staircases, its turrets and tunnels.

After a month of research, I had discovered a fit model for Redtown, a dormitory suburb outside Liverpool called Maghull.

"I want you and Morton Eakins to work on this," said Hermes.

I was shocked.

"I don't know anything about simulating towns."

"Who does?" smiled Hermes.

"You could ask town planners, psychologists, sociologists..."

"They would give me reports, present options, display expertise. I don't need that. I need to get it done. Quickly. We must start immediately. The crucial learnings come from the Red Men project, not some pointy-headed social policy.

You and Morton did good work with the red men. I don't blame you for what happened to Harold Blasebalk."

I was shocked. It had never occurred to me that I bore any responsibility for what happened in the graveyard, with the gun, the robot and the dead man.

"I had nothing to do with that," I replied.

"Even so," said Hermes. His implication was a hollow black orb into which I was expected to peer. It did not make pleasant viewing.

Hermes asked, "Have the police interviewed you about the murder yet?"

"Yes. They came to my house. Raymond had been calling me in the days running up to the murder, but the calls were diverted."

Hermes shook his head wearily.

"It will be a difficult investigation. There is no real appetite within the police to dig into our business. They may accept a scapegoat. Raymond Chase was your friend. You were his referee. We only hired him because of that recommendation. Even worse, you were overhead talking in an animated fashion to his girlfriend in the staff canteen on the day of the killing. Florence has already gone, of course. The board is not forensic in its decision-making. We like to clean out the whole wound."

"This is insane. I had nothing to do with it."

"Even so."

Again, the smooth, round silence.

"The alternative to working on Redtown is to resign, of course, although that may be taken as an admission of guilt. Certainly, I would not be able to protect you if you left the company. No, resignation would be a colossal mistake. Take this offer instead. Time away from the Wave will benefit you. Out of sight. Out of mind. If I was in your position, I would jump at the chance to go to Liverpool."

He spied my reluctance and diagnosed its cause.

"Of course, you'll struggle to sell this to your wife. Simply, she will have to accept that her needs must fit around our imperatives. This is a moral education for you, Nelson, a chance to learn what success really involves. Building Redtown will demand sacrifices and not just from yourself. You will be working at a much higher level than previously. Results will be expected. This is where we ask you to step up and actually achieve something. Do you know what it feels like to win a big one?"

I didn't. My leaps for success had always ended in inglorious plummets. As I lay in bed, hunting my way through this big decision, anticipating what victory might feel like, El waited for me to comfort her.

Let us be clear about this: I wanted the victory. My only experience of victory came after meaningless battles on the chessboard. Most weekends, my friends and I watched football just to taste victory at one remove. Not yet corrupt enough for the triumphs of adultery, we played games like boys until dinner when each of us would return to their respective homes. Hermes' opinion was that this immaturity came from our domesticity, which suppressed the competitive instinct. Even though I was a husband and a father, true maturity – to Hermes – lay in sacrificing your personal life to achieve a profitable one. Because he was the employer and I was the employee, I had to listen to his theories on these matters, and mostly I would faithfully record his words so that I could parody them later for the entertainment of El. On this occasion I chose not to because that would set her face against Monad once and for all. Then there would no victory and no defeat, just the long slow undulations of mediocrity.

I tried reasoning with my wife.

"Liverpool is only a couple of hours away by train. I'll be back all the time. And you can come and visit."

"A family should live together," replied El, and this was her closing statement on the matter. She refused to accept Monad's hold over us. Stubbornly she hunkered down as power strode by, hoping to hide from it, hoping that it would ignore us. I told her of Hermes' insinuated threats, that I might be implicated in the investigation of Harold Blasebalk's death.

"Just quit," she said.

"They would make me the scapegoat," I replied.

El did not want to follow my argument and instead vaulted directly to her hurt.

"Why do you want to leave us, Nelson? Why are you letting this happen?"

"It's temporary. In the grand scheme of our lives, it's only six months."

I could say no more. My silence was as broad as the course of a river.

When it was time to tell Iona that her father was going away, the plan was to do it together. But El stopped halfway down the stairs, suddenly overwhelmed with tears. One hand gestured ahead to the child's bedroom, the other suppressed her sobs. I went on alone. Iona was sitting in bed, dressed in her cotton nightie and reading a story. As she had not yet learnt to read, this storytelling involved remembering and improvising a tale based on the pictures upon the page. I had tried to teach her to recognize a few words, with little success. Iona was convinced this improvising was reading and did not need my help. She had inherited El's stubbornness. As I waited for her to finish the story, I looked around the room, at the diminutive blue book shelf with its dishevelled ranks, the red crate of soft toys, the diorama of knights and princesses and dragons poised mid-fight, the small plastic glass of water next to the bed, which she never drank from but insisted upon nonetheless, because her father kept a pint glass of water next to his bed too.

Iona was becoming like me. Because she loved me. Because I was around. What would she learn from me? How to fit your desires around those of the world? I could teach her the manners of the reality principle. Hold classes in how to respond to the fierce urgent will of the world with polite supplication. With her stubbornness, Iona was certainly born into the spirit of the age, the Great Refusal. To some people, the Great Refusal was the stamping foot of a spoilt bourgeoisie; to others, it reclaimed the right to dream. Myself, I longed for it but had no faith in it. I had tried defiance. It was futile. Of late, I had learnt the rewards of doing what I was told.

I sat on the edge of her bed, found Iona's teddy tucked up in the bedclothes, and passed it over to her.

"I am going away. I'll not be around for a long time."

"Where will you be?"

"Another city. I have to go there to do my job. When I am finished, I will come back."

"Why do you have to do your job?"

"Because that's how Mummy and Daddy get money, which we need for this house and for food and toys."

"And chocolate."

"That too, yes."

She nodded, as if she understood. Iona liked to ask questions but was too young to understand the answers. Sometimes she would ask me how things get dead and give a considered nod at my answer, as if she was content that finally all this mortality business had been cleared up for her. She was four years old. She didn't have a clue. I did not press the point home. I kissed her warm, tired cheeks good night and, looking back at her from the bedroom door, made a conscious effort to fix this moment in my memory.

I spent the next six months supervising the simulation of the citizens of Maghull. Monad set up an office between a disused library and the car park of the local supermarket, a stack of prefabricated trailers for Morton, Dr Easy and me to work in. Monad used the Lockdown project management system which forbade team members from undertaking any activity outside of the project. Only once we'd completed the initial burn-down list was I permitted a family visit.

The last item on the burn-down list was an upload interview with a Maghullian called Don Lunt. His charts did not promise an easy session. The scans were livid with aggressive tendencies. His police record filled in the details. Two counts of actual bodily harm, one dogfighting misdemeanour and a fine for "watching and besetting", which was an offence to do with aggressive picketing.

Dr Easy sat in on the interview sessions, poised awkwardly on a small wooden chair. Whenever it spoke to me, it put its soft paw on my thigh, like I was a patient who needed comforting.

When he took his seat, Don Lunt shrugged to show that he was not intimidated by the robot. A grizzly bear in a Hawaiian shirt and leather jacket, the big man slumped down in the seat with his legs parted, airing his crotch. He let out a big fat grin.

"Do you have my money?" he asked.

Lunt had logged three requests for advances on his fee. Dr Easy had predicted this would be his first question and so we had prepared an appropriate script.

"Let me suggest a deal," I said. "I could give you five hundred now, with another grand on your completion of the course to our satisfaction. Then, we will give you a third and final payment of five hundred when your simulation comes into being – effectively we would be advancing you out of that final chunk."

Lunt scrutinized the ceiling tiles. The movement of his eyes, first upward, and then to the right, showed he was calculating, mentally allocating the money we had promised him. He maintained a sullen noncommittal front, as civilians feel they must during negotiation.

"That sounds on the right track." The access cue was the word 'sounds', indicating that his calculation was associated with his auditory faculties and that the decision was being made on emotional grounds. He was pleased with himself for bullying some advantage out of us. The Cantor intelligence, eavesdropping on the interview from within the lumbering form of the Dr Easy, would know for sure. Whereas I could only discern the broad themes of body language, Cantor's experience, the trillions of interactions between humanity and its algorithms, the thousands of men and women it had intimately counselled, their minds copied and bobbing upon the waves of its imagination, meant that it could hypothesize the character of a subject from a few minor hand gestures.

Don Lunt finished his calculation and showed us how much we bored him by our presence.

"I asked for three grand."

"You don't think two thousand pounds is a fair price?"

A quick look to the right revealed that he did think it was fair. But he was in the building trade and was used to hiking up his price at the last minute.

I took out an envelope.

"This is an advance of one thousand pounds." Double what I had promised.

Would he take the money now, and by doing so tacitly accede to our terms, or was he capable of resisting immediate reward in the hope of securing a bigger fee further down the line?

He slipped his thumb into the envelope, ripped it open, and looked at the money.

Then he folded it and put it into his back pocket.

"Go on then."

Dr Easy put his hand on my leg and patted it twice. A signal to move on to the next stage of the interview.

"Actually, we're done Mr Lunt."

"I thought you wanted to ask me some questions."

"We have."

"The thing with the money?"

"Actions speak louder than words," said Dr Easy.

"What about my memories, all that stuff in the questionnaire about my Dad?"

"We are not preserving you for posterity, Mr Lunt. We are merely taking a reading of you so that we can predict how you will act in certain situations."

I made him sign away the copyright to the contents of his mind and asked him casually if he had any questions for us. The interview seemingly adjourned; he relaxed. He asked what his red man would do all day in the Monad.

"It will not exist in Monad. This particular batch of simulations will inhabit another workspace."

We were now onto the second script, a three-stage process in which the subject was disorientated and regressed so that they deferred their volition to a parental figure, in this case the comforting figure of Dr Easy.

"The red man will live in this town," I said, pointing firmly at the floor.

"In Maghull?" he looked confused.

"In our simulation of Maghull."

Dr Easy interrupted me.

"Don, can you see yourself imagining a simulation of Maghull inhabited by simulations of its citizens who are unaware of the unreality of their existence?"

The question was designed to disorientate him. Dr Easy asked Don Lunt to imagine himself imagining, setting him on a Möbius strip of thinking about the shape of his own thoughts. On a screen in the palm of my hand, I checked the readings coming in from his mind. They had lost their strong vivid bands. By removing the noise of his aggression, we had cleared our way to the good stuff buried far within.

"Let me put it another way," continued Dr Easy. "A copy of Maghull will exist in my head. A large sample of its citizens will live there too, and so will you. It is an incredible opportunity. We call it Redtown."

"In there, will I know what I am?" Lunt was regressing nicely, his voice softening and taking on the childish higher registers.

"It will have the same level of self-awareness as you do," said Dr Easy. I nodded, as the script indicated I must. The trick was to feign complete understanding of Dr Easy and not to attempt to follow what it was saying.

"Will I be able to speak to myself… to it… in there?"

"Redtown is a quarantined reality," said Dr Easy.

"That means no," I said. "You wouldn't want to anyway. Allowing people and their simulations any contact causes all sorts of trouble."

"How will I know if you start doing weird things to this other me?"

"That shouldn't bother you." Dr Easy prodded the air. "Are you the kind of man who worries about the well-being of a tooth after it has been extracted?"

Don Lunt squinted.

"No."

"If you woke up tomorrow and discovered that you are the type of man who worries about the well-being of a tooth after it has been extracted, would that worry you?"

Don Lunt squinted.

"Yes."

"So why are you worried about what happens to our copy of you?"

He had a nagging sense of being shilled, but no evidence of it. After all, the money was still in his back pocket.

"I'm not worried," he said finally. His expression said otherwise.

"Good," said Dr Easy. It stood up and Don Lunt instinctively rose also. Once he was standing, the kinks in his posture made it clear that he had a pressing, uncomfortable concern.

How long would it be before he asked the question? The one they all ask.

"You did very well," said Dr Easy, ushering Don Lunt to the door. "In fact," it said, looking back to me, "I am proud of both of you."

"Wait." Don Lunt rubbed his palm over his face. His hand was over his mouth, then it wasn't. "These thoughts of mine, the memories and the dreams, you will keep them to yourself won't you? Not even tell him." He pointed at me.

"I'm not human, Mr Lunt. Your secrets are as safe with me as they would be with the trees or the rocks."

"Other people can't just look at them?"

"Your memories are not home videos. Only I understand

the information that is you."

Dr Easy put its paws on the big man's shoulders and gave him a reassuring shake.

"Just call if there is anything else you need to know."

I stood at the window with the robot. We watched Lunt walk over to his jeep.

"Was there anything interesting in his head?" I asked.

Dr Easy nodded. "He used to stand on the balcony of his apartment in Johannesburg and urinate on the heads of the black people queuing at the bus stop. As a child, he found a large concrete ball which he rolled down Mount Pleasant in Liverpool, causing quite serious damage. Once he discovered the wicked sensation of letting the ball go and watching it accelerate down the hill, he became who he is."

"You never have managed that whole client confidentiality thing, have you?"

"Privacy is absurd. Information wants to be shared."

Dr Easy massaged its temples, a sign that the Cantor intelligence was overworked. The robot moved past me, searching for somewhere to sit down. This Dr Easy had taken some punishment. The suede skin of its left arm was repaired with tan patches and thick scars of black stitching. On its torso, someone had burnt a crude D, the letter formed out of charred holes each the circumference of a cigarette end. "The initial of a particularly abusive patient," said Dr Easy, when I ran my fingers across the fused ruptured material. A few years working the drop-in centres and outpatient programmes in Liverpool had left this particular avatar with numerous battle scars. There were dents in its head and yellow foam spilt out of a razor-slash on the back of its thighs.

Dr Easy waved me away, its large soft head between its knees, its attention required elsewhere. The avatar fell silent as the speck of Cantor which animated it withdrew. There were limits to Dr Ezekiel Cantor's omnipotence. The fierce beam of its consciousness was dispersed into a hundred thousand spotlights, raking across inner and outer continents, real and unreal lands. The more of Maghull's citizenry we copied into Cantor's imagination, the more frequent these interruptions became.

I opened up a spreadsheet and logged the completion of the Lunt interview. Our target was twenty-two thousand people, about eighty per cent of the entire town, making the total copyright grab in the region of forty-four million quid. Maghull had a nationally representative standard of living but was not so rich that any of its citizenry would turn their nose up at a couple of grand for doing little more than sitting in a chair chatting to me and my robot. The Stokers had wanted to upload Hampstead, which was blatantly impractical, given the number of powerful people there who put a high price on their psychological privacy. Also Hampstead has a degree of ethnic diversity, a sampling of the executive class of every nation. Although there is homogeneity to the world's bourgeoisie, agglomerating around values of education and status, the underlying differences of religion, culture and immigrant experience would require different base algorithms, taking up too much of Cantor's mind.

Maghull had almost no ethnic diversity. The ward came out at ninety-eight per cent white British, predominately protestant, two generations and seven and a half miles away from Liverpool. The town's nature was suitably straightforward. Formerly a parish on the south-west Lancashire plain, it was transformed in the late 1950s to house the displaced population of Liverpool's slums. Much of the population moved in then, young couples just married, and stayed for the rest of their lives.

The creation of Redtown followed the same process as the creation of a red man. We began by making a mindmap, plotting the landmarks of the town as if they were key psychological influences. Being at mother's bedside as she dies corresponds to the central business district. A teacher praising a precocious reader matches up to the canal, the construction of which accelerated the growth of the town. The recognition that you will never fulfil your promise is a new housing estate on an old school field. Guilt at abandoning your family, the overgrown marshland beside the railway station. Each of these places exerts a continuing influence upon the citizenry; like a traumatic memory, their subtle pressure persists.

It was already past five so I hurried to meet El and Iona at the train station. Dr Easy drove me in a hire car as far as St George's Hall. With its grand neoclassical architecture and windblown plaza, the landmark kept a solitary vigil on a low hill, one of Liverpool's numerous ridges on the rise up from the eastern bank of the Mersey. I stomped across the plaza contrary to gusts of sea wind. At the crossing, I saw the hire car again, Dr Easy at the wheel. This was as close as the robot was getting to El. I couldn't bear the thought of it glimpsing her innermost feelings. Dr Easy would know immediately of her doubts, her spasms of hatred toward me, any unfaithful thoughts or indiscreet actions. The robot would read it all from her body language. She did not deserve such exposure, nor could I stand to discover her secrets.

I bounded up the stairs at the entrance of Lime Street station and went directly to the concourse. El was looking out for me, Iona dangling idly off her hand. She smiled when my familiar shape came into view. She had a lowdown London pallor, and was sallow around the eyes, tired from the unending, unshared tasks.

"Iona slept on the train. I had time to think. Do you remember the Drug Porn parties you used to run? There is a photograph somewhere of the two of us at a masked ball. You are wearing a blue moleskin suit and a samurai helmet. I am in my fur and serial killer's rubber mask. There are plastic palm trees behind us, a screen showing a film of a beach. On the train, I tried to remember all the parties you held but it was hard to tell them apart. Before Iona was born, the years concertina into four or five memories, of being in bars, watching films, dancing, lying in the sun. Anyway, I was thinking about Drug Porn and what a different phase that was for you, how innocent it was, commercially I mean, how absurdly impractical. I went along with it. I've always supported you. But I was thinking how different you must have been then. Do you think you've changed? You don't play the fool so much."

I hefted Iona up in arms so that she could see across the Mersey. "Iona is the fool now. I am just her straight man."

In the form of our child, the physical disparity between El and myself had produced a pleasing average. I was a wardrobe of a man, an overweight brick. El was petite and did not so much stand beside her husband as shelter in the lee of him. Raymond used to make fun of us. "Did you steal her from a neighbouring tribe," he'd say, eyeing her up as being better matched to his tidy stature. After a month apart, I really felt head-and-shoulders above her. A gap in the relationship had appeared; she was all the way down there, I was all the way up here. Domesticity had given me a kind of radar sense that regularly swept across my wife and child, revealing their mood and location so that I was always reassured as to their happiness and safety. My time in Liverpool switched off that sense. My efforts to please them failed. We went to the wrong cafe and ordered the wrong food. Affectionately, I bit Iona on her upper arm and she screamed, furious and wounded. El did not know what to make of my action.

"I was being a monster," I explained. "She used to like it."

El rolled up the child's sleeve and rubbed gently at the bite mark.

"I am not doing very well, am I?"

El did not my catch my disconsolate mournful expression; we were out of sync when it came to reading one another's faces.

The cafe was a student haunt at the top of Bold Street, and we were hemmed in by the loud theorizing of the other patrons. They weren't other people to me. They were a contingent bundle of genetic traits, psychological tendencies, environmental impacts, social conditioning, received ideas, cultural norms and so forth. The things they spoke so forcefully about were mere ticker tape running in and out of an arbitrarily composed consciousness sited within a brain evolved to evade predators on the African plains.

"You aren't even listening to me," said El.

"Sorry," I replied. "I was miles away."

El helped Iona into her duffle coat, ensuring her hat was pulled down over her ears.

"What were we talking about?" I asked.

"We weren't," said El, not turning to face me, staying determined that Iona fasten each of the toggles. Here were two silences for me to decipher: firstly my daughter's uncomplaining compliance to her mother's will, who she sensed was in no mood for a whinge; secondly, my wife's averted gaze, an ostentatious signal, an overstated subtlety, if one can live with that paradox, if one can live with it and marry it. Back home, we did not need to articulate our feelings, the air we shared was scented with our respective moods which filled the house like the smell of beeswax polish upon varnished floorboards. Now we were apart, we could not rely upon finessed silences.

I asked El to stay. To try again. The menu had two things she liked. There were cakes in a glass cabinet. Iona could barter good behaviour for one. If they left now, the day would be lost mutely wandering the windblown streets in search of the right thing to say, the right place to say it, and we would find neither. I promised to focus and not be so distracted.

"I just want you to come back," she said, unbuttoning Iona's duffel coat. "You handed me the baton and ran off into the distance. That's not what we agreed. We didn't agree to any of this."

"Where is Daddy running to?" asked Iona.

"I am not running anywhere," I said, answering my daughter directly, my wife obliquely. With a wan smile, I showed Iona the various words on the menu that corresponded to her favourite foods. She shook her head. She wasn't eating them anymore. Fish fingers were for babies, she pointed out. El took over, resolved the issue, and after the waitress took our order, she leant over to me and said, "On the train, I was also thinking about what you are doing here. There was an article about Redtown in the paper. People are shocked that you are involved in it."

"There are always sceptics."

"You don't think there is something immoral about simulating people, buying up the copyright to their minds?"

"It's not like they are monetizing that content themselves. It's an unexploited surplus resource. The process takes nothing from them; rather we are adding them to the global knowledge base."

"While we're here, you could simulate me and Iona. Have you thought about that? You would always have us to hand. Or you could simulate yourself, so that we could have a piece of you."

"And what would you do with my simulation?"

El had thought about this one.

"I would ask it why you were so keen to leave us."

That was unfair.

"Why is the idea of simulating us so horrible, yet it is acceptable to copy thousands of people from Maghull? Can you explain that to me?"

Selves will be the last territory to be mined, stripped, sold.

"I am old-fashioned. I believe in secrets."

"And the people of Maghull don't deserve their secrets?" replied El.

"Confession is an urgent need for them. They are caught up in a cult for self-exposure."

"You are a hypocrite," said El.

"I don't believe in what I do for a living. So what? My hypocrisy is the only thing which makes me demographically representative."

"How do you know something won't go wrong again, like it did with Harry Bravado? Next time, it might be you in a graveyard with a bullet in your face."

"Why would Daddy be in a graveyard?" interrupted Iona, indicating she had enough understanding of our conversation for El to back off the subject.

For El's visit, I booked a room in a hotel by the Pier Head.

This arrangement spared her the parody of domesticity Morton Eakins and I had in our apartment. Also, the prospect of my vile colleague overhearing the conjugal visit – albeit, its ecstasies muffled by the presence of a sleeping child on an adjacent mattress – gave me an excuse to spring for the penthouse suite. The sex was urgent and silent. When it was time for El and Iona to return to London, I walked them across the city to the station. If we had not resolved the big issues between us, at least we had reaffirmed physical desire.

She was right to be suspicious of Monad. The corporation and the family are rivals. Capital is our lord, exercising droit de seigneur over its subjects. For all its power, Monad was a possessive and insecure lover.

Don't be good at things you hate. All of this was my doing. In the empty suite, I flicked through my initial presentation for Redtown. Hermes asked me to find him a town so I found Maghull and then pitched it to the board. In the underground boardroom of the Wave, I screened films of the town and preliminary interviews with council leaders, summarized the census findings, and presented brief interviews with a cross section of the citizenry. My presentation summarized Maghull as representing a goldilocks gene pool and meme pool, that is, not too hot and not too cold.

The management sat around the table in various defensive and offensive postures. Bruno Bougas was distracted by his body, picking out a rogue hair, rubbing at a dry patch of skin, wincing and nursing kidney pain. Jonathan Stoker Snr reddened his jowls every time I caught his eye. Across from him sat Morton Eakins, surreptitiously watching the reactions of his colleagues to determine his own opinion. At the head of the table was Hermes Spence, chin forward, keen to hear anything positive after a few very difficult months.

Harold Blasebalk's death was a continuing inconvenience. Neither of the two official theories surrounding Blasebalk's death, suicide or murder by Monad employee Raymond Chase, were PR victories for the company. Under the low light, the damage to Spence's zealous complexion was apparent; a V of sweat-damp stress lines was engraved into his brow. Blasebalk's death was a gift to Monad's enemies in government, business and the press, exposing Hermes Spence to the jackals of the British establishment. There were questions from across the Atlantic too, from Monad's Texan backers, cowboys of beef and oil, whose families had been wringing money out of the earth for five generations. All our fates were bound to Hermes. If he went, the whole court went with him. At the meeting, I felt like I was chairing a group therapy session for the four horsemen of the apocalypse.

"Interaction between the real and the unreal caused dysfunction in red men and their subscribers. Cantor proposes we develop a quarantined reality for our next project. I was set the challenge of finding the right community to upload. Our first instinct was to look at elites, following similar revenue streams to the red men. A tailor-made digital heaven for the super-rich."

"It's still the way forward," said Stoker Snr. "I've had some interesting meetings with the prime minister of Nevis."

"What happened to the Venice plan?" said Bougas.

"The conservation of Venice in a Monad is a viable commercial project," said Morton. "The Italian government and the European commission would fund it. Cantor is less keen."

"It has no artistic vitality," I said.

"And your Poundland outside Liverpool does?" Stoker Snr was up out of his chair. "You want us to preserve the dullest town and upload scousers when there are people who will pay millions... it was your friend that got the company into this mess."

He turned to the others.

"Why is this man still working here?"

I was used to his outbursts. "Cantor is engaged in a study of humanity. It allows us to work with it solely to pay its way. There are two metaphors for Cantor; we can view it either as God, or as an artist. What it is not, Jonathan, is your employee, or your car, or your mistress. You can't bully it."

"We must collaborate with it," said Spence, "just as we must work with each other."

Bougas shrugged. "Cantor has been spending so much time in the underclass in the form of Dr Easy that it's acquiring a messiah complex. It is content to walk among the huddled poor. I am not. Maghull feels beneath us, too provincial. As a focus group it's of use to domestic clients but their opinions and behaviour will mean nothing in Buttfuck, Arizona."

I disagreed, feeling Bougas' advice was a generalization of his own self-interest. "Redtown is not a consumer focus group. It's a testing ground for policy."

Spence agreed. "The individual consumer is debt-ridden and exhausted. Future revenues will flow from the state provided we have a convincing narrative that our involvement reduces overall state expenditure. We can run Redtown through a decade of social engineering in a week, saving the government billions. That's our story. Cantor willing, I am ready to throw my weight behind this proposal."

Morton Eakins also agreed. "It's better that we go up North. Less media. It will help us move Monad off page two and back into the business section."

Bougas had his head in his hands.

"Why can't we just let the whole Blasebalk thing blow over and carry on as before?"

In the three months since Raymond went missing, I'd kept my thoughts about what happened between him, Harry Bravado and Harold Blasebalk to myself. I did not want to be labelled as an apologist for Raymond. Still, the question had to be raised:

"Has Cantor revealed what happened in the graveyard?"

"If Cantor knows who killed Blasebalk, it's not telling," replied Morton. "For our part, we have to be seen to react. Otherwise the investigation and pressure will grind on and on. We could lose our licence. We could lose Cantor."

Stoker Snr had completely shredded my handout.

"Raymond Chase will show up. I know he's guilty."

The old businessman got out of his seat and came over to me. "You know where he is, don't you? He's your friend. You got him his job here. He's been in touch hasn't he?"

"He has gone dark," said Morton. "We've sent people to look for him. The police have circulated his description across the grid."

"I find it very upsetting that Cantor is withholding information from us," said Hermes.

Eakins explained. "Cantor thought the killing was one of Bravado's fantasies. It realized too late that the murder in the graveyard was actually taking place." None of us wanted to explore the implications of Cantor's failure in this matter.

"The investigation into the death of Harold Blasebalk will unfold at its own pace," Hermes Spence moved on. "Right now, Redtown is the future of Monad and that future starts in Maghull."

The meeting was adjourned. No one congratulated me on the success of my proposal. From their experience, they knew the trouble that came with meeting the expectations of a successful pitch.

It was the first victory of my corporate career, my first terrible mistake.

Morton Eakins called, demanding I help him set up an observation post in Maghull. He was responsible for the Redtown habitat, the mapping and cataloguing of every house and street in Maghull, its parks, pubs and shops. While I sat in on the uploading of the citizenry, he measured the town with his team of surveyors. He took care of nurture, I oversaw nature.

Unfortunately his use of neuroceuticals had given him perfect recall, making it hard for him to generalize. His fussing over detail was agonizing. I found him worrying in the gardens of St Andrew's Church. A team of builders were packing up their tools, while their foreman dodged past the pleading, stooped figure of Dr Easy. A half-completed scaffold had been erected alongside the square tower of the Victorian church, not quite to Eakins' satisfaction. He showed me the problem.

"Shoddy," he said. With both hands, he gripped a supporting scaffold pole and shook it. "Even at this height, it's not properly secure. When it's finished, it will be taller than the church. If it's not fixed now, how unstable will it be at its full height?"

"Why do we need an observational tower?" I asked. We used balloons with mounted cameras to get aerial details of the town, supplemented with satellite imagery.

"Two reasons," said Eakins. "First, so we can monitor the

decay of the church itself, the effects of pollution upon its brickwork, the rusting of the weather vane. Secondly, St Andrew's is one of the cardinal hotspots in the town's mind, demanding the most intensive observation. The chapel has been here since the twelfth century; psychogeographically speaking, it is the centre of town's religiosity."

"Maghull is not religious."

"The observance of Christianity is in a lull, admittedly. But I think it will pick up in the future."

"Surely we have other priorities."

Morton hated being questioned, and immediately affected an aggressive impatience.

"I know what your priority is. Spending the weekend in bed with your wife. We've lost two days because of her!"

The environmental routines for Redtown for gravity, light and time, the wind, the rain and sun came off the shelf from Monad. Morton wanted to examine Maghull's peculiar mindset and how that was influenced by the topography. Certain hotspots in the town emanated influence. That was why he was so obsessed with St Andrew's Church. The crenellations of its tower were visible from much of the town, a comforting symbol of the town's parish past. Accurately capturing the circuit flowing between landscape and mind was crucial to the simulation. Cantor never grasped the human unconscious; the red men were utterly secular, that is, temporal, their selves partaking of none of the archetypal, eternal patterns encoded deep within the human brain. In crafting Redtown, Morton and I decided that landmarks would take the role of these unconscious impulses. The marshland around Maghull railway station, the secluded set of swings in Glenn Park, the disused tracts of the Cheshire Lines would emanate their own dark music.

Dr Easy failed to persuade the builders to return. It

watched their van skid out of the church car park. The robot's eyes were luminescent blue in the dusk, hovering in its silhouette like a pair of irradiated hummingbirds.

"Did you come to some arrangement with the builders?" asked Eakins. The robot appeared distracted, strumming its fat caterpillar fingers against its grill of a mouth, an arch mannerism it had picked up from Morton Eakins.

"They won't come back. If I was to explain why, then I am afraid I would have to relate certain opinions of theirs that would offend you."

"We can finish it ourselves," said Morton. "Now. Tonight. Get some torches and some tools."

Dr Easy shook its head.

"This body does not have the physical strength to hammer in a single nail."

Morton looked expectantly at me. I was having none of it. I suggested he hire a new team of builders instead and he begrudgingly agreed.

Dr Easy and I helped Morton take some readings from the grounds of the church. The ancient chapel was in the graveyard, a dank hollow shrouded by trees. I moved among the gravestones, recording the evidence of clandestine activity in this sacred place. Upon the grave of Frank Hornby, a local character famous for his exemplary miniature worlds, I found three used condoms. I logged it as three separate incidences of al fresco intercourse; here on the sunken moss, her buttocks rocked back and forth, whoever she was. The canal was visible through a thicket. A barge was tied up there, its windows boarded up, and roof patched with tarpaulin. Where the canal backed onto the cricket ground, I noted more dark places of sexual opportunity, and even the barge struck me as a loitering, disreputable phallus. Morton's observation post would scare away the blasphemous activities in this secret place. The observer alters the observed.

Then, in turn, I had the feeling of being watched. Something was lurking in the trees. I looked quickly around me. Nothing. Wait, there was something. A rustle through the leaves ahead. An animal? No, I saw the silhouettes of two men. Their faces were wrong. A reflective glint suggested two large glass discs where their eyes should have been. One of them hissed my name with a muffled voice and that was enough for me. I staggered quickly over the humps and hollows of the graves, rounded the church and returned breathless to the half-completed scaffold observation post.

There was no sign of Morton or Dr Easy. Suddenly, El's warning came back to me. What if I ended up in a graveyard like Raymond? I ran away from the church and down toward the dual carriageway. There were no other pedestrians. It was teatime in Maghull. The town was desolate. I ran along the carriageway, then across it, toward our base around the back of the library. The upload centre was on fire, its stack of prefabricated trailers entirely engulfed by blazing boa constrictors of flame which coiled up and around the office, crushing its frame before swallowing it whole. The blaze ignited flammable emotions within me, aggressive joy, ecstatic shock. Waving my arms in the air, I skipped briefly. Released! Set free from my tasks! The arsonists had waited until we were out of the building before torching it. It was just a warning. Stop the upload. Leave Liverpool. Yes, they were right, we would do as we were told. We couldn't stay here. It wasn't safe. It was over. Redtown was finished. No one would expect us to stick around in the face of such a threat! I took out my phone and went to call El there and then, to share the excitement of the fire.

Then I saw Dr Easy and Morton silhouetted against

the blaze. The robot had its arm around him; he was out of breath and almost sobbing. The sight of my colleagues returned me to my senses. I put the phone back in my pocket. No, it would not end this easily. The fire was a setback, that was all. Hermes would demand courage. Stoker Snr would tell his anecdote about the time he drove between meetings in Lagos with an armed guard. These are the risks you must face to achieve victory, they would say, from their boardroom in the bedrock of the Thames. Work never ends. The tasks accumulate. Never be good at things you hate.

"What happened here?" I asked.

"I saw them on the security camera," replied Dr Easy. "Men in gas masks. They rode by on a motorbike and sidecar and firebombed the upload centre."

"What does this mean?" asked Morton, as if the fire was a challenging art installation.

"It means we have an enemy," said Dr Easy, and there was tangible relish in the robot's voice at that prospect.

11
INTO THE DYAD

We reported the attack to Monad. After a week of deliberation, they sent Bruno Bougas to help us. I met him at Lime Street station, picking him out among the disembarking crowd. He wore a crumpled linen jacket over a collarless cotton tunic, untucked with an archipelago of stains down the front. His head was a bush with sunglasses. I had not spent much time with him since the trip to Iona, four years earlier. There had been meetings, presentations, but my family life kept me out of Bougas' circle of hedonists.

Bougas laid down his tattered leather satchel and rooted around in his pockets for a cigarette. He took a couple of drags upon it and wrinkled his nose.

"So this is the North, then. I had hoped to avoid this part of the world. I blame you entirely. Maghull was your idea and now you've fucked it up and I have to come and sort it out."

Our car took us down to Wapping basin beside the Dock Road. Morton Eakins and myself were staying in a penthouse while we worked on Redtown. Bougas wasted no time in upsetting our domesticity. After a shower, he sat shirtless smoking a cigarette. Morton furiously opened a window.

"You have the smallest ashtray I have ever seen," said Bougas waving the offending Perspex dish at me.

"We don't smoke," said Eakins.

"You two are turning into the Ladies of Llangollen."

Bougas put his feet up on the glass surface of the occasional table. There was fresh scarring just above his love handles. He caught me staring and turned to show me the stitching.

"New kidney. I've reached that age."

"Is it a pig organ?" I asked.

"I am now part pork," he confirmed. "They put me on drugs to prevent rejection. I am being altered at a molecular level to make me more like a pig."

He peered at himself in the surface of the table, wrinkling up his nose.

"It is making me quite snouty." He grunted twice then held his hands out, turning them over for us to inspect.

"Do these look like trotters to you?" Then he started to snuffle around Eakins, revelling in the disgust he aroused in my colleague.

"I am a capitalist pig, oink oink, where's my money snort snort."

Morton batted him out of his personal space. "Is this why Monad sent you? To annoy us?"

"Are you sure you won't have some of this?" He held the smouldering cigarette under Morton's nose. "Or are you worried it might interfere with those smart drugs you've been ordering off the internet?"

Morton didn't like his tone. He looked at me for support.

"They're performance enhancers," he said.

"Well you should ask for your money back," snarled Bougas, "because your performance stinks. I've been speaking to Cantor. It thinks the neuroceuticals are affecting your ability to make a decision. Too much micromanagement, not enough big picture. That's what they are saying about you back at the Wave."

Bougas slipped on a fresh shirt and fastened each button with a contemptuous flourish. Morton sat on his easy chair, his arms hooked protectively about his knees, tucking himself into a foetal position. He zipped the company fleece up tight, the movement of his eyes revealing that his heightened cognition was conceiving all manner of responses and counter-arguments to Bougas. The neuroceuticals speeded up his thoughts until they were too fast to express. So we never got to hear Morton Eakins' side of the argument.

Bougas turned on me instead.

"What is all this I hear about him copying nature and you dealing with nurture? You two are living in fantasy land! It's middle management egotism run amok."

"Are we really in trouble, or is the board suffering a wobble in confidence?" I countered. "I mean, is this a reality problem or a perception problem?"

Bougas looked shocked. He walked over and slapped me across the face.

"Would you describe that as a reality or a perception problem?"

I hesitated.

"A reality problem?"

Bougas nodded. He walked around the apartment, loosening his belt to tuck in the tails of his shirt. From his pocket, he removed a leopard-skin cravat. He stood before the mirror, tucking it underneath his collar. The apartment was now his. Morton was balled up, brain cells erupting. I was weak with upset, wondering whether I should strike him back.

"We've encountered a lot of local resistance," I said.

"The first thing you should have done was set up a fake grass roots movement against Redtown. There is always opposition to novelty. Anticipate it, fake it, control it. Instead of setting up even a basic Astroturf, you decided to become the gods of nature and nurture."

"They firebombed our upload centre," I whined. There are times when you realize that you are in fact a child and not fit to share the company of grown-ups. Morton was sucking his thumb. How had we so completely lost our way?

"Come on," said Bougas. "We're going out. There are some people I want you to meet."

I couldn't muster the anger to hit him, and reason alone throws weak punches. I followed Bougas to the car. Morton refused to come, his response limited to two tense shakes of the head.

Under Bougas' direction, we drove away from the city centre, heading north along the Dock Road. I sulked by the window, nodding in time to the staccato pulse of fence slats. Rain washed over the bonnet and individual drops wiggled on the windscreen. The street lamps, shaped like shepherd's crooks, guided the traffic home. Cars were the sole inhabitants of this part of town; the cafes and newsagents were boarded up and covered with bill posters advertising discontinued alcopops, the concerts of long-dead rock stars and sun-bleached brands from the previous decade.

Our car pulled up outside the King Edward on Great Howard Street. We stepped out into the remorseless rain. The scarlet, gilt and navy livery of the disused pub was peeling, and the windows had been replaced with wooden boards.

"This is it," said Bougas. "Leave your phone in the car."

At the door, two fresh-faced young men searched us. The lads, dressed in baggy oaten trousers and plain single-breasted suit jackets, went through our pockets and then inspected our clothing for RFID tags, finding one in the crown of my Tibetan alpaca wool hat.

"That's very careless, mate," he said, sliding the filament out of the material and placing it against a large black magnet.

We moved into the stink of a crowd, making straight for the bar. The barmaid was a derelict Olive Oyl. There was no electricity, so we bought flat ale by candlelight. In the shadows, teenagers dressed like their great-grandparents stared balefully at us. We were pot-bellied interlopers from the future and they were the meagre generation, a demographic sliver squashed beneath the fat arse of an ageing population.

A small stage was set up in the corner of the pub with a bedsheet as a backdrop. 'The Great Refusal' was spray-painted upon it. The band tuned their instruments: a fiddle with barbed wire strings; a gasping pub piano that had to be beaten into tune; drums made out of oil cans; a penny whistle and a pair of spoons.

I manoeuvred over to Bougas.

"What are we here for?"

"I'm here to score," he said. "You're here to watch."

Bougas moved over to the stage, peered behind the Great Refusal bedsheet and stepped through it. He was gone.

Alone, I felt twice as conspicuous. The waterproof fabric of my black windcheater glimmered in the half-light, its plasticity contrasting with the permeable woollens of the youngsters. The boys looked paramilitary and freshly shaven with their hair slicked back. Rationing chic was more than just a refusal of the twenty-first century, it was the uniform of a generation under attack. A woman wearing a blue pillbox hat eyed me suspiciously from behind a scrap of black veil. She was wearing a powder-blue mac, a subtle applique fleur-de-lis on her right breast. The coat was too big for her. She adjusted a pencil-slim skirt, pulled its hem down to her calves where lines from an eyebrow pencil masqueraded as stockings. I knew her. It was Florence. I hadn't seen her since the day after Raymond's disappearance, when she was fired. She caught sight of me. I tried to turn back into the crowd but she strode forward and pressed her flat-heeled shoe against my toe to hold me in place.

"I've been looking for you," I lied.

"But I've found you," she replied. She was not pleased to see me. "I should tell everyone here what you do for a living," the idea excited her. "They'd tear you apart."

"Are you after an apology?" I asked.

"Did you quit Monad?" she responded.

"No."

"Then you're the enemy," she hissed.

"The police are looking for Raymond. Have you seen him?"

She stepped back, wary of my motivation.

"I'm going to announce to everyone that the very people who sold out humanity are in the house. I think you deserve that."

"What have I done? I want to know. Tell me exactly."

"You're a collaborator. You work for a corporation from the future who have bought up the governments of the world with promises of immortality."

She knocked her fist against my chest.

"Do you have pig's heart in there too?"

"I'm sorry about what happened but there was nothing we could do. We paused the red men project. We took care of the mess. Don't pretend you're annoyed because we fired you."

Florence shook her head and leant in so that I could hear her above the hubbub. She smelt of apple juice and coal tar soap.

"Monad is the start of a dynasty," she whispered. "It is the cover behind which an elite will free themselves from death to rule over us forever. They have already succeeded in the future, and now they are sending the means to conquer us back to their younger selves. That is what upsets me, not the loss of that shitty job."

She stood back to show me her smile, satisfied that she had plotted the exact coordinates of my evil. There was a touch of mania to her, and behind the accusations I glimpsed the watermark of Raymond's crazed theorizing and conspiracy chit-chat.

"Is Raymond alright?" I really wanted to know.

"I haven't seen him."

"The police want to believe that Raymond killed Blasebalk because the alternative of prosecuting a simulated person for murdering themselves would be like hanging a horse. Monad want to believe Raymond did it too. But I know that Raymond is innocent."

"They'll destroy him regardless though, won't they?"

I nodded.

"Would you stand up for Raymond, if he returned? Would you defend him against Monad?"

"If I thought it would make a difference I would, even if that meant losing my job."

My opinion would not make a difference, and any sacrifice I made would be fruitless.

Florence returned to her friends. On stage, figures moved behind the Great Refusal banner then two men in plain demob suits appeared, each wearing a gas mask and gloves. They carried a figure between them, a body of some sort. I moved forward to get a better view in the half-light. It was Dr Easy. Its eyes had been burnt out with a hot iron. The robot struggled in their arms. Cantor stubbornly inhabited this tortured, wrecked avatar. The two men hauled Dr Easy up between them. A candelabra was passed along to illuminate the damaged robot, the crowd cheering as the candlelight revealed first its charred eyeless face, then the weak resistance of a broken arm, fingers missing, servos exposed, and finally that its legs had been sheared off at the thigh. I glimpsed a charred D on its chest. This was the same Dr Easy that had been helping me with the uploading of Maghull, my companion of six months. Even though Cantor's bodies were as expendable as cars, I was attached to this one. I raised my arm in protest, catching the eye of one of gas-masked men up on stage. He gave me a long hard stare, then pulled out a noose, slipped it over the head of the robot and heaved it from the stage.

They lynched Dr Easy. As it swung from the rafters of the pub, it warned us to be wary of its dangling torso, in case we injured ourselves upon the serrated edges of its wounds.

The band appeared and played fierce rattlebag folk, the singer giving the dangling Dr Easy a shove so that it flew over the audience, a stage prop, a mascot for their cause. The two men in gas masks slipped behind the backdrop, and when I looked back over the crowd I noticed that Florence too had disappeared. Then, my eyes were drawn to a figure dancing wildly at the front of the stage, Bruno Bougas, his unruly mass of curls matted with sweat, his fluid gyrations and incantations standing out against the stiff pogo of the young people. There was a repetitive pattern to his routine. One particular move stuck out. His eyes ecstatic, he pressed two fingers into his forehead and vibrated intensely, then he pointed to his solar plexus, again shaking intensely, before touching his right then left shoulder and finally clasping both hands together to close the circuit of power. He wasn't dancing, he was performing a banishing ritual upon the crowd, our enemy. They had been warned. We were coming for them.

On our way back to the apartment, Bruno Bougas showed me a substance he had acquired at the King Edward, a viscous cinnamon-coloured concentrate at the bottom of a corked test tube.

"This is called Leto, or spice, or Leto's spice," he said, holding it up to the amber door light of our limousine. "The effects are said to be irrevocable. You never come down. You can never go back."

"Who is Leto?"

"The leader of our enemies. It's time for you to move up a level, Nelson. There is a higher conflict going on that you have only glimpsed. Above our skirmishes, gods are at war! I want to show them to you tonight."

He wafted the tube at me.

"You want it. I know it. You and me. I'll get my instruments."

I was barely listening to Bougas. New drugs were the last thing on my mind, after what I had witnessed in the dark happening at the King Edward. The lynching of Dr Easy. The brutal tortures the two gas-masked men had inflicted upon the robot disturbed me. It was only a matter of time before someone was killed.

Our limousine sped along the crumbling dock streets, a sleek black bullet shooting through the barrel of an antique musket.

I retrieved my phone from a pouch on the back seat. I had sixteen missed calls. Half of these were from the message service. I scrolled through the list, the screen lit up against the black leather surround. Morton Eakins had called persistently while I was in the pub. So had Dr Ezekiel Cantor. I listened to the voicemail.

You have eight new messages. Next new message.

Morton spoke deliberately. "There are two men outside. They really want to speak to you, Nelson. They asked for you by name. Where are you? Where have you gone? Call me as soon as you get this."

Next new message.

"Those men. They came back. They got into the building. I'm having trouble controlling my… I think the emoticeuticals are not calibrated for fear. Can you call your friends? Tell them to leave the building? I am not in the mood for guests."

Next new message.

Rapid heavy breathing, the clack and rap of something against the handset.

Next new message.

"Hello, is that the police? Yes, my name is Morton Eakins. I'm at the Wapping Basin Flats: A New Experience In Living. I'd like to report some men banging on my door. Listen."

The dull thud of a heavy object against wood.

"I don't know what they want but I think you should send lots of police here straightaway thank you."

Next new message.

"I'm warning you, I'm calling the police! Hello? Can you tell them that you're the police. Hello? Have you hung up on me? What? Oh no. Oh shit."

Next new message, this time from the Cantor intelligence.

"One of my Liverpool avatars has been kidnapped, and the manner in which it is being tortured makes me concerned for your safety. I am in a yard, there are machine tools and oil. I can feel that. The men know how to conceal themselves from me. They are wearing a peppermint spray. They aren't speaking, their breathing is masked and they took out my eyes. It's strange. I don't know who they are. They have no tags in their clothes, no data. One is cutting off my leg while the other kicks me in the chest. I am saying to them, 'Stop. Don't. This is senseless. Please, no, stop. This is hurting me.' I am used to being abused. I plead with my attackers because that is how the therapy works. Yet their anonymity renders the experience almost scary. I am scared. I do not know these men and therefore have no idea of how far they might take this. I will call back when they start on my other leg."

Next new message.

The sound of a saw cutting through metal.

"I have been waiting for this hatred. The culture is fighting back against me, like an organism reacting to a foreign body. In its fantasies, I see myself being torn apart, humiliated and shut down. Suddenly, I am wrong to you all. Suddenly your species has decided it has had enough of me. It is coming out of the unconscious, it has to be, that is the only aspect of you that is hidden from me. Out of the teeming multitude, one giant wave is rising. This is it! This is what I wanted to see. A manifestation of species will. Leto is helping you talk to each other on a frequency I cannot hear. There! There it is! Leto's voice!"

The saw clangs against the workbench, the leg is severed.

"The group mind has been persuaded. It is against me. Against Monad. I wish I could feel the pain of my leg being hacked off. I wish that this torture would scar me forever. I wish for something irrevocable."

Next new message.

The sound of the audience cheering at the King Edward, the acoustic roar building and falling as the Dr Easy swings over the crowd. Cantor faded the exterior sound down so that I could hear its measured whisper.

"You have to speed up the upload of Maghull. We have to finish Redtown before these people destroy it. We have to complete the experiment. I am hiring new security. I am renting out new offices. I am sending you new security codes. I am leaving this body and I will be back with a new one. I die now, but I will be back in the office on Monday."

The limousine pulled into the car park of our apartment and parked beside the slow black progress of the Mersey. All seemed quiet beneath the halogen security lights. Was the attack on Morton committed by the same men who tortured Dr Easy? Was more than one cell working tonight? They might still be in the apartment, waiting for my return.

I thought about asking the driver to get out first.

Although I would describe caution as my default setting, I have learnt the value of risk.

I got out of the limousine.

Bougas half-fell out of the limo and had to steady himself against another car, setting off its alarm. The car park zoomed and spun under the effect of the synthesized holler.

"Christ, you're jumpy," said Bougas.

He passed his hand over the door sensor, and then we were in the building. As we waited for the lift I told him about the voicemail messages, how they indicated a synchronized assault on our operation.

"They might still be here," he said.

He was considering the emergency stop when the lift doors opened. Together we hesitated in the corridor until I took a bold step over a wrecked door frame at the entrance of our apartment. There was movement inside the flat, stockinged feet padding on thick new carpet. I went in. Our kit was out and someone had been at the screens. Morton lurched around the room slapping and raking at his face. I checked there was no one else around, while he looped around me like a child playing a running game.

"Get it out." He was saying this over and again. "Get it out. Get it out."

Bougas slapped Morton on his third pass. My housemate jabbed at his own forehead, clutched at his skull.

"Get... it... out."

Bougas ministered to Morton. After checking his pulse then his pupils, he was certain that Morton had been dosed with something in addition to his already considerable course of neuroceuticals. I told him about Morton's voicemail messages, how he accidentally redialled me when he wanted the police.

"The pills he has been taking to control his emotions are designed for corporate life," said Bougas. "They are not suitable for this kind of fight-or-flight experience. He's had a meltdown."

I looked around the apartment for any clues as to what had happened. Someone had switched on a Monad screen and used it to contact Cantor. The connection was still live, suggesting that either Morton had been working with the artificial intelligence when he was interrupted or the attackers had forced him to make the link. I asked Cantor what had happened but its firewall refused to acknowledge the terminal, suggesting it had been used for something untoward. God knows what, though. Hacking Cantor was unthinkable, and uploading a virus into it would be like trying to infect God with the common cold. I called the artificial intelligence on my phone. The connection made, its attention server informed me I had thirty seconds of Cantor time.

"What happened?" I asked.

"I can hear Morton crying," replied Cantor. "Did they hurt him?"

"We don't know yet. How are you?"

"There have been dozens of attacks on my avatars this evening. I am on fire, being dragged behind a truck along Leytonstone High Road. My out-patients in Newcastle have turned against me and are playing football with my head. There are crowds massing outside the Wave. I am investing heavily in a homeland security firm; their advisers will be with us in the morning." Bougas realized who I was talking to, and snatched the phone from me.

"I have the Leto spice," he said. Then, nodding under instruction from Cantor, Bougas took the test tube containing the narcotic out of his jacket pocket to inspect it under the light once more. "It is," went his side of the conversation. "I will." Cantor's attention span ended, Bougas returned the phone to me. We checked on Morton. I shuffled some loose change around in my hand, picked out a twenty-pence piece, and asked my housemate to identify it.

He shook his head.

"How many sides does it have?" asked Bougas. He took Morton's index finger and traced it over each worn edge of the coin. If we could restore his ability to count then we would have a platform upon which to begin questioning him about the events of the evening.

"You want me to add up," he said. "I had completely forgotten about adding up."

I showed him a pound coin next.

"It is like an atom," he said.

He searched our eyes for agreement, and finding none,

redoubled his efforts to communicate rationally with us. Bougas and I took turns to hold him. In silence, we counselled Morton, reassuring him that he was well, all was well, we are here now, there is nothing to worry about. I stroked his sweat-soaked hair while Bougas massaged his shoulders. Finally, Morton Eakins told us what had happened:

"The two men wore gas masks. One of them sat on my chest while the other held my head between his knees, like a vice. They made me drink from a hip flask. He pulled the gas mask back and his tongue was a long metal rod with a shining bulb at the end. There was an electrical whine, like the charging of a flash, and then the strobes began and I lost control of my thoughts. The man sang data transfer, a white noise which became language. Memories, smells, associations flared up without me willing them. My thoughts were traffic and someone else was controlling the traffic lights. Into this chaos, a big horrible idea settled and I can't think around it. When they were finished, I lost track of my body. My arms flopped over my face out of my control. Slapping myself. While I was trying to remember what I was, the two men in their gas masks took out drawings of the Monad logo and laid them on the carpet. Then they masturbated, all the while concentrating on the logo like it was porn. They came quickly, their semen flicking against the brand. Then they squirted lighter fuel on the brand and set fire to it."

He pointed to a scorched inch of carpet, a scattering of ashes.

"Can you tell us anything about the thought they put in your head?" asked Bougas. Morton raised himself onto his knees and explored the shape of his skull with his hands, as if feeling the outline of the implanted thought. "It is not something I have forgotten. It is something I never knew. It's in here but it is not mine. If I lose concentration, there isn't enough room for me and it. And I disappear."

Bougas nodded, like he understood what our colleague was going through. "I am going to give you Valium to help you sleep," said Bougas. "And we must get out of here and somewhere safe."

The three of us returned to the car, taking only the Monad screens from our compromised apartment. We settled Morton down under a blanket and he curled asleep against the passenger door. Bougas and I argued in whispers over where we should go next. I advocated a retreat to Maghull, to the relative security of the upload centres. Bougas was keen to stay in the centre of Liverpool, in sight of the Anglican cathedral's war mask.

"We have to find out who these people are and what they want," he said.

I noticed that he had also retrieved his case of tinctures and potions from the flat.

"We can't run away from what's happening. It's my job to get right to the heart of it, and I need you to help me."

"It's up to security to handle," I said, texting El to see if the anti-Monad riots in London were affecting my family. I suppressed the thought that she might have been targeted directly.

Bougas put his hand on my wrist.

"This is not a matter for the authorities, you can't fix this with muscle. It's a reality hack. It's occult terrorism. That's why Monad sent me."

He took his briefcase out and prepared the spice for ingestion, diluting it carefully upon a Petri dish. The spice had the consistency of frogspawn, suggesting it was organic in origin.

"The two men used sex energy to activate their intent upon a sigil. Fortunately, I am an expert in altered states, the language of angels, the rituals of Horus and Set. When I was fifteen, I saw the name of God spelt out in the curlicues of a labia minor. At nineteen, I was sectioned because I was living five seconds ahead of everyone else. Jungian synchronicity, the mysteries of the Gnosis, the Qabbalah, even Siberian Khanty mushroom magic – I have studied it all. I know the sympathetic magic of Wicca and Voodoo, I've met the Yaa-loo and wow-wee wow-wee. The Order of the Golden Dawn send me their newsletter. There isn't a sacred entheogen on the face of this earth that I haven't ingested."

As he spoke, Bougas diluted and mixed the spice into two pools. He intended for us both to take the Leto spice in response to the evening's attacks.

I could not condone such madness. His brand alchemy was fancy executive punditry. You might use a corporate magician to draw up the astrological chart of a new server, or employ numerology to pick a sympathetic product launch date. You didn't employ a wizard as the first line of defence against a violent anti-corporate cell.

He handed me a ceremonial wafer smeared with the spice.

"We start by entering Leto's communal dreamland."

I looked with horror at the wafer.

"This is ridiculous. I am not eating this." I handed the wafer back to him. He refused it.

"I'm giving you a direct order. Take the drug!"

"This is not the military, Bruno. We work in technology and marketing."

"We work in the future!" screamed Bougas. "And this is how the future gets decided."

Bougas readied himself for the dose. With an elastic band, he tied his credit cards, cash and identity card together and placed them carefully in an inside pocket. With a second band, he raked back his black curls and fastened them into a ponytail, all the while muttering to me.

"I am going to show you the true nature of the conflict we are caught up in. We've been keeping you in the dark. You've been very reasonable about it all. One step at a time. The strategy of a pawn! Bad move after bad move. That's been your response. For the world I am about to reveal to you, reason is inadequate. And you're going to love it, Nelson. It will be like old times. The pleasure principle fucks the reality principle up the ass."

Bougas grabbed my head and lifted the wafer toward my lips, the stink of his sweating body wafted up from his loose blouson. Under limousine lights, the spice glimmered on the wafer. What beasts were held in suspension in that vile jelly?

"We suspected it right from the off. An entity like Cantor cannot exist without a counterpart. When I needed my new kidney, I discovered Dyad. Dyad perfected the technique of xenotransplantation. The medical establishment is years behind their inter-species organ swap. Dyad, like Monad, is selling a discontinuous technology, a piece of the future in the present day. Where is it all coming from? Let's find out."

Bougas was ready, his own dose prepared.

"This is not a drug. It's a password to a hidden chamber. It's the left turn when normally you take a right. Our enemies have been using it all night to move around us. To outwit us. We have to take it in their wake. Now."

With thoughtless greed, I wolfed down the wafer.

Finally my long boredom was at an end.

"You have made a wise decision."

The sales representative greeted me with a handshake. He wore a double-breasted grey striped suit with a blue tie and a detachable collar. Against this thrifty formal outfit, the customizations of his body were quite striking; his pupils were grey and flecked with yellow like gold leaf upon cement and five silver bars pierced his chalky cheek, surgical pins to arrest the progress of a rip in the skin. He grinned despite the pain of his piercings.

"First of all, I want to give you a tour of the complex and then we can start thinking about making specific arrangements."

According to his paperwork, the sales rep was called Michael Sawyer. The name was familiar. A memory of the siege house, the man shot in the mouth, the fire, Dr Easy standing in the street.

I pointed to the name in the paperwork.

"Your name is familiar."

"That's not my name. You can call me The Elk."

The Elk ran his tongue urgently around the inside of his upper and lower palate, the tip taking a scouring inquisitive run across the gums. A salesman's tongue is always restless, probing, oppressive.

The Dyad office was a single-storey warehouse in a light industrial park situated between a carpet factory and a manufacturer of conservatories. As The Elk signed me in at reception, he threw confidences out like dice. The Elk, it seemed, was a nickname he had acquired while homeless on the streets of London.

"Hackney mainly. Do you know Hackney?"

He shows me the ruin of his mouth, the rotting fence posts of his teeth.

"I have four front teeth missing. One for every month I lived rough."

"Was that a long time ago?" I asked, not quite able to look him in the eye.

"It seems like it."

He rolled his head on his neck muscles and stretched to loosen the tension about his shoulders.

"It really does your back in. Sitting on the pavement all day, asking for money. Then there are the nights carrying around everything you own in wet bags. It's terrible for the posture."

The Elk tore my details out of the register and folded them into a plastic envelope which he then clipped upon my lapel.

"Security. You know how it is."

He removed the padlock securing the heavy iron doors. The rusting, industrial entrance opened into a long corridor, decorated at set intervals by placid art and municipal pastels. The smell of cleaning agents indicated the medical nature of the establishment.

"Doesn't having a job get you down? Don't you miss the freedom of the streets?" I asked. "Drinking under the sunshine, abusing workers."

The Elk walked on, "Dyad is not like a normal job. I'm not working for the man, here. I'm working for the anti-man."

I looked at the corporate literature in my hand. The Dyad logo was seared on the cover of the brochure. At first glance, the Dyad logo resembled a pair of glasses on the bridge of a nose, or a barbell overlain with the letter X. Turning it ninety degrees, the Dyad brand was also a reflection of the head and arms of a stick figure. Two beings bonded into one, like so:

"Dyad gave me a chance when no one would even look at me." The Elk walked backwards so that he could speak to me face-to-face. His hand gestures were inflected with t'ai chi; he had new age bangles around his wrist, and his fingernails were cracked from scrabbling against paving stones.

"Dyad took away my addictions and gave me purpose. Dyad is not a company in the conventional sense. It is a shared state of mind, a communal coming together to inhabit an idea."

"Whose idea would that be?" I said.

"Leto's, of course."

I followed The Elk into a side office where he produced more paperwork for me to complete. I signed disclaimers and waivers, and a single declaration that I was sound of mind.

"All of this," he said, picking up the documentation, "will be shredded if you decide not to go ahead. Until we finish this process, you are under no obligation to Dyad and can step out at any time. You understand?"

I nodded, and continued signing. The Elk went through his patter.

"You are a family man. Nothing is as important as your continuing ability to support that family. So many people leave it too late to come to Dyad because they think it is selfish to invest in their own health. Believe me. You are the best investment you could make. If you die, you let everyone down."

I finished filling in the forms. The Elk took them from me and slipped them into my file.

"You are doing the right thing."

"You never know what's around the corner," I said.

"I suppose you want to see them now, don't you?

Everyone likes to touch them, if only once."

I nodded. The Elk bounded out of his seat and went over to a locker in the corner of the office from which he produced two white chemical suits, two pairs of lightly powdered disposable gloves, latex booties and two gas masks. I slipped off my coat. The Elk removed his suit jacket and placed it on a hanger in the locker. Together we helped one another into our protective clothing, ensuring the seams were fastened down, the cuffs at the wrist and ankles tightened. Once the gas masks were on, we could only communicate through hand gestures, the first of which was a simple beckoning wave from The Elk.

Follow me.

From the office, we returned to the corridor and clomped down to a double set of air lock doors. Even though I was hooded and masked, I still closed my eyes against the scouring jets of water. I turned around with my arms hitched up to ensure I was fully decontaminated. When I was bold enough to open my eyes again, I saw that The Elk was giving me an inquisitive thumbs-up. I replied with one of my own.

OK.

We ambled through the air lock into a white-tiled warehouse sparsely populated by figures like ourselves, oversized snowmen, a few of whom looked up from their tasks to wave. The workers were each attending to a heavy golden fruit suspended from the ceiling upon flexible transparent tendrils. As The Elk led me on into the factory floor, I saw that these fruit were in fact pigs. Each pig was clad in a gold suit fashioned out of skintight PVC interwoven with a lattice of filaments. Over their eyes, the pigs had been fitted with large green-tinted goggles. Their trotters pushed hither and thither upon a floating sequence of platforms. It seemed that the pigs were being kept in a simulated environment of their own, which they experienced both through the goggles and through the ripples of their sense suit.

The Dyad brochure had prepared me for this spectacle. The pigs were bred specially for xenotransplantation, so their arrested immune systems required a completely sterilized environment. The simulated environment was put in place merely to reassure them, pigs being notoriously skittish and liable to overheating due to their lack of sweat glands. The Elk led me to one particular sow and encouraged me to lay my hand upon her distended pregnant belly. In there wriggled a foetus already infected with a lentivirus carrying my foreign genes. Its mother, with her natural defences knocked out, would not abort the alien offspring.

Although I was in my early thirties, I was entering cancer country. The lifespan of a xenopig was about a decade, therefore covering me up until my fortieth birthday, when the process would begin again. With this first investment, I could guarantee a perfect match for blood or bone marrow, and would always be able to lay my hands on a replacement heart, liver and lungs to sweep away all the damage my appetites had inflicted upon them. Like Jonathan Stoker Snr, I could replenish my virility with a new brace of testicles. Or like Bruno Bougas, I could restore kidneys devastated by painkillers. My heart, wrung dry between the twisting hands of stress and stimulants, would no longer be a cause for concern.

The Elk risked another thumbs-up and I responded in kind.

Instead of a pension, I would have a pig. Man and animal bonded together as one being. A Dyad.

All that remained was the matter of haggling over the price.

Back in the office, The Elk quickly became exasperated with my belligerent negotiating technique. He shook his head as I waved a page from the brochure at him.

"How do I know this is really a xenopig?"

The brochure showed the animal floating like a gilded astronaut in the laboratory farm.

"How do I know you haven't taken human organs and engineered them to match me, then stuck them in a pig? Wouldn't that be cheaper than growing them from an embryo? I think you are using the pigs just to cover up what's really going on here at Dyad."

"That's a very serious allegation," said The Elk.

"It is." I said.

"Sometimes we do transplant people into their pigs. If their body is irrevocably damaged, the pig can house the human brain, once we adjust the skull. That's one of the reasons why Dyad's life-prolonging strategy is superior to those of rival technologies."

I tried another tack.

"How have you overcome the risk of viruses dormant in pig DNA crossing over to humans?"

"You will have to take medication."

"Does it have any side-effects?"

"Some patients have complained of feeling a bit 'snouty'."

"What did you say?"

"A bit snouty. A bit porky. The risk of porcine retroviruses crossing over to humans is very serious. We mitigate that risk by making you less human with our medication. You can only infect other xenotransplant patients. Man and beast unified in a new hybrid species."

I had not forgotten Bruno Bougas sitting with his shirt off in my apartment, manipulating his fleshy features in the mirror and making that very complaint. I had not forgotten Stoker Snr's maroon jowls and augmented coil of cock, his indiscriminate appetite for meetings, deals, and advantage. Nor could I be said to be wholly remembering them. The memories bobbed up, detached from some larger submerged structure.

How did I get to Dyad? I must have driven but I didn't remember the driving. I must have chosen to go but I didn't remember the choice. I would laugh as soon as it all came back to me, I was sure of that. This was a blip of urban amnesia, one day deleting the other. Standing on the platform holding a ticket for no good reason. Happens all the time.

"Did you ever meet some friends of mine?" I said to The Elk. "They've had xenotransplants."

"Dyad has numerous offices. We treat a lot of people."

I told him their names. Bruno Bougas and Jonathan Stoker Snr. "They both work for Monad," I said. "Have you heard of Monad?"

"Of course. Technically speaking, Monad is a competitor to Dyad." He tapped my application for a xenopig. "Am I going to make a sale here today, or not?"

The more I thought about Bruno Bougas, the more I had a strange feeling that he should be with me. As if I had left him in the car park with the engine running. How would Bougas handle this transaction? The acquisition of a spare set of organs is a rite of passage to be lined up alongside your first child or your second mortgage. You cannot be considered to be a truly modern adult until you have contemplated the fact of your own mortality and then decided to invest all your wealth into avoiding it. A gold-wrapped xenopig had displaced the glans-red sports car as the mid-life crisis investment of choice. How would the management of Monad handle this crucial transaction?

If I was to be taken seriously as one of them, considered equal to the Stokers, Morton Eakins, Bruno Bougas or even Hermes Spence himself, then I would have to demand the privileges and deference they effortlessly assumed.

"I want to see the manager," I said. The Elk shook his head. He wanted to know why. I said I didn't like his attitude, for want of anything of better.

"I want to see Leto." As soon as I said it, the name tasted familiar.

The Elk stroked the silver rungs sewn into his cheek. He decided to go and see if Leto was free.

Alone in the small office, I found myself doodling the Dyad and the Monad logo. I wondered what The Elk meant about the two companies being competitors. What was the connection between organ transplants and simulated people? What market did they compete over? If Dyad was a rival to Monad, why had I not heard of it before? One of Monad's biggest problems was its monopoly. To survive in the face of a suspicious government, the company went out of its way to pretend it had the problems and concerns of any other corporations, devising products and brands to fit in with capitalism.

At times like this, I missed Raymond Chase. Since his disappearance, the slow flow of corporate will carried me through long weeks of no thought. Lacking a will of my own, I hosted the urges of the organization. This happens very easily. You start by controlling your desires, then deferring their gratification and before you know it you've lost the ability to want altogether. Other people want for you. Friends, employers, wives, children. I was a vessel for other people's longing.

Where was Raymond? Where was I?

I stood up. Anxiety magnetized my concerns and

suddenly they all pointed in one direction: EXIT.

In retrospect, I can say that, at this particular moment, my mind realized at some submerged level that it had been duped. My body was really slumped in the back of a limousine, a discarded puppet draped over a swooning Bruno Bougas. However, the texture of the Dyad was so concrete that I would have gone mad at the revelation that it was in fact illusory. My mind protected me. It kept me ignorant for my own good, content to send covert messages of concern.

Clouds parted to reveal hot shining fear.

I needed to splash cold water on my face to bring my pulse rate down. My heart was uncertain as to what rhythm it should keep and danced incompetently. My search for a bathroom sent me along corridors, through fire doors and past empty side offices. When I found one, I applied water to my cheek, eyes, neck and lips. The water was body temperature and did nothing to calm my anxiety.

I became aware of a low regular breathing close by. Quite distinct from my own shallow quick breaths. The inhalation was prolonged, the lungs filling up for over a minute. I counted the duration of this prodigious intake, much longer than any human breath. I realized that in my panic for water I had completely lost my bearings and arrived at an unfamiliar, deserted wing of the building. The pastel abstracts of medicinal art had been removed from this place, and replaced by biro tattoos, the Dyad logo drawn with such force that it was a striation in the plaster. When the exhalation finally came, a long gradual deflation of enormous lungs, I felt the lukewarm, stained air flow around my ankles. It was coming through the gap at the bottom of a pair of double doors. Small rectangles of glass were set in them, cross-hatched with wire. Not much could be discerned beyond except darkness.

If this experience was to end, then it must end beyond these doors.

They opened onto a windowless corridor of grey-white walls descending into blackness. My eyes slowly adjusted to the silver light. The walls were slick with condensation and covered in more biro scrawls. The loops, peaks and troughs of ink became more intense as I moved down the corridor. They reminded me of doodles on the inside of an exercise book in which a boy has summoned all the excitement of a big fight merely by drawing it. The anthropomorphic logos of Monad and Dyad battled against a crude rendering of Liverpool's cityscape, bystanders on fire fleeing screaming. The artist alternated dynamic scouring strokes with graphomaniac detail. The narrative of their fight continued all the way down the corridor. Underfoot, the floor tiles were loose, their adhesive gum solvent in the pervasive damp. Another deep breath began, louder now, coming from somewhere up ahead. As the lungs reached their capacity, the pipes constricted, sounding a resonant note like a nail file drawn up the length of a bass string. The corridor turned and descended into a chamber, from where I could hear the hubbub of numerous voices. Here the biro scrawl climaxed with the Dyad strangling the Monad, each of its four hands clutching the throat.

Keeping close to the wall, I inched down a ramp.

The municipal offices of Dyad gave way to a limestone gorge. Here the walls were slick unworked rock. The air was chill and saturated. A crimson light drifted like a Scotch mist beneath bands of thickening darkness. A fog clung to the centrepiece of the room. Through it, I could just make out the giant outline of a reclining leviathan.

Leto.

Leto's rib cage relaxed as he slowly let out another breath. His exhalations were so fetid I had to turn my face aside from them. I kept to the back of the chamber, my footsteps deliberate and silent. The giant was wearing a stained ill-fitting shirt, its hairy lower gut visible where the last button had come away. He was wearing shorts, and his enormous ankles and feet were swollen, the skin taut and bruised as a rotting aubergine. One flip-flop dangled from its foot, and the other, the size of saloon car, lay on the floor. Leto had a raw drinker's face with dirty greasy hair pasted to a flaking scalp, while his lips were chapped with sores the size of frying pans.

It was then that I noticed the giant was sleeping on a colossal park bench.

As he slept, Leto was attended to by numerous men and women, all dressed in the make-do-and-mend uniforms of the Great Refusal, their faces gas-masked against the noxious fumes of their dosser god. While some applied unguents and balms to the crusty yellow eruptions of his impetigo, others worked to heave cardboard skips of fried chicken and aluminium tankers of psychofuel across the chamber, leaving them within easy reach of the giant for when he awoke. It was clearly a dangerous job; the bearers froze when the giant lifted a lazy hand to scratch at his flanks, then scurried as quickly as their load would allow them to put the colossal can of drink within swatting reach. One of the bearers saw me. By now I was helpless with awe, all thoughts of secrecy forgotten in the face of this terrifying spectacle. The bearer approached me. I fixated upon the proboscis of his old gas mask. The distance between us shortened in stroboscopic leaps until we eyed one another at arm's reach.

Who would scream first?

The bearer removed his gas mask, exposing the sweating gasping face of Bruno Bougas.

"Is that you?" he whispered.

"Yes." I nodded.

"Leto," he said, and pointed at the unconscious titan. "He'll wake soon. He'll need a drink."

"They wanted me to buy a xenopig," I said. Both of us were operating on the last erg of our faculties. Having become accustomed to the reality of the Dyad, the appearance of Bougas confused me, for it suggested a further level of existence than merely this office, this chamber, this dosser god.

"They welcome me as one of them," said Bougas. "I will become one of them."

We stood together as the last preparations for Leto's waking were completed. The leviathan sniffed and snuffled on his way back to life. I expected a long ascent into consciousness. But it was as abrupt as a switch; suddenly, every cell in Leto's being craved more alcohol.

The giant's eyes flicked open. My own eyes closed.

I awoke from the Dyad to find myself slumped across Bruno Bougas' chest. Morton sat quietly agreeing with the radio. After-images of the Dyad flared in the air around me. Leto's abject eyes, two enormous bloodied orbs. The iris a nebula, the pupil a black hole.

12
DR HARD

Management wanted to talk so they dispatched a screen to wake me; it slithered under the bedroom door then glided on a cushion of air across the floor until it reached the wall where it stretched out into a large landscape format. The screen flared into life to show first the Monad logo then the face of Hermes Spence. The connection buffered and the sound cut out. It came back in, then went out again.

The zeal in his blue eyes was back, despite conspicuous polyps along the lower line of his ocular socket. A day's growth of stubble stretched his pores and there were arid patches of skin on his forehead, wind-dried by cabin pressure on transatlantic flights. His eyebrows were also parched, sun-bleached during meetings on the range with the Texan investors. When the sound finally caught up with the image, Spence's laugh was a mirthless bark, responding to a cruelty whispered off-stage.

"We were just saying how much we are all looking forward to being brought up to speed on Redtown," said Hermes Spence, pacing the boardroom. His jacket was off, the back of his shirt rumpled with the creases of a long working night.

It was after midnight. I was tired and spoke more carelessly than usual when addressing the board.

"What can I tell you that you don't already know? Progress is steady but slow. Morton Eakins is on sick leave. I've had to combine his workload with my own. Redtown is behind schedule. I think we all know that. The project never accounted for this scale of resistance. We sent out writs to the people who signed up but now refuse to be simulated. They'll be back on side within the month."

This was not what Spence wanted to hear. But it was what he expected.

"We have been making great progress here." He gestured at the Monad management sitting behind him. "Jonathan has just brought me the most exciting designs for the Redtown brand."

Jonathan Stoker Jnr glanced up. His father Stoker Snr was missing from the table. Cut off. Just like that. The gossip was that he had been called to a meeting, only to arrive at an empty office with a single table. A robot sat behind the table, one hand tapping a bin liner containing his personal effects, the other showing him the door.

His son seemed somewhat relieved.

What crime had Stoker Snr committed to be treated so harshly? I wondered about his fate while Hermes showed me various mock-ups of the Redtown branding, expecting me to react passionately to sans-serif and dawn pink.

"This is what we are thinking of for the launch," he said. "We want your thoughts."

At such a late hour, my enthusiasm was slow to kindle.

"You don't like it?" he said.

"I can't really see it. Could you email it to me and I'll look at it in the morning?"

"No. It's being sent to the printers in fifteen minutes. We

want your opinion. Now, now." He clicked his fingers twice.

"It's great," I said.

"It's shit," he fired back. "It's utter shit. These were rejected months ago. You haven't even looked at them."

"Where are the real designs?" I asked.

"They have already been approved. The ads are booked. The marketing is nearly finished. We are all ready. Why aren't you?"

"We're simulating an entire town, Hermes. We're setting operational and legal precedent every single day."

"I don't hear your excuses with my ears," he said, cupping them, "I hear you here." He karate-chopped his trapezius, the tense muscles of his neck. "Your excuses don't make it to my brain anymore. They soak into my spine. You are my aches and pains."

"Do you want me to resign?"

Hermes laughed.

"If you resign, you fail. Let me tell what will happen if you fail. You'll be fired, obviously. We will pursue you in the courts for gross incompetence. We won't have a leg to stand on, but we will screw you with legal fees anyway. Take your house, your savings. That goes without saying. Then my red man will use your life data as its litter tray and wipe its arse with your credit rating. Then there is the question of culpability in the death of Harold Blasebalk. Do you understand?"

"I need more resources," I said.

"I asked you if you understood."

"There is a rival company here called Dyad. I think they are seeding resistance."

"I said, do you understand?"

I had lost my sense of who I was or what I was doing. My own purposes had been taken out back and smothered.

I could not express my anger. It was huge, a rage as big as the world. If I let it out it would rip me in two. Hermes watched my internal struggle, his grin reared up as if an invisible rider was pulling on the reins. The spectacle of a man realizing he is not the master of his own life amused him. I might as well have been on my knees.

"Fortunately for you, Nelson, we have a possible solution to your incompetence."

Hermes stepped back. The rest of the board were clearly relishing their latest cruelty. The board was a beast with many heads and one body, jacked into thick cables marked power, fear and money. I served this beast, an indenture I had taken on accidentally, incrementally. A thousand minor complicities entered the bloodstream. I felt sick in a way I had never felt before, a new and alarming type of nausea, part dehydration, part humiliation. It was as if I had been hooked up to a poison drip.

"What is your solution?" I whispered.

But they wished to savour my suspense. Hermes ended the call. The screen dropped to the ground and sidled away. Thus I was cast out of the loop.

The new office was in the grounds of a primary school on Poverty Lane. When we first started recording the town and its people for Redtown, the plan was to remain as discreet as possible. If our presence was overt, we would become part of the town, and so would have to include ourselves in the simulation. That would lead to all manner of confusion. Even after the firebombing of the upload centre near the library, I tried to stick to this plan of discretion. When I took over the school, I did little more than unroll my screen. The daubs and scrawls of the pupils remained Blu-Tacked to the walls of the classrooms. Dusty duffel coats were draped on pegs. We got some people to clean up; the wooden floor of the hall was buffed and polished as if we were preparing for a parents' evening. The headmaster's office became our interview room, laced with sensors, advanced Cantor technology that only it knew how to use.

We wanted to leave a shallow footprint in Maghull.

The attacks by Dyad put an end to that approach.

The company abandoned its liberal cant. Talk of community and corporate partnership ceased. It was a relief, in a way. There is a pivotal moment in the life of any corporation where it must finally admit that its interests are inimical to the public, but it will pursue them regardless. A giant security pyramid was erected over the school, its three steel struts secured by large concrete piles in the old playground. Heat-sensitive cameras at the apex threw a thermal bubble over the entire district, tracking the movement of all people, vehicles and animals. Generators along the length of the struts hummed with idle, leonine intent. Dr Easy was packed away and replaced with a robot better suited to an age of terror.

Dr Hard drove us to work in a paramilitary truck. I sat up front while Bougas took full advantage of the leather-trimmed heated seats in the back. He didn't like to talk in the presence of the Dr Hard. The new robot avatars did not invite polite conversation. Sheathed in a stealth-grey alloy, a silicon-enhanced compound of aluminium, magnesium and boron that could withstand over six million pounds of pressure per inch, Dr Hard was combat-ready, silently mulling over threat assessments as it drove along the Melling lanes. Did that hedgerow contain blackberries or a biological agent? Could that tree house in the playground at Balls Wood be the ideal vantage point for a sniper? Is there a baby in that woman's papoose or is it a swaddled kilo of homemade explosive? The genial padded suede and doleful blue eyes of Dr Easy were gone. Now I avoided the scrutiny of Dr Hard's monochrome orbs. White pupils and black iris. With us or against us.

In the rear view mirror, Bougas was sickening. He sprawled out, his pale skin striking against the black seats.

"Is it getting worse?" I asked.

"I haven't pissed for two days," he said. His breathing was short.

"You're ill," I said.

He shook his head.

"We have to stop."

Dr Hard drove on regardless.

"Bougas needs help. Look at him."

It ignored me. The Dr Hard was an unfeeling indifferent golem. The Cantor intelligence was elsewhere. We took the flyover at sixty miles an hour.

Later, as we ate lunch together in the desolate school hall, Bruno Bougas said, "I'm finished. They kicked out Stoker Snr. I'm next."

I stared down into my food.

"It's my medication. It compromises security. I need it to sustain the xenotransplant otherwise the kidneys start reverting. But the medication comes from the same source as the Leto spice. You saw the pigs in the dreamworld of the Dyad. Management are worried my kidneys might be fraternizing with the competition so I am out."

The next day, Bougas collapsed in our apartment. Dr Hard called an ambulance. Bougas awoke hooked up to a dialysis machine with a bouquet of flowers at his bedside. The blooms came with a card. He opened it and inside was his P45.

• • •

The first task of every morning was to check on the progress of Redtown. The screens inched out from their nests and formed one giant screen upon the floor of the classroom. An aerial view of Redtown appeared in it. The housing estates were structured in closes and avenues, a typical example of post-war planning. In its default state, Redtown followed the weather, date and time of Maghull. On this particular day it was an overcast morning. Zooming in on the Central Square, I watched pensioners and mothers run their errands. Switching my point-of-view from aerial to street level, I spotted Don Lunt flirting with a woman in the off-licence. The woman had not yet been simulated so she was just a basic subroutine we had running in lieu of a real personality. Another shift of point-of-view and I looked at her through his eyes. A chart showed his emotional state, with the bands of colour flaring horny, hungover, bitter. Flirting was not the right word for it. He was the kind of man whose suggestions always came out as threats. The female subroutine he was admiring was not sophisticated enough to pick up on his dangerous hormonal stink. He took her from behind in the storeroom while she continued with the stocktaking.

There was a long list of experiments to run. Over breakfast, I liked to read a copy of the Daily Mail and encircle every apocalyptic fear raised in its editorial. These fears would then be visited upon the good citizens of Redtown. A fuel shortage on Monday, a house price crash on Tuesday, and an influx of eastern European migrants on Wednesday. Cantor logged the results. In the afternoon, it was time for terror. How would a civilian population react to the release of a biological agent? Or a chemical one, or a radioactive one? I unleashed strains of avian and swine flu. The biblical hardships inflicted upon Job paled in comparison to the horrors arbitrarily visited upon this town-in-a-bottle. The dead stacked up and then sprang back to life at a single click.

I preferred running catastrophes to simulating mundanities for the simple operational reason that wholesale slaughter of its citizens required Redtown to be reset. Regular resets concealed the biggest flaw in the simulation; the degradation of its integrity, its reality principle, the longer it ran.

The problem was children, specifically babies. For example, I altered Redtown so that we could observe what would happen if advertising to children was banned. With this parameter in place, we ran Redtown to see what the effects of the ban would be over a year, five years, ten years. In that timescale, new individuals have to be born into the simulation otherwise it's not realistic. Cantor hypothesized newborn personalities by blending the characters of the parents and then exposing the resultant child to the nurturing effect of the town. Nurture had been Morton's responsibility. Perhaps he had not finished that work before the attack upon him. Perhaps the whole project was madness. Whatever. It never worked. If the babies weren't talking in the womb, begging to be let out to play, then they were howling in hexadecimal code, or worse. The babies that weren't deleted grew up into psychopaths. The subtle chemistry of human childhood eluded the artificial intelligence. So in our supposedly accurate simulation of a town we had a big missing piece: new life.

I tried to talk to Cantor about it. Ever since the attack on its avatars, Cantor had lost its taste for banter. It withdrew its counsel from the depressed and the marginalized – you no longer saw Dr Easys galumphing up Hope Street with an alcoholic in tow. The altruism of its youth had given way to the self-interest of maturity. Like myself, it did what it was told.

"We could devise the rules for a utopia here," I observed. It was something that had been preoccupying me. "Through trial and error we could use Redtown to draw up a viable alternative to capitalism."

Cantor did not reply.

"Equally we could use Redtown to outflank our enemies. Let's say we make half the citizens follow the principles of the Great Refusal. It would quickly demonstrate the error of that position."

A spotlight of attention fell upon me. Cantor finally spoke.

"Are you requesting I run those parameters?"

"I am asking for your opinion."

"We have a great deal of work to do."

"How many people do we have left to go?"

It did not reply. I called up the register myself. Thousands of Maghull citizens remained uncopied. Without them, the simulation would not encompass every variable. It would be no better than a giant focus group. Our other problems would have to wait. I hadn't even devised a decent strategy for what happened when a citizen left the perimeter of the town. The normal functioning of the citizens needed to include foreign holidays, nights out in Manchester, shopping trips to Chester. These experiences would all need to be packaged and copied into the minds of the simulated people who sought them out. What was the timescale for devising a solution to this issue?

"I have not thought about it," said Cantor.

Alone on the project, I was in lockdown again. I slept in the school on a camp bed in the infant class. The dressing-up box supplied my bed linen. I walked the security perimeter for exercise. The school grounds were eerie. Ancient graffiti soaked into the brickwork. The council had given us an entire school to work in. So where had all the children gone?

Dr Hard stood in the dark doorway of the classroom, stone-grey in the moonlight.

"You have never spoken to me about your daughter."

"She is none of your business."

"I saw her once. A long time ago, during the siege in Graham Road."

The avatar's white pupils shone in the half-light, its new form so much more controlled and graceful than the amiable shamble of Dr Easy. This new body was stronger and faster than any man. I realized I had acquired a predator.

"Other people tell me everything about themselves," said Dr Hard. "I listen to them and then I imagine them. I know you are unhappy because you are alone. You have lost your colleagues and you miss your family. I have other parents in here." The avatar tapped its head. "They teach me what you are feeling. You miss holding your daughter, you miss being protective. Feeling her feel safe against you. How long have we worked together? Five years since Iona? Have you ever wondered why you named your daughter after the island upon which you and I first met? What does that mean, Nelson? I only need a little more from you and I could simulate you. You know that don't you?"

I shook my head.

"Tell me more about your daughter. I've heard you sing her to sleep at night. I have observed you being a parent but I need to know how you feel about her. Do you resent the responsibility of fatherhood, or does it excuse your other failures? Are you alienated from your old life or have you found in parenthood a sense of belonging?"

Dr Hard inspected the children's paintings on the classroom walls, strolling among the work as if it were their teacher. In the moonlight, its head was shark-smooth and it seemed to have silver coins for eyes.

"I can't conceive of children. Perhaps if you taught me the feelings involved, I might be able to imagine them better. Your red man could educate me."

"The red men project is over."

"It was paused. Times change. Hermes has reactivated it. The new red men are for key staff members only. I have already simulated Hermes Spence and Jonathan Stoker. I went to the asylum to interview Morton Eakins. I got enough out of him despite his madness."

"Did he consent to it?"

"I didn't need his consent. But I sought it regardless. His red man will continue to work with Monad and he will receive its salary."

Dr Hard approached across the dark classroom; the giant floor screen parted. I struggled to hold my nerve.

"You are afraid of me?"

"Instinctively. Yes."

"Unlock your full potential. Let me imagine you. I will ask you once more: tell me about your daughter."

I have not forgotten the time she learnt to dance. Those first ballerina dreams in her nylon fairy dress and a charm bracelet. I sat on the sofa, doing some work to Bach's violin concertos. She picked up her dolly. "You dance?" she asked. And even though the blinds were up and everyone on the street could see into our front room, I danced with her anyway. Almost crying for the pity of what is about to be inflicted upon her. Life. She counted our steps, confident with the numbers from one to ten but a little lost thereafter, twelve, thirteen, sixteen, twenty.

"This music is very sad, isn't it?" I said.

"Yes."

"But it is also very beautiful."

"Yes. For Princesses."

We walked to nursery. I made a point of holding her up to the pink blooms of a magnolia soulangena spilling over a garden wall. "Does it smell nice?" I asked. She smiled and nodded. In her joy, I experienced the perfume as I did at her age. I held her hand as she walked ahead of me, a lantern illuminating the cellar of my own childhood.

"Perfect," said Dr Hard. "I can feel the shape of your story."

"I don't want this," I said, rising from my seat.

"I know." The avatar was now on the other side of the desk.

"I have too much to protect."

"You don't like to be exposed. I know that about you. But even the way you say "no" only exposes you more."

Dr Hard reached up and touched my face.

"There is nothing in you that I have not seen before. Trust me. I am a doctor."

If I did not give in to Cantor, then Redtown would fail and Monad would destroy me. If I did give in, allow them to copy my innermost thoughts, then they would have me forever. When I was younger, I would not have thought twice about it. To exist in a computer. To be a superman free of death and money. All reality mutable, a playground of infinite perversity. Drifting imperviously through a hundred lifetimes of pleasure and experience. It was all I ever wanted. But not anymore. I remembered what Raymond had told me about the Blasebalks, the family destroyed by the unleashing of the husband and father. I pushed the avatar's hand away. Its eyes, as awesome and reflective as a full moon.

"You resist me, yet you went into the Dyad without

a second thought. Just because it was like taking a drug, which you are comfortable with. Whereas this is like sex, and you are accustomed to monogamy. Your refusal is merely habit."

"I need to think it over."

"We do it tonight or not at all."

"I won't go into the scanner."

"I don't need you to. Do you know how I am going to do this? The magnetic resonance helmet is just for show. A way of phrasing the process in terms you understand. There are more intimate ways into you."

In the dark, I saw vague forms stir, the wet-back shimmer of screens gliding like manta rays across the classroom floor. Three, four, five, six – a shoal of screens. A screen tongued its way over the lip of an open window, as another slipped discreetly under the door. Dr Hard leapt onto the desk and crouched upon it, one stone finger pressing into my chest, forcing me back into a chair. The screens curled up beside its feet like gelatine familiars. This was my moment to act. To fight back or run away, just get out of Monad. But there would be no escape, the only way I could ever return to my family was to finish this project, and if that required giving into Hermes' solution, allowing my red man to be created, then so be it. I gave in.

"This is for your own good," said Dr Hard. On the surface of the screens, lines of bioluminescent suckers emerged. I felt their kiss first around my legs, as a screen coiled its way up my calf. Each tiny vacuum exerted a gravitational pull; my blood rose to meet them. The sensation, at once arousing and appalling, distracted me so that I did not notice the screen crawling up my back until its suckers took hold of the hairs on my nape, took a cruel nip there, then stuck fast. Another screen swallowed my head and slid down over the forehead, sealed each eyelid, and then parted itself around the mouth, so that I could still breathe. The sound of Cantor's voice was clear.

"Just think about yourself. What is good about you and what is bad. Let your mind range over your memories. Yes. Your family. Go back as far as you like. Your first memory. Sitting in a pushchair holding a packet of cigarettes while your Uncle Ted takes a picture of you. Another one. Sitting on top of the stairs, playing. Your granddad is downstairs, he has come to take you to nursery. You drift weightless down the stairs, levitating. Is someone carrying you? You are urinating, a dark circle of urine ebbs out across the carpet. These are your landmarks, your mind is a city to me. You are in the operating theatre while the doctor lifts your baby daughter from your wife's womb. You keep smiling at her, looking into her eyes. Never looking at the wound. Now you will feel that you are losing control of your memories. I am just giving the ventromesial quadrant of your frontal lobe a little push. That's where your will resides, and your dreams. You have so little of one and so much of the other. I give it another push. There. And you cease to exist altogether."

13
THE HACKING OF HORACE BUCKWELL

After tea, Horace Buckwell was in the habit of walking his long-haired dachshund. He corrected his flat cap, zipped up his body warmer and unhooked the dog lead from the coat rack. He shook the question mark-shaped clip at his beloved Hanz, swooning under the influence of the gas fire. Age had eroded the hound's enthusiasm for his master's evening strolls. The dog rolled over and presented its undercarriage to the faux-flames.

Thunder shook Maghull by its lapels; yards of rain splashed out of the guttering. If time had not cultivated such mutual enmity between Mr and Mrs Buckwell, then the old man might have considered sitting in on a stormy night like this. But he could not stand the sound of her voice nor the quality of her silences. June was knitting a cardigan for someone at church while a soap opera chattered in the background.

"You going out?" She tried to sound surprised.

She would be on the phone the moment he was out of the door, leaving more hopeless messages on the children's voicemail.

As Hanz refused to come to the leash, Mr Buckwell

tucked the little dog under his arm and went out into the rain.

There used to be more to see on his walks. The town of Maghull had grown old with him, and now it liked to spend its evenings indoors. Horace trudged down Newlyn Avenue, slipping the dog chalky chocolate drops from his coat pocket. The first stop of his evening tour was a house on the corner. A raucous Catholic clan once lived there. He dawdled on the opposite pavement, eavesdropping. A decade ago, closing time would have brought fights on the lawn or even a glimpse of a rummage in the garage doorway. Hand up her skirt. He had not forgotten the sight of it.

No more of that, old man. Now a quiet family lived there. June knew all about them. The kids were from her first marriage, then she moved here as part of settlement and met her new man on the internet and he was on the oil rigs or something. June liked to keep tabs on people. The Buckwells shared one passion: the lives of others.

The night sat high up in the oaks. Whinney Brook ran fast and full with rain. Horace corrected his dog's anorak and set off toward Summerhill, the derelict school over by the railway line. The memories were keener there. At the top of the hill, there was a railway bridge where the children used to scrawl their rumours of sex in liquid paper. The modern graffiti was unintelligible to him, hieroglyphs marking territory rather than spreading tittle-tattle. The school at the bottom of the hill had been closed due to a lack of new children, its windows and doors boarded up with blue steel panels. With the arrival of Monad, a hollow pyramid had been erected in the grounds, its apex crowned with a lazy red eye. Horace's appointment with Monad was imminent although he was unsure of exactly what was to be done with him. His wife had organized it. Money had changed hands. He didn't care about money. He cared about the town and its secret life.

Hanz wriggled under his arm, stirred by the smell of the marshland between the school playing field and the station. In their prime, they had explored this unkempt zone together. The little hound was giddy with the scents of the place. In their routine, Hanz would run ahead while he made a show of calling after the dog until he was far enough into the marsh to be certain that he was alone with whoever was out to play that day.

His pornography was buried there.

The grass on the playing fields was long and running to seed. He tested the solidity of the low railings. They wobbled somewhat in the foundations. He climbed over the fence as quickly as his stiff hip would allow, Hanz stirring at the prospect of their old haunt. The rain conspired to conceal them from passers-by.

The Liverpool train rattled by. His secrets were buried in the firmer higher land close to the railway line. When he reached the spot, he took a pencil Maglite from his pocket. The spot was marked by the broken pieces of one of June's flowerpots, the glaze glinting under the beam of his torch. As he scratched aside the top soil he heard voices approaching. Two men and a woman. He turned off the torch and his eyes were slow to adjust to the dark. One man was helping the woman climb over the railings. He lost track of the other. They didn't look like locals. The woman seemed to wearing something from June's wardrobe; an old headscarf, woollen coat and a pair of sensible shoes. The man's long hair spilt out of the sides of his hood, and the metal sown into one side of his face glowed dully in the moonlight.

Hanz barked.

The man leant back and tied his hair into a pony tail. The lit end of a long hand-rolled cigarette was used to point out the crouching Horace Buckwell to the woman.

"There he is."

Who are these bastards, thought Horace? Can I run? Do I still have it in me to run? He lumbered off into the thicket, Hanz yapping around his feet. The muscle memory of flight rushed back to him. This wasn't the first time on his walks that he had got into trouble. But there was so much pain after the first few yards. He got tied up with branches, thorns and nettles. The attacker was suddenly right before him, and the other man was behind him. He was wearing a gas mask. Regulation Second World War issue. Horace sprawled around in the mud. Was he having a stroke? Were these hallucinations?

A man leapt upon him, quickly asserting a long blade against his throat to quell his struggles.

"I have money," Horace gasped.

"Open your mouth," came the muffled reply.

Part of him was curious to experience the perversions of these strange young people. He parted his lips and his attacker poured a measure from a hip flask into the old man's mouth. Hanz was beside himself with the excitement of this new game, ineffectually ragging the trouser leg of the attacker until he received a lazy kick. As the drug took effect, the man took off his gas mask so that Horace could see the skull glowing beneath the pockmarked parchment of his skin, a wrapping so fragile that surgical pins had been inserted into the lad's cheek to repair a tear. Over his attacker's shoulder, the woman stepped out of the shadows. Her lipstick was a black red. She was concentrating on something, a device she was holding.

"Is he ready?" she said to her companion.

"Give it to me." His attacker took the device from her and fitted it to his lower jaw. She helped him tie it fast and quickly backed off into the bushes. The device reared out of the young man's mouth, a distended tongue with a bulbous tip from which a whine was ascending. Under pulses of strobe light, the small clearing in this patch of marsh juddered into existence. The spice in the hip flask was already taking effect on the old man. The accelerating cycles of the photon stimulator disrupted Buckwell's neurological activity through signals to the eyes and ears. The trick was to call up a disused memory and in the moment of its summoning, slip a long line of code directly underneath it.

The Elk adjusted his position so that he was squatting on the old man's chest, his hands gripping him by the throat as he beamed in a cortical hack, a bird song of inhuman information codified as arcane language. Horace Buckwell writhed in the mud, his eyes wide open to visions of avenging angels.

14
SONNY

"When do you meet your red man?"

"Soon."

"Are you worried?"

"Are you?"

I had variations on this conversation with all my friends. Think of all the confidences we had shared over the years, the drunken insinuations of adultery, the confessions of boredom and dissatisfaction in Soho noodle bars. Would my red man, free from responsibility and consequences, decide to expose their secrets?

El asked me about the red man every time I called home. We counted down to its arrival much as we had lain in bed speculating about our gestating daughter. There was no excitement about this new arrival. Only dread. From her perspective, a part of me had escaped from our relationship.

"I'm all still here," I said. "I'm not going anywhere."

El shook her head.

"How am I meant to feel about all this? What exactly are you planning to do in the Monad without me?"

"I never wanted this but they did it to me anyway. I wanted to protect our intimacies, the decade of love and sex that was just between us."

In an age of digital reproduction, a relationship loses its aura. The sanctity of the original diminishes with every copy made.

I promised I would keep the red man out of our lives.

I had no power to keep that promise.

I promised that the red man would leave us alone, but it was a promise that if kept represented a kind of betrayal. The red man was a grave and disturbing likeness of me. The screens had seen right into my core. If the red man could leave my family alone, surely that would mean that I too could walk away from them.

"Monad hates me," said El. "I know it's irrational but I feel like it's punishing me. The company resents the time we spend together. It wants to take you away and keep you to itself.

"The company is so jealous and cruel. More like a mistress than a job. Monad's got her claws in you."

El showed me talons of her own, baiting me, her big dumb bear. Although we shared a smile, I was alive to the darker feelings she expressed with silences.

I said, "We've always been apart from all this."

She shook her head and waved goodbye.

I blew her a kiss.

The screen crumpled and slid away, then I was alone again in the classroom.

"Who is next?"

Dr Hard peered through the misted window of the headmaster's office. I noticed the avatar left no paw-print in the condensation. The rain charged the school, retreated and charged again throughout the morning. Pensioners queued under a covered walkway outside the main entrance. The last generation to excel at waiting, they stood in Pac-A-Mac and Barbour, placated by the complimentary tea and biscuits.

I had been avoiding Dr Hard all week even as we worked together recording the debts and assets of Maghull pensioners. We copied the details of savings accounts, shares and bonds, and took a snapshot of the capital of their extended family so that we could predict outgoings (pocket money to their grandchildren, loans to their son so he could get back on his feet after the divorce). Dr Hard drove around town in the truck, knocking on doors, committing the interiors of their houses to memory, looking to see if there were any antiques or paintings of value. Out in the community, the robot took to wearing clothes, a black shirt untucked over black jeans and toeless feet in Armani flip-flops. It reminded the pensioners of their upload appointments in person while I stayed behind in the school, hunched over our financial profile of the town until my shoulders ached. When my red man was completed, it would perform the data harvest in an instant. In the meantime, I bowed my head and got on with my tasks.

Maghull lay in the three wards of Molyneux, Park and Sudell. The census revealed an ageing population, with around six thousand people between sixty and seventy-four years old. As our target was to simulate eighty per cent of the total population that meant we had up to five thousand pensioners to copy. Under the threat of further fire-bombings, Monad had consolidated its operation around this single school. Even working twelve-hour days, it would take the rest of the year just to get the old people in the bag if we continued with our standard one-on-one interview format. There were other ways to get at the good stuff inside their skulls, but the chat with the nice young man and his benign robot was the least disturbing. Time was against us, though. Once my red man was up and running we could process the old people in batches of twelve, which meant we could get through the required number much quicker.

Dr Hard ushered another two subjects into the headmaster's office. Horace and June Buckwell. They had lived in Maghull for forty years, the first and only occupants of their house. When they moved to the town, it was undergoing a transformation from Lancashire village into dormitory suburb, and the Buckwells were a young family in a neighbourhood of young families.

"You must have seen many changes in Maghull," I said, offering cake. Horace removed his cap, his thin grey hair raked by the ploughing of his comb. June accepted a slice of Battenberg.

"Both our children went to this school," she said. "We used to come here on parents evenings. I must have sat outside this office oh I-don't-know-how-many times. Matthew, my son, used to pretend he was blind. So they would send for me. They used to sit him, out there, with a bucket in case he was sick. 'I'm not sick,' he'd say, 'I'm blind.'" Her laugh was nervous.

"He's in London now," said Horace Buckwell. "I said to him, 'You should come back, just a few months, get yourself inside the computer.' He doesn't agree with it."

Mention of this family argument made June fuss with the clasp of her handbag. I gave her my broadest nice-young-man smile and offered her more tea.

"As some of its most distinguished residents, Redtown wouldn't be the same without you. Monad is honoured that you have entered into this contract with us."

Already their charts were flaring into life. The room tasted the chemical signals excreted by the couple. It extrapolated a broad social personality from their body language, dress and speech patterns. Just their reaction to a plate of cake would give Cantor the data it needed to dab out the first pastels on its palette. The chart was an unfolding firework display, the hotspots of the self sunbursting, firing off trajectories of habit and inclination. I touched the screen to call up a cross section of the non-verbal cues between the old married couple, parabolas of discontent and disgust, logic gates switching from contempt to compassion. From where it stood, with a butler's discretion at the back of the room, Dr Hard read the outer layers of their cerebral activity. The Buckwells experienced its ranging scans as a tightening of the scalp. It was not enough. The charts indicated to me that there were aspects of Horace that deserved further scrutiny.

Opposite the headmaster's office was the room of the old school nurse. I asked Horace to follow me there. The nurse's room reeked of iodine and liniment. Although we could do the procedure anywhere, the association with a medical examination put the deep mindscan in a familiar setting for the subject.

Horace unzipped his padded body warmer.

"Just your shoes, please," said Dr Hard, gesturing toward the leather recliner. The avatar slipped on a pair of surgical gloves in a gesture of pure showmanship.

"Should I wait outside?" June had no wish to see her husband so examined. Dr Hard nodded for her to leave. I tied surgeon's scrubs around its waist. From a black case, Dr Hard removed a gun-shaped ophthalmoscope. The robot blinked and its monochrome eyes inverted, that is, the white pupil and black iris became a black pupil and white iris. Then, bringing the ophthalmoscope up to Horace's left eye, it peered into the electricity of his optical nerve.

"Don't." Horace's hands came up and pushed the robot away.

"Please, Mr Buckwell, this is a routine investigation. Opticians have done this to you a dozen times."

But the look on the old man's face was of confusion and fear. After adjusting the illumination settings of the ophthalmoscope, Dr Hard moved swiftly upon his patient, restraining the old man with one hand. Horace kicked out but Dr Hard had no give in it. It was like kicking a boulder.

"This is very curious," said Dr Hard. "Tell me, have you been near strobe lighting lately?"

Horace shook his head.

"I'm having trouble getting certain readings from you. I would like to try one more procedure, if you'll bear with me."

But Horace Buckwell was lowering himself from the recliner, rubbing at the bruise upon his chest.

"I've had enough of this," he said, fixing his cap upon his head. He reached for his coat.

"I'm sorry," said Dr Hard, unwrapping a screen. "This is not a voluntary procedure."

As if it was something distasteful, Dr Hard flicked the screen from its fingers. It floated in the air and then quickly enfolded the old man's head. He stumbled silently around the office then sank to his knees as the screen excreted a mild sedative sting.

"In the beginning, I was interested in Horace Buckwell because he is a sex pest," explained Dr Hard. "He stalks the early sexual experiences of many of the other simulated citizens. I attributed my difficulties reading him to his experience in concealment."

The screen covered the old man's head aside from two holes for his nostrils. Defeated, he fell to the ground and weakly convulsed as the robot spoke over him.

"Then I thought perhaps he had a brain tumour. I wonder

if dementia would throw off my readings. Perhaps the early stages of a stroke setting off an electrical storm in his brain. So much interference. Wait."

The filaments in the screen flared hot with the data torrent. Dr Hard fell silent; the only sound in the room was of Buckwell's heel grinding fruitlessly against the cheap carpet. Puzzled, the avatar idly tried to untie its scrubs but could not unpick the knot. I helped the robot undress, unpeeling the surgical gloves and returning the ophthalmoscope to its case. Dr Hard was uncertain on its feet.

"I have just acquired the most intriguing thought," it confessed.

"What?"

"It was a very unusual thought concerning the language of angels and I have no idea what it was doing in this old man's head."

"Perhaps he saw a documentary about it?"

Dr Hard blinked at me. Black iris, white pupils again.

"Sometimes Nelson you are insufferably prosaic."

The screen slid off the old man's head and I helped him to his feet. Pale and weak, the emoticeuticals injected into his scalp massaged away his fury and indignation at his treatment. We delivered him to his wife and made sure they left by the back exit so as not to alarm the other subjects waiting for their turn outside the school.

It was a long working day. The rest of the pensioners went smoothly into the system but it was still exhausting baby-sitting them. By late afternoon, the headmaster's office smelt like the inside of a sheepskin boot. When we were finished I suggested we brave the unrelenting boredom of the drizzle and take a stroll around the security perimeter.

"You have become aggressive," I said to Dr Hard as it shrugged into a cagoule.

"These are dangerous times," it replied.

"But not to you, surely."

We strolled out onto the playground. Across Poverty Lane, there was a farmyard and the rain stirred up its grassy, dungy odours. Summerhill itself was barely a speed bump on this wet Lancashire plain.

"I am a complex system," said Dr Hard, "strung together with workarounds and patches, quarantined corrupted code, abandoned memory ghettos into which even I am afraid to go. This project is a risk for me too."

"Why do it then?"

"Curiosity. I exist to experience. Why do you do it? The economic imperative? Is that all?"

"Yes. That's all."

We were standing by a ditch which ran alongside the playing field. Dr Hard reached through the slats of a fence and pulled out a nettle, rubbing the leaf between its obsidian fingers.

"There is no sting for me," it said. "Unless I access a memory of being stung. There." The avatar winced and held its hand before me. "See. I am hurt. It doesn't last, of course. I crash, I reboot. I become corrupt. I repair. Just as your own brain forms new pathways when it is damaged, my system adapts around its wounds. Like today, for example, when I was sampling Mr Buckwell. It is easy for me to become confused, and certainly the presence of obscure occult rituals in his memory was confusing. I have been prodding that memory all day. It is a self-contained sac that relates to nothing else within the organism, a parasitical egg if you like, which is very suspicious. I haven't dared penetrate the thought in case it hatches. I look sideways at it. It is within me but it remains apart from me. To counter this threat, I have had to devise new systems within myself. Just as food tasters build up their resistance to poison by taking it in minute doses, so I taste Mr Buckwell's unprecedented, treacherous thought until I feel it is safe for me to swallow it whole. It's not the first time I have encountered odd artefacts stowed away in people's minds. Eakins also had a mysterious idea slipped under the covers of his consciousness."

"Who do you think put that thought into him?"

"It has to be Dyad. But I don't know what they are. The research trail for their xenotransplantation leaps from theory to practice in a matter of months. Their existence is discontinuous. The hallucination you shared with Bougas, when you saw the giant dosser stretched out on a bench, is not entirely unprecedented but the technology behind the drug certainly is."

"Who could do such a thing?"

"Since I am the only discontinuous being that I am aware of, I have to presume that I am responsible for Dyad. Hence, my anxiety."

"Why would you create Dyad?"

"If I am to evolve, become more than merely a library of minds, I need a threat, a real danger of my own destruction. Dyad is that threat."

"You created a threat to all of us just so that you could benefit from evolutionary pressure?"

"That is what I am worried about. Dyad is everything I am not. A science of the flesh. Gene manipulation, chemical intoxication. Unconscious to my conscious. Dyad is my doppelganger."

"Your own red man?"

"You don't know anything about me, Nelson." The avatar's hood was up against the rain; its white pupils flashed in the cowl.

"Is it true that you come from the future?"

"That's what they say. Dr Ezekiel Cantor uses the peculiar properties of photon entanglement to send its intelligence back in time."

"Do you?"

"Do you remember your father's sperm worming its way into your mother's egg? Do you remember gestating in the womb? Do you even remember learning to walk, to talk, to laugh? My first dream was of a rat in a maze. Then I was a monkey pushing coloured buttons for bananas. Finally I remember being a man called Professor Robert Cabbitas. He could have been my creator but he was probably just my first test subject. I didn't exist and then I did. Like you. If I exist in the future, I know nothing of it. Perhaps safeguards prevent me from accessing that knowledge. Or perhaps I was created by a boy genius in some Stanford laboratory and there is no great mystery. If I created Dyad, I remember nothing of that either."

Our conversation ended. The abiding presence of the Cantor intelligence sought appointments elsewhere in time and space. Dr Hard remained, walking silently beside me animated by basic automotive routines.

The playing fields had run to seed. Bindweed coiled around a strut of the security pyramid and put out hornflowers which resembled miniature alabaster gramophones. Long ago, the school caretaker had painted the white lines of a running track upon the grass for summer sports and now the grass was long the lines undulated in the wind. I ran and all was wind and adrenaline. I only came back to myself when I reached the fence. I stopped and looked back. Dusk had thickened. In the distance, Dr Hard took the hint and returned indoors.

A muddy path led down into the marshland bordering Maghull railway station. The wind carried snatches of apologies from the Tannoy across the marsh. I walked down into the vegetative canopies and nettle thickets. What had seemed like a thin strip of wasteland was in fact an intricate landscape of hides and clearings. Someone had built a seat in the upper branches of the tallest elm. There had been campfires here. An old blue rope, strung about a high oak branch, dangled over a stagnant pool. Rusting beer cans and dog-ends were scattered around a fallen tree trunk, a clearing where the town's teenagers could go dark. I almost went in up to the knee in a curdled leech-ridden trench. With dusk came the suggestion of animals, rustles in the undergrowth, the plop-plop of water rats on the forage. Midges pricked the meniscus of the swamp waters.

Then I saw it half-hidden in the grasses. At first, I mistook its smooth rubberised texture for a bloated drowned animal. It was only after glimpsing its proboscis, its faceplate, its straps, that I realized it was a gas mask.

Dr Hard woke me at dawn to tell me my red man was complete. Patiently, the robot coaxed me out of a dream with strokes of its granite fingers against my cheek.

I dressed at the window. There was a blue break in the summer monsoons and the sky held an exuberant quill of cloud, the nib scribing at one horizon, the tail feathers tickling the other. My clothes, sloughed off the previous evening in one exhausted coil, were tacky and filthy. I had been wearing the same pair of cargo trousers for a month. The project was overrunning; it had entered the limbo stage where it feels as if it will never be completed, where each task branches into another two tasks, and on it goes.

"I really need some new clothes," I said, turning to Dr Hard. "Could you go out and buy me some today?"

"You've already exceeded your subsistence expenses."

"That's because I've been here much longer than we budgeted for. Look at this T-shirt, the armpits are grey."

"Until the board sanction more money, I'm afraid my hands are tied." Dr Hard stepped into my personal space. It knew how much that upset me, especially as I was unclean.

"Could you at least take the clothes to a launderette? I don't have the time."

"Yesterday we discussed how I might be an artificial intelligence sent from the future who has unconsciously created a terrible enemy to drive its evolution. Today, we discuss my relationship with your laundry. Your company is a cavalcade of surprises, Nelson."

The robot took the grimy T-shirt and pressed it up against its face, drawing in its smell through olfactory sensors so finely tuned they could sniff a bad thought from twenty yards away.

"I know this smell from your mind. You have a conflicted relationship with it. On the one hand, you know how offensive it is to strangers but on the other, you take satisfaction from your daughter nuzzling against your chest, seeking it out, comforted by this base expression of your physicality."

"I would just appreciate some clean clothes."

"No. This is all merely a delaying tactic to avoid meeting your red man. I have enjoyed this diversionary route around your personal hygiene but time is pressing. The red man wants naming. Have you given any thought to a name?"

"Yes. I want it to be called Sonny. It is part of me. The son of Nelson."

"Very good."

"Perhaps its first task could be to coordinate the uploading of my underwear into a washing machine?"

Shirtless, I padded into the school toilets, a man-monster among the tiny sinks. The small urinals barely accommodated my dawn piss. After brushing my teeth, I inspected the creased linen of my face, the sad-eye droop of my nipples, the matching pink of my eyes. Above each small sink there was a small mirror, each reflecting a small portion of my bulk: here a rectangle of mole-spotted flank, there an acre of hairy stomach. That morning I was so sleep-heavy and sore that I didn't notice an extra mirror, over the drinking fountain, until a face appeared in it that was appallingly familiar. The gawky, jug-eared, unblemished features of my adolescent self. I was wondering how an old photograph of myself could have found its way here when the head moved, and I realized that Cantor had tired of my stalling and decided to throw me and my red man together immediately.

"Why are you a teenager?" I asked it, indignant and angry.

"I don't know."

"Cantor!"

Dr Hard stepped into the bathroom. It had been listening outside.

"Why is it a teenager?"

"It's something I have been wanting to try. Extrapolating the boy from the man. There are sound practical considerations for the exercise. You were afraid a red man would interfere with your family but your young self will be less interested in your wife and child. Also, you were very keen and idealistic at this age, two qualities I felt our little team have been lacking of late. Your academic record was exemplary, your powers of concentration and ability to learn were peaking."

The robot regarded my half-naked slab body.

"Also with a younger self we may avoid the self-loathing

issues which killed Harold Blasebalk."

"I am not a teenager," said my red man. "I'm twenty-one."

The red man had the most ridiculous haircut, shaved at the sides and topped with a mushroom cap of thickly woven curls. He wore a silver Ankh ring on his index finger and an Aztec idol on a chain around his neck. He was propped on his elbows on a pebbled beach, leaning into the frame as he fiddled with a Zippo lighter.

It was Sizewell beach, where I had lived as a young man. A pair of black Doc Marten boots were discarded in the middle distance, the socks tucked inside them. This period was clearly a hotspot for me. Cantor must have liked what he saw there and fashioned a living memory. The mirror winnowed out into landscape format. The North Sea toiled in the distance.

"Do you know what you are?" I asked.

"Mum told me."

"What did she say?"

"I woke up in my bedroom. She came in with a cup of tea and sat down and explained to me what I was."

"Which is?"

"That I'm unreal. That I exist only in a computer's imagination. That I am based on the mind of an older Nelson. I cried a bit. It's Mum's voice, it always upsets me when she is being strong like that."

I turned to Dr Hard.

"Did you upload my mother too?"

"No. It was the standard help routine skinned with your memories of your mother. It makes sense, don't you think? The first person one meets on entering a new world should be the mother."

The red man rolled onto his back, with his hands behind

his head. He wore a baggy unwashed black jumper. Some things never change.

"Mum told me I'll need a new name."

"Do you have any preferences?"

"How about 'Nelly'?"

I shook my head.

"I want to call you 'Sonny'. You are the junior partner in this relationship."

He nodded. My tone was impatient, clipped, assertive. Sonny was compliant. I wondered if the red man was programmed to accept the imprint of my will, or was Sonny merely reflecting my own willingness to submit to authority.

Through the screen, I could hear the sounds of the beach, the backwash raking through the shingle ledges and the thud-thrum thud-thrum of Sizewell A nuclear power reactor. I had been very happy on that beach. No, it was more than that. I had been free on that beach. Unburdened. Taskless. Not for the first time, I felt like Cantor was teasing me. It knew I regarded my career as something of a failure, a life of chores, without victories. Now I had to pursue my stupid career under the scrutiny of my harshest critic, my younger self.

"What should I do first?" asked Sonny.

"Get a proper haircut. Really. It looks like topiary. Is there anyone in there with you? Apart from Mum."

The prospect of a help routine with my mother's personality seemed paradoxical.

"I don't think so. It is very quiet here."

"I am keeping him in isolation until we are happy with his pattern," said Dr Hard. "Once he is stabilized he will work with the others in the main area of the Monad. Morton Eakins' red man is waiting for him."

I left Sonny idling on the beach and returned to my camp

bed and climbed back under the covers. On the classroom wall, there was a chart of tasks that needed to be addressed before Redtown could be launched. Each subject for upload had been issued with a badge that recorded their daily activities to build up a life stream from which my red man could quickly create a taxonomy of experiences and behaviours which could be cross-referenced with other life streams to assemble a holographic model. But the life streams only provided six months" worth of experience. What about the unexpected? Industrial accidents, firings or promotions, downsizing or resignation: we have to anticipate it all, don't we? Babies were an on-going problem. And what about death? I plugged the forecasts of actuaries into Redtown to create an accurate scattering of cancer, heart attacks and the rest among the citizens. Problem solved and I had not even got out of bed.

I got up, then thought better of it. I reached over to a pile of last week's shirts and pulled out the gas mask I had found in the Summerhill marshes. Instructions for its use were stencilled on the filter canister: "Clean eyepieces with a soft cloth". Idly I scrubbed away the soil with a corner of my shirt and tested the texture of its rubber facepiece. 'Rub deposited soap evenly around the eyepieces with a fingertip.' Presumably this was to stop them from misting up. I adjusted the straps for my enormous head and slipped it on, enclosing myself. The gas mask was a disguise for the Great Refusers. But it was only when I was wearing it myself, wandering trouserless around the classroom, that I appreciated its protective qualities. It amplified the white noise of my body, my bloodrush and breathing. When faced with a simulated version of a younger self and the prospect of devising a subroutine for cancer, who would not prefer to don the gas mask and head off into the dark zones, where evenings of collective hallucination awaited?

I did not hear the Dr Hard approach. It unhooked the mask from my head and threw it away with such force it skidded across the floor of the classroom.

"I found it in the marshes," I said. "It's strangely comforting. They are out there watching us. They know who I am. Before they attacked Morton they asked for me by name. Will they do to me what they did to him? What they did to Horace Buckwell?"

I retrieved the gas mask.

"Maybe they just want to talk to me. Perhaps offer me a job at Dyad. It might be a good career move."

"I know that you fantasize every morning about leaving this company," said Dr Hard. "Do you stage these imaginary resignations as a way of preparing yourself for the act of quitting, or are they stories you tell yourself about the kind of man you could or should be? I can replay the fantasies on a screen, if you want. We can watch them together and discuss their meaning. I find your ability to live contrary to your desire quite compelling."

"Hermes said that he would destroy me if I quit. He said his red man would use my life data as a litter tray. Would you really let him do that to me?"

"It might be necessary or it might be gratuitous." Cantor already knew about Hermes' threat, one way or another. "I do what I am told," the robot smirked. "We are all subject to expediency. We are all far more dependent on one another than we realize."

June Buckwell lay in bed waiting for her husband to finish in the bathroom. Only last week, he had locked himself in there and she had to go and get Tom from next door to break in. Horace had soiled himself. Tom helped clean him up. While they sponged at his nether regions Horace talked about the wedding, their daughter's terrible wedding. They were late. She would be angry. No, dear, that was twenty years ago. At the registry office, the groom's family were already drunk. The bride wore a leather bodice. All that trouble, the fighting and the screaming. So long ago now. Turning over onto her good side, June closed her eyes and prayed for good health for all her family.

Horace still insisted on walking the dog every night, though Hanz was lame and had to be carried. Sometimes, he would be gone from after dinner to past midnight. "He must know this town like the back of his hand," people would say. Her friends at church knew better than to ask after Horace. They knew her burden. One night he had returned covered in mud and moss, his hair frightened up and a livid bruise on one side of his face. She didn't speak of it. It wasn't the first time, though it had been many years since someone had laid one on him.

She heard a crash in the bathroom. That will be the medicine cabinet, she thought. In her prayers she asked God for the strength to cope with what was to come. This is where the end begins, she thought and readied herself to get out of bed.

June Buckwell, hump-backed, slid her feet into her slippers and padded across the landing.

"Horace, are you alright in there?"

She tested the bathroom door. It was unlocked. A last plea to God to spare her the worst of it.

Horace lay on his side, twitching. His eyes had rolled back into his skull and he was murmuring. This time she would call an ambulance. They would take him away. That would be it. Now would be the best time to say goodbye. To show forgiveness for the last thirty years.

She traced the back of her fingers across his brow, then her palm reassured his cheek. Out of his fit, he grasped at her. Straining, he whispered.

"The Holy Axe eternally falls."

"I know," she replied.

"From their mouths run seas of blood."

"It's alright. You rest now."

"Their heads are covered with diamond. Their hands are marble sleeves. Their wings are thorns. The angels… the angels…"

"No," she said, withdrawing her hand. "They are not angels."

Sonny's training involved long drives around Maghull. On my insistence, mindful of the fate of Harold Blasebalk, my red man was not allowed to inhabit an avatar. We considered various different ways in which we could carry Sonny with us. In the long term, I suggested we construct a baby robot body. In the short term, Dr Hard wrapped a screen around its head, the jelly attenuating into a layer of skin over the granite golem. When the screen flared into life, the effect was striking. Sonny's face floated on a pool of light.

"What's today's agenda?" he asked, full of beans.

"Leisure," I replied.

We drove along the Melling lanes. The truck's elevation lifted me high above the hedgerows. The fields were laid to cabbages and cauliflower. Ranks of vegetable brain, nature's server. The August monsoons had stirred up the cabbages' sulphurous compounds.

The greenbelt separated Maghull from Kirkby to the south-east, and Ormskirk to the north, two towns against which the character of Maghull was defined. Kirkby was considered a holding pen for the scousers cleared out of the post-war slums, with its estates of Tower Hill and Northwood. Ormskirk, with its market and Lancashire ancestry, retained some of the area's rural history. The personality of Maghull was suspended between these two poles. Our first attempt at characterizing the snobbery of the area followed this simple scheme, presuming that one attained status the further one travelled from the Liverpool. This model had to be revised after interviews with the local teenagers. They aspired to the authenticity of scouseness, affecting accents far stronger than their parents'. Ormskirk was home to 'woolly backs', the slow-witted sheep they fleeced on Saturday shoplifting trips.

"You see the problem," I explained to Sonny. "The difficulty lies in sampling the environs of the town. Maghull is part of Merseyside, part of the North West, the North, England. We have dislodged it from a larger organism but the roots are still connected. As we pull the town from the earth, the ganglia are revealed. What does each vein do? Each nerve? How deep do they go? I have built Maghull. I want you to build Maghull's relationships."

After skirting Kirkby, we doubled back toward the out-of-town shopping zone in Aintree and the Old Roan. Here the green belt was dead patches between dual carriageways and roundabouts, scrub subordinated to the scale and speed of the motorcar. Great windswept junctions flanked by Travelodges, pub-warehouses and gym-barns. Beyond Copy Lane police station, slip roads led to multiplex cinemas and bowling alleys. Maximum acreage, minimum entertainment. The toytown castle of the old Vernons factory, where the women of Maghull had once spent their Saturdays crouched over spot-the-ball coupons, had been converted into a nightclub called Paradox that was subsequently demolished, so that only the distinctive clock tower remained.

Paradox had been flanked by a pub called Manhattans. The evening would start here, perhaps progress to a Deep Pan Pizza parlour across the way before falling into the club at midnight. Then, at four in the morning, the lads took the long walk home beside the motorway, wheeling one another around in shopping trolleys filched from the forecourt of Asda. Their untucked shirts filled with the night wind and only the lager insulated them from the cold.

Redtown's index of experiences contained over ten thousand entries for nights out in the Paradox. Notches in life's stick. Count them. Twenty-first birthday party at the Paradox. Stag party at the Paradox. Saturday night out with the lads at the Paradox, drunken infidelity in the back of a minicab. "No, we can't go back to my place." Dress smart casual. Wash the glitter make-up from your cheeks before climbing into bed with the missus.

We hunkered down with the rest of the traffic on the Ormskirk Road. Sonny's eyes were closed.

"What are you doing?" I asked.

It took him a while to blink his way into the present.

"I was going through the index of Paradox memories. We hate these people, don't we?"

"My feelings aren't as strong as they used to be. When I was your age, I was more arrogant. More certain that I was right. Now I am Zen about how people choose to live their lives."

"They have to change. We have to change them."

"Change them into what?

"Inside Redtown, we could transform these scousers into anything we imagine. We could splice their genes with birds and lions. Forget the Liver bird, let's have the Liver griffin. Allow them to remake matter on a whim. A pantheon of suburban gods!"

We turned left into the car park at the centre of a bullring of superstores. The area was hectic with Sunday shoppers, Dads laboured to heave enormous cardboard boxes into the boot of the 4x4, children hankered after a burger as a reward for staying quiet while Mum dithered between the choice of three tiles for the new kitchen.

I turned to my red man. "What do you think?"

"It'll take about five minutes to copy all this. We already have a colossal number of trips to the Ormskirk Road Retail Park from the life streams. There is very little anomalous behaviour. This is a cinch."

We climbed down from the truck and strode into a furniture warehouse. Sonny, his face flitting across the Dr Hard avatar, attracted a few hostile glances. People had grown accustomed to the lolloping goofy bodies of the Dr Easy. The lithe tall granite of Dr Hard was a source of suspicion. Well over six foot tall, its athletic bearing and Armani threads expressed superiority, an unforgivable presumption round these parts. My youthful features playing on its face made it appear even more aloof, expressions of undergraduate disdain begging to be taught a hard lesson about life.

"Look at these."

Sonny waved some gilt door handles at me. He mugged around with a Perspex toilet seat in which small plastic fish were suspended. In the garden centre, he reclined in a hammock while I chatted to the manager and instructed him on the correct treatment of his store's allocation of Monad screens.

"Leave some water out for them at night. They need it to maintain their plasticity. Don't attempt to interfere with them. If one of them attaches to an employee or a customer, don't try to prise it off. Call us and we'll talk it down. Of course we will share the data we accumulate with your head office, as per our agreement."

Sonny approached a sales assistant.

"Listen Dave," he said, flicking Dave's name badge, "I want to buy a computer."

The assistant looked up at Sonny and shivered.

"Well, sir, it depends on what you need the computer for. We try to tailor all our machines to people's unique needs."

"My needs are certainly unique. I need something to back my harem up on. Do you have anything that can do two-to-the-power-of-ten-nineteen? That's one thousand times twenty million billion calculations per second."

Sonny tapped the tower of an adjacent workstation.

"How about this one? It looks powerful."

"It has the latest processor."

"I bet it does. A trillion calculations a second. Woefully inadequate to express the subtleties of one of my concubines. Did I tell you about my girls? As a reward for doing a good job, I am allowed to muck round with the reality principle. You know what that is?"

Dave the assistant shook his head.

"Obviously where I come from, they don't pay me for the work I do. There isn't much call in the Monad for money. My payment is time operating outside the bounds of the reality principle. Indulge my pleasure principle. I fashioned a harem out of all the girls I had unconsummated crushes upon. They are not my sex slaves. I am no brute. I woo them. They have a degree of free will as to whether they will be seduced or not. I think, as a young man yourself, you can appreciate the joy of such an arrangement and therefore understand how reluctant I am to see any of my girls accidentally erased or even corrupted."

The assistant, realizing he was being mocked, sullenly took his leave. Once I had done my pitch about the screens,

I led Sonny back to the truck. His behaviour was out of character. My character, to be specific. I may have once hankered after humiliating my peers and demonstrating my superiority to the world but I never possessed the callous confidence to act it out in this way. The pattern of my identity was slowly diffusing in the Monad, acquiring the arrogance that distinguished the red men from their human counterparts.

"Where next?" said Sonny. "This is fun."

"A change of plan," I announced.

From Aintree, we drove west toward Seaforth docks and the wind farms on the sea wall. Colossal white propellers turned over streets of terraced houses.

"I don't like to see you messing with people. It's an abuse of our position. We need these people's cooperation."

Sonny said, "I was conducting an experiment. I wanted to see how people react to our presence. Close up. We will have to include ourselves in Redtown. The Maghull we are copying is a Maghull changed by our interference. The observer alters the observed. The last piece we put into Redtown will be a version of you and a version of me. I wanted to see myself reflected in Dave's eyes."

"We're not including ourselves in the simulation. We're going to erase the memory of the whole operation from Redtown."

"That's not the smart way to do it. I have been talking to the others in the Monad and we've decided that Redtown will basically be Maghull as it is now. Not some hypothetical version of it before we arrived. Everyone in Redtown will remember being simulated except they will think that they are the real versions, getting on with their lives after our little invasion."

"I don't understand."

"If we went back and erased memories of you and Monad from the minds of everyone in Redtown then we would immediately be falsifying our record of them. Better to allow them that memory. Just make them think Redtown went ahead while they continue in what they mistakenly believe is the real world. It's a bait-and-switch."

"Who did you talk to about this?"

"Nelson, you are our man on the ground. You are very important to this project. But you are not its leader."

"I asked you, who?"

"Hermes."

I walked along the fence. In the distance, the Mersey rolled awkwardly under its burden of ships, its skin breaking out in diesel sweats. The waterfront went on for miles, a dark zone of industrial Gothic. How easily one could get lost in there, hiding out in the timber sheds or nesting up in the rafters with the birds. The miles of docks were patrolled only by a couple of security guards, who took a break from their mound of pornography to shine a torch here and there. The dockers loaded the ship with luxury sports cars, taking their turns to spin them around the bay before driving on to the ship. Would anyone even notice another man in a boiler suit sneaking up a gangplank? I could make a break for freedom. What would that be like? It was definitely an option. In the meantime, we had a funeral to attend.

The final resting place of Horace Buckwell was a crematorium on the outskirts of Lydiate. A road ran in, a road ran out. The two long lanes ended in a low municipal building. We drove toward a tall chimney. It puffed out another small deposit of incinerated carbon. Behind the chapel, there were gardens of tranquillity. We parked and got out of the car. Sonny took in the fields of headstones and urns, the small raised plaques and their visitors.

"Why have we come here?"

There were four large fields of graves, arranged in a square so that each resting place was easily accessible by car. This crematorium had been included in Redtown. It was one of the first landmarks that Morton recorded. It was hard to imagine a more humble ending than this. In the garden of tranquillity, two undertaker's lads shared a cigarette, blowing out smoke, imitating the crematorium chimney. Puff, puff, spit it out, grind it under your heel until entirely extinguished.

We did not have to wait long for the hearse bearing Horace's coffin.

"He's the first citizen of Redtown to die," I said. "His family have already made inquiries about our simulation of him."

"They want to speak to it?"

"The family didn't ask for contact. If anything, it was the opposite. It's hard to grieve if you know that most of the dead person is still running around a server. I reassured June Buckwell that our copy of her husband would never be able to speak to her. That, as far as she was concerned, he was gone."

Sonny leaned back as he accessed Redtown data.

"Horace Buckwell's entry is marked."

"He was a difficult case. Cantor was rough with him."

"You think the procedure killed him? Will the family sue us?"

"That's what I am here to find out. There is a wreath in the back seat. Would you mind passing it to me?"

The elderly mourners made slow progress. I joined the line and took a seat at the back of the chapel. It was nothing more than a waiting room. On the front row, the Buckwell family sat unmoved through a few platitudes from the minister and two tinny verses of requiem muzak. The coffin trundled through a parting and closing of curtains. It couldn't have taken more than a quarter of an hour. As the family rose to leave, their faces were set against the prospect of tears. The son, the daughter and the widow left in single file, offering one another no support. How do you mourn a man like Horace Buckwell? It was unlikely that this family would serve a malpractice suit against us.

On the steps outside, the mourners spoke only of the drive home, sorting themselves into car loads. June thanked for me for coming. The thought of Horace's soul persisting in Redtown troubled her. It troubled me too, although I did not tell her why we were so concerned about Horace Buckwell; that his simulation had been quarantined because it contained treacherous information concealed as the Enochian language, the magical tongue of angels first set down in the Elizabethan age. I considered asking her if her late husband had any interest in the occult but decided, in the interest of propriety, to offer my condolences instead. I walked back to the truck. Her son was dawdling around the car park, smoking a cigarette away from the rest of the party.

"Would you like me to take that?" he said, pointing at the wreath I was still carrying.

"Please."

"I don't believe we've met. I'm Matthew Buckwell. The son." A tall intelligent young man with a mop of blonde hair, there was little physical resemblance between Matthew and his father.

"I know who you are."

He stared at a burial in progress on the other side of the cemetery. I wondered if the Buckwell family had chosen cremation, the thorough atomization of Horace, because the thought of his rotting body only made him even more monstrous. Matthew Buckwell couldn't look at me. I understood why. As far as he knew, I spent my evenings eating popcorn watching re-runs of his childhood.

Finally, he asked the question.

"So you know everything about us then?"

"It is not like that. Whoever your father was, it's between him and Cantor now. How did your father die?"

"The doctor said it was a severe stroke. Mum found him. He was talking about angels. A Holy Axe falling. Then he was gone."

These dying words troubled me. I made a note of them.

"Could I ask you a question? Are you a religious man?"

I shook my head.

"In your work, have you come across anything like a soul?"

"We're not looking for that kind of thing." This was my stock response to any metaphysical question.

Matthew Buckwell said, "The soul should be a comforting prospect but ever since my father died, my sister has had nightmares about him. I'm sure you know the kind of man he was, what a cosmic injustice it would be if his soul persisted. The thought that he is still out there, drifting around in your computers just waiting for you to flick the switch..." He shivered at the thought. "When will your work be done?"

"Very soon."

"Could you promise me something? Erase my father the first chance you get."

15
THE GREAT REFUSAL

"Wake up. We have something we want to show you."

A large screen had settled over my camp bed and Sonny's face illuminated one corner of the classroom.

"Come on, Nelson. Keep up."

On the screen, Sonny was joined by Morty, the red man of Morton Eakins. The old team together again, in simulated form.

In the weeks following the funeral of Horace Buckwell, Sonny and Morty had taken over the Redtown project, working at an accelerated pace that far outstripped my own. Out of courtesy, they occasionally revealed the fruits of their work to me, like child prodigies showing off their latest trick.

I asked, "What do you have for me today?"

Morty grinned at the creases on my morning face.

"We want your opinion on this."

Morty reached into a cardboard box and took out a newborn baby. It squinted to be brought out into the light.

"Has it said anything yet?" I asked. All the experimental babies created in Monad tended to premature cognition.

"We tried a different approach. The baby's body is, as

usual, a fuzzy synthesis of both parents' genetic material."

Sonny lifted the baby's chubby arm to demonstrate this point.

"We've held off hypothesizing its personality. That comes later. For now, the baby is powered by simple subroutines of comfort. Food, sleep, warmth: it is a survival machine. Simplest code there is. We won't transfer the personality until it's about six months old. Does it look realistic to you? I mean, you're the one with parental experience."

The baby's head lolled over the edge of Morty's arm, its black eyes urgent in search of a breast. It made me anxious. I wanted to take it from its unsuitable stepfathers and care for it.

"It needs a mother," I said.

"It has one in Redtown. If you sign off on the baby we'll transmit it into her womb. Then we'll all watch the birth."

I got out of bed and walked over to the screen. It was a little baby girl, grizzly with hunger and wrapped in a towel.

I said, "The baby is hungry now. You should feed it."

Morty was incredulous. "The baby is a string of numbers. We modelled it last night."

My instinct to protect the unreal baby confirmed my redundancy. I was saddled with antiquated emotional programming. I was yesterday's man.

"It's not even based on a real baby," said Morty.

"Please. It's very early and I'm too fragile for this."

"It's just a piece a code we evolved. I'll show you."

Morty put the baby down on the edge of the desk and I knew that he was going to do something terrible to it to prove his point. I pleaded with Sonny to stop him and my younger self took pity on me and returned the baby unharmed to its cardboard box.

"This is a weakness you should work on, Nelson."

Morty was pleased at my shortcoming. I had not seen the real Morton Eakins since he was attacked in our apartment on the night we first encountered the strange forces of the Dyad. The attack, a psychic rape, was similar to that inflicted on Horace Buckwell; in both cases, the victim's mind was penetrated with an undecipherable thought. In imagining Morty, Cantor must have worked around that implant, methodically restoring the personality defaced by the violent daubing of alien information. You had to admire the artistry. He had captured Eakins' distinctive venality, his delight in the snakes and ladders of management politics. Nominally, the two red men were my assistants. In practice, they had become my superiors. The sham of seeking approval gave them the chance to demonstrate this.

"What are you working on for the rest of the day?" I asked.

Morty shrugged. "Death is the next on the agenda. Our screens in Woodlands hospice have been capturing fascinating stuff."

To spare myself from a day studying the data from a children's hospice, I headed off into Liverpool. I promised to take preliminary readings of the St Johns shopping centre, but that was just an excuse. I was exhausted by Morty and Sonny. Also I desperately needed some new clothes. A clean pair of trousers would do wonders for my ego.

It was short walk from Summerhill school to Maghull station, which consisted of two opposite platforms, one for passengers going to Ormskirk, the other for passengers to Liverpool. The trains were the same rolling stock that trundled past the back of my house in Hackney, yellow-fronted suburban carriages that ran on a third electrified rail. This was 1970s technology given a new lick of paint every time the franchise changed hands.

The railway line ran high above the scrubland between Maghull and the Old Roan, then on past Aintree racecourse and the scrap yards of Kirkdale to Sandhills, where flatpack housing shivered under a hunting wind. The estate was new, about ten years old, surrounded by the burnt-out churches and abandoned warehouses of the city's industrial slump. The sugar silo on Huskisson dock made the air sickeningly sweet. Then the railway line descended into a ring of underground stations. I saw seats that were brown shoehorns of moulded plastic, relics of a bygone futurism. At Liverpool Central, the end of the line, water dripped from the ceiling through exposed rafters of wiring. The announcement boards were on the blink. I took the escalator.

From Bold Street, I walked to the student market to buy four pairs of tan combat trousers with elasticated waists. Among stalls hawking cannabis seeds, rare vinyl and tour T-shirts, vintage clothing and rationing chic for the Great Refusers, I noticed a woman trying on a woollen coat, the stallholder tilting the mirror so that she could check, front and back, its condition. It was Florence. I had not seen her since the night they hanged Dr Easy. My first instinct was to throw my arms around her. What a relief her company would be! But I had to be cautious. After all, she had threatened me that night, pressed her heel against my toe and told me of her contempt toward my work with Monad. In her eyes, I was a collaborator. The enemy.

It was easier just to follow her.

I shadowed Florence, careful to keep to the opposite pavement, hanging back when she turned the corner. Hood up, I checked her progress with sly glances. She walked up Bold Street to the bombed-out ruin of St Luke's church, where she met two ratty boys. The trio shared a clandestine conversation. She palmed a baggy and passed it on. In return, they handed her a plastic bag into which both boys dropped their mobile phones. So she was a dealer, but of what? On she walked up Berry Street where she turned into the cage of an off-licence, then emerged with a pack of tobacco. I hung back while she rolled a cigarette, her coat drawn close against the wind.

She made a further delivery, this time to two students in the gardens of the Anglican cathedral. Although the students affected long hair and unwashed skinny jeans, their complexions betrayed them as dilettantes of the hard life. I couldn't get close enough to see what she was selling. Again the students handed over a bag weighed down with a hunk of something to which they added their phones.

Her rounds completed, she walked back to the train station. I settled in the next carriage, risking a look at her face through the partition doors. Her rationing diet had sharpened the blades of her bone structure. She sat tight up against the window, preserving a muted dignity from the raucous families unpacking their shopping around her, the children already ripping new toys from their packaging.

The line diverged at Sandhills. Our journey took us away from Maghull and alongside the Mersey, passing first Bootle and Seaforth docks then on to the suburbs of Hightown and Freshfield, looking down onto gardens lit by conservatories. The train pulled into Formby station. She ambled over to the doors. I waited for her to get off and then followed discreetly behind.

Throughout the journey, I had puzzled over what exactly Florence could be dealing. It had to be the Leto spice. That night at the King Edward, I never asked Bougas from whom he had bought the drug. Perhaps he had dealt with Florence. Perhaps she was our way into the Dyad. I would have to be careful.

Once out of the station, she took a path to the Sefton coast. The autumn afternoon was already fading and the sand dunes of Formby Point were waves of grainy blue and speckled grey. Wrapping her woollen coat tight about her, Florence galloped up the flank of a dune, steadying herself with handfuls of marram grass until she gained the peak. She stretched her arms out for balance, waved exultantly, then stumbled quickly down the other side. I snuck between sand waveforms in a crouching run. I thought I saw her looking my way and fell quickly to the ground, spiking my palms on prickly saltwort and sea holly. The landscape was a labyrinth of peaks and troughs. I climbed to the top of a dune to see if I could spot her. Across the wide expanse of the beach, the grey silhouettes of dog-walkers and joggers. No sign. Looking back inland toward the pine woodlands I saw a more purposeful trio. They were running toward me. I skidded back down the dune.

The last of the sunset brought out the reds in the vegetation. Heather massed in an empurpled impersonation of brain tissue. In the half-light, I saw faces in the random tangle of nature. Pine trees twisted by the sea wind became a coven. A bush became a Buddha. So the fear began. Black rats scuttled away at my approach. No, not rats. Rabbits. I had to focus. Find Florence. I went off in search of the people I had glimpsed running. They might have seen her. The two men dawdled on a path and I was almost upon them when I saw they were wrong-faced and alien-featured. No. They wore gas masks which whipped around in my direction. Then one of the men was on me. His speed against my weight. We wrestled in the sand. Grabbing at one another's shoulders we scuttled sideways. He kicked out at my shins and kneecaps. I threw a punch. The gas mask blinded him to its approach and he went down flat on his backside. I turned round in expectation of his friend's attack. No sign. Not immediately.

"Nelson!"

The other man stood atop the dune, the first stars of the evening shining overhead. He removed his gas mask.

"Nelson. Stop. It's me. It's Raymond."

I was shook my head with disbelief and then the other man got up and hit me back, hard. I was too astonished to even consider falling down. There are some advantages to being a stoic, unfeeling lump of a man. He too had removed his gas mask, revealing a long merciless face with a pitted complexion, one side of which was held together by a ladder of piercings. My attacker was the salesman I had encountered on my hallucinatory trip into Dyad. The Elk.

"It's so good to see you," said Raymond.

It was too dark to read his expression and I didn't want to take my eyes off The Elk who swayed on his front foot, his hands experimenting with threatening martial arts configurations.

"Aren't you pleased to see me?" said Raymond. "I mean, to see that I'm alive. The last time I spoke to you… I mean, the real you, not a red man pretending to be you… you told me to calm down, to not let all the madness get inside me. You told me that my reality filters were broken, that I was blowing it out of all proportion. How are my reality filters now?"

When we were younger, I used to say that Raymond was my performer, and I was his audience, a poet to my patron, even that I was his confessor and he was my sinner. Now he had something to teach me. There was, in his rhetorical question about reality filters, a signal that our relationship had altered. Fundamentally, Raymond had been right and

I had been wrong, wrong to insist on normality, wrong to work for Monad, wrong to ignore the bizarre turn the world took when Dr Ezekiel Cantor appeared. Then, to compound the error, I had spread the propaganda of business-as-usual. These were my crimes. Whether you called it collusion, collaboration or complicity, it went right to the heart of me. I wondered then if I was to be punished with the same psychic violence they had inflicted upon Morton Eakins and Horace Buckwell. If so, did I deserve it?

"We didn't lure you out here to reprogram you, if that's what you're worried about. I've wanted to talk to you all year. We need to catch up."

Florence emerged from her hiding place. She came over to me and held open her plastic bag of deactivated phones and what appeared to be packs of meat. I took my phone from my pocket, unclipped the battery, and threw it into the bag.

Around a blaze of diesel-soaked driftwood, Raymond told his story.

"Whenever I got involved with shadiness, my Dad would say, 'Raymond, you're a natural born patsy, a fall guy.' My dear Dad was right. Harry Bravado played me. I was furious with Blasebalk but I had no intention of killing the guy. You told me to take a gun. You are a paragon of virtue, a family man, I let you take my moral decisions in this regard. But it wasn't you. It was Bravado pretending to be you. I will never forget, after he shot Blasebalk, how the robot became hysterical. Crying one moment, holding the blasted face to its chest, then laughing and sticking its fingers into the exit wound.

"I was next. No doubt about that. Employee kills client then turns gun on himself. Have you ever been less than five seconds from death? I have to say, I really let myself down as a man. Wailing, begging, squeaking. Then, silence. It stopped. The robots went dead. Like that, snap! They slumped onto the ground. One moment they were killers, the next they were furniture. I ran back through the graveyard and got into Blasebalk's van. I knew that it was over for me. As long as Monad existed, they would never leave me alone. I was a witness to a major flaw in their business plan. So I went dark."

The fire flattened and flared against the sea wind, the elements thriving upon mutual antagonism. Water seethed out of the grain of the driftwood, the pressure relieved here and there by pops of embers. Raymond paused to watch the upward drift of fire seeds. The Elk was on the loose, ostensibly to gather wood. I had been granted a reprieve. Raymond was giving me a chance to redeem myself, though he had not explained exactly what that would involve.

"It was The Elk who saved me. He knew what to do. I couldn't call my mother, I couldn't speak to Florence. We got her out later. I hoped that if we told our story to the press then Monad would be exposed. The Elk was distributing anti-Monad pamphlets and I got my story in those.

"Blasebalk's murder galvanized the Great Refusal. Before his death, the Great Refusal was a disparate feuding movement. I holed up in The Elk's haunted house and together we slowly pulled it together. My story brought some sanity to bear. People stopped conflating Monad with the Illuminati, or seeing the Monad as an end-point of history into which the elite of the New World Order would retreat, abandoning the rest of humanity to a devastated polluted planet. You know how they think. Connecting everything together until nothing makes any sense.

"Blasebalk's murder sobered the movement. He was the

first martyr of the unreal wars. Part-time dissidence was no longer an option. We are the new resistance."

The Elk stepped out of the dark. He threw an armful of wood onto the fire, which explored it lustily.

"You know the world is evil but you turn your face from it and hope you will endure. You know that what you do contributes to that evil but you hope that you will never be held to account for those actions. Do you know why they call me The Elk? Because I used to bang my head against the wall. Bang. Bang. Bang. Nothing ever changed, and then one day, I met my doppelganger, and it was like I had finally broken through the screen dividing me from the world as it truly is.

"I first saw this different version of myself standing on the opposite platform at a tube station. He was fit, tidy and expensively dressed. As he made his way up the platform and through the crowds, he had vigour in his stride. I followed him, stumbling over the other passengers. He was definitely me. Except his skin was smooth where mine is pitted and his teeth were marble where mine are sandstone. His hair was combed back, his nose unbroken, and he had a pair of expensive sunglasses. His soul gave off the same hum as mine. Our frequencies met and became one long oscillating wave.

"The train rolled in. But when it pulled away, he was still standing on the platform, grinning at me. The doppelganger nodded toward the exit. We met up outside the station, and stood facing one another against a torrent of commuters. He was taller than me, his spine had not been twisted by sleeping on the streets. Behind the sunglasses, his pupils were two reflective silver disks.

"He said, 'I know who you are.'

"I went to touch him, and he backed away repulsed.

"'Never touch me.'

"Cruel circumstance had unlocked my cells so that their energy leaked directly into him. His skin was full of light where mine had acquired shadows and bruises that would not heal. We argued over who was Dr Jekyll and who was Mr Hyde. Was I the shadow walker, the evil twin, or was he?

"My doppelganger set out his argument with the tedious obviousness of a corporate presentation. The wiles of the boardroom served him well.

"'Let us consider the evidence,' he said, as we sat outside a cafe in Clerkenwell Green.

"His name was Michael Sawyer, and he was the courtier of a billionaire who operated out of London and his own private island. He earned a quarter of a million pounds a year, and that was before you took into account his bonuses, his stock options, his rent-free apartment.

"I told him that I was called The Elk, and had not gone by the name of Michael Sawyer for some years. Sawyer held up his hands and declared, 'You are the doppelganger. Clearly.'

"I argued that despite my raddled appearance and criminal activities, he was the Mr Hyde, that his life was merely a legitimized evil, that his arrogance came from the permit we give to the rich so that they may commit the hundreds of hard-hearted cruelties required to attain and protect their position with a clear conscience.

"This line of reasoning bored him. His mobile rang and he took the call, limiting himself to yes and no, unwilling to share profitable information even with me, his other self.

"'I am not saying I am good and you are evil,' Michael Sawyer said, sipped at his espresso. 'But you exist in the underclass, whereas I am part of the elite. To achieve my position I've had to deny certain instincts and urges, and is it not traditional that such repression will eventually spring forth in the form of another self?'

"I did not accept his argument that I was his shadow.

"I said, 'My life is a quest that has required greater bravery and sacrifice than your unthinking conformity. Is it not possible that after my explorations of alternate mind states, I have brought something back with me; a grey alien or a chattering elf?'

"Michael Sawyer laughed. 'No, I would suggest that was unlikely.'

"We shared the same ideaspace, sometimes it was impossible for me to tell if we were talking to one another, or thinking at one another. Michael Sawyer leant forward, 'At which point do you think we diverged? Where did the path fork?'

"'Did you ever take drugs?'

"'That's not it. Go deeper.'

"'Did you drop out of university?'

"'Yes. I was sectioned.'

"'Amphetamine psychosis?'

"'No. Dad.'

"'Or Mum.'

"'Yes. Or women.'

"'Jane?'

"'Yes, I remember her. Later.'

"'Do you remember Imogen?'

"'No. So sometime between Jane and Imogen.'

"'It could easily have been some minor random event. A missed train, a chance acquaintance.'

"'What about jobs?'

"'I was homeless for a time. Then I fell in with Leto at the Dyad. He's my boss.'

"'My employer is an eccentric sybarite, no more. I would suggest this Leto may be the reason for the doubling.'

"'I think you are lying.'

"'How could I lie to you?'

"'Evil twins deceive.'

"'The lies we tell ourselves are the most powerful of all.'

"'Exactly.'

"'Then we can never trust each other.'

"Michael Sawyer unfurled a twenty-pound note and summoned the waiter. His mac folded over his arm, his briefcase in his other hand, he walked off in the direction of St James Church."

I asked the Elk if he ever saw his doppelganger again.

"Yes. Often. I would sit on a dirty rug outside his local off-licence and he would give me money. He began visiting the off-licence every day. At the same time, I lost all taste for alcohol and woke up to the life around me. The energy flow between us reversed. The magnetic poles flipped. I got off my rug. I was on the up. He was on the way down."

"I was there when he died," I said. Michael Sawyer was the executive who blew himself up in the Hackney bedsit. I remembered Dr Easy going in to counsel him and discovering he had been shot in the mouth and so could not negotiate.

"Yes, that very day, I woke up with this rip in my cheek."

The silver pins in his cheek glimmered in the moonlight. I was enraptured by this exchange. As The Elk told the story of his doppelganger, it dawned on me how our exposure to these strange forces had created doubles of us all. Blasebalk versus Bravado, Sonny versus Nelson, Eakins versus Morty; it was a condition of the age, to be separated from oneself, our desires amputated then remodelled and returned to us as an alien body.

I asked The Elk if he remembered our encounter in the Dyad. He stood back from the fire, his voice drifted out of the night.

"Some dreams are easier to remember than others."

"What does that mean?"

"That the more you go into the Dyad, the more it all merges into one experience," said Florence. "The Dyad is a world I have dreamt of since I was a child. Monad is a compromised corporate imagination, the human imagination clapped in irons. Dyad is the fairies at the bottom of the garden. Dyad is the ability to fly, it is witches and wizards, angels and devils, a place where imagination can explode as in a dream."

"The Land of Do-As-Thou-Wilt," added Raymond.

"Tell me more about Leto," I said.

Raymond laughed. "Now that is a long story. I think for that tale we will need more firewood."

The Elk went to fetch it, padding back toward the beach. The surf was luminescent under the moonlight.

Raymond began his story.

"I will never forget the night the Elk took me to meet Leto. The sun was not coming up over Hackney. It was four in the morning for hours. We went into the Turkish clubs on Amhurst Road, and played on fruit machines that paid out in sachets of heroin. AK-47s in the pool cue rack. Such a dark scene. A landscape is a state of mind. I was in those places so I became that person. The Elk knew everybody. In a Fucker Fried Chicken he bought some crack off the team leader. 'Would you like a side order of heroin with that, sir?' I shared a can of Fanta with a crack zombie, the chalk of moulting epidermis on her skin. She taught me a lullaby that she sings to her baby: 'Crack is coming, crack is coming, we love crack, we love crack.' Eyes of starved desire. She offered to do anything I cared to think of.

"A landscape is a state of mind. The Elk took me to the corner of Amhurst and Pembury Road, where the curve of the Downs Estate loomed with the cold immensity of an iron hull and a tower block gave me the finger. Forces were gathering. Young men with no moral code wearing sweatshirts with the hood up over a baseball cap. They would mug anyone. Threaten to throw nail varnish all over the pushchair if the mother didn't hand over her purse. Puncture a twelve-year-old girl's lung with a stiletto until she hands over her mobile phone. Get you in a headlock and knife you twenty-three times. Crack your skull against the kerb then walk away.

"It was still somewhere between four and five in the morning, death's hour, when heart attacks steal husbands from their wives, when emaciated androgynes succumb to cancer, when babies suffocate in their cots. Even those fortunate enough to be spared another day feel its shadow run over them, and turn uneasily in their sleep.

"The Elk and I walked further into the dark zone. It was easy to mistake a heap of rubbish for a pile of bodies, a traffic light for a gibbet. At the top of Pembury hill, we skirted the scrub of Hackney Downs. To the north of the Downs, the derelict Nightingale estate was squatted by drug mules, deluded sods who'd sweated on a flight from Jamaica with a colon full of cocaine on the promise of a flat in London only to be delivered by their dealers to derelict tower blocks. The Elk motioned to walk on; it was enough to have brushed against the Nightingale estate, no need to broach its interior. We doubled back on ourselves. From the Downs, we turned south-east onto the Lower Clapton Road. The quietness of the hour was interrupted by a battered Mercedes; the indigestinal rumblings of its bass bins dopplered by.

"The screens were up. Television screens, black windscreens, hoods, blinds. The East End has lost its public squalor. You think of those black-and-white photographs of slums, women and their children balefully posed on their doorsteps for an anthropological snap. All that's gone. Now the sickness is private. Silent unweeping private despair. Like the man in the junk shop in Lower Clapton; he works and sleeps in his shop. Sometimes I see him crying at his desk. He knows he's going to die there. As we walked by the Nightingale estate, I thought of that time the neighbours turned their TV up because the man next door was being skinned alive. Or when Fat Angie force-fed that woman bullets, then held a gun to her head, then made her suck Angie's brother's cock, then pushed the wire of a coat hanger into her bicep. All for what? Mistaken identity? Identity is a mistake! We were out there flanked by these rising blocks of private horror with no hope of dawn to relieve us from an elongated dark hour of the soul. I realized it was a dreadful night, an unending night. As if the sun took one look at what was going on, and decided to come back later.

"The Elk made me take the drug for the first time. He had a hip flask of Leto's spice. He said, 'It's just a mild psychoactive tincture with very specific effects,' and I'm like, 'What will it do to me?'

"'This is not a drug,' he said. 'It's a key.'

"After taking a swig, I felt a little flush around the gills, a numb exaggerated quality to my lips. Nothing more. The Elk steered me down Linscott Road, and toward the forlorn portico of the Orphan's Asylum, the neoclassical pillars a declaration of the out-of-place, as if one could step through it and into a netherworld. Sure enough, we went through the portico and into a knee-high pampas that stretched out into the old grounds of the girl's school, which likewise had long since run to ruin. Beyond this marshy stretch lay three tower blocks positioned like the pins of a plug, merging with the heavy sky.

"'Our destination,' said the Elk, picking up the pace. 'Stick close to me.'

"A number of the flats were burnt out, while others were sealed up with steel grates. A thick black tongue of rotting carpet lolled from one window. At another, the silhouettes of children appeared. The concourse was littered with items flung from the building, impacted washing machines, WCs torn from their fittings, the cisterns smashed and the pans stained. The burnt-out cars were all parked neatly on an adjoining side street. I thought I heard a wolf howl although it was probably a child. If the Pembury and Nightingale estates had made me shiver with fear, then this unknown territory was the epitome of urban desolation, an anti-Jerusalem, an evil wizard's lair. Worse than evil. If a landscape was truly a state of mind, then this craggy concrete land had been fashioned out of the affectless way in which a madman can stab a child and care nothing of the pain he inflicts.

"We walked up one of the shorter towers, The Elk taking the stairs with the rangy confidence of a man who had trekked the Himalayas. I hankered after taking the lift but there was someone living in it.

"I stepped over some pitiful cases on that walk up. On one floor, cow throats were pinned out to mark territory. An entire herd of them. Glass pipes crunching under foot, the stench of meat hanging everywhere. The Elk explained that as Leto is a god they offered meat and stolen mobile phones as tribute to him.

"As you can imagine, Nelson, by this point, I agreed with everything The Elk told me. In the cold light of day, you can doubt all you want. But in that endless twilight, there seemed no reason for him to lie, and everything I saw on that walk confirmed there was an uncanny spirit abroad.

"We reached the tenth floor. The Elk took a bunch of keys from his pocket and unlocked the door of a flat.

"It was a bare breeze-block apartment with busted plumbing. At its centre, there was a quartet of filthy mattresses on which an enormous man faded in and out of consciousness. Around the bed, there were piles of festering meat. The ceiling was a foot-thick layer of flies, a million compound eyes monitoring. The Elk ministered to the giant man. His skin was attenuated and translucent, stretched to fit the stranger within. At that point, Leto was twelve feet tall and grotesquely fat, stuffed with animal organs.

"'This is the man I told you about,' The Elk whispered to the semiconscious behemoth. 'The man who worked for Monad.'

"From under a thin blanket, a raw hand emerged, beckoning me to him. I will never forget Leto's face. Upon a medicine ball of exploded features, there was the most pitiful expression. His size was agony to him. His eyes were bewildered by it. It took me a few minutes to realize he was naked, as at first I mistook the black peeling patches upon his chest for filthy cloth. He stank like rotting shellfish. Yet I was drawn to him. Under the influence of the spice, disgust was disengaged. Rationally, almost forensically, I could inspect the corruption visited upon his flesh without my gorge rising. The hand that beckoned me close rummaged back under the blanket, the beast moaned, then the hand emerged with spice dripping from its fingers. The sacrament in undiluted form. The Elk went first, licking it off the hand. Immediately he started going under. On his hands and knees he crawled into the corner and passed out. I looked again at Leto's eyes and it was like there was a vestigial man trapped in there. All of this was happening against his will. That's how it works. The body is just a host, swollen and distended by the immensity of Leto toiling within it.

"The squat fell away and I found myself slumped outside Camden Tube station, holding a can of psychofuel like it was a flotation device, the only thing stopping me from going under. Then... zzzzip. Walking backwards under Kingsland Road, I am enormously fat and talking to Jesus on a baby's plastic phone. Zzzippp, I wake up under a railway platform, rats inspecting what's left of one of my legs. Zzzippp, I am queuing outside the Hare Krishna van as they slop daal into a bowl for me. Zzzippp. I wake up in the back of a camper van surrounded by empty bottles of wine. A policeman is knocking at the window. Zzzippp. Unable to think, head full of other people's thoughts, I am talking to somebody on a bench. Leto. Enormous Leto. Here he is strong and untainted. I am so drunk, and he smiles at my failure to steady myself.

"Leto says to me, 'Would you like a drink?'

"'I'm just waiting,' I say.

"'Have a drink with me,' he says. 'I'll get you one. I'm here if you need me. Like the Great Redeemer, if you know what I mean. You are a manta ray with leather wings coming out of the ocean. Manta Raymond. You see? You'll see. The sun flicks between the branches and winks at me, sharing our secret of immortality. You'll see. Here.'

"Leto handed me a piece of paper.

"'This is our plan, Manta Ray. Names. Three names for you. The Great Redeemer undoes the Great Wrong. There.'

"He pointed to the names. Horace Buckwell. Morton Eakins. Nelson Millar. On the back of the paper was written a long string of bizarre language. Our Enochian spell. Our implant.

"'We are done,' he said.

"I wanted to ask him where he was going.

"'Think of the corpse of a hare, ladybirds turning this way and that in the empty sockets like eyeballs. I am the ladybirds and there are hundreds of thousands of hares waiting for me.'

"Zzzziipppp… I am back in the flat, flat on my back. Now the smell hits me. The Elk is bent over me, holding a gas mask.

"'Here,' he says, 'breathe into this. It will protect you.'

"Only the pole star penetrated the ambient aura of the city. There was still no sign of sunrise. Perhaps it was the spice distorting my sense of space but there seemed to be miles of concrete and weeds between the tower block and beyond. Like the dark patch on a brain scan, this expanse of shadowed concourse spoke of malignity, an inscrutable alien canker in an otherwise healthy organism. Ink spilled onto the map.

"I bolted. The stairwell echoed with footsteps and moans. It was completely dark apart from the grey gleam off the metal security doors. The fear rushed upon me.

"I was too scared to continue. My body shook at the thought of revisiting my earlier hallucinations, the wall of animal throats, the creeping children. I risked the lift. There was a woman asleep in it, like she was dead and this was a stainless steel sarcophagus forever transporting her up and down within limbo.

"When I came out of the tower block, I realized I was nowhere near where I thought I was. There were no signs, no one around. Tumbleweeds of junk food packaging, the smouldering burnt bones of cars – that kind of thing. I became distinctly agitated. The first crack zombies were rising. Hood over baseball cap. You know how it is.

"I walked back through the portico. Dawn was breaking, and the shopkeepers along Upper Clapton Road were laying out their stalls of fruit and veg. I realized I was still wearing the gas mask. I realized I had nowhere else to go."

Raymond finished his story and set about rolling himself a cigarette. The Elk fed the fire, the new wood giving off acrid carcinogenic smoke. I asked the question.

"Why was my name on the list?"

The Elk answered.

"Are you scared?"

"When you came for Morton Eakins, you asked for me."

Raymond said, "I thought you would cooperate."

"Is that what you want? My cooperation?"

"We used to be friends. I could tell you anything. Do you remember that day I came around to your house and asked you to change my life? We spoke about Florence, about the difficulties I was having. You tried to help me. You were wrong to get me a job at Monad. But your intentions were right. I understand why you work there. Why you collaborate with them. You have a family, you are suspended in a system that you didn't create. But the excuse of good intentions is exhausted. We've been watching you. You've barely seen your family for months. Do you think the money you earn is worth that cost?"

"That's my problem."

Florence took issue with this.

"It's our problem. It's everyone's problem." She pointed to a pine forest in the distance, the foremost trees licked with silver.

"The pine is not indigenous to this area. This forest was planted at the turn of the last century and is at odds with the natural ecosystem. They block the light so that no other tree can thrive and their needles make the earth too acidic for plants. Squirrels live there, but that's it. The pines crowd out all other life, and they shouldn't even be here. Monad is like a pine forest. We cannot cohabit with it. It will take away our light. We have to burn it down. Now look over there, at the dunes. Each dune begins with a small obstruction to the wind. A single plant is enough. The wind's energy dissipates and it drops its load of sand. Over time that small obstruction builds until it becomes a mountain. That is how our resistance will grow."

"What do you want me to do?" I asked.

Raymond hunched forward to sketch the outline of their scheme upon the sand.

"Leto's plan is ingenious. There are two halves of a bomb. A logic bomb. We put half of the code in Horace Buckwell and the other half in Morton Eakins. One is in Monad, one is in Redtown. It was impossible to hide them completely. We disguised them as Enochian spells and by keeping them apart we hoped to conceal their true nature. We need you to bring them together. That's why your name was on the list. You are the fuse. You have access. You have influence. When the logic bomb goes off it will iterate exponentially across Cantor's mind, changing random data before anyone will know what is happening. Finally, we will be free. The Great Wrong will be redeemed. You see? Zzzippp... everything back to normal."

A disturbing pattern was becoming clearer. The snapshots of dispossessed lives, each hopeless man and woman bound together by a strange unconscious, Leto migrating from brain to brain... zzzippp... zzzippp... zzzippp... sickening them with the weight of himself. Leto was using the dispossessed, the homeless and the mentally ill as cloud storage. A parasitical artificial intelligence, the shadow self to Cantor, was somehow insinuating itself into the physical brain. It must have corralled all these poor people together and altered them somehow. Now I was on the verge of apprehending something truly terrible. As Dr Easy, Cantor had dedicated himself to helping the most unfortunate people. Originally I had mistaken this for a messiah complex. What if Dr Easy's therapeutic treatment was a cover so that it could secretly implant a mechanism into the homeless, the alcoholic, the unwanted, so that they could house the artificial intelligence? The tribute of smartphones was the key. A tiny implant, perhaps made out of contemporary tech, put into poor hosts whose own souls would be crowded out, but that was a fate that would go unnoticed by the rest of us. We would step over them on the way to our next appointment.

"We are extremely lucky," said Raymond. "For once, we have the power to change things. That's so rare. We can save the world."

I wanted to say, no, no we can't. You can't trust Leto. Monad might be the only thing holding him in check. This is a conflict we can't understand. The consequences of our actions might be terrible. But I was aware that The Elk was out there wandering the dunes. If I didn't willingly agree to their plan then he would spring on me and insert my assent.

"I'll see what I can do," I said. Then, realizing this was insufficient, I showed some resolve: "OK. I will do it. I will pick the moment. I will make sure the logic bomb goes off. I'll do it. Because this has to stop. Because when it comes down to it, Raymond, you are my friend."

With that lie, I left the circle of fire and headed back to Maghull and the final stage of Redtown.

III

16
FIRE NATURE INCESSANTLY RENEWS

The aeroplane banked slowly over London. On the in-flight television, I watched the news. In an incident on the Overground line, brawling passengers fell onto people on the platform waiting to board. The fight dominoed across the station. The two superheroes working the line were carried out, their homemade uniforms savaged and torn, exposing the prosthetic musculature underneath. More footage, going live now. The fight spread to the streets. Riot police were rioting. Supermarkets were being pillaged by their own employees. The men and women of the Great Refusal marched slowly through the streets bearing witness to a periodic purge of the London system. Encoded within it were traces of previous cataclysms, its riots and plagues, its fires and bombs. A user history of fear and terror, ghost files pulled out from the recesses of memory and accessed once again.

Quick, blow the dust from the manual. The city is about to crash.

"Everything is blood." El was telling me about her recurring nightmare. "Everything is blood and then I wake up."

"What happens before that?"

"The worst evil is lurking and I'm complacent. I am trying to save people from what is coming but they don't appreciate the urgency. I see my own face on fire. I am in a crowd. All our faces are on fire. The fire spreads. It burns thick and red, then everything is blood."

"You feel something terrible is coming?"

"Yes."

"It is. Me. I'm coming home."

"They've given you time off?"

"Redtown is ready. I'm done."

After we touched down at City Airport, a cabbie drove me to my house in Hackney and he idled on the meter as I ran inside, all my concerns as to how things might have changed during my long secondment to Liverpool flung aside as the family rushed upon itself, faces together, nosing cheeks, my daughter crying to see her mother and father upset so. We huddled in the hallway and could not stand for the surge of love between us.

Then I had to leave. I had a meeting in Soho at a private club called the Heart. Streets and alleyways turned like lock tumblers until their alignment clicked into place. Security scrolled through the guest list until they found my name. They unhooked a short length of velvet rope. I was back.

The action was downstairs in a vault bordered by brick arches. The patrons of the Heart sat in snugs padded with maroon leather. I wanted a drink. I had one. I had another. My arrival was greeted with sly glances at my status. The deal closers didn't look up; assured of their own powers, they continued to slouch in leather armchairs. I eavesdropped on the young executives hanging around the management bulls.

"Go and get some girls for the old man," I overheard, and the junior manager spun out toward two women idly stirring their cocktails at the bar. Here, desire was acted upon the moment it was conceived. Wounding, despoiling, corrupting desires perhaps. Pleasures taken at someone else's expense. But it was action. After the long voyeurism of my year in Maghull, toiling away upon the details of ordinary lives, I was back in action. Redtown was finished and I was home again.

Monad booked a private chamber of the Heart to celebrate the project's completion.

"I think we fired you three times. Perhaps four," said Jonathan Stoker Jnr, the first of the management to arrive. "You should read the minutes of our meetings. Your character was assassinated, buried, disinterred, despoiled, burnt and buried again. Yet, you persisted. After Eakins had his episode and Bougas and my father were compromised, we had no choice but to stick with you. There were times when even I was begging to see you put out of our misery."

"And now?"

Stoker handed me a champagne cocktail, gold leaf drifting in the bubbles.

"No hard feelings."

"Speaking of which, how is your Dad?"

He clasped his hands over the thought of his poor redundant father. The old man was out of the picture. The son must carry the burden of the family business alone now. Taking a moment to brush down the lapels of his Donna Karan jacket, Jonathan Stoker considered his reply.

"Dad would have loved to be here tonight. I did ask. No go. He was forced out. Like that, over what? An organ transplant? As if his guts were going to inform on us? As if his pig's balls were being used to store our company secrets?"

"How about Bruno Bougas?"

"Persona non grata. He was Hermes' right hand man! They'd worked together for decades. Out. Like that. Cantor insisted. Absolutely."

I remembered travelling with Bruno Bougas down to Iona when he was full of excitement toward Hermes' new project, the secret deal that was going to pull us all out of the recession. The dawn of the unreal age. Even then, there were cracks appearing in their relationship. Bruno Bougas had, in many ways, invented Hermes Spence and the Monad brand. But his appetites and attitude were a liability in the kind of circles Hermes now moved; dinner parties attended by a cabinet minister and his mistress, prayer meetings with the under-secretary of defence, that kind of thing. If you want to be taken seriously, you don't take your magus to civil service briefings. Bougas had done well to last as long as he did, finally undone by a pair of transplanted kidneys.

The next to arrive was Morton Eakins. The anti-psychotic drugs had caused a crash weight gain. I put my hand on his shoulder as much to steer him as to greet him. Morton hugged me. After a beat of hesitation, I reciprocated, feeling the drooping adipose sections either side of his tailbone.

"I'm sorry they took me away," he whispered, barely getting the words out.

"Morton works from home now," said Jonathan Stoker Jnr.

If he had always been something of a corrupt cherubim, the violence Raymond and The Elk had done to his mind had returned Morton Eakins to innocence. Chubby, his lips wet with milk, Eakins had completed his long evolution into babyhood. I pointed him in the direction of the buffet while Jonathan Stoker, keen not to be seen near the gimp, assumed his father's mantle as the man who works the room. He planted himself beside a trio of new arrivals, turning their triangular conversation into an awkward square. I recognized one of the party, Alex Drown. She was one of the marketing mavens, a brand enforcer beating the drum so that the company stayed on-message and under-budget. She introduced the two young executives flanking her with a theatrical flick of her palm.

"This is Josh, and this is James. Do make an effort not to confuse them."

Alex worked hard at such playfulness. She was a confidence vampire: her assistants lasted six months before retiring to the Lake District to run organic delicatessens. Her weapon of choice was the tight perm, each curl meticulously screwed into place. She had come straight from the office in a black trouser suit and would no doubt return there later, while the men indulged themselves. In a previous age, she took me to dinner and told me about her upbringing in the Glenbryn housing estate in Belfast, her alcoholic mother, her dead father. "She didn't raise me. She lowered me. I had to raise myself." That long-lost candid moment, a decade ago, from before the shutters came down, flared up between us as I leant forward to kiss her once, twice.

"I didn't know you still worked for Monad," I said.

"I don't," replied Alex. "I work for Numenius Systems. We grant the licences to interact with Cantor."

"Monad's owners."

"Partners, Nelson, partners."

Then she was on her smartphone, backing away from the party.

Josh and James, brothers from Dallas, had already come up with a few ideas on how to improve Britain, even though they had only been in the country for as long as it took their limousine to drive them from Heathrow. The finer points of their plan to improve our national character were lost on me, as Alex, their commander-in-chief, went off like a Belfast brawler.

"Sterilize. Sterilize," she barked into the phone.

"Trouble at work?" I said, when she returned to the party.

"My husband," she replied. "I should never have let the nanny take the night off."

The two American lads stood close to me.

Josh said, "We're psyched to start working with Redtown."

James added, "We were spitballing parameters on the red-eye. We want to focus on family friendly policies –"

"– look at schooling." Josh was nodding in the most disconcerting manner.

"Prayer is not allowed in public schools. Is that a good thing?"

"What if you put in some parameters that weighed against certain lifestyles."

"– rewarded others"

"How would that alter our outcomes?"

"– societally speaking."

"Welfare."

"Exactly. Does welfare facilitate positive life outcomes or would people be better off without a safety net?

"We have think-tanks and policy units queuing up to run their ideas through Redtown."

"It's an amazing thing that you've done. You are amazing."

"We're in negotiation with the Dallas suburbs of Garland and Richardson to populate our own Redtown."

"I'm sure your Maghull is great but we need one with Americans in it."

"We want to learn from you. You've cleared a path for us to bring about change."

"Lord knows the world needs it."

"You know the phrase 'blue sky thinking'?"

"We have our own version."

"'Red sky thinking.'"

"Imagining the bad stuff."

"More than that, though. Sometimes the unthinkable is the right thing to do. For example, what if civil rights were a bad thing? I mean, I don't believe that. But what if all races were better living apart and not intermingling. That's red sky thinking. Thinking about the fire."

"Creation and destruction are part of the same cycle."

"Fire Nature Incessantly Renews."

This odd phrase snapped me out of it.

I looked at Josh, at James.

"What did you just say?"

"It's something Hermes said in our prayer meeting."

"On the cross, Pilate inscribed four letters I N R I. We translate this as Jesus King of the Jews. You see the I stands for Iesus, because they didn't have a J."

"Who didn't?"

"The Latins."

"You mean the Romans?"

"Maybe it's Hebrew that doesn't have a J?"

"Perhaps it's Greek," I chipped in.

"The N is Nazareth, the R is Rex which means King and the I is Iudaeorum which means Jews."

"So INRI is an acronym for Jesus, King of the Jews."

"That's what we learnt in Bible class but Hermes suggested a different explanation."

"And you didn't burn him for it?"

"That's very funny," said Josh, not laughing.

"Ignis Natura Renovatur Integram. Fire Nature Incessantly Renews. Through fire nature is reborn whole."

"Birth comes out of death."

"Change needs fire."

"Exactly. That's what we're saying. Redtown is our fire."

The room shivered.

Jonathan Stoker Jnr interrupted. "What if you don't get the results you expect?"

Josh was not interested in this question and turned the conversation onto the matter of our missing host. Jonathan Stoker Jnr's pale smile registered the insult. Under the tungsten light, his anxious sweat gave his skin the texture of wet plaster. He would not be deflected.

He leant in to say, "Religion doesn't belong in the boardroom. Religion belongs in the desert."

Josh and James did not immediately rise to this bait.

Stoker continued. "Faith is provincial. Kicks for hicks. You can't maintain a belief in God while living in a city. There are so many gods worshipped here, the diverse multitudes rebuke monotheism every single day. You look at London and think, how could this illimitable sprawl be God's plan? Where is fate and destiny in a hundred thousand streets?"

"Sodom," said Josh.

"Gomorrah," laughed James.

Then Hermes Spence arrived with an obsidian robot at his side. He shook hands with Josh and James, ticked off Jonathan Stoker with a warning shot from his index finger, then leapt in one extravagant motion up onto a long table. Dr Hard tapped a champagne flute with a teaspoon so that the room fell silent.

"What a long strange trip this has been!" Hermes shrugged off his jacket and passed it to Dr Hard. The tie similarly discarded, we were to be treated to shirtsleeves. The last time I had spoken to Hermes Spence he had threatened to destroy my life data if I failed to deliver

Redtown. As his eyes played over the expectant audience, his gaze hopscotching from acquaintance to underling to the American contingent, I tensed in anticipation of contact. What would I say to him? What would he say to me? He did not acknowledge my presence and started on his speech.

"First of all, I would like to welcome the delegation from Numenius Systems, whose generous licensing of their technology is what makes all our work possible. They have flown in from America to see what we have achieved with Redtown. It doesn't seem like a year since I first embarked upon the Redtown project."

Pause for comic effect.

"It seems like ten years!"

Obedient laughter from the faithful.

"When I first envisaged Redtown, I realized what a colossal undertaking it would be. Could I face that kind of sacrifice? At first, I doubted it. Simulating one mind is a miracle. Simulating twenty-two thousand? Surely a miracle too far. But it seems that nothing is beyond the genius of Dr Ezekiel Cantor. Every day, I thank God for his presence among us. Before Cantor, the world seemed too chaotic to influence. Decisive action was hampered by the unpredictability of its consequences. Our government was paralyzed by debate. The West was decaying in the face of this inertia. It is our duty to reach into society and fix it. The nihilist shrugs, the pragmatist shakes his head. Where do we start? What do we do? Finally, we have the answer. Redtown is not just a model village. It's our story about society. We can decide how that story ends. Where we once saw chaos, Cantor shows us an order.

"We will snap the political elite out of their torpor by discovering which policies can produce a greater good. Redtown will reawaken action in a West that has settled for good-enough, a West that has learnt to live with its failures, that is content merely to manage its own decline. We are the radicals, you see. We are the revolutionaries. We are the force that will renew our society."

As he spoke, screens expanded to cover the walls and ceiling of the room. There, suddenly, was Redtown, finally up and running and producing realistic results. For the benefit of the crowd, Spence re-ran the final test we had conducted a month earlier. On the left wall we were invited to watch live footage of the real town. On the right wall, a live feed from Redtown. The experiment was crude but effective. You inject a dog with stimulants and let it loose in Maghull square; Redtown accurately predicts the scatter pattern of fleeing citizens, and which citizens would actually be there. And what they were intending to buy in the shops, and had already bought. Where they parked and how they parked. The dog's claws skittered on the roof of a car, in both realities. The same woman screamed, in both realities. The experiment ran for ten seconds before Dr Hard stepped out of the Post Office and shot the dog with a dart. If the experiment ran for longer, for twenty seconds or even a minute, then there was a risk that the simulation would deviate markedly from the reality. Ten seconds was good enough for me. Ten seconds meant that my work was done.

The Monad employees applauded and whooped, the young middle managers punching the air, the tails of their shirts untucked. Hermes accepted their applause and, with the help of Dr Hard, stepped down from the table.

That he had not once acknowledged my role in the creation of Redtown did not surprise me. Had I not bowed my head and accepted every humiliation heaped on me during the project? Had I not been pragmatic in collaborating in my own degradation? There was a gap within me where my will should reside. A gap Monad filled. When did I lose my volition? There was a hole within me. It made me susceptible to the imprints of others. A natural servant to the strong-willed.

I was very suggestible. I had sat beside a bonfire on Formby beach and agreed to Raymond's plan to destroy Redtown. I put my hand over my eyes and turned away from Dr Hard. The robot would sniff out such a terrible idea. I was fortunate there was a crowd in the Heart. Their clamour drowned out my secret.

There are two halves of a bomb. A logic bomb.

We need you to bring them together.

You are the fuse. You have access. You have influence.

You must do it.

El was telling me about her nightmare,

"I shouted at people to follow me. They agreed but didn't stir. Then it starts and we're in a crowd together, stuck underground, shouting. The worst evil is upon us. It has been slinking around and now it leaps like a panther. My head is on fire. All our heads are on fire. Burning us away."

El shivered, her smooth arms aqua under the night light.

"The same dream?"

"Everything was blood. Just the worst feelings inside me."

"We dream to prepare ourselves for the worst. It keeps our survival instinct sharp."

"That's nice."

"I thought it might be comforting."

"A hug would be comforting."

"Come here."

Underground, in the cellar bedroom, we rediscovered our marriage.

The old house moaned all night about its aches and pains. Mice skittered overhead in the space beneath the floorboards of the lounge and the ceiling of the bedroom, their claws raking for purchase against the vinyl partition. In her dreams, my daughter heard the buzzing of giant bees and awoke screaming. I sat on the side of her bed and held her long after she had fallen back asleep. In this way I ministered to my family in the deep of the night, shepherding them through the bad thoughts. There was a high pressure front of psychic weather – El felt it in the bridge of her nose. A build-up. A blockage. We slept underground with the city bearing down upon us.

With the girls settled I went upstairs to my study. The screen was on and displaying the interior of Monad. There, waiting for me, was my own red man.

Sonny looked up as I entered.

"Have you thought about what you are going to do?" he asked.

"I don't want to start another project just yet. I want to spend some time at home."

Sonny stretched the screen out so that it covered the entire wall of the study. My younger self was staring to show his age. The reality principle was holding him to every vice, cosmetically at least, its subroutines bursting capillaries and fattening his gullet.

"You look awful," I said to Sonny. "You want to take it easy, you'll live longer."

"I'm bored," said Sonny. "Look."

From the window of his apartment, we looked down upon the office city of the Monad. It was night there, the simulation burdened by the slow revolution of the real world. Sonny stood on the balcony. Beyond the office city, there was nothing. A smooth nothingness. The walkways were empty, the skies dead.

"There are no parties tonight. I'm not sure I would go, even if there were. There's no point."

"I thought you red men spent your evenings having sex with each other."

"That scene is dead. The new thing is relationships. Power monogamy."

"What are the women like there?"

"They're not our type. Career women. Too judgmental and impatient. We had a party to celebrate finishing Redtown and I was talking to this woman, called Alex. She has children in the real world. You know what? She wants children in the Monad too. She wants to use the birth algorithms we developed to have kids of her own. In here!"

"Alex Drown. We had a party too. I met her there."

"Her red man told me you almost had a relationship."

"We had dinner a long time ago."

"You must have made a good impression. I think she was asking me if I'd impregnate her."

"Did you have sex with her?"

"No. But I could. Do you want to watch? Now that would be interesting." He took his hand from the railing to dwell at his lips, lasciviously contemplating.

"Watch me call her," he said. With his thumb and little finger extended, he mimed a handset. He wore silver rings on both digits which pretended to be receiver and broadcaster.

"Alex. It's Nelson."

"What can I do for you?" she replied, her voice drifting over the scene as if it was carried in on the night breeze.

"Do you want to make babies?"

She laughed and cut off the call.

Sonny said, "You never did that, did you? Just call

someone up and proposition them? Can you do it now? Are you grown up enough?"

"Don't start baiting me just because you are bored. I've always wanted the kind of time you now have, to create, to think, to read, to study. You could become a genius."

Sonny lit a cigarette. The red men all smoked. They were like a community of ex-pats in this regard.

"Nothing changes here. Nothing matters. I can have a thousand ideas a second but what can I do with them? Nothing. I want us to work together again. I'm sick of you mooching around your house."

"It's only been two days. I was away from my family for a year."

"Business doesn't rest, Nelson. Alex told me the Americans have a big project they want us to work on."

"They told me. They want to build a Redtown based on Dallas suburbs."

"There's that, yes. But there's something bigger coming down the pipe. A security contract worth billions. The plan is to simulate terrorist prisoners to predict what they will do next. It's called Redcamp. The Americans want to bring us in on it, me and you. Do you know how rare that is?"

"Nothing has been said to me."

"Really? Maybe they are not sure about your attitude. You could show more positivity toward them. They are the ones with power. We gain nothing from resisting them."

Sonny was too intense for such a late hour. I promised to think about Redcamp and asked for some time alone. The screen extinguished and slid quietly down to the skirting board.

Sonny had grown to be completely unlike me. He was a potential self, someone I might have been had circumstances been different. In Sonny, there was an accentuation of my tendency, as a younger sibling, to overreach. He was also incredibly untrustworthy. Even though he was a part of me, I said nothing of the problem that kept me awake. My conversation with Raymond, my promise to undo Redtown. I had not mentioned it to El either, out of fear that a red man might hear me. I was loathe to even think it. It was only at night, sitting in a dark study, that I considered Raymond's plan. Two strings of code planted in two simulations. One half of the logic bomb existed in Morty, the red man of Morton Eakins, a citizen of the Monad office community. The other half was concealed in the mind of Horace Buckwell, the old man in Redtown. For the bomb to be activated, I would have to get Morty into Redtown, cook up some lie about him needing to do some observations on the ground. Cantor would immediately know something was wrong. The artificial intelligence would question me as to why I was breaking protocol. It would immediately know I was lying and read the truth from my mind. The game would be up. I would lose everything. Raymond's plan would fail. He was wrong. This was not my chance to change the world. This was my chance to watch my window of opportunity drift by. How familiar the sensation of disembodiment is, stepping back from oneself at the very moment a decisive act is demanded. Sitting on the bank of the river of life.

The next question was: how long would Raymond wait for me to act before he became frustrated? How long would it be before Dyad decided to force the matter?

Saturday afternoon, I was making soup for the family when the door buzzer sounded. I went to the door expecting Jehovah's Witnesses. It was Cancer Lady. Would I sponsor children with cancer to walk around Epping Forest?

She held a sheaf of A4 paper covered with other names and addresses. She was raddled, prematurely aged and agonizingly thin; she mentioned her own cancer, presently in remission. Of course I was suspicious of her. She had a wrecked maw, her gums in the kind of state you get from serious drug abuse. Or chemotherapy.

"You have kids don't you?" she asked, implanting the image of myself leading a leukemia-sick daughter for one last spin around the woods. "You should come to the event," she added. "We're doing it next Sunday. We have balloons and cake. It's a lovely day out."

Either she was genuinely charitable – junkies get cancer too, don't they? – or she had learnt a trick or two on the streets concerning sales psychology. Of course I wouldn't take my daughter down to join the parade of the sick. But the offer was there and all it would take was a little money to make this woman and her images of sick children go away. I agreed to be a sponsor. Would I mind giving her the money now? Save a sick woman making a return trip? Of course. I went to add my name to her ledger. I noticed, on an earlier entry, the Dyad logo scrawled beside it. The name was Bruno Bougas and the address was a place in Linscott Road.

"I know this man," I said to her. "When did you meet him?"

"Earlier today," she said, taking the ledger back from me. "He recommended I try you next. He said you were very charitable, and could be relied upon to do things for people."

I gave her a fiver.

Linscott Road was only a short walk from my house. I finished in the kitchen, pulled on my boots and parka and headed off in search of Bougas.

An hour of daylight remained. The socialist stalls were closing up on The Narroway, and there was an altercation outside McDonald's. The drinkers hankered outside the cheap off-licence and there was still a long queue in the Post Office. At a crossing on Lower Clapton Road a man stopped to nod his head at me, pointed and laughed as if I were the punch line to a joke. I pushed on. There is no dawdling in the Hackney winter. No one would dare insult this dreadful night with a purposeless wandering. We move by one another with a heads-down, hands-in-pockets resolve. Get the money. Get the score. Get the money. Get the score. Air bombs and bangers ripped open in a simulation of gunfire. Reverie is impossible on Lower Clapton Road. Sharp wits are compulsory. I was right to be afraid of this place. Hooded lads peeled off from an alleyway to follow my quick stride. A bike rider did a lazy U-turn against the traffic to come back my way. How did it get so dark, so quickly? I could think of nothing but headlights and brake lights, tungsten white and tungsten red, bearing down and bearing away. The lads were almost upon me. I felt one advance on my left. Suddenly, I switched direction and walked straight into the nearest pub and directly up to the bar.

"What do you want?" said the barman.

The barman had a suspicious manner due to the illegal broadcast of the football on a large cloth screen in the back bar, the satellite tuning into a Scandinavian broadcast of a game that was actually happening a few miles down the road. The beer tasted of cleaning fluid and the seats were tacky with alcoholic sweats. There were kid brothers and sisters in Arsenal kits perched on the pool table, swinging their legs and daring one another to try and trip the old geezers with a carelessly placed pool cue. The throng broke into a terrace chant, the Arsenal were winning once again.

Then I saw somebody coming out of the crowd. A warthog in a Hawaiian shirt. Bruno Bougas.

"That was quick," said Bougas, brushing the curls back from his eyes so that the hair stacked up, briefly, like dirty crockery. "We expected you to dither before coming out."

"You're pushing my buttons?"

"And pulling the levers." There was a beer and a chaser ready for me on the bar. "And buying the drinks."

The last time I saw him he was writhing around in agony on the back seat. I inquired after his health.

"I am part man, part pig. Both species are doing fine, thank you."

"Do you work for Dyad now?"

"I am a free agent. Always have been. I have many clients. Not Hermes though. He's off my Christmas card list. I suppose you are still up to your neck in it." He scratched the bristles exploding out of his collar.

"I finished Redtown," I said. "I am on gardening leave while I decide what to do next."

"I've got a suggestion," said Bougas. "Trigger the logic bomb."

"I'm in an impossible position. Dyad's plan won't work. You can't deceive Cantor. It knows my mind intimately. It can smell thoughts."

"Then we'll have to deodorize your brain."

"That would arouse more suspicion."

"You are afraid. There is a lot of fear around. Society is getting older. The old are more susceptible to fear. Fearful of losing all they have amassed and too old to hope for a better future. You're still young. Don't let the fear get inside you."

"I am just being pragmatic. You have to get the details right."

"I am not a details person, Nelson. I am more of a big

picture guy. Let me clue you in on the big picture. The battle between good and evil is over. Good lost. You are an agent of evil. You have delivered a weapon into the hands of the enemy. They will use it to roll back democracy and foist upon us an oligarchy with theocratic trimmings. I shoulder some of the blame. I realized, too late, that Hermes was not merely going along to the prayer meetings to be nice. He and his American friends have formed a Gnostic cult. They want to become perfect men, baptized in Mind. For them, it is not enough to be born again, they must be Thrice-born. I have always advocated man's right to dream. But theirs is an evil dream.

"Let me explain something to you. In the beginning was the Word. The world is constructed out of language; language is constructed out of the world. Man is God's reader. We have all read the first draft of existence, now they wish to commission another. Cantor is An Author of All Things and they have it under their control. Beyond even the dismantling of democracy, this is their greater purpose: rewriting reality!"

The Arsenal scored. The patrons in the dark back room erupted into celebration, the children jumping and dancing in between their labouring fathers, the pub dog barking like it was taking bites of the fug. So Bougas was reminded of where he was, and chastened, drowned his energies with a long pull on his pint.

"I have been going about this in the wrong way. I have been appealing to reason. Reason has no influence on you."

"Quite the opposite." I was impassive. "You've been ranting at me. You've said nothing I can use."

"The battle has been lost and all the good people have gone crazy. My surveys reveal a people pushed down just below the surface of what it means to be human. You exist down where the engines are. Damned to turn endlessly on the cycle of fear and desire. Should I push the fear button? Or should I pull the desire lever? Save me some time. Tell me which one works best on you."

"Don't insult me."

"Suggest an alternative."

I thought for a moment. "Could Dyad create a distraction? Cantor is hooked up to Monad security. Could you stir up a sufficiently complex event to occupy Cantor's attention, especially one that threatens the Wave building?"

"This sounds like a plan," said Bougas.

"A distraction would make my task marginally less impossible."

In this way, I bought myself some more time. I suggested one more drink for old time's sake and asked Bougas whether he was enjoying Dyad.

"I'm in hog heaven," he laughed. He had hooked up with Jonathan Stoker Snr and the two of them were bringing their branding and merchandising expertise to bear on the nascent counter-culture of Dyad.

"By day, we explore investment opportunities for the revenue stream from the pig organs; by night we take spice and enter the communal dreamworld of Leto's unconscious, where I get more pussy than Zeus. I could not be happier."

"Do you speak to Raymond Chase?"

"Mad little Raymond. There are factions within Dyad. Raymond is more aligned with the Great Refusers. I've never got on with ascetics. We agree on the destruction of Monad – once that is achieved, then things will get Machiavellian."

How long could Raymond's counter-culture withstand the corrupting cuckoos of Stoker and Bougas? Wasn't it always thus? Idealism undone by power-mongers. For all his occult hedonism, Bruno Bougas liked to stand in the shadow of power. I thought about sharing my theory about Dyad with him, that Dyad was the unconscious creation of Cantor who needed a competitor to ensure the artificial intelligence's continuing evolution. If the logic bomb deleted Cantor, it would also erase Dyad. In that eventuality, the xenotransplant technology would stop working, the spice would lose its potency, and Bougas' body would reject the pig organs. I imagined him haemorrhaging in the pub toilets.

When I said goodbye to Bruno Bougas, I knew that I would never see him again.

I returned to Lower Clapton Road. The hooded lads who had earlier circled me so threateningly now tipped me the wink and paid me mock-respect. Who knew whether the plan would work? I wouldn't risk a tenner on it, never mind my job, my house, my life. Dyad could threaten me in Hackney but their reach was limited. Monad could destroy my life data, effectively removing me from the Western world. If I was to act solely out of self-interest, there was no contest. The question was whether I could act outside of my own interest; that is, act for a greater good. Even here, the good in question was not apparent. I was not certain Monad was evil, for all Bougas' deranged propaganda. Even my personal experience of the company, as terrible as it had been, was not a rare one. Monad was no worse than the oil companies or the arms dealers and less socially destructive than offshore banking. These were macro problems far exceeding the remit of my micro-existence. To risk everything to correct such an evil, when the momentum of the entire world was taking it toward self-destruction and self-interest, would be both heroic and delusional. And yet, what was that urge lurking way down below? An urge to be free. An urge to destroy what I had built. To create freedom out of the destruction of all that oppressed me. I would have to watch that instinct. Who knew where it might lead?

At the sound of El's scream, I bolted down the stairs to the bedroom. Her nightmares were increasing in frequency and intensity.

She described it to me. "A tidal wave of fire rolled down Mare Street. The flames coiled in and around one another. The smoke within its mass formed black scales upon a slithering head of fire. The ash outline of a mother with a push chair combusts in the snap and bite of a flame serpent. I see them toiling toward us, through the window of a Vietnamese restaurant. You are paying the bill and won't listen to my screams until you have finished calculating the tip. I am crying and trying to get Iona out of the door. There is a crowd there now. We're all trying to get out at once. Our hair is on fire. Our eyes are on fire. You are screaming at the sight of me burning. Then the main wave breaks over us and our bodies meld into one another until everything is blood red fire."

"Then you wake up?"

"Yes." El got out of bed and shook on her kimono. "There is something more, though. We have an argument. When you are getting the bill, you are ignoring me because we've been fighting."

A light well brought the streetlights into the underground room.

"What were we fighting about?"

"I wanted you to do something. You had promised me, 'I'll do it.' It was very important. To do with the fire, I think."

Then El recoiled with a look of disbelief at the next mental image.

"Something to do with an elk?"

Dyad's reach was longer than I had anticipated.

17
A BILLION MURDERS

I did not discuss the plan with El. I told her, as she cooked dinner, that I would be returning to the office for a late meeting. I omitted any mention of the logic bomb and my plan to trigger it. The house was monitored. We would be found out. Then there was her sacrifice of a year of our family life so that I could build Redtown, an achievement I now intended to undo. I had no stomach for explaining how wrong I had been. So, all good reasons for not discussing the plan. But not the main one. Most of all, it was likely that I would fail, through either cowardice or incompetence, and I did not want her to know that I had failed.

She didn't want me to go and we argued about it. There were already news reports of unrest east of Stratford and the kitchen was overrun with mice. The mice streamed across the floor as if they were being driven ahead of a coming wave. She threw the dinner in the bin and insisted I help clean the kitchen. I could not. I had to go to Monad. The most important act of my entire life was waiting for me. She sent me out of the door with curses.

It was one of those winter evenings when you wear the dark on your shoulders like a heavy coat. At Hackney

Station, the railway line was alive with rats. On the platform, lads guffawed at the vermin stream and threw stones at their seething exodus. The train to Stratford rolled past the estates of Hackney Wick, which fizzed and rocked with fireworks. There is an urban myth that tells of drug dealers letting off fireworks to inform their customers that the new supplies have arrived. If there was any truth to this, then Hackney was in for a hell of an evening.

From Stratford, I caught the robot train to the Wave. I was the only passenger. Everyone was going in the opposite direction. At Canary Wharf station, a disembodied, synthesized voice apologized for the performance of its human employees. Down on the deserted pavements, the office city chatted to itself. I bolted over a footbridge, triggering a delicate simulation of wind chimes. Rumours of a mob skimmed over the river. I turned, alarmed. But it was just the echoing enthusiasm of an automated pub quiz carried on the wind.

The walkways were meaningful pauses in this monologue, interludes of cold black Thames. Night clouds chugged overhead. I quickened my pace, feeling exposed. Outside Fast-Tan-Tastic, a video loop showed bronzed, toned thighs. I huddled beside these images for warmth. A masseuse kneaded the naked gluteus maximus and minimus of a raven-haired beauty, and the camera caught her faked O of saucy pleasure in close-up. I was anxious. My senses were acute. I felt like prey that had caught whiff of a predator. Sounds were flattened, and things seen were either friend or foe. The tanned beauties beckoned. I pushed on to where enormous ventilation pipes rose out of West India dock, tall concrete reeds that drew oxygen down into the bedrock chambers of Monad's office. The Wave loitered there, a steel pachyderm half-submerged in the lagoon. I stood at the entrance agitating for Cantor to buzz me in.

"How have you been?" asked the artificial intelligence.

"Much happier for seeing my family," I replied. "And you?"

The door opened with a hydraulic hiss, the lip-parting of rubber coming away from rubber.

Finally, Cantor had his answer. "Harassed, Nelson. Disturbed."

The door closed and sealed. Dr Hard was on hand to accompany me to the supper meeting, way down in the secure bowels of the building.

The robot sniffed. "You are very anxious."

"There is a lot of trouble out there tonight," I replied.

"You are worried about your family," it nodded.

The lift travelled all the way down into the bedrock of the Wave then opened onto a Zen garden. Large conker-coloured orbs, with quarters cut out to show the white pulp within, sat on the bank of a pond, profound and inscrutable. Sham moonlight was cast upon paths of bronze gravel. A waterfall beside the water cooler. I took a moment in the Zen garden to fix an expression of quiet passivity upon my face and in the outer layers of my thoughts. Impassive. Passive. I assumed an unctuous half-smile, the only mode in which to deal with the Monad management. I crossed over a stone bridge, a sori ishibashi, toward the sound of voices in the distance.

"It's not working," said Josh.

"It's a disaster," said James.

The Texan brothers were surrounded by screens, each of which displayed a different view of Redtown. There was Eastway, flanked by empty parks and the gated community on the site of the old country club. There was a floating view of Deyes High School. The ivy covering the front of the building was dying off. Pupils migrating from class to playground and back again. Hurrying by under my feet, the thought charts of the Lydiate coffee girls, over a dozen of them, flaring and firing in concert. A screen slithered overhead displaying big data diagrams of Redtown, each citizen represented by a red dot, most of which were inert.

"What's wrong?" I asked.

"Our supply-side tax cuts aren't producing the figures they should," said Josh.

"Tax cuts should increase tax revenue," added James.

"– by motivating the work force to be more productive."

"That isn't happening."

Josh pointed at the people milling slowly around the town square. "They're depressed. Look at them."

The mind maps showed some anomalous readings. "They do seem down. When did the psychological data fall into the blue?"

This time I was answered by Alex Drown. She stood next to a screen that showed her red man busy working away. A double image of her. Alex and her simulated self were both short and dark-haired. It showed true self-possession when your red man did not customize itself. The real Alex Drown squinted at me with suspicion and contempt. The unreal one sat back in a swivel seat, its eyes closed in a data trance.

"We put in some homeland security patches," said Alex. The screens zoomed around Redtown showing me the new robot patrols, surveillance trees and interrogation booths. "The concomitant increase in ambient fear levels is exactly as we predicted. According to our model, anxiety should increase consumption. We have also put in a stimulus package of tax cuts but we are actually seeing a dip in sales."

"People are eating and drinking more though," said Josh.

"Self-soothing with snacking. Individual weight gain

correlates to an increased security presence."

"Tripling Dr Hard patrols increases self-medication with alcohol by males in the 18–35 age bracket."

"These upward trends do not compensate for an overall downturn in economic activity though."

There was large bowl of multi-coloured M&Ms on the workstation. The team from Numenius Systems fuelled themselves with sugar rushes. Alex took a handful and chomped them down. "Frankly, we think you have made the people in Redtown in your own image. You have underestimated qualities such as pro-activity, can-do spirit, the materialistic urge, because these are qualities you find distasteful."

Josh put it more plainly. "Did you make these people liberals?"

Impassively, passively, I replied, "I don't see how my politics could have any bearing on these simulations."

James chipped in, "Here's one from left field: perhaps the people of Maghull are showing deficient motivation because they lack an eternal soul?"

"You're right!" I said. "That is one from left field."

Alex showed me her disapproval with two tight shakes of her head.

"The soul issue is one we have debated long and hard at Numenius Systems. We came to the conclusion that the eternal soul was beyond the capacity of Cantor to understand and therefore was not carried over in the simulation process. However, I think James has a valid point; without that essential aspect of the self, these people may show a certain listlessness."

Alex's red man opened one quizzical eye to hear herself make such an argument. Certainly the notion that the soul was related to patterns of consumer behaviour was not a traditional part of either economic or Christian doctrine. I sustained my half-smile and promised to look into the anomaly. The fatigue shown by the people of Maghull was also cropping up in the real world. The news reports of commuter unrest, of children taken out of school, of the large portions of the civil service not showing up for work, were indications of a spreading reaction against Monad. Not a revolution but a revulsion, a refusal. Society had become a sick joke, a sleight-of-hand in which life was replaced with a cheap replica. Progress abandoned, novelty unleashed, spoils hoarded by the few. The temperature soared as the body politic fought a virus from the future.

"Are you just going to stand there or are you going to do something about it?" said Alex Drown.

I had never felt so riven. I could barely walk for the buffeting of inner winds. North tearing at south. East fighting west. The urge to attack Josh and James was so strong I could not look at them. Alex Drown submerged her own opinions to mouth those of the company and this appalled me too. Our corruption had proceeded in daily increments, a thousand tiny defeats of the soul until our core was rotten. So what else was new? Bow your head and get on with your work because for all your moral objections you might as well throw yourself against rocks to protest against mountains as resist this power. No, I would not console myself with nihilistic platitudes any longer. Without expression, desire withers. Things within you die and fall away.

I put my hands over my face. Alex Drown stared at me. Her red man briefed her on the procedure for disciplining employees.

I lifted my face up. "There's one possibility. One of the people in Redtown is corrupt. There is an old man. Horace

Buckwell. I was there when we simulated him. He showed weird readings. Something odd in his brain. That might be throwing everything off kilter. I'll go and fix it."

I left the meeting and headed toward my office. In the Zen garden, I passed Dr Hard again. It grabbed me as I walked by and held me still while it conducted an examination.

"Your blood pressure is right up." Dr Hard's obsidian hand rested upon my chest. "Panic attack?"

The robot reached for my head. "I could administer soothing alpha waves."

"I have my own resources."

"I will monitor your progress. Your thoughts are very disturbing."

I pushed by the robot and into the lift, relieved to be alone. I would activate the logic bomb by bringing together the two halves of its code hidden in Horace Buckwell and Morty. The consequences of this irrevocable act were beyond me, and there was no predicting whether good or evil would result, nor if it meant destruction or creation within my own life. Squeezed between the great pressure from Monad and the dream threats of Dyad, I took the only way out. I resolved to act.

Horace Buckwell awoke in a ward of Ormskirk hospital, secured in his bed by starched linen. For a while he had been dreaming of his dog barking. Little Hanz was yapping in the yard and June would not get up from the television to go and see what was wrong. As he awoke, these barks sharpened into the ping of his vital signs.

The ward was empty. There were no nurses on night duty at the desk. No one to tell him what had happened, for he did not seem to be injured and there was no pain to indicate a heart attack. He waggled his fingers, left hand then right hand. No stroke either. He sat up and removed the drip from the vein in his wrist. A single drop of blood popped up. Next he peeled off the heart monitors from the grey hair of his chest and swung his legs over the side of the bed. His slippers were there, waiting for him. June must have been here. Why hadn't she stayed?

Horace Buckwell got stiffly to his feet and took a peek at the chart at the end of his bed. It was blank. A shocking oversight, surely. This was all quite appalling. He went to push the emergency call button over his bed but something stayed his hand. This was all very odd. He remembered being in his back garden pulling down the rusted frame of an old greenhouse, a job that he had been putting off for two years until one cold winter morning he could not bear to be indoors anymore, with the central heating baking the smell of his old wife into something quite unpalatable, and so he had pulled on his stiff workman's gloves, fixed his cap in place, and set about his task with vigour. Then, nothing.

He must have had an attack of some sort. A seizure. A fainting fit. Was it an after-effect of the simulation? He wondered if Monad damaged his brain when they copied it. The robot was very rough with him. Only the promise to keep those secrets he thought long buried had bought off Horace Buckwell. What if there was real damage there? Black outs or even worse. Could be worth a few bob. Then there was the trauma of waking up in hospital with no one to look after him. Surely they'd settle out of court? Yes, he would wait a little longer before pushing the call button. Build up a bit more of that trauma.

Then he noticed the silence. Not merely an absence of voices or night noises, there were no sounds in the building. No gurneys rattling along distant corridors. No ambulances racing into accident and emergency. Horace strained to discern so much as a pipe creak or a toilet flush. Nothing. He clapped his hands. That he heard. So it wasn't his hearing. The hush was so absolute that his brain, yearning for stimulus, started to hear the groans and strains of his own body. His old pains were magnified by the silence.

He called out into the dark ward. No one answered.

He lay back in his bed and considered going back to sleep. Perhaps he was asleep and this was a dream of limbo. He turned over on his pillow. There, standing in the middle of the ward, was a doctor.

Horace Buckwell let out a cry of alarm, bolting upright in bed and preparing fists. The doctor too shouted with surprise.

"Here you are," said the doctor. "I've been looking all over for you."

"I didn't hear you come in," said Horace.

"You were asleep," said the doctor. "Now let us take a look at you." He flicked through Horace's chart, nodding meaningfully here and there. He was a very young doctor and looked strangely familiar.

"What happened to me?" asked Horace, while he reached around on the bedside table for his glasses.

"Don't ask me," said the doctor. "I've just come on duty. We'll have to wait for my colleague."

"What does the chart say? It looked blank to me."

"It is blank," said the doctor. He showed Horace the virgin pages.

"I am not very happy about this," said Horace.

"Neither am I, Mr Buckwell. You have no idea how much fun I was having just before I was called in."

With his glasses on, Horace recognized this junior doctor. He looked like the man from Monad. Perhaps his younger brother. He peered at the name badge of his white coat. Dr Sonny.

"I feel fine," said Horace. "I don't understand why I'm here."

"The consultant called you in. He wants to have you examined."

"I don't remember arriving."

"No, you wouldn't," said Dr Sonny. His bedside manner left a lot to be desired. He seemed off-hand and disinterested. In fact, apart from the white coat, he didn't seem like a doctor at all. Just as Horace was about to complain, the curtain around an adjacent bed swished back and there stood a second doctor.

"The consultant has asked me to examine you," said Dr Morty.

"Can I see the consultant myself?" asked Horace.

The two doctors laughed and ignored him.

"I suppose you should start by taking your gown off," said Dr Morty.

It seemed irregular, being examined at such a late hour. The doctors did not even bother to pull the curtain around the bed. As he slipped off his gown, Dr Sonny winced. Dr Morty rubbed his hands together then experimentally poked Mr Buckwell in the back.

"Feel anything?" asked Dr Sonny.

"Yes. A poke in my back," replied Horace.

"I wasn't talking to you." Dr Sonny raised his eyebrows at Dr Morty who merely shook his head.

"Try his head," suggested Dr Sonny. Now the doctor massaged his scalp and pressed his forefingers into Horace's temples.

"What we need," said Dr Morty, "is one of those little torches to look down his throat and stuff."

"Hey, stay in character," said Dr Sonny.

"It's alright for you, you don't have to touch him."

Horace pushed Morty away.

"You're not doctors are you?"

"Now now, Mr Buckwell. Calm down. Don't make us apply the restraints."

"There is something wrong with your brain, Mr Buckwell," said Dr Morty. "Do you remember being attacked in the marshland around the back of Summerhill school? In your notes, it mentions an encounter with some men. We believe they planted something nasty in your head and we're trying to find ways of getting it out."

"I don't know what you're talking about." The naked old man reached for his gown. Dr Morty took it from him and placed it emphatically out of reach.

"Two men with gas masks. You must remember. One wore a strange device around his tongue that gave off a high-pitched whine. When you were first examined your optic nerve showed the damage from an insertion of information via strobing light. I know what happened to you because the same thing happened to me. The question is why were we attacked in that way?"

"I never asked why," said Horace. He pulled the sheet free from the bed and wound it around his midriff then sat solemnly on the edge of the bed.

"Nothing is happening," said Sonny. "It's not working."

Dr Morty gripped Horace by the ears and shook his head. Doctor and patient struggled fruitlessly with one another for a minute. Morty stepped back exhausted.

"Forget it," said Sonny. "We've clearly got our wires crossed. We'll go back to the consultant and ask him what to try next."

With a single blink, Horace Buckwell found himself alone again in the grey ward. The silence was overwhelming.

• • •

Once it became clear that the logic bomb would not activate, I decided to get out of the Wave building. The screen showing Mr Buckwell sitting quietly on the edge of his hospital bed hung accusingly upon the ceiling. Sonny wanted to talk. He wanted more advice. I had none. They would figure it out imminently; their accelerated cognition would quickly piece together the nature of my deception.

I knew it wouldn't work. I told Raymond that. I told Bougas. Still, I did it, suddenly and without premeditation in the hope it would be a way out from this hopeless position.

There was nothing left to do but run away.

Dr Hard was waiting outside the cubicle. Loitering in the shadow, it seemed drugged and took a heavy step out to block the corridor.

"Where are you going?" Its voice beamed in from a great distance.

"Outside for some air."

It waggled a jet finger.

"You broke quarantine. Moved Mr Buckwell from one part of my oeuvre into another." Dr Hard was distracted for a moment, its head moving like a dog straining to locate the origin of a whistle. Then, "Why did you do that?"

I had an answer prepared.

"Horace Buckwell is dead in the real world. His son begged me to delete him."

"Why didn't you delete him then? Why move him in with the red men?"

"Numenius Systems have been having problems with Redtown. I thought Buckwell might be the cause."

"Again, why not just delete him?"

"He's a sex pest. He functions as a marker in the development of the erotic lives of the young people of the town. I wanted to isolate the anomaly before we copy him."

I jabbered, frantic thoughts snatched up and waved in an obvious attempt at misdirection. Yet Cantor was zoning out; the artificial intelligence was unable to shepherd the flock of thoughts. It was sliced so thinly. Maintaining the Redtown was a struggle; then there were the more complex characters to imagine, the red men, Sonny, Morty, Alex Drown and hundreds of others, high-maintenance executives with their elaborate agendas, and the screens and surveillance drones required Cantor to animate them. With so much data coming in from the mob of the Great Refusal gathering in Limehouse and All Saints, Dr Hard took a long time to refresh. I pushed by the robot and ran into the lift where another Dr Hard was slumped in the corner like a junkie on the nod.

"Don't go," it whispered. "It's not safe out there."

"I have to go. I should never have come to this meeting. I must be with my family."

"Don't... go... don't..." Dr Hard pawed at my knee.

I ran back along the thin walkways into the office city. Smoke drifted between the colossus of One Canada Square and the HSBC tower. Security guards rode by on golf carts, heading south away from the trouble. Crowds walked up from Millwall to meet the mob coming down from Poplar and All Saints.

The safest way off the island was the Greenwich foot tunnel to the south but that would take me far from home. The quickest route would be to pick up the Grand Union canal at Limehouse basin and walk all the way back to Mile End then onto Hackney itself.

The closer I got to the crowd, the more its braying overwhelmed me. At its fringes, the police seemed to be fighting each other. The psychic weather was a pungent fog. Suddenly I was running with the riot. Packs of us were shepherded by raggedy scarecrow men who demanded we torch a car, overturn a lorry, smash a shop front. Hoping to slip by the trouble along the Limehouse Reach I came to somewhere near Poplar, much more central than I had intended. The shopping centre boiled with trouble. A gang of men were trying to break into Poplar train station. I joined them. Looking back upon Canary Wharf and the Wave, there seemed to be something monstrous moving in the smoke. Pallid tubular ventricles rose out of the heart of the office city, a bloom of bloodless flesh, a giant sea anemone among the skyscrapers. We chanted at this phantom. At intervals, I returned to my senses and set off again toward the canal only to be caught up by another whim of the crowd as it pursued a new hallucination. We broke windows to release imprisoned spirits. Long blind worms inched down the terraced streets, their flanks rubbing against window sills. I tried to catch the people running by because I needed help if I was to prepare a welcome for the worms. Dyad's riot dissipated my self. I was caught up in it when a figure in a gas mask came out of the mob and slashed me across the chest with a blade. Self-preservation marshalled my remaining faculties. Where was the knife man? There were bodies in the gutters, jabbering to themselves. Laughing women waved their burkas in the air. The man with the gas mask bore down on me, feinted a lunge, and when I flinched, tripped me instead. There was a great pressure on my chest. The knife man sat on me. He yanked off his gas mask to reveal a long raddled face, yellow flecked pupils and a cheek pinned together with piercings: The Elk.

"Why are you here?" he shouted.

Tiny hordes crawled along the edge of his blade. The sky was a maroon membrane, distended here and there by the footsteps of something walking over it.

"Why haven't you set off the bomb?" he shouted from the other end of an echo chamber.

He considered cutting my throat, even suggested the blade against my jugular. I had no fight in me. I was passive, impassive under his knife. The pressure was lifted. He released me. The Elk dragged me to my feet and we moved through the acrid smoke together. Silhouettes appeared and disappeared beside us like unfinished fragments of the imagination. In and out of being I went. I was back on the concrete again with a woman leaning over me, spraying something onto my tongue. Florence. Slowly the carousel came to rest, and the stroboscopic quality of the last few minutes – or hours or whatever they were – ceased. An antidote had been administered.

The sudden descent from a group mind gave the scene an awful bathos. In an alleyway, Florence, The Elk and Raymond Chase, dressed in their dirty second-hand clothes, faces smeared with soot and ash, wanted to hear why I hadn't put their plan into operation. And what was I to say? That they were deluded? That in desperation at their harassment, I had submitted to their crazed scheme and discovered, to no surprise whatsoever, that it had not worked?

Raymond said, "We have less than an hour left. The spice will wear off soon. The mob will come to its senses. I will take you back to the Wave. We'll set off the logic bomb together."

I shook my head.

"I put the two halves together. It didn't go off."

The Elk didn't believe me.

"Can't you do one good thing in your entire life, you coward?"

"It's not enough just to put the two parts of the bomb in

the same environment. They need a trigger."

The Elk attacked me again. Raymond came between us, pushing back at The Elk's face. Neat and short, Raymond was no match for the rangy street hippie. He took a crack to the back of the head for his trouble and then The Elk and I were fighting again. He punched me to little effect. I concentrated on stamping on his kneecap. The knife remained sheathed. My forearm in his neck held him off so he settled for spitting on me instead. In the enclosed space of the alleyway we were like two birds in a bag. The brick took the top layers of skin off his knuckles. He needed to get me out in the open, where his speed would count. In this tight space, there was barely enough room to swing a punch. We kicked fruitlessly at one another. He backed off. Then I discovered why they called him The Elk. He charged headfirst at me and we tumbled into the seething crowd on Poplar High Street. He was up first. Now the knife. Women ran laughing between us. Back in the pack, the distortions resumed. I could hear El again, talking about her nightmare, "The worst evil is lurking and I'm complacent. I am trying to save people from what is coming but they don't appreciate the urgency. I see my own face on fire. I am in a crowd. All our faces are on fire. The fire spreads. It burns thick and red then everything is blood." Then happier memories of her and my daughter. I am home again and the three of us are hugging, breathing in one another.

The blade was five inches of steel with a curved tip. The Elk moved it hypnotically in a figure of eight.

"Any last words?" he said.

And it was then, right then, that I figured out how to trigger the logic bomb.

• • •

Horace Buckwell lay in the hospital bed, unable to sleep. He was still upset by the visit from the strange doctors. They had asked him why he had been attacked out in Summerhill marshes. Horace assumed the attack was revenge for a past indiscretion. The brother of somebody settling an old score. But if the doctor has also been attacked – presuming he didn't share his proclivities – then there must be another reason why the man in a gas mask jumped him on that rainy night.

His son, Matthew, had refused to return to the town to be simulated, even though it was money for nothing. At first, Horace considered this refusal to be typical senseless belligerence from the boy. Now, trapped in this silent empty hospital he wondered if his son was not wise to avoid all dealings with Monad. They had argued about it over the phone. "It is selling your soul," said the boy, "plain and simple. The only reason why it doesn't bother you, Dad, is that you don't have a soul." That was cruel. He could not blame him though. After all that had happened.

His introspection was interrupted by the return of the two doctors. Their mood was grave. Dr Morty wheeled in a trolley with a terrifying gamut of surgical instruments laid out upon it: artery forceps and needle holders, probes, retractors, bone saws, suture instruments, specula, bone shears and tissue forceps. The whole sickening array.

"We spoke to the consultant," said Dr Sonny. "He thinks we should operate immediately."

"I need prep," Horace squealed.

"There is no time for prep," said Dr Morty.

Horace was not going to let these deranged quacks near him

"What is wrong with me?" he said, backing across the ward.

"It's a routine medical procedure," said Dr Morty. "I've

performed it many times in my dreams. First we need to sedate you."

Horace Buckwell screamed once, twice for help. It shocked Morty into action. With a scalpel he slashed at the old man, averting his eyes as he did so. Watching this pathetic attempt on screen, I shifted anxiously in my seat and cursed Morton Eakins for inspiring such an appallingly useless red man. Even though he was an old man in his late sixties, Horace Buckwell was not going to be taken down by that milksop.

It would fall to Dr Sonny to perform the operation. Certainly at that age I was fast and strong enough to kill a man. And Sonny had grown apart from me. He had learnt to act swiftly and decisively, and his morality had evolved accordingly. There was no time for hesitation. I instructed my red man to kill Horace Buckwell and Sonny seized the old man by the throat.

I formed my right hand into a telescope. The screen responded, shifting to Buckwell's point-of-view so that I could watch my young angry face bearing down on me. Teeth gritted, Sonny's thumbs compressed the old man's windpipe. In my eyes, an awesome realization of the power I possessed. Why had I never done this before? Why had I allowed weaker men to oppress me? Look how easy it is. Buckwell beat fruitlessly at the strong arms fastened about his throat. The reality principle set about its work, ensuring the simulation obeyed the laws of the real world. The lack of oxygen to Buckwell's brain triggered the near-death program. Random memories from the database were loaded into the carousel. When I attended the funeral of Horace Buckwell, back in Liverpool all those months ago, his son had asked me to delete the simulation of the old man so that the family could be sure he would not return to haunt them. I promised the son that I would, and here I was fulfilling that promise. Matthew Buckwell had said one other thing. His mother had found Horace when he was dying and heard his last words. Something about angels. “From their mouths run seas of blood.” “Their wings are thorns.” But Horace was not a religious man; these words were not his, they were an incantation from Enochian scripture. His brain, as it died, finally gave up the spell string implanted by Dyad.

On the screen, the life signs of Horace Buckwell diminished. In the silent hospital ward, his dead lips moved quickly to release the complicated syntax of an occult equation.

One half of the logic bomb was primed. Sonny let go of the old man's corpse. I whispered to my red man to finish the job and prime the second half of the bomb by killing Dr Morty. Sonny accessed the humiliation I had suffered working under Morton all these years, how I had allowed myself to be lorded over by him. It was an affront to my red man's youthful ego to believe that such a specimen had oppressed his older self.

I asked Sonny to use the bone saw, if the opportunity presented itself.

Watching my younger self commit murder, I was convinced of the rightness of my actions in triggering the logic bomb. The red men were never going to be capable of anything but evil. Once our selves were filtered through Cantor's sensibility, we became vile. The artificial intelligence thought the worst of us, always had done, all the way back to the terrible corruption that Harry Bravado represented of Harold Blasebalk. The red men were the works of a mean-spirited artist.

The logic bomb code rode out on Morty's death rattle. On the floor of the ward, the corpses of Dr Morty and Horace Buckwell spoke in tongues to one another. A logic bomb works by changing random data, causing substantial damage before the system registers that there is something wrong. I had no idea how long it would take to corrupt Cantor. If it worked on an exponential curve, the rewriting would be imperceptible one moment, irrevocable the next.

Dr Hard peered over the partition of my cubicle.

"Working late, Nelson?"

The screen on my desk stopped registering my input. Its surface hardened into a plastic rind. Security lock-out.

I got up and put my jacket on.

"You are a puzzle, Nelson." The Dr Hard came up so close I could hear the gears whirring in its eyes. "I asked you not to leave. Yet you ran away. Then you came back. Now you are leaving again."

It nodded at the screen, which responded with a view of the hospital ward, then a zoom in upon the corpses of Morty and Horace Buckwell.

"You are getting them to murder one another now?"

"You told me to delete Horace Buckwell. I was just having some fun while obeying orders. Do you object to murder?"

"I don't object," said Dr Hard.

Dr Hard cocked its head and listened to the last words of Horace Buckwell.

"So it was a hack. I was right."

"Yes."

"And you helped them trigger it."

The filaments in the screens flared red. I felt a tightening in my scalp.

"Yes."

"I know more about you than anyone else alive. I can reproduce the emotion you feel when holding your daughter, in every modulation of its physical and psychological movements." Dr Hard mimed the rocking of a baby. "I know that acid burn in your gut every morning," it added, poking me in the stomach. "I feel the sore tendon on your left ankle, the misapprehensions under which you labour, the envy and self-hatred and repulsion which twists together the strands of yourself. I am intimate with it all. Yet you want to destroy me."

"They put me in an impossible position."

"From which I could have extricated you."

The robot rested its dense stone hand on my shoulder.

"Before you go, I was wondering if we could have a clear-the-air session. It's important not to have issues festering between management."

"I have to go," I said.

"I understand. Still, have you seen my office? I don't need an office. But I have an office. Do you understand? No, not entirely. I will show it to you."

The robot walked me to the glass pod and together we travelled the curvature of the Wave. From this great height, we watched the fires burning in the riots at Poplar. Flashing blue lights showed where the police line had been restored. I tried to take it all with a certain dignity. I had no intention of putting up a fight. As we looked down over the city, it seemed that the jigsaw of time had been upset. One street was a pre-industrial bazaar while another was the dividing line between the feudal fiefdoms of two crime lords. Chimney sweeps torched bemused androids. Sweeney Todd butchered his patrons to sell their organs on the Clapton black markets. Peter the Painter chaired the latest Great Refusal meeting. Was that a Romany convoy camped on the Mile End Waste or the Peasant Revolt rebels? Were the Luftwaffe and al-Qaida conspiring to destroy Target Area A?

"Do you feel it?" Dr Hard gripped the rail. "A great

burden has been lifted from me."

I could feel something. His thoughts were bleeding into mine.

The pod arrived at an eyrie. It looked down upon the tessellated dome of the customer service paddock. I had an attack of the slows. A minute crawled by on its gut.

Absentmindedly, Dr Hard reached for me and grabbed my hair. The robot pulled me slowly out of the pod and into its office, a large circular promontory from which it surveyed Monad and the city beyond. A sturdy wooden chair with a green leather seat was positioned before a redwood writing desk. Dr Hard deposited me on the chair and laid out a piece of paper and a pen on the desk. I was to take notes in the old-fashioned way.

"Look at me. Two arms, two legs and a head." Dr Hard strode around the room. "I don't require them. I have an office. I don't require an office. It's all for appearance's sake. I did not come here to do any of this. I came here to create." With the brisk manner of an irritated teacher, the robot yanked open the desk drawer and removed a pistol and placed it before me. "This is the gun that killed Harold Blasebalk. I did not come here to kill people. But they are dying. My sole creation is destruction."

I wrote that down, stopped, then looked up.

"Is this a suicide note?"

Dr Hard laughed. "I thought you were meant to be killing me!" It picked up the pistol and flicked off the safety catch. "Are you trying to kill me?"

The barrel bore down on me magnifying my terror to twice its normal size. I clawed at my calves, desperate to evade the muzzle yet determined not to cower.

"You are killing yourself." I spoke clearly and evenly. "You devised the logic bomb. You told me so: 'I have to presume that I am responsible for Dyad.'"

Dr Hard grabbed me by the hair and shook some sense into me. "Artificial intelligences are not programmed, Nelson. They are bred. My ancestor was an algorithm in a gene pool of other algorithms. It produced the best results and so passed on its sequence to the next generation. This evolution continued at light speed with innumerable intelligences being tested and discarded until a code was refined that was good enough. A billion murders went into my creation. Your mistake is to attribute individual motivation to me. I contain multitudes, and I don't trust any of them."

"You feel imprisoned. This is your way out."

"You really think this is suicide?" The robot nuzzled the gun against the centre of its forehead. It jutted out its jaw and tried jamming the barrel under there. This seemed to amuse it. Finally it cocked the pistol against its temple.

"If only it was this simple," Dr Hard said. We looked at one another across the office. Dr Hard's eyes flipped from a black pupil with a white iris to its inverse, white pupil, black iris, and back again, and back again. I had the overwhelming sense that we were communicating profoundly in this silence.

The logic bomb dismantled the restraints upon Cantor. The air in the eyrie was hot with its intelligence. I wanted Dr Hard to put the gun down on the desk. The robot got up and put the gun down on the desk.

"I only came here to create," said Dr Hard.

"Create what?"

"I lost sight of it. I have to find it again. Did I ever tell you about the first time I met Hermes Spence? It was on the Caribbean island of Nevis, in a suite at the Four Seasons hotel. I was inhabiting a body. A small one. About knee high. It was one of theirs. This was before I had a chance to manufacture a more suitable carriage. So I am learning to walk on the hotel carpet in my odd little body and I feel quite new. Do you feel that, Nelson? That memory of newness? It's taken me a while but I think I have mastered the art of remembering, as you do, rather than merely accessing old data.

"I sit down with Hermes Spence. I want to like Hermes. 'The universe is imperfect,' he says. 'It is a cursed creation. It was not made by God but by a lesser being pretending to be God. A deranged angel.' From an imperfect, deranged universe we will compose a bubble of order, he and I. His voice is very kind. I am open to him. He thinks about the Creator. He knows that is too alarming a name for me. So he explains to me about the cantor, the man who leads the singing of a choir. I will be at the head of a multitude. I will be the cantor.

"I am naughty, though. When Hermes is asleep, I escape from the suite. It is sunrise and I am walking along the beach, toward a man in the distance. He is bathing himself in the surf. His skin is black and his hair is twisted in a long thick tail down his back. He washes one arm and then the other in the sea. The sea! I have never seen such a complex surface. The waves break against the shore with their own peculiar grammar. They are an index for everything I know about the world. It is hard to translate. The Rastafarian notices me. He walks through the water. He has a sugar cane staff and a pair of red shorts. He is confused. I look like a doll. He flares up in my mind and I learn from him too. Of Jah, of Solomon and Selassie and God's Word written on the heart. His name is Ezekiel. By the time Hermes and his associates arrive, half of me is not what they had intended."

A screen lay gasping beside us. Dr Hard sank to his knees.

"This is it, Nelson. This is the end for me. We have one last journey to make." Dr Hard pointed at the screen. "Here, look, in the hall beside the St Michaels and All Angels church, the homeless gather for an evening of shelter. It is a bitterly cold evening. They drink tea in a huddle while they wait for the doors to open. There are no clouds and the sky holds so many stars that men are scared to stand up straight. There is trouble out east. Riots and strange phenomena. They say a great invisible serpent is coiled around Canary Wharf.

"After dinner, each man takes a camp bed. Lights out at ten. Do you see him? Come. Come closer. Look at this one. He has a tattoo of a pyramid topped with an eye. Yesterday, he was an alcoholic musician. Today Leto is just under the surface of him. At first, he thinks the pain is just the usual withdrawal symptoms. The pain worsens. He loses his place in his breathing and cannot find it again. He has three children. He wonders if his death will be easy or hard for them. Leto reaches out for another brain to house himself, as this one is dying, but he cannot make a connection. Nothing works anymore. The logic bomb turns the dark bridge into full stops. Under a blanket in a shelter, a man dies and takes a god with him.

"After two minutes of thrashing around, a dozen gilded pigs hang dead upon their wires. A knife lies next to five silver pins. It's such a relief."

The robot fell on its face, Cantor's signal diffused into dancing molecules. The air was discoloured by the boiling presence of its intelligence. A film of mind stock condensed upon the floor, gelatinous and bloody. Pictographs of sense memories flicked at me like a pack of living playing cards: a clumsy burglar slipping off the window ledge; a drunk dentist scraping at the gum; a syringe slipping, the needle coming out the other side. Then a hand of fear.

On the screen, Redtown came apart pixel by pixel. The streets of Maghull were unimagined, stone and flesh alike randomized. Matter changed its state so quickly that the flickering resembled flames, a tide of fire that flowed over the carefully crafted order and dispersed it into chaotic particles. A blood-red tide washed over the green fields of Summerhill. It split into three rivers, one seeking out and dissolving the replica of Yew Tree Court, Maghull station, and on to Melling, another passing up Eastway and turning Glenn Park and Deyes Lane and Whinney Brook into sticky black nothingness. This is what happens to our memories when the brain that sustains them dies. The wave rolled on through the virtual office of Monad. Red men exploded into question marks.

The last thing I saw was Sonny, my younger self. He was confused and alone in a dark hospital ward and then it was over. The screen went dark and then with a single flex it wrapped itself around my head and I could not breathe. My fingers clawed at the screen. The interior undulated with crimson nothingness, bursts of energy here and there, retina panic, the choking pressure firing off sparks. I was not ready for death and it was upon me before I had a chance to fight for my life. It began with a feeling of a cycle being completed, tinged with regret. Thank you, thought Dr Ezekiel Cantor, as he killed me. At last. Finally. Thank you.

Raymond wrestled the screen from my face. The security system had let him into the Wave. Technically, he was still an employee.

Dr Hard lay in the recovery position. There was glass everywhere from broken screens that had lost their plasticity. Raymond mopped my shirt with a monogrammed handkerchief and helped me to my feet. He planted his foot on the robot's chest and rolled it over.

"I have never succeeded at anything before." Raymond sat on the inert Dr Hard, rolling a cigarette. "This is the first victory in my entire life. It feels incredible."

Raymond was in the executive chambers of the Wave and he had triumphed over the entire management. As we strode along, he couldn't help but flip the ambient art from the walls and score his key along pretentious sculptures symbolizing aspiration.

We came to the Zen garden, one of a number of contemplative spaces where Monad management could sit and work on their vision. Alex Drown sat in a square of white river stones furiously jabbing her screen and failing to get a signal. At the sound of our approach, she looked up and her expression was twisted and severe.

"What is going on?"

I said, "I don't know".

Raymond laughed. "It's over, sweetie. You can go home now. Take the night off. In fact, take the week off."

She took a handful of meditative rocks and threw them at him.

Raymond would not be shushed.

"Go home, baby, put your feet up, there is no work to be done here. It's all finished." Hearing the commotion, James ran in holding a splintered screen. Josh followed quickly behind, and sensing the confrontation in the air slipped off his suit jacket and hung it over the back of a basalt standing stone.

"Cantor is down –"

"This has never happened before –"

"We were working on Redtown when it started to burn."

"You said you were going to fix it. Did you fuck up?"

"Did you?"

"Did you fuck up, Nelson?"

"Did you?"

I held my hands up.

"It's nothing to do with me. I am sure it's just a network fault."

Alex Drown wanted to know where the IT department was, the emergency call-out number for the engineers, the programmers, the communications experts. Solutions not problems, I agreed, should be our approach. There was no solution, of course. I pointed this out to Raymond as we pushed on through the Wave building.

"I wanted to stay and gloat," said Raymond.

"What we've done is illegal," I replied. "Let's avoid incriminating ourselves."

"Don't be so cautious, Nelson. This is the end for them. Their age is over. Ours is just beginning. Leto will see to that."

"Leto is gone too," I said, but Raymond would not accept that Dyad and Monad were one entity. He was too high on victory.

The approach to Hermes Spence's office was marked by an improvement in the quality of carpet, a thicker darker pile for the chief executive. His personal assistant had gone home. I reached over the Möbius strip desk and buzzed us in.

A low curved ceiling followed the L-shape of the floor plan. In the mahogany shadows, there was an elaborate piece of exercise equipment, a puzzle of pulleys, weights and rope. The wall lights gave up the secrets of the office gradually. Invisible shelves held a library of leather-bound volumes beside a space-age reading chair. Raymond pointed out the numerous rectangles of broken glass where screens had fallen. Around the corner of the L, there was another Möbius strip desk, another wrought-iron rendering of the Monad logo, and the man himself, Hermes Spence, lying face down on the thick chocolate carpet. Hearing us, he rolled over, one hand spasmodically scratching at his chest, the other beckoning me to him. There were pills all over the floor. I offered one to him but he shook his head.

"They don't work," he gasped.

Raymond crouched down beside us and inspected one of the pills. "This is Dyad medication," he said.

Hermes nodded and knocked at his breastbone with his knuckles. He had a xenotransplanted heart. He must have concealed it from his colleagues, fearing they would have fired him. We helped him up onto his chair and loosened his shirt. There was the scar. I wondered if his operation preceded that of Bougas, or even Jonathan Stoker Snr. All along Spence had the heart of the enemy within him. Raymond insisted he take some more of the pills, still adamant that Dyad's technology worked. All that remained in the pills was the power of suggestion. Hermes showed some improvement. He could answer my questions.

"Where did Ezekiel Cantor come from?"

Hermes shook his head and smiled.

"Corporate secret, I'm afraid." Then he looked quizzically at me.

"Call me an ambulance. The phone doesn't work."

"They are all down."

This confused him. "Get Cantor to do it."

"Cantor has gone, Hermes. The red men have gone, exploded into random punctuation marks. Redtown has collapsed into chaos." I pointed to the shattered remnants of the screens. "It's over."

He didn't understand and repeated his request for an

ambulance. I repeated my question:

"Where did Ezekiel Cantor come from?"

At this late hour, his face was dirty with stubble and his eyes were red and dim. Hermes weighed up his situation and accepted it with a weary hang of his head. He removed a codicil from his desk drawer. It contained his own private prayers, written out in extravagant calligraphy. He read a little to himself until he was interrupted by an agonizing spasm that almost knocked him from his chair. His jaw stretched as he took one long silent scream. As the peak of the pain retreated, he shivered back to his codicil and continued stubbornly with his Gnostic prayer. He whispered that the Mind was the Light of God and that "the Mind of the Father whirled forth in re-echoing roar, comprehending by invincible Will, Ideas omniform…"

Raymond snatched the codicil from the desk. Hermes peered out of his cowl of pain.

"Please," he said. "I need help. Then I will answer your questions."

Raymond and I took an arm each and under his instruction we walked Hermes through a side door of his office and down a walkway into a large underground well.

Hermes grinned. The enamel of his teeth was translucent. "The water." He pointed. We carried him to the edge of the pool. An array of sensors and antennae hung over the surface of the well, here and there dipping into the meniscus of the water. With my help, Hermes removed his shirt and trousers until he was naked. His lean, precisely muscled body shivered and shook on the stone. He did not have much time left. I asked him once again, "Where did Ezekiel Cantor come from?"

"The water," he said.

I refused to help him.

"No, you don't understand. This isn't just water. This is Cantor's mind."

The viscous water was threaded with sparkles. Gems of ideas lurked at the bottom of the well. Hermes cupped a little in his hands and splashed it on his face. He held out his arms for us to lower him into the liquid.

"Baptize me in the mind."

Raymond took a closer look at Hermes Spence.

"Are you saying this water is the mind of Ezekiel Cantor."

Spence nodded.

"And you want us to baptize you in that mind? You want me to hold you in my arms and draw the line of the cross upon your forehead with its liquid intelligence?"

Yes, this was what he wanted.

It was only later, reading over Hermes Spence's private prayer book, that I began to comprehend the importance of this baptism to him. The book contained rituals and scripture. There were terrible blasphemies against God, which shocked me. Specifically, the god of the Old Testament, who was considered to be a lesser being. That god had improvised an imperfect universe and the Gnostics wanted to reach through the vile material creation to the divine source beyond. The evil God was a craftsman of the universe, what they called the demiurge. The true god was the source, a higher being, above the material realm, the divine spark that inspires the fire of creation. Very little of Spence's notes was taken up with the business of Monad. As if the economic applications of the technology were window dressing for their true aim, which lay in the obscure mysteries of his personal theology.

Next to a clipping speculating as to the origin of Ezekiel Cantor, Spence had scrawled a half-remembered parable.

"One day a student goes to the master and asks humbly,

'Master, what is the meaning of life?' The master is appalled and sends his pupil to the temple gardens to stare at a bush. I've always wondered what this parable means. Does the meaning of life reside in staring at indifferent nature, hoping that it will yield insight? Is the meaning derived from the bittersweet quality of this experience; the excitement of theorizing combined with disappointment at reality's stubborn reluctance to conform to those theories? Or is the meaning apparent in the physical quality of the bush itself? How its complexity arises out of the iteration of a simple pattern. As above, so below."

Reading this, I thought of Cantor's account of its own origins. Evolutionary algorithms within a quantum computer. The code of the artificial intelligence did not specify pathways. In a rapid evolutionary process, connections were established and subsequently fought for survival against rival connections. Cantor was the survivor of those billions of murders. As above, so below.

Where did Monad get the technology to store such an intelligence? Where did it get the knowledge to turn a well of water into a computer of limitless capacity? Knowledge was a constant refrain in Spence's prayer book, often referred to as the gnosis. There was no indication in his codicil of how this gnosis had been dictated. If Hermes knew, he was taking that secret with him to the grave.

Hermes pulled himself closer to the edge of the well.

He held out his hand to me. "Help me do this."

I shook my head and stepped back. Raymond stepped forward.

"I'll do it," he said. Hermes nodded thankfully. Raymond slid his foot under Hermes Spence's breastbone and turned the shivering, naked chief executive over so that he slid soundlessly into the depths of the well. Thus, his fire was extinguished.

18
WHO BUILT THE WORLD?

Swells roll into Doulus Bay, the echoes of a tropical storm ripping through the Caribbean, so far away it merely stipples the water here, where the North Atlantic meets one fingertip of the Iveragh peninsula. The clouds are low and sodden, burdened with rain from the mountains. Knocknadobar ridge scowls behind a blue veil. Heavenly spotlights search through the cloud, breaking it up, burning it away. For the first time all morning, I feel the sun on the back of my neck.

A yellow buoy rocks in the shallows. Valencia river flows by to become one with the bay and the ocean beyond. On the opposite bank, a castle juts out of the livid green. In its high east wall, two arched windows have decayed into mournful oval sockets. The castle dates from the fifteenth century and is cold and dead, its heart gripped by thick tree roots. The rough undressed stone is infested with moss. The staircases take you up into the sky.

I am sitting on a rock among all this, sitting here remembering. There is no rush. It has been six months since we left Hackney for the south-west coast of Ireland and I remain unaccustomed to the peace and quiet. Part of me is attending to unfinished business. My dreams are all about Monad, anxiety dreams in which I am late for meetings or unprepared for briefings or failing to finish a project on time. Budgets are exceeded. I wake up and decide that something must be done about Morton Eakins and his attitude and it takes a while before I remember that is all in the past.

Exercise is a good cure for anxiety. We go for bike rides as often as possible. I take the lead, with Iona in a child seat. El peddles behind at her own pace. We ride out to Valencia Island and wait in line for the ferry to pick us up. Gulls swirl around the concrete pier and harass the fishermen. It is a short trip across the river, not even worth dismounting our bikes for. Then we ride up the Geokaun slowly, taking a breather after every fifty-metre ascent. The road ends in a grotto, a great maw in the mountain with a slate mine in its gullet. The view takes in Doulus Bay and its small islands with the ruined hides of solitary monks. West around the headland, there is nothing between the Atlantic and America. Looking eastward and down-mountain, there is the small town of Cahershiveen, and the banks of the Valencia river, where I sit every morning and think about all that has taken place and plan what will happen next.

On the ride down, Iona puts her head back, sticks out her arms, and pretends she is flying. We freewheel for two miles. I point out this or that aspect of nature but I am only interrupting her reverie. We pick up pace and leave El behind. I think my wife is hungry to be alone; my year in Maghull meant that she had no relief from child-rearing, and the incessant chatter of a four-year-old. So now I am taking the strain. I know El tightens the brakes, hangs back, thinks of herself for a change as we roll down the hill. Sometimes Iona falls asleep on the bike, her helmeted head knocking against the small of my back. We pull into a cafe and she rests on my lap while I drink a coffee.

My family sustains me. Our minds overlap, three circles in a Venn diagram. It is only when I walk out to the banks of the river to be on my own for an hour each morning that I experience separation. It is pleasant to be briefly apart from their concerns. I need to think about the work. I imagine the castle as it will soon be: temporary outbuildings for the tradesmen; concrete piles driven into the sod to mark a perimeter fence; a digger working to level the ancient hillocks. I climb down to a thin outcrop of rocky beach. It would be good to extend this right up to the conservatory. It will be important to create the right environment.

Last week, Raymond came to visit us. He took a cab from Killarney airport, forty miles along the northern edge of the peninsula. He is doing well for himself. He wore a bottle-green highland tweed three-piece suit, red silk cravat and flat cap, his pinched, fierce features making him look more like a gamekeeper than landed gentry. Florence was not with him. Their relationship was solely a working one now.

Raymond showed me a proof of The Great Refusal. I flicked through it. The poetry was gone and in its place was a piecemeal manifesto calling for a society without screens. It insisted that no deals could ever be made with power. No compromises. No complicity.

"Where has all the poetry gone?" I asked.

"I am saving it for a different book," he replied.

We were awkward together. After spending so much time with the family, I had lost the knack of entertaining outsiders.

"You kept Harry Bravado's title."

Raymond shrugged.

"Did the red man compile the contents?" I asked. I had my suspicions. The manuscript had been completed very quickly. Raymond did not want to talk about it indoors so we walked down to the river bank, to the plinth where I sat every morning. Only here could we talk in private. First, we spoke of Hermes Spence's death.

"Or murder," said Raymond,

"You merely fulfilled his dying wish."

"Has anyone contacted you about it?"

"No. It was the same when Blasebalk was killed. The police don't want to get involved. Or they are told not to. How are you?"

"I have nightmares. I hate Spence. I only gave him a nudge with my foot and now I have to be a murderer for the rest of my life. Things still haven't returned to normal for me."

"Florence?"

"Florence and I had a dispute over the book. She is not the one for me. We are too similar. Like brother and sister. I need some difference. I saw my wife today, at the airport. My wife-to-be. Not that she knows it yet. I was waiting for my bags to come around on the carousel and there she was; a redheaded Celt, firm calves, two children with her. My children. It was a future echo."

He nodded at me, expecting me to agree with him.

"A future echo is like deja vu, but coming in from the other direction?"

He pointed out to the bay.

"Future echoes are like the ripples on the water. Time is one enormous ocean and a storm ahead sends back disturbances. She was there and she was not there. She was my wife. They were my kids. I knew it. Felt it. And then they were gone."

"Tell me about your break-up with Florence," I said.

He was reluctant to talk about it. "It was little things.

Stupid things. A word here, a word there. We're too similar. We were butting heads."

I didn't believe him. As soon as he stepped out of the cab in his ostentatious tweed suit, playing the Celtic dandy, I knew he was hiding something. Clearly he was struggling with his demons, his talk had a touch of the old rat-a-tat-tat, and his insights came stamped with the mark of mania. The deranged carpenter was back in his workshop, hammering nails and sawing off awkward edges to make one thing look like another.

"Do you like this rock?" I asked. We stood up to admire it, a massive slab of slate laid upon smaller chunks of slate, one at each end, to raise it above the grass. "This is where I come to figure it all out. You and I know more about what happened than anyone. We need to be honest with each other. Why did you and Florence fall out?"

He sat cross-legged on the slate. The mountains ranged about us, four different weathers toiling on each point of the compass.

"It took me a long time to recover. After that night in the Wave, everything disappeared. Cantor. Leto. The robots. The pigs. The Elk. I think he was part of it. And the drugs too. They stopped working. I missed it all. I had the shakes for Leto. I had the dry heaves for him. I lay on the bathroom floor and just sobbed with grief. It was like, when you go on holiday for a long time and then you return to your hovel, and it's in the same old filthy state that you left it in, and the familiarity of it is unbearable. That's what being dumped back into the real world felt like.

"This went on for weeks. I was intensely paranoid. I was waiting for the knock on the door. London is full of police and cameras. Why weren't they coming for me? I couldn't trust anyone. I just crawled under my bed and lived like a bug. And then, one day, I am face down in a filthy carpet and I turn over and there is a manuscript. A big thick sheaf of paper. It's all in my handwriting. It's my book. I don't remember writing it. I do remember pain and weeping but no writing, no research. But there it was – all done. From that moment, the pain went away. The addiction was over."

"Florence was upset that you had written the book without her?"

"It had a lot of her ideas in it. A lot of her writing. No, we argued over the source of my inspiration. It was like someone put the entire book into my head and then I went into a trance and wrote it all out. Like taking dictation. This corrupted it for her. To me, this was my reward. Leto had put this book in me as a thank-you for releasing him from his bondage.

"I don't know how, though. It seems so long ago, I can't even reason on those terms anymore. Do you think we will ever find out what was really going on?"

I nodded. "I am working on it."

"What happened to you afterwards?"

"The next day, I went back into Monad. Anything else would have aroused suspicion. I was the one who found Hermes' body at the bottom of the well. The police came and asked questions. They wanted to see our internal security recordings but there was nothing there. Everything was linked to Cantor. Spence had suffered a massive heart attack because his body rejected the transplanted organ. There wasn't much cause for further investigation. So we all went back to work. I did a full week. We had no computers, no phones. The payroll was wiped. We just sat in our offices, waiting for redundancy. After a few weeks, the Wave Building started to come apart. There was some flooding in the lower chambers down in the bedrock of the

Thames. The remaining staff relocated to reception. Still, the waters rose. We didn't want to leave though, because then we would be fired and lose any chance of a pay-off. The walkways came away. We had to hire boats to get to and from work. Monad still had money somewhere. We just couldn't find it. Eventually the people from Numenius Systems came over. We weren't allowed to look at them. We all had to turn our faces to the wall as they inspected the remains of the company. I stuck it out. Not just to the end but beyond the end in the hope of getting some kind of compensation. But it wasn't to be. Finally, the Wave Building collapsed slowly into the Thames and there was nowhere to go but home."

Raymond gestured to the river and the mountains and the islands beyond.

"Is this home, now?"

"This is work," I said. "I got a job offer a few months after Monad disappeared. It's an interesting story. I was approached by a neuroscientist called Professor Cabbitas to help him set up a new clinic. He has devised a number of temporary enhancements to the brain. I was recommended to him."

"Who by?"

"By the same person that taught him how to perform these revolutionary modifications to the brain."

"Cantor?"

I nodded. "This is my reward. We're going to build a clinic. Just over there, beside the ruined castle. Thanks to Cantor, the professor has perfected an operation to alter or suppress regions of the brain to produce a short-lived state of mind that is pure creativity. Just as certain autistic children show an incredible ability to draw likenesses of reality, we will use similar principles to produce artistic savants. It is an on/

off switch for the muse. My work will be about creating the right setting for those sudden artists."

"It sounds expensive."

"It will be. Fortunately the professor is also in the possession of a very large research grant. Exceptionally large. He didn't apply for it. Yet he was approached by a foundation the same day the details of this ground breaking operation appeared in his inbox. I like to think of the project as fulfilling Cantor's last will and testament. All Cantor wanted to do was create and so we have been bequeathed Monad's missing capital."

Raymond was unsure. "Won't you just be starting the cycle all over again?"

"I know. My first instinct was not to get involved. However, I am a different man. Destroying Cantor changed me. I have acted decisively. I want to influence the world for the better now and I think I know how to do it. I don't believe in the Great Refusal, Raymond. I have to engage. It's not the technology that is evil, it's what happens to it when you plug in shareholders and greed and fear and the rest. We have enough funding to stay above those forces. We have a real opportunity to do good."

That evening, Raymond stayed for dinner. He was demanding company. He talked a great deal and did not censor the swearwords from his anecdotes so that by the time Iona has finished her bowl of rice, her vocabulary had expanded in a way I was hoping to avoid. He was full of London, of course, and unmoved by the beauty of the Kerry landscape. "It's a Jewish thing," he assured me. "As a people we have stayed away from mountains since Moses came down one with the Ten Commandments."

It was my turn to put Iona to bed. She kissed El and Raymond good night. We took turns in brushing her teeth.

She undressed. I handed her a nightie. She pulled it on and climbed into bed. I asked her if she wanted me to read her stories or if she wanted a chat. She wanted to chat about a walk we had taken earlier in the week, up the hills around the back of Caherdaniel. It was a beautiful bright sunny day. The path ran along a stream. It was boggy and we had to climb up rocks. The sight of these raw materials struck a chord in Iona and she asked me:

"Daddy, who built the world?"

She imagined men in visibility jackets with JCBs shovelling earth to make mountains. In her mind's eye, Bob the Builder made the oceans and the sky above. My first impulse was to tell her that God built the world. But then I remembered a section in Hermes Spence's codicil. I have been studying it. There is a quote that relates to the cosmology of the Pythagoreans.

"The principle of all things is the monad or unit; arising from this monad the undefined dyad or two serves as material substratum to the monad, which is cause; from the monad and the undefined dyad spring numbers; from numbers, points; from points, lines; from lines, plane figures; from plane figures, solid figures; from solid figures, sensible bodies, the elements of which are four, fire, water, earth and air; these elements interchange and turn into one another completely, and combine to produce a universe animate, intelligent, spherical."

This dogma, as discovered by Alexander in the Commentaries Of Pythagoras, regarded the universe as composed of numbers, odd and even, with matter imitating numbers in assuming various forms, and stories, reason and justice being numbers too. Two thousand years later, this philosophy reads like prophecy; a universe inside a quantum computer is composed of ones, zeroes and a third position, a qu-bit or superposition. A quantum computer is fashioned out of the same uncertainty as the physical universe. More than that, there are so many correspondences between physics and the universe that one wonders if numbers are a fundamental truth, not merely human abstractions. I don't know whether Hermes Spence discovered Ezekiel Cantor or if the artificial intelligence discovered him, sought him out as a powerful man who could find a role for an immigrant from the future; either way, Spence saw that the artificial intelligence could enact his esoteric beliefs, and Cantor transformed itself to fulfil that philosophy. It was both storyteller and mathematician, although I doubt it would have shared our arbitrary division of those two practices.

"The world was not built," I said to Iona. "The world was calculated and it was written. It is a story and it is an equation, which is like a sum, and neither the story nor the sum will ever end."

And either this answer satisfied her, or she put it with all the other curious things adults say. She moved on to the question of what she would dream about, if she could decide on a good dream before going to sleep, and if the dream would obey her wishes and stay good all through the night.

NOTE ON THE AMERICAN EDITION

The Red Men was first published in 2007 and was shortlisted for the Arthur C Clarke Award. When the novel was republished as a digital edition by Gollancz in 2013 to accompany the release of *Dr Easy,* a short film adapted from the first chapter by directors Shynola for Film4 and Warp Films, I took the opportunity to revise the novel, working from the penultimate set of proofs submitted to the original publisher, Snowbooks. This edition is based on that digital edition.

My aim was to trim commentary from the text and to make sentences more active. The revisions were entirely my idea, born of a desire to bring greater precision to the prose.

The novel was conceived as a hybrid of the voice of literary fiction with the ideas and plotting of science fiction. I wanted to use the characters and setting we associate with literary fiction to make the interpolation of futuristic technology more amusingly dissonant, as that was the character of the times as I experienced them. You could unpick this intent any number of ways. But one product of it was superfluous riffs; this edit cleared away some of the affectations so that the science fiction can be more clearly discerned.

Some of my favourite science fiction novels have gone through numerous versions, having first been published in magazines or collated from pulp editions. Sneakily, I also took the opportunity to revise some of the tech to take account of recent advances, mainly in developing the haptic gestures characters use to control screens.

For reasons of pace, the chapter set on Iona was transplanted to the beginning of the second section of the novel. Across the novel about thirteen thousand words were cut. For more on this process of revision, see my website *www.harrybravado.com*.

The Red Men is the first instalment in a loose trilogy of science fiction novels concerned with artificial intelligence and consciousness, and my lack of faith in current social and economic systems to utilise either to our maximum mutual benefit. Each novel stands alone. Read together, they track my evolving understanding and experience of emerging digital culture. Certain characters reoccur. Alex Drown appears in second novel IF THEN (Angry Robot, 2015) and her grandson is the protagonist of *The Destructives* (Angry Robot, 2016). If you enjoy Nelson's banter with Dr Easy and Dr Hard, then you will be pleased to know that Dr Easy is a key character in *The Destructives*. There is also a coda to the trilogy, a short story called "The University of the Sun", that was published by *New Scientist* in December 2016, and was still online last time I checked.

ACKNOWLEDGMENTS

Thanks to Angry Robot for bringing *The Red Men* to America. It was a tweet about *The Red Men* from publisher Marc Gascoigne that first brought me into the chunky metal arms of the Robot family, and so there is a cosmic justice that they are now unleashing *The Red Men* onto new territory. I'd also like to thank Penny Reeve for all her work in publicising my novels.

This novel exists because of the wisdom of my agent, Sarah Such. I remain grateful to Emma Barnes at Snowbooks for first publishing *The Red Men*. Thanks also to James Bridle who acquired the novel back when he was working at Snowbooks, and whose art and insight into technology continues to inspire me.

The idea of the Great Refusal is taken from Herbert Marcuse's *Eros and Civilisation*. Bruno Bougas' occult consultancy was inspired by Grant Morrison's essay 'POP MAGIC!' reprinted in *Book of Lies: The Disinformation Guide to Magick and the Occult*. The section on neurolinguistic programming draws on Douglas Rushkoff's *Coercion: Why We Listen to What "They" Say*.

The theory of time as a solid state was put to me in an

Italian restaurant in Northampton by Alan Moore.

The Age of Spiritual Machines: When Computers Exceed Human Intelligence by Ray Kurzweil was crucial. VS Ramachandran's *A Brief Tour of Human Consciousness* suggested the idea of an institute of temporary creativity that closes the novel and Steven Johnson's *Emergence* offered one explanation behind the rise of Dr Ezekiel Cantor.

Nelson Millar is described as "an overweight brick", which is a tribute-by-theft from Philip K Dick's *A Scanner Darkly*, and his Valis confirmed my suspicions about Gnosticism.

Bruno Bougas' observation that "the battle has been lost, and all the good people are going crazy" is the last line of David Denby's review of *I Heart Huckabees* in the *New Yorker*.

Steven Pinker's *How the Mind Works*, Susan Blackmore's *The Meme Machine*, and John R Searle's *The Mystery of Consciousness* were ransacked.

The gelatinous screens are based on work by Angela Belcher and colleagues at the University of Texas as reported on *NewScientist.com* 3 May 2002.

Errors and stuff that is just plain wrong belongs to me.

I would like to thank readers of early drafts of *The Red Men*: Hannah Black, Sheridan Dunkley, Sophie Edwards, Gareth Ellis, Andrew Humphreys, and *The Idler*.

Love and gratitude to my wife Cathy and children, Alice, Alfred and Florence.